JOSIAH WOLFE

Overall Cover Design by: BJ Moore

Contributing Cover Graphics obtained from Pixabay.com

Reader Advisory:
Adult Content, Adult Situations, Sexual Violence, and 1890's Racism is all dealt with, and contained within this book.

"Racism, and Sexual Violence should never be tolerated in our society. The author relished in putting the perpetrator of such actions in this book to his grizzly demise. We are all created equally on this earth, and in my opinion, we should all be treated as such."

DEDICATION

This book is dedicated to the three people in my life who have always stood with me no matter what. Those who have encouraged me in everything that I have ever done, and who over all, have allowed me, to just be me and do what I do.

First, I dedicate this novel to my parents, my late father, David Moore, and my mother, Bonnell Moore. Both who have always been there for me through thick and thin. They encouraged me, and gave me the confidence to follow my dreams of being a published author. My father passed away almost exactly one year before this book was to come out in print, and though he is no longer with me, I know he is still encouraging me, and watching over me from Heaven.

I also dedicate this novel to my husband, Calvin LaPier, who has always stood by me right from the beginning with my first book, "The Culebra", and who kept encouraging me to do what I needed to do to make my dreams of being a published author come true.

Without the love and support of these three people, this book would never have evolved beyond just being a story idea written down on paper. It never would have made it into print, nor would you be sitting here reading it today. So, I say Thank You to all of them from the bottom of my heart for all the love and their support they have shown me. They will never know how much their encouragement has meant to me in the past; and what it will still mean to me in the future.

Author's Note....

I am a story weaver, a spinner of dark tales. What I am not is an English Major, nor a professor of such. In my books you will not find perfection, for the world is not perfect, and neither am I. What you will find are scenes that will make your skin crawl, your heart beat faster, and leave you terrified of what you now think could lie hidden within the darkness around you. Do you dare blink? For in the blink of an eye, your vision will fade to utter darkness. Your inner uncertainties will grasp a hold of you, your heart will beat faster. It is then that you realize that you are completely alone in the darkness, and the horror of your own fear riddled imagination.

If you like to be scared, a journey is now placed before you. Only you may choose the path you wish to take, but in the end, no matter which course you choose to go on, all paths still lead to the same ultimate frightful destination. Once you are ready to harness your fear and venture forth alone into the darkness that lies before you, your journey through horror is ready to begin.......

B.J. Moore

Are Dogmen Real?

Some of us are believers, some are not. There are countless unexplained occurrences happening out in the world around us on a daily basis. From the unexplained mauling of livestock, to the sudden disappearance of experienced hikers and hunters. There is something mysterious, or possibly even nefarious, out there that is responsible for it all.

You say that you have never seen a Dogmen? Well good, you probably wouldn't want too. Some that have, say that once you do, it can change you forever, and not in a good way.

New species of animals are being discovered every day around the globe, and we as humans don't know how many more undiscovered species that there are still out there, and we probably never will. But who knows, maybe the Dogmen is just one of those many unconfirmed, yet to be discovered species like all the rest yet to be verified.

What you choose to believe about the existence, or the origin of Dogmen is up to you. This book is just about one possibility being tossed out by its author, and it is just one amongst many, many other theories out there as to where the origin of the Dogmen began. This story is intended for entertainment purposes only, and is not based on any verified factual research, or research material seen or read by the author.

So, now as you turn the pages of this book, please sit back, get comfortable with the beverage of your choice and enjoy your journey into the world of the Dogmen, and into the life of the one such Dogman named, "Josiah Wolfe".

INDEX

Chapter One

Bright golden yellowish eyes, illuminated by the moon's steadfast presence high in the sky, peered out from the depths of the shadows and into the darkness of the night. The subtle glow from the full moon cascaded downward towards the earth, and danced lightly across the open field. As it did, the lunar glow lit the way for the animal's keen sight to be able to scan all that lay in the vast expanse before it.

In the twilight, a cool wind wafted across the field, and the tops of the various pasture grasses swayed back and forth as the light breeze blew gracefully around them. It was a breeze that as it blew by him, carried many hidden messages with it, some were interesting to him, but many were not. These mixed messages that drifted by his nostrils, were readily picked up and taken in by the highly sensitive beast that now lay hidden under the cover of an old downed apple tree.

Lazily, he gradually raised his muzzle slightly up into air. The creature's nostrils twitched as he inhaled a long, deep breath that flowed over his olfactory sensory organ. Many scents

1

were present that night, but none that drew his immediate attention, or even spiked any interest at all in the nocturnal creatures that had left them behind.

Concealed by the darkness of the night, the creature stretched out his weary limbs. The popping sounds emitted from the manipulation of his joints, echoed as they broke the silence of the night around him. Relaxing his strong muscles and drawing his stiff limbs back in close to his body again, he continued to patiently wait. *"Soon, very soon,"* he thought to himself as he waited for his long-anticipated prey to eventually come into view. *"Patience,"* he told himself as he licked at one of his front paws, *"Patience...."*

The creature had hopes that he would eat well this night. It was a full moon, a good night for a hunt, and his belly was now all but empty. The rumbling within his body gave evidence to the deep craving of nourishment that it wished to have fulfilled. At this moment though, his hopes were beginning to fade as it seemed as though the opportunity to feed this night, would possibly once more elude him. Not yet allowing himself to feel defeated though, he would continue to lie low and keep a watchful eye out for even the slightest movement in the field before him that could possibly lead to a much-needed meal.

The creature as well, kept a sharp ear out for any sounds that may find their way into one of the two pointed appendages that rest upon the sides of his massive head. Any sound, even the slight rustling of minute foot falls hidden from sight, could perhaps give away the presence of possible prey moving around in the heavily shaded, unseen areas along the fields edge. He just had to have patience, bide his time and wait until the time was right. The time when an unsuspecting prey would make a fatal mistake.

Patience hasn't always been a strong point in his life; and it never will be. But tonight, for him to be successful, that is just what he had to do. He had to be patient and wait, wait for something outside of his control to make the move first.

Anymore, most times he preferred that his prey would come to him, he had learned long ago that the meat would taste sweeter if he didn't have to chase it down to make the kill. If he was forced to pursue his prey for any distance before making the kill, he knew that the adrenaline from the chase would taint the meat, and ruin its normally delightful flavor. Not only that, but to hunt in the open field that lay before him during a full moon, he would be taking a very risky chance. If he were to be seen and discovered by the two-legers, it could mean trouble, and that was trouble that he did not desire.

While the large creature continued his vigilance, he laid his muzzle down upon his front legs and closed his eyes. Though he no longer visually watched over the field before him, his other acute senses took over the watch. The creature's large pointed ears were held erect above his head, and were constantly slowly rotating from one direction to the other as they continued to take in the sounds of the night. Not only were his highly tuned ears listening to the sounds of the night, but with every breath, his keenly developed nose constantly took in and processed the scents that were forever changing in the breeze.

3

The soft sound of laughter and the indistinguishable constant chattering of faraway voices could now be heard off in the distance. The sounds irritated and disturbed the massive creatures rest as he continued to lay in wait.

With the faraway voices stirring him from his peaceful slumber, the creature took a deep breath and slowly raised his head and opened his eyes to peer out across the wide-open field in the direction that the noises had emanated from. *"The two-legers are up early this morning,"* he disgruntledly thought to himself as he squinted his eyes and stared intently in the direction of the sounds.

A small village lay just on the other side of the tree line at the far edge of the large open field. The creature had been to the village many times in the past, but he no longer chances going anywhere near it. That is where the two-legers live. They infest the entire area that lies within its boundaries, and with each passing day, their numbers continue to grow. *"They are as irritating as fleas, and they multiplied just as fast,"* he grumbled to himself as he gave a small disapproving grunt.

Squinting his eyes, he continued to stare across the field at the village. He didn't like the two-legers. To say that he despised them would be grading his feelings towards them far too lightly. He stayed away from the village where the two-legers lived for a reason. There were far too many dangers that lurked there for a creature such as he. Every so often, one or two of the two-legers have been known to disappear at night, but that was not any of his doing. There are other dangerous predatory animals in the area that prowl the land at night besides him. Many follow the same

4

predatory patterns like he does, hunting while being concealed by the darkness of the night, but some don't, and they chance hunting during the diurnal hours of the day.

Tonight though, tonight he would just lazily continue to stay under the downed apple tree that concealed his view from others. There, he would just wait for his prey to come to him.

Many predators are not as careful as he is, some carelessly throw caution to the wind and foolishly take their chances at being caught. They get the bloodlust into them, and they get the craving for human flesh. Not him though, he is smarter than they are. He has seen many rogue wolves hunted down after taking advantage of such human opportunities. He has seen them stalk vulnerable human two-legers, and when they find them alone and the opportunity presents itself, they hastily acted upon their wild urges. With his own wary eyes, he has witnessed the two-legers taking down the same man-killing wolves. They tracked them relentlessly for days and after finding them, they returned to the village with their prizes in hand, which were the detached heads of their foes.

The two-legers took the dislodged heads of their enemies back as trophies to their village to show them off, bragging the whole time about what great hunters and protectors they themselves had been to be able to kill those that had threatened their village. "*The two-legers have no respect for nature, no, not any of them, not now, nor have they ever. Nor do they have any respect for those like me who dwelled within it. If they did, they would not be so cocky with themselves, and instead they would fear the unseen dangers that lie within the darkness of the woods around them. If they only*

5

knew…,*" he thought to himself as he continued to stare begrudgingly at the village.

Unlike the rogue wolves, he was nowhere near desperate enough for food to go for the humans he could hear, nor that foolish either. That would only succeed in giving away his presence, a presence that he has tried so hard to conceal. But it is not to say that in time, that it won't someday come to such measures. The longer he stayed in this valley, the more the old resentments from years past were beginning to build and fester from deep within him again. They were like a cancer, a cancer that was slowly eating away at him from the inside out. The time of decision, his decision for what the future was to hold for him, was now drawing nearer and nearer by the day. For tonight though, he would force himself to put his intense loathing of the two-legers aside, and temporarily push the anger festering within him out of his mind. He was both tired and hungry, and all that he wanted to do at this moment was bide his time and wait for his prey, any prey, to cross his path. After scanning the field before him one last time, he lowered his head back down onto his forelegs once more, and closed his eyes while he continued to wait in silence.

While the creature lay in wait, he thought he heard the sounds of twigs breaking that came from behind him. Lazily lifting his head up, he turned to look into the darkened woods where the noise had come from, but he saw nothing. Putting his nose to the air, he sniffed the breeze as it wafted past him. He started to pick up a scent, a scent that he didn't like. Rising up onto all fours, he turned and stared off into the shadows of the wood line.

The noises were getting louder as the animal was getting closer. The thud of its footsteps gave away its huge size as it moved through the brush. Carefully, the creature took a few steps towards the wood line and stopped. He knew from the scent that was carried in the breeze what the animal it was that was now approaching him, and he knew of its power.

Taking a few more steps towards the wood line, he heard a low guttural growl emanating from the trees. The creature bared his teeth and returned the menacing growl with one of his own. A large bruin stepped out from behind a huge oak tree and stared at the creature, eye to eye. Aggressively, the huge 700-pound black bear stood up onto its muscular hind legs and roared. Swinging its massive front paws into the air, it demonstrated its fearlessness to the creature that stood before it. Locking its eyes on the creature, it snarled aggressively down at him. The creature, showing no fear of his own, snarled back at it and refused to back down. Cautiously step by step, the creature continued to steadily approach the large bear, readying itself to defend his territory from the interloper.

The large bear dropped back down onto all fours and began to run towards the creature for a fight. Not backing down, the creature began to run towards the large bear as well. The sound of brush breaking beneath their feet could be heard echoing off the trees around them. When the two huge animals impacted, it was as if two solid objects powerfully collided.

A great struggle ensued between the two masterful predators. Pushing each other back and forth, they wrestled with their front limbs wrapped around each other. Their snarling easily drowned out all other noises of the night.

Clawing and biting at each other, neither animal was giving way to the other. The creature seeing an opening, leaned in and bit down hard onto the front shoulder area of the large bear. As blood began to run from the wound, the bear roared in anger and turned and tried to swat at the creatures. Seeing the bears claws coming at it, the creature released the bear and quickly moved off to the side and out of its reach. Enraged, the bear again roared out in anger at the creature.

Furious, the bear swung its own head around to try to bite down upon the creature's body, but his opponent was far too agile for it, and he quickly backed away out of the bear's reach. The creature then turned, and by using one of its huge forearms, it quickly swept one of the bears hind legs out from underneath it. The bear was caught off guard and thrown off balance. After losing its footing, it fell down onto the ground and rolled over onto its side.

Quickly getting back to its feet, the bear again charged at the creature. Dodging the bear, the creature swiftly jumped off to the side, turned and jumped up onto the bears back. He was less bulky and far nimbler than the bear was, and he used that to his advantage.

After biting down hard on the bears shoulder area once more, the bear painfully cried out in frustration. Shaking its head back and forth, the bear roared out angrily at him. Rising up onto its hind feet, the bear snarled loudly at the creature as it tried to reach him with its long front claws.

Swing its head around, the bear saw the large oak tree just off to the side of them. Swinging its body towards the tree, it forcefully smashed the creature's body up against it. The shock from powerful impact caused the creature to lose his grip on the larger bears back, and he fell from it down onto the ground below.

The creature looked up at the bear hovering over it as it readied itself for attack. Raising its front legs up into the air, the bear flung itself forwards as it tried to stomp down on top of the creature with its claws and canine teeth flaring. The creature quickly spun around and rolled away from underneath it.

Still snarling at each other, both of the opponents continued to size up the other challenger. The large bear stood back up onto its hind legs and again loudly roared at the creature. Taking note of the now exposed underbelly of the bear, the creature quickly charged at the bear and rammed it in the abdomen with his right shoulder. The impact cracked one of the bears ribs and knocked the bear off its feet. Flying backwards, the bear skidded to a stop on the leaf littered ground below.

Enraged and badly injured, the bear got to its feet and let out a loud angry roar. It was furious and beginning to froth at the mouth from all the fury it was feeling towards the creature. Its eyes seethed and hatred spewed from them.

Wildly charging at the creature, the bear was again sidestepped by it, and ended up crashing into the thick brush before roughly coming to rest against a large tree. It was then

9

that the bear began to realizing that despite his size, this was a fight that he was not going to be able to win. The creature was both stronger and quicker than the bear was, and it knew it. The bear was exhausted, injured and bleeding profusely from its front shoulder area. It had expended all the energy that it had left in his body during its last charge, and it could go on no more.

Still slightly huffing at the creature, the bear slowly began to back away. The creature mock charged at the bear to solidify its point, and to ensure that it would not return in the future. The bear only momentarily paused to snarl back at him, before it slowly began backing away from the area where the creature was still standing his ground. With its shoulder badly wounded, and a broken rib, it wanting to avoid any further confrontation. The large bear slowly began to limp away as it lumbered off beyond the tree line. Pausing momentarily, it looked back one last time at the creature before dropping down over the knoll and off into the darkness of the night.

Only after the bear was out of site, did the creature begin to calm down. Adrenaline was racing through his veins, and though he really wanted to run after the bear, he knew that there was no need for it. The bear knew it had made a mistake to confront an apex predator that was much larger and stronger than it was. It was a mistake that nearly cost him his life, but lucky for the bear, it didn't need to come to that.

The creature returned back to where he had been lying, and licked the bears blood from his claws. He could have easily killed the bear and eaten its meat, but the meat of a predator is not like the meat from a pray animal. It isn't sweet, but instead it is strong and vile. He was choosing his meals carefully, and for now, the large black bear wasn't on his menu.

A few hours later, with his heart rate back to normal, he was again relaxed and resting underneath the old downed apple tree. A rustling sound in the tall grass off to the left of the creature caught his attention. Slowly he opened his eyes and cautiously turned his head to look in the direction of where the noise had emanated from. Though accustomed to the darkness, the light of the moon did not help him pinpoint what was hidden by the tall, thick switchgrass. Continuing to listen, he tuned out all other noises but for the one that he just heard.

Carefully the creature raised his head up and put his muzzle into the wind to see if he could catch a hint of what was hidden within the shadows just beyond his sight. His eyes squinted and his nostrils flared as they attempted to pull in the various aromas from the cool breeze wafting past him. Regrettably for him though, the slight breeze was blowing in the wrong direction. It drifted away from him instead of towards him, and any effort to pick up on the scent of what lay in the tall grass before him was useless. The effort had failed to offer him any clues at all.

After intently watching and listening for any more signs of whatever was out there, more light rustling could be heard coming from the same area as before. The creature's ears perked up in attention and rotated towards the area in an effort to get an exact location from where the noise had

11

come from. Catching sight of a slight movement off to the side, the creature quickly began to fixate his attention towards a particular patch of switchgrass. As he watched the native grass, his keen eyes saw that sprigs of it were moving ever so slightly opposite of the direction of the wind. Though the grass barely stirred, his sharp vision was able to hone in on the movement, and he now knew where his prey was concealing itself.

For now, he chose to continue to lay motionlessly and wait. He now knew where his prey was, and he was going to try his best not to give away his own position to the animal that lay beyond. *"Not good to rush things, not good at all,"* he silently told himself. He didn't want to spook what might be his only meal of the night by foolishly moving into position too soon. Seconds turned into minutes though, and minutes turned into agony as his stomach ached in anticipation of a meal. It had been days since he had eaten anything more than field mice, and the occasional hare. He needed more than a measly pittance of a meal to sustain him, he needed much more than that to provide the nourishment that his massive body required. He was even beginning to second guess his allowing the black bear to back away and leave his presence alive.

Again, more rusting drew his attention back to the spot where the animal was hidden. Keeping a close eye out on the area, all he could do was to just patiently wait. This time it wasn't long though until the animal slowly began to wander into his view. It was a young fawn, not long out of spots, but yet well fattened up from the shorter wheat crop that the two-legers had planted in the field years before. He suspected that it had gotten separated from its mother and the others in the herd that it had been with. He looked at it and knew that being it was the only deer in his view, that it would be an easy quick kill for him.

The fawn, sensing something was wrong, suddenly froze in place and lifted its nose up towards the horizon. Slowly rotating its muzzle from one direction to another, it tried to read what was in the breeze, much like the creature did earlier as well. Unlike the creature though, it was now clearly being told a tale of what lay ahead of it, but it was confused by the signs that it was given. The scent that the breeze was carrying was different, it had a foreign, unknown scent to it. It was one that the fawn had never smelled before, and because of that, it couldn't decipher what dangers were hiding in the darkness ahead of it.

The young deer should have been suspicious of the unknown scent, but it wasn't. Instead, due to the lack of experience and wisdom on its part, the young fawn unwisely chose to throw caution to the wind, and ignored the unknown dangers that possibly lurked before it.

Now with the young deer finally within his sights, the situation had become a battle of stealth between the hunter, and the hunted. It would be a battle of patience for the creature now, he knew that it would be hard for him to control himself, and the building tenseness that he felt deep within. As his stomach suddenly grumbled and threatened to give his presence away, he put his hand on it, trying to silence the emptiness that it felt within. To not spook the young deer before he would have a chance to strike, he only had to be still, quiet and implement patience. These three nearly impossible acts for him, were all that stood between him and this fawn being his next meal.

When the creature did not immediately make its move, and silently held fast to his position, it gave the fawn a false sense of security. Without its mother, the young deer lacked the knowledge it would have been given in situations like this. As the young deer began to became more at ease once again, it began to mistakenly surmise that whatever danger had been in the vicinity, was now gone.

Looking around one last time, and seeing no impending dangers lurking, the young fawn lowered its head and foolheartedly started to once more graze upon the tender meadow grasses and grains that grew at its feet. To the young deer, for all it knew, the warnings could have been from an old presence, one that was long gone by now. Because of its lack of knowledge and the instructive influence of other deer, it did not have the experience to know the difference between true danger like it now faced, and situations of unimportance.

Wandering aimlessly from one spot to another as it grazed, the young deer slowly began to stroll its way across the open field as it foraged.

Watching the young deer slowly approaching, the creature began to salivate in anticipation, and as it did so, the spital began to drip from his mouth and dampened the meadow floor below. Not taking his eyes off of the young deer for even a moment, he continued to watch it intently. As it proceeded to graze, it continued to move in various paths until it ultimately began to work its way in his direction.

The young deer proceeded to meander through the field while feeding on the vegetation at its feet. Nibbling on the most tender grasses, it was oblivious to the danger that it was quickly approaching. As it continued to move in the direction it was walking, unbeknownst to it, it continued to get closer and closer to where the creature was concealed.

Excitement began to set in and the large beast began to quiver. Realizing what he had done, he tightened his muscles and again froze in place. Now with his muscles back under control, he silently went back to staring in the fawn's direction. Though it was close to where the creature lay, it had not noticed its unvoluntary movements. *"One more step closer is all I need"*, he silently told himself. One more step was all that he needed to be able to reach out and grab the deer without even leaving the spot where he sat hidden behind the tree.

"One more step...just one more step," he continued to silently tell himself. Excitement began to again build within his body, his muscles began to ache as he tightened them even more in a conscious effort to control their movement. With the young deer as close as it now was, any movement at all would give his location away to it. The longer it took the young deer to advance, the harder it was making it for him to remain still and to hold his position.

The inexperienced fawn, still ignoring all the previous warning signs that were brought to it by the breeze, slowly took that one last step that would lead it to its death. As the young deer moved forward, it quickly caught movement off to its side, but it was too late. In a blink of an eye, the creature struck out with its large clawed hand, and the young deer was immediately scooped up from the meadow floor, and into the grasp of the deadly predator.

The young deer, now wide eyed and in a state of shock, had no idea what had just happened to it as it was snatched up from the spot that it had just stood only seconds before.

Looking up at the great beast, the young deer cried out in fright as it struggled against the creature's firm grip. The young deer lashed out with its hoofs as hard as it could, it tried to kick at the creature, but the fawn's defensive actions yielded no effect on it. The creature was far too large, and too strong to be affected by the simple blows of a small animal's hoofs.

Holding the still squealing fawn tightly within the grip of its left hand, the creature reached out with its other hand and placed it around the throat of the still struggling animal. Exhausted from the struggle, the young deer weakly bleated one last time as it looked back up at the creature standing before it. Showing no pity in his heart, the creature looked deeply into the eyes of the frightened young doe that he now held within his grasp, and without showing any emotion, the creature dug its claws deep into the flesh of the young deer's neck. Feeling his claws tear through the connective neck tissue that held the fawn's head to its body, he quickly and mercilessly ripped the fawns head off. Upon that, death was instant for the young deer.

Bright red blood instantly began to pulsate and spray from the gaping wound where the young deer's head had just been a few seconds earlier. The animal's heart, now emptying itself of all of the life sustaining blood that it had previously pushed through the young deer's body, quickly ceased to beat. With the blood no longer being pushed throughout the fawn's body, the young deer's life was snuffed out, and its body now hung limp in the creature's hands.

The creature looked down at the fawn's head that he still held within his hand. Lightly huffing at the head and determining it useless to him, he let loose of his grip and allowed it to roll off the ends of his fingers. As it rolled off of his fingertips, the head landed on the ground and rolled a few feet away from where he stood before coming to a stop.

The creature turned and looked out into the night; he was scanning the area cautiously before he began to eat. He wanted to make sure that there were no other predators that had been drawn in by the young deer's cries. Seeing none, he turned his attention back to his prey. He could smell the fresh blood that was still slightly dripping from the wound. It smelled enticing to him, and it woke him up inside. His stomach started to rumble louder as he began to lick at the blood pooling at the top of the severed neck. He enjoyed and savored every drop of the crimson liquid as he lapped it up into his mouth. It was warm and sweet and he shivered with excitement. Nothing tainted this blood; it was fresh and pure as it could be.

Licking his lips in further anticipation, the creature looked at the side of the dead fawn's body. Taking one of his large clawed hands, he firmly wrapped his fingers around the hair covered skin, and quickly jerked it outward. He easily tore the skin open and expose the meat underneath before then peeling it back and removing it from the dead fawn's body. He didn't enjoy eating the hides of animals. They were tough and the hair held nothing of value that he desired.

Looking down at the fresh layer of fat and meat that was now exposed, he again licked his lips as the saliva once more began to drip. Bringing the carcass up to his mouth, he took a large bite out of its side. The immature rib bones made a muted snapping sound as they were broken up under the pressure of creature's powerful jaws.

Eating quickly, the creature barely took time to swallow what he had in his mouth, before he took another bite of the tender venison. He continued to ravenously eat until nothing remained but scattered patches of the hide, and a few gnawed upon bones and the young deer's hoofs. Looking off to the side, he saw that the young doe's head still laid by the base of the tree where it had rolled. He wasn't interested in the head, there wasn't enough meat that remained on it for him to bother with, but he still didn't want it drawing attention to his den. Walking over to where the head now lay, he reached down to picked it up. Turning to look at the trees behind him, he tossed it as far back into the woods as he could get it.

Placing one of his clawed hands upon his stomach, he could feel the small food bump that he had just created underneath his fur covered hardened skin. The young doe didn't provide a large meal, but it was enough to silence his growling insides.

18

Turning to once more face the darkened field, he let out a small sigh of contentment into the night. If felt good to him to have eaten something larger than the usual field mice and rabbit that he had come accustomed to.

The creature turned away from the field and sat down on his haunches as he leisurely took his time licking his hands to clean of the blood that was left on them from his kill. His meal was good, he would give it that, it warmed his stomach and settled the cavernous rumbles that had been coming from deep within his midsection, but this meal would not last him long. The fawn was not that large of a kill for a predator of his size, and it didn't provide him with the nourishment that a full-sized doe would have, but it was enough to satisfy him for the moment.

What he had just consumed would hold him over for a day at the most. But the aching need, and the blood-lusting hunger would then take over again, and the desire to hunt would once again rise up from deep within him. At that point he would need to venture back out of the safety of his den, and enter back into the world of the two-legers. That thought alone made the creature unconsciously curl his lips up in a snarl. He despised being anywhere near the two-legers. He wanted absolutely nothing to do with them, but for now, he had no choice because of where he chose to live. The two-legers not only inhabited the field, but they also hunted the same game as he in the woods behind where he lived. There was nowhere he could go that he was safe as long as he was in the valley. One day he would leave this place behind, and rid himself of his constant irritants, but until then, he would just put up with their horridness.

The next time that he left the safety of his den, he would leave with the intention of hunting for a more substantial prey. He had gotten lazy as of late, settling for only morsels of food, instead of larger and more satisfying prey. He knew that he needed something that would last him much longer than the crumbs like what he just consumed this night, and by hunting under the cover of darkness, and far away from the two-legers, he hoped that he could find such an animal that would fulfill his needs.

The large beast now comfortably laid back down in the same spot that it had previously been laying while waiting for his meal to come to him. Feeling no immediate need to return to his den as of yet, and being that the darkness still covered all the land around him, he chose to continue to relax under the glow of the full moon, and enjoy the cool refreshing breeze blowing over him until the morning light would once again begin to rise, and the moons glow would begin to dissipate and dip down past the horizon.

During the early morning hours, darker clouds containing rain had silently begun to slowly move in above him. The darkened sky overhead now almost completely blocked out the shining of the stars above from his sight, and threatened to do so with the moon's golden glow as well. As the dark clouds continued to form and get thicker throughout the night, a dampness took over the air and a light mist had begun to fall from the clouds above that put a layer of moisture on everything it touched.

The creature rested underneath the old downed apple tree all night as he waited to see if something else would randomly wander past. But with the smell of death now lingering all around the area, it was as if there was a beacon indicating a stern warning to others that no animals should dare approach this area. Rolling his eyes, he silently admonished himself, telling himself that he should have known better than to be lazy enough to hunt this close to where he now lived. Even if the two-legers weren't smart enough to know that he was there, all the prey animals in the area now did.

Slightly disappointed with the lack of another meal, the creature rose up onto all fours and began to stretch his body out. As he stretched, all of his joints made popping sounds as they manipulated themselves back into a more comfortable, natural position for him. The creature then lifted both of his front legs up from the ground one at a time, and as he extended them, he felt them pop back into place. Then with one loud crack from his hip area, he arched his back and swung his body upward until he now stood in an upright bipedal position. Pulling his shoulders back to reposition his arms, he also twisted his neck and waist, manipulating the joints in his body, back and forth. By limbering up his thoracic back muscles, and bulging frontal pectoral muscles, it helped to release some of the stress upon his body during his upright transition. And as the heavy muscles extended and stretched, he let out with a loud, low pitched growling type sigh of relief. With his now towering eight-foot muscular stature, he felt even more powerful than before.

Still hungry, the beast turned and looked back out over the field towards the village of the two-legers beyond. As he stared out into the dim light, he allowing his mind to wander.

He was from this area at one time, and he had lived for many years amongst the two-legers that he now despised so much. They proved themselves to be a rather cruel and untrustworthy race. They beat him, mocked him and imprisoned him until he was fortunate enough to finally escape. After he escaped, they relentlessly pursued him, and drove him from the valley that had been his home for many years, and into the mountains high above.

They had pushed him upward and tracked him up into the surrounding mountains that lay beyond the great lake. That is where he was finally able to secure his freedom. He made himself a home there in the mountains, not one like he had before, but in a cave where he could have protection from the harsh elements, and it was there that he was able to live peacefully for many years. His years there in the mountains now held both good and bad memories for him. Much had happened to him while he was hiding out in the mountains, and this new freedom that he had been able to obtain from the two-legers had come with a large price. Endless hunger and the intense fear of everything around him turned out to be his constant companions there, but even they seemed like an insignificant tradeoff when it came to his freedom.

The constant hunger and solitude of being on his own quickly begin to wear on him, and it was if it was chipping away at his soul. In the beginning he was nowhere near as cunning and fearless as he was now. Back then he was inexperienced with the ways of nature, and he wasn't able to hunt the way he does now. He had no tools or weapons to use to bring down game animals, or anything to even use to defend himself with against the many larger predators that roamed the mountain side. The one weapon that he did have with him was lost during the battle for his freedom, and there was no way to get it back. He felt lonely and fearful there. At night, after darkness loomed over the mountain, the night sounds would begin. That is when it was the most dangerous for him there.

He lived in a constant state of fear from both man and animal. During those early days he mostly lived off seasonal berries that he would pick at the edge of the forested area, or raw fish if he was lucky enough to corner one in the shallow area of the creek. Once in a while, he would be fortunate enough to kill a squirrel or small rabbit with a well thrown rock, but little else ever made its way through his lips. Fresh venison, that was what he needed, but again, he had no way of obtaining it.

Eventually over time, and after changes had been made, he did become more accustomed to the way of life that he had to live in, and he began to flourish in it. He mastered different skills that he didn't even know that he possessed, skills that now come naturally to him. He learned to refine his natural instincts and trust in his own newly found abilities.

After some time had passed, he found that he had changed both physically and mentally, he had become stronger in body, and wiser in mind to the ways of the woods. Through watching the pattern that the animals moved in, and where their weaknesses were, he had learned how to use that information to his advantage, and he no longer had to worry about ever going hungry again. He had rightfully gained the respect of all of the animals that lived in the forest with him. But in the end, man stepped in again. The two-legers encroached on him once more and began interfering with his life to the point that he could no longer stay.

Because of the two-legers, he once again had to leave what had become his home, and his sanctuary. He was now forced to leave the existence that he had been able to etch out for himself, and the security that the mountain had provided him, along with everything he needed to survive. Because of the two-legers, and because of what they now were doing, they not only were forcing him out, but they forced the wild game from the mountain as well. And because of the two-legers increasing infestation of the land high above the lake where he had been residing, the same game that had been chased from the mountains, was now the same game that was dwindling here in the valley as well. And now, the two-legers were once again to blame for his deep and constant unfulfilled hunger.

He felt that the two-legers were at fault for everything bad that had happened in his life, not only the hunger that he now continuously felt within the pit of his stomach, but with also the way that he now had to live. That fact alone ate away at him on a daily basis, and the more that he obsessed about it, the angrier he was becoming.

For him the two-legers destroy everything that they touch. They ran off his food, and what they didn't push away, they hunted and killed for themselves. They killed off so many of the prey species that all that was left were the predators. Many of the predators began to go hungry, and that led to them fighting amongst themselves. Inner fighting all because of man and their so-called progress. The two-legers have always been at the root of all his problems, and because of this, his long held obsessive hatred towards them ran deep, deeper than his soul itself.

The impeding gloominess in the sky had finally given way, and the first rays of the rising sun now edged their way above the horizon, and a new day, a brighter day, had begun to emerge. As daybreak approached in the valley, the birds began to sing their morning songs as they left their roosts and fluttered down to drink from the droplets of dew that still remained on the leaves of the trees around him.

Realizing that he had been lost deep in thought, the creature yawned and lazily turned and moved away from the downed apple tree where he had been silently standing. Pausing momentarily, he turned and sadly looked over his left shoulder at the waning darkness that now only existed in the shadows of the trees.

Seeing the new day about to be born, the creature slowly made his way back into the shadows of the tree line. Before reaching the trees though, he turned and took one more look out over the field. He stood and watched as small puffs of white smoke rose from the stone chimneys on many of the two-legers buildings. The two-legers were beginning to stir. Squinting his eyes, the creature curled his upper lip and quietly snarled at the village that lay at the other side of the field. This place now only held agony and painful memories for him, this was where the two-legers lived that ultimately ruined his life and drove him his home. Angrily, he jerked his head away from where he had been staring, and headed for the security of his den.

The creature's den was a cave that sat depressed within the side of a small knoll not far from the field. Well hidden within the shadows, the opening was mostly obscured from outsiders by the overgrowth of dense vegetation that skirted both sides of it, and a thick layer of tightly woven vines that also cascaded down over the front of the entrance way, creating a thick veil of greenery that obscured it from sight. A large hornet nest also hung nearby, further securing his home from discovery by unwanted guests.

A large black bear, possibly even the one he had just done battle with earlier, had once lived in what was now his home. When he first moved into the secluded den, he knew that it had been long deserted by whatever animal had lived there. There were no fresh scents, or signs of scat left in the area to be found. He could still tell thought from the old, almost diluted scent that barely still clung to the walls around him, that it was a bear that had lived there. Once the creature had moved into the cave though, he marked it as his own. At that point, no other creature would dare question its ownership. For them to do so, or worse, to attempt to take it as their own, it not only would be foolish, but it could ultimately lead to their death.

With his stomach still not full after the small fawn he consumed, his insides once more began to grumble as it called out for more sustenance. He had no choice but to wait until the darkness of the next night came to hunt though. The day light didn't belong to him, nor did it belong to any of the night time dwelling creatures that lived in the shadows of darkness. There was only one race that the daylight hours belonged to, and that was the two-legers.

Instead of thinking about it any further, he chose to try to put his anger and animosity towards the two-legers out of his mind and take advantage of the coziness of his den. Placing his head down upon his weathered hand like paws, he stared towards the front of his den and watched as the veil of ivy gently swayed in the breeze. Though hunger still panged at his stomach, he was able to push the desire for food out of his mind, and think of other things instead. Knowing that he was safe from the prying eyes of the two-legers, he closed his eyes. Night time would again come, but for now it was time for him to rest.

Rest never came easily for him, and this day was not any different than any other. Instead of sleeping, he often found himself just staring out at the entrance of his den. His thoughts were always agitated, and in the place of sleep, he would lay awake and allow his mind wander. On this day he obsessively once more thought about his life and the hardships he had gone through, and about the revenge he hoped to someday enact upon those who had made it that way. The more he thought about it, the more his anger would grow within him. The two-legers just will not allow him to live in peace. Continuously they tormented him, they took over his hunting grounds, they took his food, his freedom, they took everything, and one night, when they don't expect it, he just might take back all of what was once rightfully his in retribution for the relentless torment that they caused to him over all the years.

As the creature's eyes now finally began to became heavy, his frustrations began to give way to weariness, and he started to slowly drift off to sleep.

27

Many years ago, too many to count, the bright sun light of the daytime had begun to bother the creature's eyes, it made them water and made it hard for him to see clearly. It was then that he had made the decision to become a creature of the night. He has now lived in the darkness for so long, that over the years, he has come to realized that at times, he could barely remember it being any other way.

A slight whimper escaped the muzzle of the creature as he sporadically jerked his head from side to side. Low growls were trailed by more light whimpering that followed each of his muscular jerks. Though he slept, his sleep was never restful, good dreams were occasionally dreamt, but more often than not, only disturbing, hurtful ones occupied his unconscious mind instead.

Most likely due to the fact that he was now living so closely to the two-legers once more, his slumber was often troubled by bad dreams. He just didn't like being this near to them, nor did he trust them. The two-legers had no idea that he was here though, or probably that his race even truly exists, but unaware, they naively continue to carry on with their basic daily lives.

As the creature continued to sleep, his dreams had drifted off to a time long ago, back to a different life than he had now, and to a different time, a time of great sadness. His dreams took him back to a time when he lived amongst the two-legers himself. He was once a man like them, a tall slender man that worked the fields off to the side of where he now hid. This was his land, his land fair and square. He came here early on and moved onto this acreage. He got his property through a government land deal in 1899, and then through hard work, he was able to claim deed to it, and it became his own. He once had a family too, a wife that he had brought with him onto the land, and two children, both daughters, that were born there. For him, it seemed like it had all happened a life time ago, and in a way for him, it truly did.

Though consciously only retaining small parts of his memory from that time, most of his memories now only came back to him in his dreams. Consciously, what memories he did have of his past life were now beginning to become blurred to him, and some even being erased by the ravages of time. In his dreams, he remembered that he had been a farmer, working the fields, turning the soil and planting the seeds for the crops all on his own. Not being from the village, Josiah minded his own business and stayed to himself and his family as much as possible. He never had the need to ask others from the village for help, and they looked down upon him for being nothing but a dirt farmer. He didn't care what the villagers thought of him though, he was a proud man, proud of what he had been able to achieve, and proud of what he had accomplished all on his own.

One hot summer day when the sun was high in the sky, and his work was done, Josiah came in from working the wheat fields with a cold cup of water from the nearby well pump on his mind. As he approached his house, he paused to scan the beauty of his fields. He was proud of his fields of grain that he had grown, and the food that it would provide for his family. He looked from one boundary of his land to the other, taking in the beauty of all that it held. He was very pleased with what he had accomplished for his family and himself. Starting from nothing, a poor orphan boy with no family and nowhere to live, then being adopted into a Dutch speaking farming family from the next town over, to now being a land owner with a farm and a family of his own. Smiling to himself, he proudly considered himself as being one of the richest men he knew. Not in money, but in other ways that mattered even more.

As he turned around and headed back towards the house, he started to hear a ruckus coming from the barn, the cattle were mooing loudly and stomping the ground as if something was frightening them. Josiah turned towards the barn and took a few steps forward. As the bellowing got louder, he began to run towards the barn to see what was going on with his livestock. Hurrying in, he saw that his cows were nervously pacing back and forth and shoving each other with their bodies and butting each other with their heads to get the others out of their way.

Looking around, Josiah couldn't see anything in the barn that would have set them off like that. Climbing the ladder to the loft area, he cautiously peered over the edge to see if there was something, or someone hiding up there. Seeing nothing he climbed back down and inspected the stall areas. Satisfied that nothing was in the barn itself, he walked back out the door and went around the backside of the barn. He looked around as he scanned the fields adjacent the barn. Seeing nothing there, he looked down at the loose dirt surrounding the sides of the barn to see if there were any animal tracks there that might give him any indication as to what had upset the cows so much. Several feet in front of him, Josiah saw something out of the ordinary. Walking up to it for a closer look, he saw that it was a track of a large animal, and it was fresh.

"What the hell is that?" he quietly asked himself as he bent down to get a closer look. "Another damn wolf," he told himself under his breath. "Another big one at that," he continued to say to himself as he put his right hand down next to the track. The track was elongated, and unlike any other wolf print that he had ever seen. The nails at the front of the track were large and spanned at least half an inch across at the base of the toe pads, and the foot area itself appeared to have a second back pad that sat not far behind the first, that gave it the look of having an almost human like heal.

"Damn, it really is back. this looks just like that same damn wolf track that I saw before when we lost the stock. This track is far too big to be a regular wolf though," he thought to himself. Looking closer at the heal section of the foot print, Josiah scratched his head. *"This has to be a wolf, but yet what is wrong with its feet?"* he asked himself. *"If this really is a wolf track, then this isn't a normal wolf, and whatever this thing is, it has to be huge,"* he thought to himself as he continued to stare at the print.

Standing back upright, Josiah turned and looked around the field again to be sure that whatever had been there and left the strange tracks, wasn't there any longer. Seeing nothing else out of the ordinary other than the strange wolf type tracks, Josiah went back into the barn to check on the cows. Several of them were still pacing back and forth and showing signs of uneasiness, but some had begun to settle down. Not

31

seeing any signs of physical injury to the cows, he was hoping that it meant that whatever that strange wolf type animal was, that it had just been outside right before he got back in from the fields, and that it didn't actually have time to get in the barn with his herd.

Thankful that his cows were safe, Josiah gave a sigh of relief as he closed and secured the barn doors. He couldn't afford to lose any more of his herd to this strange wolf. Taking one last look around the fields, he turned to head for the house.

As he walked towards the house, Josiah paused to look back over his shoulder towards the barn and again scan the field for any sign of the strange wolf. He could still feel the odd uncomfortable feeling inside of him that had started when he began to hear the cows bellowing from inside the barn.

Josiah could still hear nervous bellowing and mooing that was coming from inside of the barn, but it wasn't a panicked sound like it had been before. *"Why won't they settle,"* he wondered to himself as he stared at the barn. *"Maybe they can feel it too,"* he thought. He had been a farmer long enough to know that this was very unusual behavior for his cattle. Other than the last time that he suspected that this wolf was here, his cows had never been this upset, not even when there was the occasional smaller wolf or mountain lion roaming in the area. That fact in itself told him, that whatever this was, it was back.

As Josiah turned and looked towards his house again, and as he did so, a sudden wave of panic entered his body. His chest tightened up, and he felt as if he couldn't breathe. The realization that his wife and daughters were alone in the house with this thing roaming around had just hit him. Josiah froze as he looked towards the house that now seemed as though it was miles away from where he stood. The need to get to his family pushed him forwards. Breaking out into a sprint, Josiah ran as quickly as he could towards his house. Keeping his eyes glued on the doorway that led into his house, Josiah accidentally stumbled over a rough patch of earth and tumbled to the ground. Unable to get his hands out in front of him in time, Josiah fell face forward down into the gravelly soil. Hitting hard, Josiah groaned as he rolled over onto his back. With his face scratched and his nose bleeding, he did his best to get back to his feet. Regaining his balance, he unconsciously brushed himself off and when he did, he noticed that his shirt was ripped and covered in blood, blood that was dripping from his own nose. Using his sleeve, he wiped his nose and then without even thinking, he lifted his shirt tail up to try to stop the bleeding.

Looking towards his house again, Josiah felt a knot forming in the pit of his stomach and he let out a small sob. He could feel it deep inside of himself that what he was going to find in the house, and it wasn't going to be good. Taking a deep breath, Josiah stumbled forward as he again began to awkwardly jog towards his house.

As he stumbled onto the porch, Josiah collapsed forwards and placed both of his bloodied hands on either side of the screen door to catch himself from falling. Lifting his head to look in through the screen, time instantly slowed down and came to a total standstill. A large lump began to form in his throat and he could barely breath as in horror, he saw his wife's motionless bloodied body lying before him on the kitchen floor.

"Sara! No!" he cried out to his wife as he grabbed the handle on the door and flung it open. Running into the kitchen he cried out again, "Sara, no, no, no…"

After running to his wife's side, Josiah fell down to his knees. As he knelt down, shock began to set in and everything thing around him now seemed to be proceeding in slow motion. Tears began to well up in his eyes and stream down his face as he looked upon his wife's lifeless, bloodied and broken body.

"No, no, no," he cried out in agony. "Why would somebody do this to you, why?" he cried out through his pain as he raised his hands up to the sides of his face. Tears now ran uncontrollably down his face as he looked at Sara's lifeless body. Raising his arms up, he used his shirt sleeves to try to dry his tears.

Looking down at his wife, he could clearly see that she had been raped and severely beaten. Her torn and bloodied dress was still pulled up around her waist, with the skirt part of it thrown over her and covering her abdominal area. Looking at her, he noticed that her undergarments were gone as well. Biting his lower lip, Josiah slowly turned his wife's face towards him. Upon seeing his wife's face, he let out a sharp gasp. He could see that his wife's once beautiful face had been slit open from the corner of her mouth to her left ear, exposing the insides of her now gaping mouth. There were several other deep scratches on the right side of her face as well that were both above and below the one that opened up the left side of her face.

Staring at his wife's face in shock, he began to momentarily disassociated himself from the situation. Thoughts about what could have happened began to run through his mind. He cocked his head and began to wonder what had caused the cuts on his wife's face, but he didn't think that the damage was from a knife, it had been from something else, something sharp at tip, but yet wider and cruder with duller edges that had snagged the flesh and caused the slightly ragged cut. As he continued to stare at his wife and cry, a noise from outside momentarily caught his attention. It sounded like the hinges of a door creaking, but when he turned his head and looked through the screen door, he saw nothing. Looking back down to his wife, he began to cry even harder.

"Who did this to you? Who....?" He cried out as he raised his left hand up and pushed his fingers through his hair. Feeling a tacky type resistance, he pulled his hand down from his head and saw that he not only had his own blood covering it, but his wife's blood now as well. Staring down at his now blood-soaked hands, he became nauseated, turned and gagged. After throwing up onto the floor next to where he knelt, Josiah looked down at his hands again and anxiously wiped the blood off of them onto the front of his shirt and pants.

Looking back down at his wife, tears continued to run from his eyes, and drip down onto his wife's now severely disfigured face. Leaning forward, he lightly kissed her on the forehead and then using his thumb, he attempted to wipe away some of his tears that had fallen onto her face. As his tears continued to flow and drip onto the floor, he once more leaned forward and put his arm around his wife's body before placing the side of his face down onto her bare chest and sobbing into it.

Josiah's wife Sara, had been a beautiful woman. She had long flowing blond hair that cascaded well down past her shoulders to the middle of her back. It was a total contrast against Josiah's own unusual dark jet-black hair. Sara also had the face of an angel that had the ability to turn any gentleman's eye, even from a distance away. Though the years on the farm had been hard on her, she never lost the glow that haloed over her. She was his gift from God, but that gift had now been taken away as she now laid on the floor of their house, lifeless in a pool of her own blood. Patches of her long blond hair that had been ripped from her scalp, now lay indiscriminately tossed onto the floor. *"Who would do this to you, who???"* Josiah asked himself over and over again as he continued to scan the floor about him for any signs at all.

Taking in a deep breath, Josiah tried to regain his composure. Forcing himself to remove his gaze from his wife's face, he scanned further down her body and watched as the last of the blood still remaining in her body, drained and expanded from both sides of her corpse. Out of the silence that now consumed his house, Josiah thought he could hear a drip, drip, drip. As he listened closer, it came to him what he was hearing. His wife's life sustaining blood was now seeping down between the cracks of the wooden floorboards, and was trickling down drip by drip onto the damp, musty sod below.

Now feeling numb inside, Josiah closely looked at where his wife's clothes were shredded and bloodied, it looked as if a very sharp tipped hand rake had been taken to them. Reaching down, he pushed his wife's skirt from her midsection back down over her exposed genital area to protect her dignity even in death, and it was then that he again gasped as he saw that his wife's stomach had been split open. With the initial shock that he felt from finding his wife's butchered body, this is the one thing that had never entered his mind. He hadn't even thought about the unborn baby that she had been carrying. Never would he had thought that someone, something, would go as far as cutting out an unborn baby from its mothers' womb.

"No! No, no, no, no!" he cried out over and over again as he took his fist and pounded it, and pounded it again onto the bloodied floor beneath him, all the while splashing more blood onto his own clothing, and onto his own face. "No...no...no....," he cried out again as he lowered his head in agony. "Why take our baby...why..." he sobbed.

Time now crawled at a snail's pace for Josiah. After what seemed like an eternity, he began to regain his composure again as the numb feeling once more took over his body. It was in that moment that another wave of terror washed over him. What about his children, were his children? His daughters had also in the house with their mother.

Taking a deep breath, Josiah turned and looked over his shoulder at the doorway behind him. Slowly crawling to the entranceway, he took hold of the framework the stood between the kitchen and the living room and managed to pull himself up onto his now trembling, unstable legs. Still suffering from shock, he felt weak and very unsteady on his feet. Supported by the doorway, Josiah looked back at his wife's body, and then back towards where the children's rooms were. Biting his lower lip and inhaling deeply, he gazed at his oldest daughter's closed door. *"Please God, let them be okay,"* he silently prayed over and over again.

Josiah and his wife Sara had two children, both little girls, one was barely three years of age, and the older one was five. Both girls were the most important things in their parent's lives. The baby that his wife had been carrying, was to be their third child, and it was hoped that it would be a boy, at least that is what the midwife had told them that she thought it would be due to the way that his wife was carrying it within her womb. The midwife, Ms. Dixie, she owned and ran a small diner in the village. She was a very kind woman and went out of her way to be kind to them. She had been there to help with the delivery of both of his daughters as well.

Josiah stood in the doorway listening for any sounds, any sounds at all that would give him hope that his daughters were safe and unharmed. Trying to steady himself, he slowly began walking through the small living room towards the far wall where his oldest daughter's bedroom was. He paused outside the closed door, afraid to open it. Drawing upon his inner courage, he slowly reached out and grasp the metal door handle and lifted the lever to unlatch it. Standing motionless, he took another deep breath before he began to push the door open. The old metal hinges creaked loudly as he slowly pushed the wooden door open. Looking in, he saw his five-year-old daughter lying on her bed in front of him.

She appeared to be peacefully sleeping on her side as she facing away from him.

"Anna?" he called out to her in a voice barely louder than a whisper. "Anna? Anna where are you?" he said to her again.

Gripped with fear when he heard no response, Josiah felt faint and had to lean against the door frame for support. Closing his eyes for a moment and taking a deep breath, he slowly regained some balance again and proceeded to walk forward to his daughter's bed. With a shaky hand he reached out to her, and touched her on the shoulder. As his hand made contact with her arm, the young girls still warm lifeless body rolled back towards him, and she came to rest flat on her back on the bed.

Startled by the sight of his daughter's appearance, Josiah cried out in anguish and stumbled backwards from the bed. Catching the heal of his left boot on an uneven floorboard, he fell backwards and struck his head against the wall. The impact left him dazed, and unable to get up.

Josiah sobbed as he sat on the floor looking up at his oldest daughter. The sight of her lying before him with her throat cut open, and with what looked like a deep knife wound in her abdomen, was too much for him to bear. He saw that the top of her dress had also been shredded in the same fashion as her mother's dress had been, and that she too had scratches on her face and arms.

Regaining his strength, Josiah slowly got up and again approached his daughter's dead body. He knelt down beside her bed and gently took her little hand up into that of his own. Bringing it up to his face, he lightly kissed it and paused in agony as his lips touched her cooling pale skin. Tears continued to run down his face as he stroked her small, delicate hand with his fingers. Her skin was pale like her mother's was, and she had shared all the same features of her as well, with her glowing beauty being just one of them.

Standing back upright, Josiah reached down and took the covers from the bed in his hands and began to pull them up over his daughter's dead body. Pausing for a moment, he looked down at his young daughter's face and her flowing blond hair. It was her mother's hair; she had gotten her golden hair from her. *"At least she didn't have to suffer like her mother did, she wasn't, she wasn't... raped. She was spared that indignity,"* he thought to himself as more tears began to run from his eyes and drip from the end of his nose. Reluctantly, as if saying a final goodbye, he finished pulling the covers up and over his daughter's face as he let out a choked-up sob.

Just as he began to take a step back from his daughter's bed, a flash of something shiny caught his eye. Cocking his head and looking in the direction of the reflection, he focused in through his tears and saw that a bloodied knife was lying half concealed in the bedding. He then realized that it was the knife that had been used on his daughter, and it could have been also used on his wife, Sara, as well.

Josiah slowly reached out and picked the knife up, wrapping his fingers around its handle. Holding it in his hand, the knife felt heavy and cold. As he gripped the knife firmly with his fingers tightly wrapped around it, his anger and hatred began to boil over for whoever did this to his family.

Josiah turned and stared at the doorway leading out of the room for a moment before walking over to it with the knife still in his hand. Looking back at his daughter's bed, he got a far away, disconnected look in his eyes. Reality was being questioned in his mind right now. He so badly wanted all of this to be nothing but a bad dream, but in his heart, he knew that that was the furthest thing from the truth. The truth was, this was his reality now.

Josiah slowly walked down the hallway until he came to another shut door on the right. Pausing as he had before, he said a silent prayer in his mind before reaching for the cold steel latch. This was the room of his younger daughter Ava. She had just turned three years old the month before, and they had given her small party to celebrate the occasion. It was just the four of them, but that is all they needed. Her mother had baked her a cake and they had gotten her little pink candles from Ms. Dixie for on it for her to blow out. It was a joyous day, one that he would treasure for the rest of his life.

Holding his breath, Josiah pushed downward on the latch and the door slowly creaked open. Already numbed by finding his wife and older daughter murdered, Josiah braced himself for how he may find his youngest daughter as well. Peering in, he called out to his young daughter.

"Ava?" he quietly called out. "Ava, are you in here?" he asked with fear rising up in his heart. Hearing no response, he again took a deep breath before pushing the door open a little further and looking in. From where he stood in the doorway, he couldn't see anything out of the ordinary, so he pushed the door open the rest of the way and slowly walked in. Standing just inside of the entranceway, he called out to his youngest daughter once more.

"Ava?" He called out. Still no answer came. Slowly he walked over to the young girl's bed. Her bed was empty. He looked on the floor on the other side, and again he saw nothing. Josiah then knelt and got down on one knee so that he could look underneath the bed. The young girl was not in her room. Turning, he ran from the room and went to his own room that he had shared with his wife thinking that maybe the young girl would be in there.

"Ava!" he shouted loudly as he ran into the room, but not a sound came in response. Not seeing the girl there, he ran back to the door and ran out. Panic started to set into him as he ran throughout the house calling out to her, but there was no sign of the little girl anywhere.

The house felt heavy now. Death had come to visit, not once, twice, but three times, and the mystery of the missing girl also filled the air. The smell of freshly spilt blood seemed to cling to everything that Josiah had touched with his own bloodied hands and clothing as he stumbled through.

As Josiah made his way back to the living room, there was another pungent odor in the air that he just noticed for the first time. It was a stronger, more overpowering musky type smell. It smelled like the smell of an animal. To Josiah, it smelled as if something had purposefully marked its territory there. The odor was strong and over powering, almost taking his breath away. Putting his hand up to cover his nose, Josiah backed away and headed for the kitchen where his wife still lay.

Not knowing what to do, Josiah went over to the table and pulled out a kitchen chair, sat down and sobbed. Through his tears, he looked down at his wife still laying in a pool of her own blood. As he continued to look at his wife's body, his thoughts then wandered to the sight of his older daughter lying lifeless on her bed, and then to Ava.

"Where is Ava? Who would have taken her, and what do they want with my daughter?" he silently asked himself. As he sat on the kitchen chair, feeling numb inside, his tears began to slow, and he felt empty inside.

Forcing himself to look away from his wife, he instead looked down at the knife that he still held in his hand, he ran his fingers over the crudely made hand-carved wooden handle, and the double-edged steel blade. It was a roughly made knife, forged in an ancient way of days gone by. Looking closer at the handle, he could see it was made from a very hard wood, possibly teak, and from the patina on it, it appeared very old as well. It was then that he noticed that on the side of the handle there appeared to be a worn face and upper body carved into it. Looking even closer, he saw that the carving wasn't that of a human, but instead what looked like a crude rendition of an odd-looking upright standing wolf. As he turned it over in his hands, the features began to became even clearer for him. The carving was definitely in

43

the shape of some kind of a strange looking wolf, an animal that he had never seen before.

Josiah was still staring at the knife when he heard the sound of horses galloping up his drive. Quickly he got up from the chair and ran over to look out the window to see who was approaching. The men were still too far away for him to recognize who they were, and another nervous knot began to form in the pit of his stomach. Cautiously he peering out from behind the curtain that covered the window. He feared that it might have been the murderer returning with his friends to finish him off as well.

As the horses turned the corner, Josiah could see through the swirled pane of glass that it was the sheriff and some of his deputies that were approaching. *"Who, how did they know?"* he thought to himself.

Seeing it was the sheriff, Josiah stood upright and slowly walked to the door. Opening it cautiously, he stepped outside to meet them. Upon seeing Josiah standing before them, the sheriff and the other men pulled up on the reins of their horses, dismounted and drew their weapons.

"Drop it!" the sheriff yelled loudly at Josiah. Looking down while still in a daze, Josiah saw that he was still holding the ancient knife in his hand. Not comprehending the order that he was given, Josiah just looked up at the men blankly and continued to stand where he was on the front porch.

"I said drop it!" the sheriff again bellowed at Josiah as he tried to get him to let go of the knife.

Still in a state of shock after seeing the grizzly scene of his family's murder, Josiah continued to not fully comprehending what he was being told to do.

"My family!" Josiah cried out in a thick Dutch accent as he took a step forward and pointed back towards his house with the knife.

"Damnit Josiah, I said drop it," the sheriff again ordered.

Josiah unconsciously took another step towards them and the sheriff fired off a warning shot from his smaller caliber pistol into the air.

"My family," Josiah said as he took another step towards the armed men.

With that, the sheriff fired his pistol and hit Josiah in the left shoulder. The bullet only grazed him, but he was hit hard enough that the impact of the bullet spun him backward and almost knocked him off his feet.

Josiah turned back towards the sheriff with knife still in hand, and again stumbled forwards. The sheriff again took aim at him.

"What, what are you doing?" Josiah stammered as he stared at the sheriff. "Why did you shoot me?" he questioned.

"Damn it man, I said drop it, now!" the sheriff ordered just before he shot off one more bullet, this time dropping Josiah where he stood.

Not knowing where he was, Josiah woke up in a jail cell two days later. He was lying on his back on an old ratty cot that smelled of old sweat and whisky. His left shoulder throbbed and upon looking down, he saw that his arm was being supported by a homemade muslin sling. Through his hair, he could feel that he had a bandage on his head where the second bullet had left a deep gash in his scalp above his left ear. Raising his arm and putting his fingers up to the bandage, he winced in pain as he touched it. Feeling confused, he started to nervously look around to try to figure out where he was.

"Well, lookie here, nice of you to finally wake up from your little nap Wolfe."

Seeing Josiah put his hand up to his head and winch, the man chuckled and continued speaking. "Don't worry, you've just been grazed," the sheriff told him through the bars on the cell. "You sure ain't goin' to be dyin' from that," he added.

"What happened? Why am I here in this cell?" Josiah asked the man as he slowly sat up on the cot.

"What? Are you tryin' to tell me that you don't remember why you are here?" the sheriff asked as he turned and spit tobacco into the spittoon next to his desk. "Well, speak up boy, cat got your tongue?" he growled at him.

"No, no I don't," he stammered. "Why am I here? Where is my wife?" Josiah asked as he looked around the jail house. Seeing his surroundings, fear began to rise up from deep inside of him.

46

"You won't be seein' your wife anytime soon, that's for sure," the sheriff shot back at him with obvious hatred in his voice. Spitting tobacco off to the side of him again, he shook his head and chuckled at his prisoner.

"Why, what do you mean? I want to see my wife and I want out of this cell!" Josiah demanded with the thick Dutch accent to his voice.

"Not goin' to happen Mr. Wolfe," the sheriff told him as he pulled out a heavy wooden chair for himself and sat down at his desk.

"Will you just please tell me what is going on! I need to know!" Josiah shouted angerly at the man.

"You mean to tell me that you really don't remember what you did?" the sheriff asked with a snide, cruel sounding chuckle to his voice. "We found you two days ago standin' out in front of your house, bloodied and holding a knife, the exact knife that you had just murdered your wife and daughter with!"

"No! You're lying to me! Tell me the truth, I deserve the truth, why am I here and where is my wife!" Josiah shouted as he got up and moved towards the bars that stood between him and the sheriff.

Seeing Josiah getting up and moving towards him, the sheriff slapped one hand down onto the top of his calf and got up from his chair. He pushed the chair back away from him with such force, that it toppled over backward and skidded on the worn wooden floor before coming to rest against the wall. As the sheriff took two steps towards the cell, he put out his hand and pointed his finger right at Josiah and snarled as he spoke.

"Well now, you listen to me you low down good for nothin' dirt farmin' scum! Your wife is dead! Your daughter is dead! And you are the one lyin' here, not me!" the sheriff told Josiah. "And one way or the other, I will get you to admit to that! But what I want to know from you right now is, where the hell is your other daughter?" the sheriff demanded. "What the hell did you do with her? I suppose you are goin' to claim that you don't remember what you did with her either, huh! You perverted maggot; we know your kind. You come here from who knows where, you settle on our land and expect us to automatically accept you. You low down immigrants can't even speak English proper. You with your funny accents and funny way of talkin'. Y'all should be just all sent back to where you came from. We don't want your kind here, and this is exactly why! Now I'm goin' to ask you one more time, where the hell is your daughter?" he screamed at him now only inches from Josiah's face.

Taken aback by the verbal attack put forth by the sheriff, Josiah took a few steps back from the bars, and away from the menacing face of the sheriff that was now staring him down with absolute hatred in his eyes.

"I was born here in this country just like you!" Josiah yelled back. "I was raised by Dutch farmers and that is why I talk with an accent! I am no different than you are!" Josiah yelled at the man in anger.

"That still doesn't mean that you didn't kill your family now does it!" the sheriff shot back at him. "Now, tell me why you did it, and where the hell your youngest daughter is!" he said as he sneered at the man.

"I don't know what you are talking about! I was out working in my fields, and the next thing I remember is waking up here. I don't know what you are talking about!" he said as his heavily laden Dutch accented voice started to crackle with emotion. Josiah turned and sat down on the cot and bowed his head. Without looking up at the sheriff he asked, "Is it true, is my wife and my daughter really dead?"

"Yes, they are, and you are bein' blamed for it. We know you did it and there is no denyin' it. We caught you with the murder weapon in your hand, and your wife's blood all over you. You made a real mess in that place. We also found your bloody hand prints in both of you daughter's rooms, and there is no way that you are goin' to explain that fact away! No way at all. You're lucky, we should have just hung you right there and then."

"How can you blame me? I didn't do it. I couldn't kill my family! You know I couldn't do it!" Josiah said as he pleaded with the man.

"No, I don't know that, how would I know that. None of us know very much about you or your family Mr. Wolfe. You and your wife weren't exactly neighborly to any of us here now were you. You and your family all kept to yourself all these years, and rarely even set foot in town. Hell, the only time you even came into town when you needed somethin' from us, and that was about it. You never associated with anyone, or said anythin' to anyone unless you had to. We don't know you Mr. Wolfe. How are we to know what you are capable of, and what you aren't. But after what you just did to your family, now I guess we do, don't we!"

"Just because I preferred to stay to myself and keep us pure from a lot of the worldly things that your towns people are accustom too, that is why you think I killed my whole family? That is no reason!" he told him.

"Are you sayin' that you are better than we are? You needed to keep yourself pure from us heathens! You worthless piece of shit! You are goin' to rot for this one Wolfe, and I'll see to it that it happens soon!"

Josiah could only sit on the edge of his bunk and silently look up at the sheriff. He didn't know what to say, or how to even try to defend himself.

"Now, I didn't say that you killed your whole family, not all of them anyway. I said that you killed your wife and daughter. Your youngest one there, now she is still missin' and what I want to know is what you did with her."

"I don't know what you mean. I didn't do anything with her. I left Anna and Ava in the house with their mother when I went out to work the fields. The girls were playing in their rooms and Sara was doing some canning. It was hot working in the field and so I was coming in for some water," Josiah started to recount. "I remember on the way in, I was hearing the cows bellowing for some reason, so I walked up to the barn on my way in. They were pacing back and forth very nervously about something. I went into the barn to have a look around, but I didn't see anything, and after that, I just can't remember anything."

"Well, maybe durin' all that time that you 'don't remember', you killed your wife and daughter. You ever think of that! You sliced them both up, and then you gutted your wife like a pig!"

"No! I didn't do it! I couldn't have. I love my family, I could never harm them," Josiah screamed as he stood up and faced the sheriff again.

"Did you kill your little one too? You keep sayin' that you love your family, if you love them so much, you'll tell me what you did with your youngest, and where she is now," the sheriff pressed on. "Well, are you goin' to tell me what you did with her or do I have to beat it out of you?" the sheriff yelled at him.

"No! I can't, wait, I don't know!"

"Now wait a minute, are you now admittin' that you did somethin' with her now?" the sheriff asked Josiah acting rather pleased with himself. "Are you ready to finally tell me what you did with your youngest daughter?"

"I don't know. You are trying to confuse me; I don't know anything anymore!" Josiah said as he pounded his fists in the air. "Will you at least please tell me what happened to my family? I need to know!"

"Bein' you don't seem to remember, or at least you are claimin' not to remember anythin', I will refresh your memory for you. We believe that you came in from the fields and you were upset. We surmise that you had gotten into a fight with your wife. Maybe she didn't want to put out for you or somethin', we don't know. But you raped your wife right there in the kitchen and then you sliced that pretty little lady's face wide open from her mouth to her ear, probably so no other man would ever look at her again. That would be enough to turn any man's stomach if you ask me. But then you weren't finished, you also cut out your unborn child from her belly! You butchered her like she was an old fat sow!" the sheriff screamed at him. "That is another mystery too, where is that baby? What did you do with it? After butchering your wife, still mad, you went to your eldest daughter's room and you cut her up too. After that though, we don't know what you did. We don't know what you did with your unborn baby, or what you did with your youngest daughter either, we searched for both of them, we even looked down your well, but we never found either.

We had reports from your closest neighbor of screamin' and that is what brought us out to your place that day. If it weren't for that, you might have gotten away with it. But when we got there, there you were, comin' out of the house with the murder weapon in your hand. I ordered you to drop the knife, but you wouldn't listen. I even gave you the benefit of the doubt and shot a warnin' shot off into the air, but bein' the stupid fool that you are, you just came at us with it. I had no choice but to shoot you. The first shot grazed your shoulder there, the second shot is what took you down. If I would have had the notion to kill you like I do now, you wouldn't be sittin' there on that cot right now, you would be six feet under in the pauper graveyard where your kind belongs, lyin' next to your wife and daughter."

Josiah sat silently in disbelief. He couldn't believe that he could have done such a thing to his family. It was more then he could comprehend and mentally grasp. He loved his family more than anything, more than life itself. He told himself that there was no way he could have killed his family. No possible way. Leaning his back against the wall, Josiah brought his right hand up to his face and sobbed.

B.J. MOORE

Chapter Two

The creature laid back its ears and whimpered as he cried in his sleep. The fur below the part wolf, part human's eyes dampened as its tears flowed down his face. Nightmares were a common occurrence for him. In his dreams he relived the past, and in his unconscious mind, he replayed the horrors of it over and over again. He was haunted by a memory of one particular day, as well as the many days that followed it. His life as he knew it had ended the day his family was slain. All were gone but for one, and the that one was possibly still out there somewhere. No one knew for sure what had happened to the little girl in his dreams, all that Josiah did know for sure though, was that he didn't kill her, nor did he kill any of them.

The nightmarish dreams continued to haunt Josiah's thoughts throughout his daylight slumber, until the crepuscular hour once more began to approach.

Awaking and opening his eyes, Josiah slowly raised his head and look out towards the mouth of the cave. He instinctively knew that the light of day was again beginning to fade, and that the darkness of the night would yet again soon be making its presence known.

Sitting up so that he could get a better view of the outside world, Josiah could see that the evening hues in the sky were turning a purplish pink. Soon, very soon, the daytime would give way to the shadows, evening would finally set in and his time would be at hand. The crepuscular hour was his time, the time that spanned from dusk to dawn. This is the time when the animals of the night are the most active, venturing out into what they consider the safest time for them to feed and wander about. But for the prey animals, the darkness of this hour is also what makes them easier targets for the predators such as he.

It was during the crepuscular hours that Josiah would occasionally venture out under the cover of darkness, to keep an eye on what was going on with the two-legers in the village. Though he loathes them, he felt the need to sporadically keep tabs on their coming and goings, and to hear their conversations from the cover of darkness. He listened for any mention of a mysterious creature in the area, or a premise that there may be something different going on outside of the village. Talk like that could lead to misfortune for him if he didn't already know, and the early warnings would give him the chance to quickly depart from the area.

Early on, Josiah would hear his name mentioned now and then. The two-legers would speculate as to what had happened to his family, and what had happened to Josiah himself. Those that had mentioned his name talked of him and his mysterious disappearance. The majority surmised that he had possibly fallen prey to the rogue wolves that were strewn about in the woods beyond the valley. To them that was the most likely explanation to his demise, but being there was never any body, no one ever knew for sure. But those days of idle chatter have all passed now, he and his family, a family that he can barely remember himself, have now all been but forgotten about, and for that he is glad. Now the two-legers conversations have changed to other subjects, subjects that he is disinterested in to say the least, so he rarely feels it is worth it to take the chance to continue to go back.

Though not totally nocturnal, if the clouds hang heavy in the sky and block the brightness of the day, he can still venture out into the world. A daylight outing for any predator is always dangerous though. There is constantly a chance of human interaction in doing so. Though he was an expert with blending in with his surroundings, and almost being able to totally disappear into the trees, there was still the chance that a two-leger could possibly catch a glimpse of him, and if that happened, he would have no choice as to what he would have to do. He could never allow a two-leger that had seen him full-on to go back to the village alive, not when they would be carrying stories to tell of a great part wolf, part man like creature that walks on two legs.

The chance that anyone would believe the two-legers stories were slim, but with the death and dismemberment of the village's sheriff several years prior, and a witness that swore to seeing a great beast resembling a huge wolf running from town the same night that he died, those accounts all could very easily be brought up again. So, for Josiah, he decided it was best to err on the side of caution, and to remain hidden during the daytime hours, and live a nocturnal life as much as possible. That way, the daylight can be for the arrogant two-legers, and those unlike himself.

Josiah stretched out his limbs as he rose up onto all fours. As he laid his ears back and closed his eyes, a massive yawn escaped through his lips. Settling back down upon his haunches, a low rumble was felt rippling throughout his abdomen. It was a signal from his body indicating his need for nourishment from deep within. The young deer that he consumed from the night before was just a small pittance of what his body actually needed to survive, and what had been left in him of it, had already quickly passed through his system and was expelled. So, this night he would hunt once more for something more nourishing, and a considerably much larger and sustaining meal to consume.

For the most part, Josiah had been surviving on rabbits and woodchucks while living in the valley, but that was nowhere near what he really needed to feed his large body and to survive. The occasional deer would wander by while he was on the hunt, but even they were becoming scarcer of late. There just wasn't the same amount of prey animals that there had been at one time in the valley. The two-legers once again had over hunted the game, taking more deer than they had needed to feed their families, and they weren't allowing the species time to recover and repopulate as they should have.

He was going to have to hunt for larger prey soon to satisfy his increasing cravings. The taking of smaller game was more easily hidden because they were plentiful, and the two-legers didn't notice them missing, but the larger prey animals, being they were still fewer in numbers, or even cattle, they would leave more evidence and draw more attention to the fact that there was something large once more living in the valley.

The evidence of the loss of larger prey would signify that there was a new predator in the area by way of skeletal remains. Though he was sure that the remains would be blamed on the occasional grey wolf roaming through the area, he didn't want anyone to wonder if there was something else out there in the darkness of the forest as well. Josiah wanted to keep his presence hidden for as long as he could, or at least until he himself decided that he was ready to move on.

Standing upright again within the large interior of his den, the silence of the night was broken as Josiah's bones began to start to snap and crack as they worked their way back into place, and he once again became bipedal. Walking over to the mouth of the cave, Josiah knelt down and looked out at the last glimpses of light that remained of the setting sun. The remnants of the thin streaks of light slowly dwindled until they were eventually snuffed out by the tree tops on the horizon. With that, the crickets then began to chirp their evening melodies, and the last of the song birds had settled in for the night. Placing his arms over his head, he again yawned and stretched his extremities, his bones cracking with every manipulation of his massive form.

Josiah's hairy arms showed signs of age and experience. Under the layer of dark fur were scars from previous battles fought, but yet battles that he always managed to win. One scar in particular remained with him from his old life, a deep divot above his ear where a misplaced bullet had grazed his skin. His chest, as with his arms and legs, were very muscular and were covered with the same thick dark charcoal grey/black fur as the rest of his body. His hands and his feet were both elongated, and where he used to have nails, he now had thick black claws that extended out two inches from his finger tips and toes. His head and face were what had taken on the most dramatic transformation over time. He now had the upright ears of a wolf, one on either side of his head, pointed and tall. His jaw and nose had both been shifted forwards as his skull was reformed and shaped to create a well-structured muzzle. His human teeth were dislodged and pushed out and replaced by those that were now more wolf-like in nature, with long sharp canine fangs jutting out from his upper and lower jaws. His eyes were also no longer his own either. They had changed from his natural dark brown human eyes, to eyes that were more golden amber in color, that now likewise also shown a luminescence reflective glow in the moonlight.

After the sun had gone away and fell below the tree line, that is when the world would open up for him, and when he was at his best. With only scant lighting at times, he could still spot a rabbit moving at 100 yards as if it were right in front of him. He had the best of both worlds, the craftiness and the agility of the wolf, and the intelligence and perceptiveness of man.

Still standing at the entrance to his den, Josiah stuck his muzzle outward and took in a deep breath of the cool night air. Nothing was coming to him; no messages were riding the breeze yet that night. It was evident that the other night time creatures haven't descended from their burrows up till now either. Back on all fours again, Josiah slowly crawled out of his lair and walked down the rocky descent from his cave to the fields below.

Josiah was not far from his den when he heard a noise. Freezing in place, he slowly rotated his ears towards where the noise had come from. Through his well-tuned ears, he picked up on what sounded like whispers being carried in the breeze. He could hear laughter and then faint talking following it. They were speaking in a language that he had no reason to use any longer, one that his vocal cords were not formed to speak anymore either. But he still knew it and understood it well. What he was hearing was the language of the two-legers.

As the voices that he heard got closer, Josiah quickly moved and crouched down behind the old downed apple tree. The voices were both male and female, but yet sounded different to him, their words were quite slurred, mixed in with high pitched laughing. He had heard the two-legers talk like this before in the village though, so he was well aware of what caused them to talk like this, they were both very drunk.

The scent that heavily clung to them in itself, was proof enough of their drunken state. The scent of the man was as rancid of an odor as Josiah had ever smelled. The sour scent of whisky filled his nostrils with disgust. The scent of the female though, her scent was different. The female two-leger still had the same rancid odor of alcohol that clung to her, as it did with the male, but there was another odor, a sweeter odor, that mingled with it. Though it piqued his interest, he wasn't immediately sure what this new scent was. In the back of his subconscious, he felt that at one time in his past that he had known it well, but now he wasn't sure. It had been far too long since he had been in the presence of a human female to immediately recognize it.

Drawing the air deeper into his lungs, the woman's scent was now becoming almost intoxicating to him, and the feeling just kept getting stronger as the couple began to approach closer and closer to him. It was then that a dawn of recognition all at once flooded over him, and he knew what was so stimulating about the woman's scent. The source of the uncontrollable feelings that were now increasingly racing through his body, began to become plain to him. He realized what it was that he was sensing from her. He now knew that the female two-leger was in season. Deeply drawing in another breath of air to fill his lungs, Josiah could smell and almost taste that irresistible scent of hormone laced blood that the female was shedding.

Josiah had to struggle with himself at this point to stay hidden. All he wanted to do was to go for the woman, but he knew that he couldn't. He started to feel a strange, strong burning sensation from deep within his groin that began to grow and increase in intensity, and as it did, it triggered a long-forgotten animal instinct from deep within him. That animal instinct made his body ache for her. He lightly groaned as a deep-seated aching feeling that virtually hurt him from within began to surface, an aching that begged for a merciful and speedy deliverance from it. It was all he could do not to open up his mouth and cry out as he again deeply inhaled and tasted the sweet aroma in the air.

Not since his wife was alive, had he had the pleasure of being in the company of a human female. There had been other females that he could have had his way with if he had so chosen to. But not human females, human females were special. It had been such a long time ago, that he had forgot what it was like to even be around a human female in heat, and to be able have her as he longed to. The urges he was feeling now were growing stronger within him, and he desired this female so badly that he painfully ached for her from deep within.

Digging his massive claws deep down into the soil beneath him, Josiah tried to keep his desires under control. He made a tight fist in the damp soil and squeezed it tightly as he tried to fight the raging hormonal urges growing from deep within. Josiah could feel the pressure growing stronger from within his groin, and the pain from the pressure was almost more than he could bare. As the sensations grew and got stronger, a small whimper managed to escaped from deep within his chest before he could stop it.

The two-legers heard him and the air got quiet as they both stopped speaking. Slowly turning around to look in his direction, they scanned the field between them and the tree line beyond. Afraid to move, they listened intently as they waited to see if there were any more sounds to be heard.

"Did you hear that?" the woman quietly whispered to her partner standing next to her.

"Yeah, I did. What was that?" he asked in a more sober voice.

They both quietly stood and stared at the spot where Josiah hid behind the brush of the old downed apple tree. Now he didn't dare to even move a muscle for fear that they would see where he was hidden. He was thankful that the evening had already begun and that it was now very dark out, for if it weren't, there would be no way that he could have managed to have concealed himself so well.

"I don't know, but I don't have a good feeling right now. I'm scared, let's get out of here okay," the woman pleaded nervously to the man beside her. "I really don't feel comfortable here anymore. I want to leave. Please, let's just go," she begged to him without taking her eyes off the downed tree and the brush where Josiah was hidden.

The man silently nodded his head and took the woman's arm in his hand. Backing up a few steps, the man forcefully pushed the woman behind him to protect her. While listening for more sounds to be emitted from the area beyond, an old great horned owl began to hoot and it startled them. Turning their heads upward, the couple looked for it in the tree line.

"Maybe it was just the owl we heard," the woman quietly told her suitor from behind.

"I don't know. Let's just keep walking okay," he told her as he again glanced back to where Josiah was hidden.

As the man continued to slowly walk backwards, the woman panicked and began to run towards the village. Realizing that he was now alone to face whatever it was that they had heard, the man then too turned and bolted back towards the village. Only after he got to the trees at the edge of the village did the man pause to turn to glance back in Josiah's direction. Staring out over the field, he saw nothing moving, and nothing nefarious that was stalking them in the dark. It was only then that he allowed himself to calm down, and he gave a loud sigh of relief.

The woman that he was with was already safely inside one of the buildings that stood along the streets edge, and satisfied that they weren't followed, the man turned his back and headed there as well. Just before shutting the door behind him, he once more scanned the field on the other side of the trees. It was as if he could feel himself being watched, and it made him edgy. As the man began to close the door behind him, he thought that he heard the sound of the owl hooting once more, and then the sound of a wolf howling off in the distance.

Josiah had watched in silence as the couple sprinted back to the edge of the field, and then back into the village where they felt again safe. Though he thought about it, he knew that there was no way he could follow them. Deep down he had wanted to give chase and kill the man so that he could take the woman for his own, but that would have only given his presence away.

Josiah admonished himself for feeling so weak, and for almost allowing himself become discovered. The scent of the woman though was just so powerful, and exciting to the point of being like an intoxicating drug that he couldn't get enough of. Her scent was so fresh, and so enticing that it made his insides churn up into knots. That feeling alone was almost more then he could control. Just from the scent that the woman was leaving in the air around him, he had felt an inner pressure in his groin begin to build, and then he felt himself growing stiff and hard in her presence. His sacks had begun to feel like they were filled with fire, a fire that needed to be expelled to be extinguished. He wanted to badly to be able to extinguish it with the human female, but he didn't dare. That feeling and inner turmoil created by the aching and the desperate longing for something that was just outside of his physical reach, is what had caused him to accidentally whine out loud. That feeling was something that meant much more to him at this moment, than any hunger pangs he still felt within.

As Josiah watched the two-legers quickly rushing out of the field and run back towards the village, he subconsciously started to slowly rotate his pelvis back and forth from the uncomfortable burning sensation coming from within his groin. As he put one of his large hands down to rub his aching sacks that hung from between his legs, the feelings and the excitement grew. Moving his hand upward towards his penile sheath, he unconsciously began to thrust his hips. As the feelings from deep within grew stronger, he began to thrust his hips quicker. As the strong desire began to become more uncontrollable, he desperately wanted to give chase and claim the human female for himself before it was too late, but she was already gone from his sight. With his feet firmly planted in the soil and his nails curled under, the frantic desire of relief washed over him, and Josiah thrust his head up into the air and let out a long mournful howl.

When Josiah began to calm down from the woman's presence, he sat back and sighed. Reaching down, he rubbed himself where he had felt the pressure building earlier. Upon touching his fur, he found that his crotch area was wet and covered in a warm, slimy fluid. He hadn't realized it at the time, but just the scent of the human female in heat, and in such close proximity to him had been too much. The subconscious rocking motion back and forth that he had done, and the rubbing of his hand on his penile sheath, had caused him to release the building pressure from within, and he freely ejaculated onto the ground.

After smelling the scent of the two-leger female, Josiah realized how much he needed and wanted a female of his own, how much he now yearned for the sensual touch of a female, and the warmth of having her body lying next to his. All of these thoughts began to work on his animalistic desires, a desire to take a female, any female that came near him, and breed with her. He knew that no human female would ever willing want him ever again, but he knew that his animal instincts would take over and he would force her to mate. And because of his newfound desires and lack of self-control, he knew that his days in the valley were now numbered.

As Josiah sat back, he quickly began to doze off, and his mind began to wonder. It took him to a place that seemed like a life time ago. Back to a time when Josiah had a woman of his own, to when he was married. In a way, these memories almost seemed foreign to him now, they almost didn't seem real, but he knew in his heart that they were. It was a time that he had everything a man could want in life, a loving wife, two daughters and another child on the way. He worked hard on the farm that he and his family lived on. He owned the land, and he raised cattle and other livestock as well. The farm is what gave them the life style they desired, and the freedom and the peacefulness that they had dreamed of.

Josiah recalled back to the spring just before their second daughter Ava turned three, it was then that they started to have some problems on the farm with some of the livestock. First, they started out mysteriously losing some of the chickens, and then the turkeys went missing as well. The birds were fine one day, and then in one night, half a dozen would suddenly come up missing. He saw the foot prints of a very large dog in the mud and blamed it on the neighbor's large sheepdog that lived at the farm over the hill. When Josiah confronted the man about it, the two had almost came to blows. The argument ended though when Josiah found out that the man's large sheepdog was found dead two days before his chickens had started to disappear. The dogs throat had been ripped out and the carcass was left lying in a pool of its own blood behind the man's barn. At that point Josiah had no idea what he was now dealing with.

After Josiah lost most of his chickens and all of the turkeys, some of the other live stock began to turn up missing as well. First, one of the dairy goats went missing, only to be found a few hundred yards from the barn. It had been killed and left half eaten, then a four-month-old beef calf was taken as well. It was then that he realized that he didn't have a dog problem, he had at least one large grey wolf on his land.

Setting out to catch the wolf, or wolves, Josiah set out leg hold traps in the areas that he thought that the wolves might be travel through to get to his barn. He was correct in his choice of areas, and he in fact did catch something that first night, but whatever he caught didn't stay in the trap for very long. When Josiah checked his trap the next morning, he found it mangled to the point of being beyond reuse. On the teeth of the trap, he found blood and coarse dark brown hair that measured at least 4 inches long. Whatever had gotten into the trap, it was big and extremely strong, and it was also now dangerously injured. From the looks of the damaged trap and footprints left in the dirt, what had gotten caught, obviously was bigger than any wolf that he had ever seen before. The tracks that the creature had left when it had been caught, were at least four times the size of any ordinary grey wolf, and they had an odd elongated appearance to them as well.

After the mangling of the steel trap, Josiah and his neighbor that had lost his sheepdog, went together to talk the sheriff about the rampant killings that was going on, on both of their farms. They had both hoped to at least get some help to track and kill the massive beast, but instead they were met with ridicule and disrespect. The two men were told that in no uncertain terms that if they had a problem with a wolf, that it was what it was, their problem, and their responsibility as well and to deal with it on their own. The sheriff told the men that a rogue grey wolf wasn't a legal issue, and if they couldn't protect their stock, then that was their own problem, not his. Before kicking them out of his office, the sheriff told them gruffly that he had better things to do with his time than to waste it talking to two damn dirt farmers about some damn stupid animal that he had no stake in, and that was also none of his concern.

After another week of losing several of his animals, the killing stopped as suddenly as it had begun, and Josiah believed that the wolves had finally moved on. Days turned into weeks and weeks turned into a month. Nearly two months after the last of his livestock had gone missing, the day came that changed everything for him. The day that Josiah's entire world came crashing down upon him.

It was early in the day and Josiah was out working the fields to bring in his first crop of hay. There were strong storms moving in from the west according to a telegraph that had come into the general store the week before. If the warnings were true, and they received the same weather that the towns further west had, Josiah knew it could possibly destroy their entire crop that was left in the field.

Josiah had been putting in long hard hours, working from sun up until sun set in the fields. On this day, while his daughters happily played in their rooms, his wife Sara was busy canning of some the crops that she had harvested from the garden just off to the back of the house. Sara was now into her eighth month of being with child. Being a strong, devout woman of faith, rearing her children right, and taking care of her family meant everything to her. And their newest child that she now carried in her womb, he would be looked at no differently.

Early on during the harvest season, Josiah had gotten into the habit of coming in for a late lunch so he could check in on his wife. This pregnancy was more difficult for her than the first two were. She was very ill in the beginning, but as time went on, it seemed as though it got easier on her. Still though,

70

there was something in the air, an uneasiness, that Josiah had picked up on. Though his wife didn't say anything, he could tell that she was uncomfortable and feeling it too.

As Josiah continued to sleep with his back against the tree, he went on to dream about his family and what had happened that dreadful day. He had no way of knowing the details that led up to what had happened in the house when he wasn't there though. The details from prior to him coming in from the fields, they were all recollections of another, one that he didn't know.

The scent of the female with child is what drew the wolf-type creature that had been praying upon Josiah's livestock to his house, he was able to smell her scent from miles away. When he had first caught the scent of the woman, he knew that he was where he was supposed to be. Though it was the scent of the two-leger female that drew him there, it was the availability of food that kept him near while he waited. It was him that had been preying upon the animals on this farm, as well as from the other farms close by. It was also him that killed the sheepdog as it was trying to do his job and protect his flock. The whole reason he was there fully centered around the human female, and nothing else. He knew that he had to patiently wait and just watch from the shadows until the time was right, that is what a voice from in his head kept telling him to do.

The creature had found an abandoned bear den just inside the woods, and it was there that he spent most of his time when he wasn't hunting, or spying on the female two-leger. The creature hunted by the light of the moon, and remained

71

in his den during the brightest part of the day. He had regularly taken animals from the different farms to sustain him, but when the farmers began to notice that there was something out there targeting their stock and they set traps, it was then that he had started to hunt for deer instead.

The longer that the wolf type creature stayed in the area, the more agitated he was becoming, and his frustration only got worse as the scent of the woman became stronger the closer that she came to giving birth. The restlessness that he was feeling, had begun to become almost unbearable to him. His animal instincts, and deeply set urges were getting harder and harder for him to fight off.

On this particular summer day, the sky was beginning to turn gloomy with the approach of the darkening clouds of the impending storm. The bad weather that was due to come over them later in the week, now appeared to be coming in much earlier than it had been expected to do so. With the sky now darkened, and the bright light from the sun being covered up, the creature decided to leave his den and get a closer look at the farmhouse. When the male two-leger left the house earlier in the day and headed for the far side of the field, the creature knew from watching his habits, that the man would not be returning any time soon.

The creature's animalistic cravings had been getting stronger the longer he remained in the valley. He would sit in the opening of his den and stare down at the farmhouse knowing that just inside the white, wooden walls stood a female that was left alone. After watching the woman come and go day after day, the creature was having a harder time fighting off his desires. He would sit at the mouth of his den and let his mind wander. As he thought about the female, he would feel the pressure building up in his groin area. He would stroke himself in an effort to relieve the pressure, but it did nothing for the desired of flesh-to-flesh contact. And now, with the male two-leger once again out in the fields, he knew how easily he could go down to the house and slip in unnoticed.

Seeing the woman walk outside and dump a pan of water onto the ground, the creature stood up. Still beyond the woman's sight, he decided that he needed to be closer to the woman. He told himself that by going closer it would give him the chance to better observe the female. In his darkened heart however, he knew what he wanted, and he knew why he wanted to be closer to her, and if the time was right, and despite what he was there for, he would take her, and fulfill his animalistic desires.

Under the cover of the darkening clouds, and by using the barn to help block the view, the creature made his way down to the farmhouse. As he knelt down, he peered into the window and watched the human female as she moved back and forth from the wood-fed cookstove to the table with something in her hand. Every time she would turn, he would observe the large protrusion coming from underneath her apron. For a moment it caused a glimmer of a memory to come back to him, but he didn't remember what it was about. At this point, his attention was fully on the female, and the desires he was feeling for her from deep within.

Sticking his muzzle towards the door, he took a deep breath and breathed in the essence of the female. The aroma caused a deep-seated desire to be pulled up closer to the surface, and the now familiar sensation began to build up inside of him again. *"Wait,"* he heard from deep within his head. *"Wait until the time is right,"* he heard again. Shaking his head, he drove the words out of his mind. *"No!"* he growled just under his breath.... *"Will not wait..."* he grumbled.

Staying low to the ground, the creature silently made his way on all fours from the side window to the doorway. It was a warm morning, and the only thing that stood between him and the human female was the old wood-framed screen door. Now closer to her, the aroma of the woman was absolutely intoxicating to him as he drew in another deep breath. He had never smelled anything so delicious, so sweet before in his life. He knew he had to have her, and he wanted her now.

Josiah had been due in from the fields shortly, when Sara heard the front screen door slam shut. She had been standing over the cook stove with her back to the door as she lifted the next to last jar of tomatoes from the hot water-bath canner. Carefully setting her hot jar down on the table, she covering it with a cloth and called out to her husband.

"You're in early. I thought you were staying out a little longer to stay ahead of the weather?" she said with her back still facing the door. "I have to finish getting the last jar of tomatoes out of the canner, and then I will get your lunch, okay?" she told him as she reached in and took the last hot jar of tomatoes from the canner. It was then that she heard a low rumbling noise coming from behind her. At the sound of the growl the woman froze in terror.

When what she assumed was a wolf didn't approach her from behind, she slowly turned around to face it. What she saw was a hulking part wolf, part human type creature standing upright on two legs towering over her. The creature stood at least eight feet tall and snarled at her as it looked down its muzzle at the woman. The hot jar of tomatoes fell from her hands and exploded as it hit the floor in front of her. Sara screamed and threw the tongs that she was holding at the creature as she tried to turn and run away, but the beast reached out with its large clawed hand and grabbed her by her hair and pulled her back to him. With her back turned towards him, he leaned in closer to her, he put his muzzle almost against the skin of her neck, and inhaled deeply. Sara was frozen in terror. As the creature continued to sniff her, Sara could feel his acidic smelling breath wafting against her skin as it filled the air around her with its stench.

Standing this close to the human female, and with the added heat of the morning magnifying her lovely fragrance, her scent only increased in its alure for him, and it was making the temptation of the woman more than he could handle. He knew in the back of his mind that he was there for a reason, another purpose, but with the enticing womanly hormones filling the air around him, those reasons no longer held any significance to him, and were now totally put out of his mind. All that he knew or cared about now, was that this female was alone, ripe and ready for the taking.

As the large creature sniffed her neck, the aroma of the female two-leger made the creature begin to salivate. Spittle began to drip from the corners of his mouth and fall to the wooden floor below.

Holding her closely in front of him, he moved one of his clawed hands down her sided and around her engorged midsection. He could feel the baby from within her moving beneath her skin. Looking down from over her shoulder, he looked at the natal bump under his hand. The woman whimpered and quivered in fear. Huffing deeply next her ear, the creature moved his hand back over to her hip before then moved it to one of her buttocks. Cupping her backside in his hand, he squeezed her right cheek and as he did, his claws penetrated her skin. As Sara cried out in pain, she reached down with one of her own hands, and shoved his wrist forcefully to try to get his hand off of her.

The creature growled at her and swung her around to face him, and as he did, several locks of her hair snagged on his claws and fell to the floor. Tears ran down the woman's cheeks as the large creature stared menacingly at her. Continuing to hold her firmly in place, he slowly moved his eyes up and down her body. Moving his face to where it was only inches from hers, he lifted his lips, exposing his massive teeth to her as he widely grinned.

Sara turned her head and looked away from him as he started to lower his muzzle to her chest area and began to roughly nudge her breasts one at a time with his nose. Drawing in deep breaths as he moved from one to the other, he could smell the milk that they were in the process of producing, and to him, it smelled delicious. Taking his free clawed hand, he raised it up and roughly cupped one of the woman's swollen breasts within it. The woman tried to jerk free, but he held her tightly with his other hand so she was unable to move. Once more, he leaned in and took another deep breath. She whimpered as she could feel his hot breath blowing against the fabric of her dress.

The woman let out a loud cry and took her free arm and pulled it back to swing at the creature's face. Seeing the woman preparing to strike out at him, the creature pulled back its muzzle from her breast area and quickly moved it to within just half an inch from her face. Squinting his eyes, he snarling at her and chomped his teeth together. Again, the woman cried out as more tears steadily flowed down her face and she dropped her hand back to her side. A feeling of hopelessness overcame her as she felt that no one was going to come to save her, and that her fate was now sealed.

Moving his muzzle from the woman's face, the creature then directed his attention to other areas of the woman's body. He spent time sniffing her more closely in certain areas than he did in others, until he came to stop again at her hips. This area was extra enticing to him, and it made his groin area enflame and throb with excitement. Taking his hand, he placed it upon her engorged abdomen. The woman protectively took her own hand and tried to swat his hand away, but he was too strong and again he looked up menacingly at her and growled.

Grunting, the creature continued to sniff the female, breathing in deeply to get as much of her scent into his nostrils as possible. He wanted her, deep in the recesses of his mind he knew he shouldn't, but he didn't care, he had to have her. At this moment, he wanted her more than he had ever wanted anything else in his life. Taking his hand away from the woman's stomach, he moved it down lower to her hip area and then to the middle of her groin. The woman trembled from his rough touch.

Quivering with fear, the woman's body began to get wobbly as she began to go into shock. Her legs began to shake and they started to give out from underneath her.

"No!" the creature silently bellowed at her. *"Stand woman!"* he ordered her with his face only inches from hers. The creature lifted her back upright onto her feet and held her there before him. His muscles tensed up and rippled beneath the layer of dark brown fur covering them. Shocked, Sara looked deeply into the creature's hate filled eyes. She saw that they were the eyes of a soulless creature, no softness, no pity, only the look of evil was contained within them. When she looked at the creature as a whole, all she saw was a part wolf, part human type abomination with dark amber eyes. She saw the blackness in its heart, and the long threatening fangs that jutted out of its mouth. Evil had invaded her home in the form of this creature, and evil was there to kill her and her unborn child.

"Words, how could this creature form words and speak? Its mouth is not moving, but yet it still speaks, are these words really in my head? What kind of demon is this animal? Josiah, where are you? I need you now more than I've ever needed you before," she subconsciously cried out as she faded back and forth in consciousness.

The half-conscious woman watched in terror as the creature took one of his clawed hands and in one smooth curl of a claw, ripped off the apron she was wearing around her waist.

Tossing the apron to the side, he slowly reached out to her again. This time he laid the back of his hand against the fabric of her dress, and slowly ran it up and down her body while feeling the smoothness of the material against his toughened skin.

Turning his hand over, and using his nails, the wolf like creature snagged one of the buttons on the front of her dress and ripped it off. As the button fell to the floor, it bounced and rolled under the cook stove. Sara bit her lower lip in fear. Then one by one, the creature continued to slowly rip the rest of the buttons off her dress, and then curiously watched as they fell to the floor and disappeared.

As her dress gapped and fell open to just below her breasts, Sara brought her hands up to cover her now bare chest. Whimpering in fear, tears began to once more fall from her eyes.

The creature reached out and roughly swatted her hands away to expose the pale skin of her bare breasts. Blood began to seep out of the wounds where the creature's claws had just raked her tender flesh. Her upper chest and breasts began to glistened with the small droplets of the oozing scarlet liquid that now seeped from her wounds. Leaning in, the creature sniffed the fresh blood and then licked his lips. Sticking out his tongue, he slowly put it against her bare flesh and began to lick the blood from her body. He wanted to savor this new unexpected event, and relish the flavor of fresh hormone infused blood entering his mouth. Crying out, Sara brought her arms up to her chest and pushed the creatures head away from her. Snarling at her, he quickly rose up and angrily struck out at her and shoved her arms back off to the side as tears of terror continued to run down her face.

The creature looked at the tears running down over Sara's cheeks and now found them interesting as well. Cocking his head slightly to the side, he watched as more tears formed and ran down over her face. Sniffing the tears, and smelling the saltiness of them, he then licked the woman's face. Instinctively the woman slapped the beast across the face with her free hand, and with that, he struck her back and knocked her backward off her feet.

The sudden jolt caused a sharp pain in her stomach and she groaned in agony. Sara grabbed for her belly, only to have the creature again roughly swipe her hands away. Now kneeling on the floor, he bent over her and glared into the woman's eyes. She was frozen with fear. She tried to scream but nothing would come from her mouth but a whimper.

The creature swung at her again, and this time he caught the corner of her mouth with one of his razor-sharp claws. When his claws hit, he ripped her face open from the corner of her mouth to her ear. Sara screamed out in anguish from the pain she felt. Putting her left hand up to her face, she felt the gaping wound and let out a loud sob. The creature seemed to be pleased with her reaction to what he had just done to her. When the shock of having her face ripped open began to set in, and the fright became too much for her, mercifully she passed out.

With the woman no longer conscious and able to fight back, the creature sat on his haunches and stared at the lifeless appearance of the woman lying before him. Nudging her bulging abdomen with the back of his hand, he got no response. The object of his animalistic lust could no longer fight back. For him the game of cat and mouse had been half the fun, but now that the two-leger female was unconscious, it was going to make what he wanted to do to her easier though.

Using his claws, he flipped up the skirt part of the woman's dress, exposing her from the hips down. This caused his interest to be peaked again. Looking up at the woman's face and then to the floor, he saw that the blood was still flowing from the injuries that the woman had suffered. Leaning down over her lifeless body, he again began to lap up the tasty red fluid from her chest and face.

After he finished cleaning up the fresh blood, he again looked down at Sara's partially naked body. The woman's scent was still strong. Leaning his muzzle down to her lower abdominal area, he took in several deep breaths. He felt that same throbbing feeling beginning in his groin, and the intense fire started to burn in his crotch. He was getting excited again, and his hands were beginning to tremble.

Reaching down, he grasped the woman's underclothes and yanking them upward. His clawed fingers quickly ripped them from her body, leaving her lower body now fully exposed. Wanting to draw in her fragrance, he lowered his muzzle down closer to her pubic area. Her scent filled his nostrils and sent a pleasant shivery feeling down his spine. Sticking his muzzle even closer, his groin began to instantly throb, and saliva began to drool from his mouth.

Breathing deeply, the wolf like creature picked up the woman's hips with is muscular hands, and brought her limp body up to meet his. As his excitement grew, his penis became harder as it began to grow and extend out of the penile sheath. The expectation and excitement of what he was about to do, was almost more than he could bear.

It was then that the woman began to regain consciousness. She looked up at the creature, and seeing him holding her close to him, she began to scream hysterically.

"No!" the creature growled at her as he reached his massive hand out and covered her mouth. Terror was spewing from the woman's wide-open eyes. She could see the creature's engorged penis and she knew what was about to happen.

Moving his hand further up her face, the creature now covered her nose as well as her mouth and cheek areas. Her eyes grew wider as she tried to turn her face away from his in an effort to dislodge his large hand, but he held it firmly in place. Sara couldn't breathe, he had blocked any access to fresh air that she had. She tried again to scream but it only came out muffled. Grabbing at his arm and large hand with her own smaller hands, she couldn't budge either one. After only a short time, Sara quit struggling, her eyes lost their life's luster, and her head tilted off to the side. She was gone.

Removing his hand from Sara's face, the creature once again looked down at the woman's partially naked body. The strong urge he was feeling within his groin was still there, and it once again began to burn with his animalistic desire. Though the woman was now dead, he didn't care. Her life meant nothing to him. He had male needs, and she didn't have to be alive for him to fulfill those needs. Roughly grabbing her by the hips again, he lifted her up to where he could easily control her body. Pulling her closer to him, he thrusted himself hard into the woman, tearing the lining on her hymen and causing her to bleed.

As he felt himself insert into her limp body, he let out a low rumbling howl. Now panting, he continued to roughly thrust himself into the woman until he burst forth and ejaculated into her. Though finished, the canine type bulbus glandis tissue at the base of his penis kept them locked firmly in place. Still panting, the creature sat down on the bloodied floor with the body of the woman laying limp between his legs. Because of the pain it would cause him if he withdrew, there was nothing for him to do now but wait.

Closing his eyes and taking deep breaths, the creature tried to relax. When the swelling in his penis had receded, he pulled back out from the woman and a gush of blood and semen poured out of her. Looking down at the new situation, he bent down and sniffing her again, and then he looked up at her stomach. A vague memory was still trying to come back to him, but he just could not recall the meaning of it.

Looking further at the maternal hump within the woman's abdomen, he reached up with one of his massive hands and placed it over her stomach. He could no longer feel the baby moving inside of its mother. The unmoving child felt foreign to him. Animal instinct was beginning to kick in again. He knew that the female two-leger was with pup, but that pup was not his. He instinctually knew that in the animal kingdom, when a female was carrying the pup of a less dominant male, that the dominant male was to destroy those pups and impregnate that female with the seed of his own loins, and in his mind, he now considered himself to be the dominant male.

Reaching down to the woman's abdomen, the creature took one of its claws and inserted the sharp tip down through the fabric of her dress and into the woman's stomach. In one swift motion, the creature tore through her skin and opened her up from her upper stomach to just above her groin, exposing all the tissue that lay between the fetus and the outside world. Not seeing any movement coming from underneath the newly sliced open area, the creature stuck one of his hands down into her bloodied womb, and lifted out the unborn pup. He looked at the baby closely as it laid helplessly in his hand. Sticking his muzzle down to the infant, he smelled it. It smelled of its mother, but it also had a different smell to it. He wasn't sure what the other smell was, it was a smell all of its own. He didn't smell of his father, the creature knew it's father's smell well. But the pup definitely had a smell all of his own.

Not knowing what to do with the child that he now held in his hand, he closed his fingers around the body of the little boy and held him tightly. The baby didn't move under the compression that he exerted on it, but the pressure caused the amniotic fluid to spill out of the dead baby's nose and mouth. Looking at the umbilical cord that still bound the dead pup to its mother, the creature reached out with is other hand and ripped it from Sara's womb. As if knowing that the voices in his head would say that he had done wrong, he reached out with one hand and flipped her skirt back up to cover her deflated abdomen.

Bringing the dead baby up to his face, he again sniffed its lifeless body and smelled its scent. He looked closely at its face and body. He had never saw a baby before and didn't know what to think about it. Using one of his fingers, he then lifted each of the baby's arms and legs one at time before letting them drop limply to the infant's side. It was as if he were playing with it and satisfying his own curiosity about the dead infant.

After staring at the dead baby for another moment, the creature became bored with it and opened up his hand and allowed the dead infants body to fall from his hands and onto the bloodied floor. Inside his head, he could vaguely remember there was something that he was to do with the dead pup, but his mind was now clouded over. The echoes in his head that he once heard were no longer, and he just couldn't remember no matter how hard he tried.

 As the creature stood back up, he caught another scent. Turning round to look to where it was coming from, he saw a young child of five years of age standing just inside the doorway to the other room. She had been standing there, frozen in horror as she watched her mother's lifeless body being violated by the creature, and then her baby brother being extracted from her mother's womb.

Rising to his feet, the creature slowly took a step towards where the young girl was standing. Seeing that the creature was now walking towards her, the young girl backed up against the door frame and trembled in fear. After quickly glancing over at her mother lying dead on the kitchen floor, the young girl turned swiftly around and quickly ran towards the back of the house to hide from the creature.

Knowing that there was now a witness to what he had done, the creature quickly followed her. Looking around in what was the living room area of the house, he didn't immediately see the little girl. But he saw that there was only one direction that the little girl could have gone. On his way to follow the young girl, he slowly walked past the couch and he paused to look out the large picture window behind it. He could see that the young girl's father was still on the farthest side of the field cutting hay. He knew that with the noise of the horse-drawn sickle mowers that he was using, that he couldn't have heard his wife's screams. Sniffing the air, he could smell the male two-legers scent on the furniture, and it disgusted him. Looking down at the furniture, the creature first leaned over the couch, and then the chair, and as he did so, he urinated on the cushions where he knew that the less dominant male two-leger would have sat.

"Time," the creature mumbled to himself as he continued to stare out the window. With the darker clouds now lifting in the sky, he knew that the little girl's father would stay out in the fields long enough for him to do what he now needed to do.

Turning and going back into the kitchen, the creature pushed open the screen door and bent down to retrieve a very worn large leather satchel that he had been carrying when he first approached the house. Upon viewing the female human through the window, he had set it down and forgot about it until now. After reaching down and picking the large bag back up, he placed his hand inside to make sure that what it had contained in it, was still there. Reaching to the bottom of the old satchel, his hand quickly came to rest on an old knife. He remembered taking the knife before he left, but now he had forgotten why he had brought it. His memory was no longer clear of what his purpose for coming here even was.

With the large satchel and knife now in his hand, the creature went back into the house to look for the young girl. On his way through the kitchen, he paused and again looked down at the dead infant laying on the floor next to its mother. A slight inkling of a memory again tried to break through his subconscious, but it quickly faded as soon as it tried to materialize. Reaching down, the creature once more picked up the body of the dead infant and stared at it as it laid in its hands. After staring at the lifeless infant for a few more seconds, the creature looked off to the side of where its mother lay. Laying off to the side in disheveled clump was its mother's apron. Reaching over to pick it up as well, the creature then proceeded to wrap the dead infant in its mother's bloody apron before then he quickly placed the now bundled up infant in his satchel.

Looking towards the doorway to the other room where he had last saw the young girl, the creature headed in that direction. Walking through the living room, he went into the hallway that led to where all of the bedrooms were, but stopped in front of the first bedroom that he came to. After sniffing the air for the little girl's scent at the first door he came to, he knew that this is where she was hiding. Reaching down, he firmly grasped the metal handle to the door. He paused only momentarily before gradually pushing the lever down and slowly shoving the door open.

A small blond girl was crouching down and whimpering as she peered out at the creature from around the curtains that hung over her bedroom window. Upon seeing the small child, the creature took a step towards her before stopping. A foreign emotion had suddenly made its presence known to him. Hidden for years beneath the tough animal exterior, a twinge of sadness had begun to surface. This was a new emotion for the creature, and it was one that he was not knowledgeable with, or had felt before.

Continuing into the room, the creature slowly approached the child. Putting her hands over her eyes, she turned her face away from him and began to whimper loudly. The creature reached down and carefully took the child by her hands and gently pulled her up from the floor. Once standing upright on her feet, she looked up at the creature that towered over her and bit her bottom lip in fear. The child sniffled and uncontrollable tears began to run down her cheeks.

The creature gently led the child over to her bed. He felt empathy for the two-legers female pup. The sight of her fear tugged at the last remaining bit of humanity that he had left within him.

"Name?" the creature silently asked. *"What do you go by?"* he questioned again. Upon hearing his voice in her head, the young girl looked up at him in astonishment.

"Anna," the young girl whispered through her tears. Like her mother had, she too was hearing the creature's questions in her mind, and not through verbal communication.

Taking one of his clawed fingers, he carefully brushed away a lock of the girl's golden hair that had fallen into the child's eyes. He motioned for the child to lay down upon the bed and close her eyes, and she silently obeyed him. As the young girl leaned back away from him, one of his claws accidentally snagged her dress and tore a long slit into it. She looked down at her torn dress and then looked back up at him in fear. Again, he nudged her to make her lie back upon the bed and close her eyes. After placing his hand over the child's eyes, he stood next to her bed and stared down at the small child that was so innocent and sweet. He was wavering inside as to what to do about the young girl, but the animal side of him was so strong and dominant that he was having a hard time fighting against it.

With his hands shaking from the inner turmoil that he was experiencing; he reached over and removed the knife from his satchel and lifted it up and placed the tip of it on the child's abdomen. She could feel the pressure of the knife on her stomach, and he felt her beginning to cry underneath his hand that was still covering her eyes. Picking the knife back up off of her stomach, he continued to fight against what he knew he had to do. She was a witness to what had just happened with her mother. He could not allow her to live. Two-legers can't know of his existence.

Taking in a deep breath to gain the strength that he needed for what he knew lay ahead, the creature closed his own eyes and before he had a chance to change his mind, he quickly plunged the large knife deep down into the young girl's abdomen.

The young girl weakly cried out and grabbed at the creature's arms with her own frail little hands. Struggling against the creature was of no use, the damage was already done. As the young girl got weaker, her cries faded and her little arms and hands dropped limply to her sides.

Removing his hand from the young girl's eyes, he again reached over to push another lock of her golden hair from her face. In doing so the tip of one of his claws accidentally scratched her face and blood droplets began to form. Pulling his hand back, he stared down at the fragile young child that he had just killed, and he felt a pang of remorse from deep within. After looking at the child for another moment, the creature reached down and withdrew the knife from her lifeless body and laid it off to the side. The young girl's blank empty eyes were still open and now stared at him accusingly, as if she was saying to him, "I still know what you did, I saw everything." Taking a deep breath, he reached out and gently closed the young girl's eyes to break her empty accusing stare.

"Sleep little pup," he told her. *"Sleep."*

After closing the young girl's eyes, he rolled the little girl over onto her side to make her look as if she was truly sleeping peacefully. Satisfied with her positioning, he then he drew the covers up over her body, leaving only her blood hair showing.

The creature had never killed a child before this day, but this child knew too much. She had seen him. He knew that she saw him as he both raped and murdered her mother. He also knew that she had witnessed him cut out her baby brother from the safety of its mother's womb. He didn't like what he had to do to the child, and he fought against the urge, but he couldn't have her telling the other two-legers what she had seen, he couldn't have the two-legers coming knowing about him.

Picking up his satchel, he went back to the doorway. Glancing out to make sure that there was still no one else in the home, he walked out of the room. It was then that he picked up on another scent he hadn't smelled before. It smelled like a two-leger, but there was something different about it. With his curiosity peaked, he turned and headed down the hallway further until he came to another door. Reaching out, he quietly unlatched the door and slowly pushed it open. Once the door was open, he could see another small child lying in a smaller bed than the other young girl had been in.

Quietly approaching the bed, he looked down at the peacefully sleeping child. This child also had long blond hair and the face of an angel like her sister. To him, this little human pup seemed as though she was much younger than the other young girl. The creature stood above her and stared at the peaceful child below. That same feeling began to grow inside of him that he had with the other child, but this feeling was stronger. This time being more careful of where his claws were positioned, he cautiously he reached down and touched the child's cheek with the back of one of his fingers. Her skin

91

felt soft and smooth against his own rough and weathered skin.

Feeling her face being touched, the young child's eyes began to flutter, and then open. She looked up at the creature with a wide-eyed wonderment that only a child can have. Unlike her older sister, this child was not afraid of him. She reached out a chubby little hand and stroked the fur that was on the back of the creature's hand and arm. She ran her fingers through his fur, and felt the stiffness of the guard hairs that stood out.

Turning her face upward, she looked into the creature's face again. A calming effect came over the creature and he began to relax in the small child's presence. The little girl then reached her small hand up towards the creature's face. The creature knelt down to get closer to the little girl, and then leaned forward to meet her little hand. Using one of her little fingers, she outlined the various lines and angles of his face. She stroked his strong protruding muzzle, and then looked deep into his eyes. The creature was entirely taken aback by this child, and his heart softened as he found himself drawn in by her.

The child then reached out to the creature with both hands. Looking down at what the small child was doing, he then in turn reached over and carefully picked her up. Sitting down onto the edge of the bed, he lifted and sat the little girl on is lap while she played with his fur. He was mesmerized by the golden-haired child and couldn't drag himself away from her. He was mesmerized by her and could feel something growing stronger from deep inside of himself that was drawing him to this child for some reason. Being in the child's presence, his internal anger calmed, and he felt something inside for this little girl he had never felt before. He knew he shouldn't, but she had now become something that he couldn't, and wouldn't give up.

Still holding onto the child, the creature rose up to his feet. He looked around the room and took a blanket from the young girl's bed to wrap her in. He then saw two small dresses laying over a rocking chair and he quickly shoved them both into his leather satchel. Now with the young girl in his arms, he went to her door and as soon as he stepped out into the hallway, he heard someone entering through the kitchen doorway, and then he heard a man scream.

The creature looked around wildly in search of another exit out of the house. He knew he couldn't go out the same way he had come in, not now that the male two-leger was back from the fields. Looking further down the hallway, he saw that there was another exterior door off to the side of the house. Covering the little girls head with the blanket, he quickly headed for the door. With the little girl still in his arms, he decided at that moment that there was no doubt that he was going to take her with him. She belonged to him now. She was now the dominant male's pup, and no one where he came from would dare to even try to question that, or try to take her away from him.

Before exiting the house, the creature carefully pushed the screen door open far enough that he could peer out from around the corner of the door to see if it was safe to slip out. From where he stood hidden, he could see in through the door to the kitchen. He saw the two-leger male kneeling down over his wife's dead body. The man was kneeling with his back facing the doorway, so he knew that now was his chance, his only chance, to escape without being seen.

Quietly as he could, the creature pushed the door open and stepped onto the porch. As he took another step, one of the floorboards creaked under his weight. Looking over towards the male two-leger and seeing no reaction from the noise that he had just made, he felt assured that the two-leger didn't hear it. As the still crying two-leger male remained bent over his dead wife's body, the creature took another step and was off of the porch and running for the wood line beyond the barn. From behind him as he ran out past the barn with the young girl in his arms, he could still hear the man who was left kneeling in the kitchen crying out over the loss of his wife.

Chapter Three

When Josiah awoke a short time later, he had a feeling of sadness in his heart. He didn't remember what it was that he had been dreaming about, but it left him with a sense of great sorrow. Standing back upright onto his hind legs, Josiah looked out into the field around him and huffed. While staring at the golden wheat lightly swaying back and forth in the field in front of him, he caught movement off to his right. Cautiously Josiah came out from his hiding spot and went to investigate what it was that had caught his attention. It was a handkerchief belonging to the two-leger female. Even without picking it up he knew it was hers by the scent that lingered heavily on the woven fabric. Reaching down, he carefully picked it up and gently rubbed the silky fabric between his callused fingers. Bringing the handkerchief up to his nose, he closed his eyes and drew in a deep breath, savoring the woman's scent that had owned it. Moving his hand, he then placed it against his face so he could feel the smoothness of the material against his skin. After enjoying the feelings that his new acquisition had brought to him, he started to again get that aching feeling from deep within.

"No!" he told himself as he felt the strong carnal urges begin to once more build up from within himself, and the familiar aching in his groin was again beginning to escalate. *"No! I can't think of such things,"* he told himself as he quickly took the piece of cloth away from his face.

Still holding the handkerchief in his hand, he rolled it up into a ball and buried it in his massive fist. He knew the temptation that came along with this piece of cloth, and what it could lead to. He also knew far too well what the outcome would be, if he allowed himself to act upon those desires.

Frustrated, Josiah turned and left the area that he was in for more secure cover. He didn't want to linger out in the open any longer than he already had in case the two-legers had told anyone about what they thought that they may have heard. Though it was still dark, and it was usually his time to be out, he still had to be careful. If he wanted to remain in this area for a little while longer, he could not take the chance of being discovered.

On his way past the mouth of his cave, Josiah tossed the balled-up handkerchief just inside the entrance. He didn't want it with him any longer, he didn't need the trouble it could bring to him, but yet he wasn't ready to totally part with it either though.

Josiah decided to hunt on the other side of the hill that night, away from the two-legers, and away from the village beyond the field where he lived. He thought that the hunting may be better in the denser woods anyway because of less human pressure. And because of that lack of human presence, the prey animals may be more at ease in their surroundings as well.

Though his mind was no longer on hunting, he knew he still had to eat. He had been subduing the feeling of the growing emptiness within the pit of his stomach for quite a while. He was hungry all the time now. He no longer was able to acquire the easier game he was accustomed to hunting; he had just about depleted their numbers in the short time that he had been in the valley. Tonight though, tonight he would hunt for something larger, something more fulfilling, and more of a challenge than the ground birds and small animals that he had been catching.

Josiah moved quickly. He was able to move far more rapidly than any two-leger ever could. His strides were long and fast. He could walk upright, or he could travel on all fours, whatever he needed to do, and whatever worked out the best in whatsoever situation that he was in. But, by traveling all fours though, it did give him the ability to move with the quicker speeds, the stealth, and the agility of a true predator.

Once on the other side of the hill, Josiah stopped and slowly looked around. Wilderness, pure sweet wilderness, even the air was unblemished here. Not a two-leger house in sight, nor any of their irritating chattering noise to be heard. Josiah was in his element there in the woods, here, he was the king of the forest.

As Josiah walked through the timber, he began to wonder why he just didn't move to this side of the hill and leave the cave that he was now living in. The heavily timbered area in which he stood, offered him everything he needed, but yet there was something holding him there in the valley, something that drew him to the other side where the cave was. It was a feeling, or a deeply ingrained longing, he didn't know which. But it was as if it held the key to the last piece of his old life, and what little bit of his humanity, that he still had left in him.

The sound of rustling leaves suddenly caught his attention and brought him out of his deep thoughts. Quickly crouched low to the ground, he listened to see where the noise had come from. Once more, a few seconds later the rustling sound broke the silence of the night.

Listening closely, he now could tell where the noise was coming from, but he still couldn't get the visual that he needed to enable him to make out what it was that was being masked by the darkness. Staying perfectly still, he patiently watched and waited for more signs from his possible prey. Not even blinking an eye, he continued to stare out into the darkness.

Again, the rustling noise came, and this time his keen eyes spotted the area of its origin. Out of the shadows, a large doe stuck her head out from behind a large oak tree. Still not moving a muscle, Josiah stared intently at the animal. Taking one step, then followed by another, the deer slowly made its way out of the trees, and into the small moonlit clearing. As the doe nibbled on the sparsely growing green grass, the deer had no idea that just downwind from where she was now grazing, a deadly predator was just biding his time and waiting for the right moment to pounce.

Still on all fours, Josiah leaned back and got ready for his attack. The deer raised its head and twitched its ears as if it had heard him moving. It looked in Josiah's direction, but it couldn't see him hiding in the shadows. As the doe lowered her head back down to continue to graze, Josiah leapt out from his hiding spot, and within four springs, he was on the deer.

Jumping onto the doe's back with his upper body, he immediately sank his large canines deep into the muscular neck of the animal. The deer reared up and fought him, kicking and loudly bleating into the night.

Sticking his claws deep into the flesh of the deer's front quarters, Josiah held on to it tightly. There was to be no escape for the doe now. His size alone had already sealed this deer's fate. The doe snorted loudly and continued to try to buck and kicked at Josiah with its back legs as it tried to dislodge the unwanted creature from its back.

Wanting to quickly end the hunt, Josiah swung one of his large clawed hands around to the front of the doe's neck. Digging his claws into the flesh on the other side, he easily ripped through the doe's juggler vein, and within seconds, its life sustaining blood sprayed into the air and onto the ground below it. The doe quickly began to get weaker as it bled out. After one last fleeting attempt to kick at its attacker, the doe's legs buckled out from underneath her, and its now lifeless body fell to the ground.

Once the doe was on the ground, Josiah withdrew his claws from the animal's body. After nudging it with his foot to make sure it was no longer alive, Josiah reached down and grasped it by its back legs. Looking over his shoulder, he looked for a good place to take his newly won prize. Finding a suitable spot, Josiah pulled the animal from the small clearing that he was in, to a safer spot in the woods that was under the cover of darkness.

After pulling the deer into the shadows, Josiah paused and looked around out into the darkness for any signs of prying eyes. Satisfied that there were none, Josiah knelt down and began to feast on his new acquisition. He would eat good tonight, and gorge himself on the fresh venison until he could eat no more.

After Josiah was done eating his meal, he got an uneasy feeling, and he began to feel like he was being watched from somewhere in the shadows. Looking out into the darkness, every so often he would catch sight of a set of yellowish amber eyes watching him from behind the safety of the tree line on the other side of the clearing. The owners of the amber eyes had nothing to fear that night though, for he no longer needed to hunt. After what had seemed like far too long, his belly was finally full, and he still had plenty leftover to sustain him for yet another day.

Seeing that the suns impending rays were beginning to glow above the dense forest canopy, he knew that he needed to leave his kill so that he could get back to his den before the sunlight began to brim the horizon. He also wanted to get back before the dawning of the new day, when he knew that the two-legers would also begin to rise and leave their homes once more.

Josiah turned and looked for a good hiding place for what was left of the doe's carcass. He saw that there was a large dead log on the forest floor not far away from where he stood, and he knew that he could make good use of that. Going over to inspect the large log, he reached down and rolled it over and found it to be hollow on the bottom of it. Satisfied that there was enough room in which to hide what was left of his kill, he returned to the partial deer carcass, took it by the hind feet and easily pulled what was left of the deer over to the log and placed it securely beneath it. *"Leave no sign, leave no mark, leave no evidence that you were here,"* he told himself.

After he hid what was left of his food, Josiah started his journey back to his cave on the other side of the hill. He felt so much stronger, and so much surer of himself than he had in a long time. He decided that he would no longer hunt only the smallest of the creatures of the food chain, he would go after the larger prey that suited him much better. He was a predator, an apex predator, not a lowly scavenger. After years of being beat down and intimidated by mankind, he was now beginning to once more realize, that he was the most dangerous predator in nature, and that it was time that he acted like it.

It didn't take long for Josiah to make his way through the forest and return to his cave. Glancing over at the village of the two-legers, he huffed at them before going back inside. On his way into his den, Josiah reached down and picked up the handkerchief that he had tossed just inside the entrance on his way past earlier. Holding it in his hand, he ran it back and forth between his rough fingers. Snagging the material with one of his callouses, he ripped a small hole in a corner of it. *"Not worth it, maybe someday, maybe never, but not worth it now,"* he told himself as he began to feel the pressure in his groin. Looking over towards the left side of his cave, he tossed the torn piece of cloth over in that direction, and it landed on top of his bag.

He was very pleased with himself after his hunt. It felt good to have his belly full again. It had been a long time since he felt this good, and this strong. It was a feeling that he rarely had gotten to enjoy lately, but now, with the venison he had just consumed beginning to digest and spread its nourishment throughout his body, he had no worries of where or when his next meal would come. He was now done with small pittances; from here on out, he would eat like the dangerous predator he is.

Now again back down on all fours, Josiah moseyed to the back of his cave and stretched out his weary body onto the cool ground. Running his hand over his now extended belly, he could feel the hard food-bump made from the procurement of his latest hunt, and he relished in the feeling. As he closed his eyes, sleep was not far from him on this day, it beckoned to him, and he happily complied. The muffled sound of the crickets chirping outside of the den, and the call of the mourning doves from across the field soothed him until his eyes became heavy and his breathing became peaceful and steady.

As Josiah slept, his mind began to wander as it did on most nights. His dreams this night took him back to the time when he dwelled amongst the two-legers. Back to before what he was now, back to when he was still human like them.

"You are a lousy piece of garbage; you know that Wolfe! Nothing but garbage!" the sheriff yelled at Josiah as he leaned in close to the bars.

Josiah, ignoring the sheriff, sat on the cot in his cell and silently wept. He cried for the lost lives of his wife, and for those of his children. And then, he also cried for himself as well.

"Come on you pansy, you can't ignore me, I'm the law here! Why don't you just stand up here and face me, and take it like a man!" the sheriff yelled at him again as he raked his baton against the cell bars. But Josiah couldn't bring himself to even look up at the man, and that just infuriated the sheriff further.

"You know, you are just a waste. You aren't even a man! You are just a good for nothin' piece of horse shit! We should have just shot you dead and gotten it over with when we found you covered in your wife's blood."

"Then why didn't you?" Josiah calmly asked as he looked up from the cot where he sat. "Why didn't you just kill me?" he now shouted.

"Oh, believe me, I wanted to take you down right there and then, but that ain't the law now is it. And after we found out that your young one was missin', if I had shot you, then we would never know what you did with her now, would we? Hell, we can't even find that unborn kid the two of you were goin' to be havin' either. And that, you piece of dirt is the only reason that you are still alive."

103

"I told you before, I didn't do anything with Ava, or the baby!" Josiah shouted back as he stood up and took a step towards the bars glaring at the sheriff.

"Come on boy, come on over here and I will give you somethin' to be mad about," he told him as he tried to egg Josiah on.

Josiah stood in the center of his cell and glared at the sheriff.

"You aren't even man enough to face me, huh? Can you only hurt women and children; you aren't man enough to take on another man are you; you pansy!" he cackled at him.

Josiah only continued to glare at the sheriff with anger in his eyes. He never hated another man before in his life, like he hated this man now. He wanted to reach right through the bars and strangle the man with his bare hands, but he held back. He had to find out what really happened to his little girl, his little Ava, and he knew that if he gave into the sheriffs prodding, he would never get the chance. In his mind, the sheriff was the only garbage in the room. He is the one that deserved the gallows, not him.

"I didn't think so," the sheriff said as he gave a loud belly laughed at Josiah before turning and walking back to his desk. "Total waste of human flesh," he mumbled to himself as he sat back down in his chair with his back to Josiah.

Minutes later a very pretty young dark-olive skin-toned girl, appearing older than her young 15 years of age, knocked lightly on the old wooden door of the jail and stuck her head in around the door. She had only moved to town the previous winter with her father in search of work. It wasn't long after they moved, that her father caught pneumonia and passed away. Ms. Dixie took her in and gave her work at her diner to pay her way.

The young woman entered the jail carrying with her two trays of food in her hands. She wore her long dark hair neatly drawn up into a tight ponytail on the back of her head, that was then twisted into a bun. She also wore a long flowing light blue dress that Ms. Dixie had made for her that came down to just above her ankles.

"Hey sweetness, what did you bring me darlin'?" the sheriff asked the teenaged girl as he made eyes at her and look her up and down.

"Ms. Dixie fixed you two up some meat loaf and mashed tators for your dinners," she told him.

"Well, what are you waitin' for, bring them on over here little lady," the sheriff told her. "Let me get a closer look at what you have there."

Doing as she was told, the young woman walked over to the sheriff's desk with the two trays of hot food. The sheriff was standing off to the side of his desk at this point, and was intently watching the young woman's every move.

"Just sit them over there on the side of the desk little darlin'," he told her as he pointed in the direction with his baton. Obediently, the young woman leaned forwards to place the dinners on the corner of his desk. As she did so, the sheriff took his baton that he still had in his hand, and tucked it up under the back of the young woman's skirt and quickly lifted it up to expose her bloomer covered buttocks. Feeling her skirt being lifted, the young woman quickly stood back up and pushed her skirt back down as she turned to face the sheriff.

"If that is all you need sheriff? I really do need to be getting back to work now. Ms. Dixie is expecting me to come right back," she told him now red faced, and looking down at the floor to avoid making eye contact.

"Well, what's your hurry little lady? I'm sure Ms. Dixie can wait just a few more minutes for you to get back. How about sittin' a spell with me and my prisoner. We get a little lonely here you know," he told her as he glanced over in Josiah's direction.

"I'm not supposed to stay, I need to get back to help Ms. Dixie at the diner," she told him as she quickly began to back away from him.

"Naw, I think that Ms. Dixie would understand if you were just a few minutes late," he told her as he took a step closer to her. As a reaction to his approach, the young woman took another step backwards herself to create more distance between them, even at that distance though, she could still smell the stench of his vile breath.

The young woman backed up a few more steps in an effort to put more distance between her and the man, until she found her back against the wall. The sheriff positioned himself just in front of her, blocking any escape routes that she thought that she might have had. Feeling like a caged animal, and not knowing what to do, the young woman looked from side to side in a panic.

Sneering at the young woman, the sheriff reached down with his baton, and picked up the front of the young woman's dress. Lifting one of her hands, she quickly slapped it away. The sheriff laughed at her actions and quickly grabbed her by the arm and held it tightly off to the side against the wall, limiting her movements.

"What's the matter little Darlin', haven't you ever had a man lookin' at you before?" he asked her as he once more took his baton and roughly rubbed it up against her leg as he lifted up her skirt.

"No! Let me be, I have to go!" she screamed at him in fear as she took her other hand and slapped him.

"That was a mistake little lady," he growled at her as he struck the baton against the wall just to the right of her face.

Again, putting his baton under the young woman's dress, he lifted it up until he stopped at mid-thigh, he looked up at her face and laughed at her before rubbed the baton back and forth to tease the young woman. A tear began to run down the young woman's face as she stood frozen in fear of what was to come.

Seeing that she was not going to fight him anymore, he began to raise the baton even higher up on her inner leg until he felt it come to a stop. The young woman began to whimper lightly as he began to move the baton back and forth again between her legs.

"Such a sweet thin' ain't ya," he said to her as he leaned in and licked his lips.

Bending over slightly while still holding tightly on to the young woman's arm, he took ahold of the woman's skirt with his index finger and lifted it so that he could see what lay beneath.

"Do you like that," he asked her as he continued to torture her. "I bet you do, don't you," he continued with a smirk.

The young woman again took her free hand and swung at his face, slapping him hard across the cheek.

"Damnit woman! You are goin' to regret that!" he yelled at her menacingly.

Holstering his baton, he turned her away from him and grabbed both of her arms and pushed them behind her back where he could hold onto them both with just one of his large hands. Sticking his face off to the side of hers, he roughly lifted her arms until she cried out in pain. Using his free hand, he then reached down, grabbed the young woman by groin area and pulled her tightly back against his body. He relished in the feel her young body up against his.

The young woman tried to pull away from him, and as she did so, she managed to pull one hand free, but that still left him holding onto the other though. Roughly swinging her around to face him, he quickly grabbed her by the neck with his other free hand. Forcefully pulling her to him, he leaned in and kissed her roughly. The young woman tried to squirm away from him, but he was too strong and continued to hold her firmly against him.

"Damnit woman, stand still!" he snarled at her as he hit her hard across her face. The forceful open-handed hit split her lip open, and a trickle of blood began to run down her chin and drip to the floor.

Putting her hand up to her lip, she saw the blood on her fingers when she drew it away. Looking up at him, and fearful for her life, she again slapped him and continued to struggle against the larger man in an effort to gain her freedom.

"That's it. Come here you!" he told her forcefully as he grabbed her around her waist with one arm and half dragged, and half carried her screaming towards the back room.

"Leave her alone!" Josiah yelled at him. The sheriff stopped and slowly turned his head around to glare back at Josiah.

"If you know what is good for you boy, you will stay out of this! This here ain't none of your concern!" the sheriff growled at him in anger.

The sheriff turned back towards the door and jerked the young woman in front of him. Opening up the door, he forcefully pushed the crying woman into the darkened room that was just off to the side of the cell area where Josiah was.

All Josiah could do was watch as the sheriff slammed the door shut behind him.

Through the closed doorway Josiah could hear the young woman screaming and then the sound of a hand slapping bare skin before the room went temporarily quiet. Josiah put his hands over his ears and walked over to the far corner of his cell. He didn't want to hear what was going on in that room, and his hatred towards the sheriff boiled inside of him even stronger than before.

Slowly, and with his back now against the corner of his cell, he slid down the wall until he was in a squatting position on the floor. With his ears still covered, he closed his eyes and waited for it all to be over.

"Look at me you whore!" the sheriff yelled at the young woman once they were inside the room. The young woman tried to pull away from him, but he still had her fast in his grip.

The only light in the darkened room came from the tiny window off to the backside of the building. Darkness had already set in, but the glow of the full moon was all he needed to see by.

"No, leave me alone!" the young woman cried out into the darkness.

"Don't you be tellin' me what to do woman! Who do you think you are?" he shouted at her. "You're all the same, women like you, you're nothin' but a tease, and you all need to be taught a lesson! A woman's only purpose in life is to please us men and bear our offspring! You have no say so in anythin'!"

Holding the young woman firmly, he grabbed the back of her dress and yanked it down roughly. The fabric ripped and tore apart down to her waist.

"Well, look at that little thin', you seem to of ripped your dress somehow," he said as he chuckled at her.

The young woman cried out and whimpered. As she tried to pull away from him, the sheriff placed his hand upon the bare skin of her back. She began to shake as he moved his hand further down her back and slipped it underneath the fabric of her bloomers and onto her bare buttocks.

The young woman squirmed as he firmly squeezed one of her bare cheeks.

"You like that don't you, I know you do," he told her as he continued to torment her.

The young woman knew what was about to come for her, and she also knew that she couldn't do anything to stop it. Taking both of his hands, the sheriff reached up and pulled the front of the young woman's dress down to expose her bulging breasts.

"Now look at that. Hard to believe that you're only 15 now darlin'. But even 15 is more than old enough for what we're goin' to do," he said as he began to ogle her chest.

Reaching out to the young woman, he placed both his hands on the young woman's breasts. As he did so, the young woman closed her eyes and sucked in her lower lip as she took a deep breath.

"Now I know you like this," he told her as he roughly messaged her breast. As he crudely handled them, he could feel her heart beating rapidly beneath her skin. "See, I told you that you liked this, I can you feel your heart beatin' with excitement? I bet you can't wait to have a real man!"

Bending down, the sheriff tried to kiss the young woman's breasts, but she slapped his face away from her. As soon as she hit him, he stood up and slapped her back brutishly across the side of her face causing her to cry out in pain.

Now standing, he gruffly put both of his hands on the young woman's shoulders and roughly pushed her backwards onto the spare cot in the corner. The metal springs creaked under the pressure of her falling upon it. Pulling the young woman's skirt up, the sheriff reached down and ripped off her bloomers and tossed them off to the side. Then placing his hands down between the young woman's legs, he forced her thighs wide open.

The young woman looked away and concentrated on the light coming in the window, trying in her mind to go to a different place, and relenting to what she knew was about to happen.

Sticking his hand down to her crotch, he grinned nastily. "Ahh, you must be pure huh. Tight as a whistle," he said as he laughed at the young woman. The young woman didn't respond to his actions at all, and only continued to gaze out the window.

"What's the matter darlin', cat got your tongue?" he asked as he roughly molested the young girl. "You know you are takin' all the excitement out of this for both of us. You are goin' to be missin' all the fun if you don't start to pay attention to what is going on here little darlin'," he continued to say as he sneered down at her.

The young woman wouldn't give the man the satisfaction he would receive from her looking up at him, so instead she continued to stare out the window in silence and wait for what was yet to come.

"Hell, I ain't waitin' for you to come around and join in on the fun. I know how to make my own fun when it comes to a woman," he told her. Removing his hand from her crotch, he reached up and undid his belt, unbuttoned his pants and pulled them down to his knees. He was already erect and firm. "Do you want to at least take a look at what a real man looks like?" he asked her as he firmly slapped her upper thigh. "The hell with you then, you might not want to look at it, but you sure as hell are goin' to feel it!" he said when he still got no reaction from her. "Let's see if this gets your attention," he said as he let go of the waist band and allowed his pants to fall down to the floor.

Climbing up on the cot with the young woman, he shoved her legs even further apart than before and placed his engorged appendage up against her. "You ready for this little darlin'?" he asked as he roughly just before shoving it into her.

113

The young woman gasped out in pain as she felt the man's penis forcefully enter into her. Tears began to run down her face, but she did not remove her eyes from the barred window on the far wall.

"You had me goin' there for a second there little darlin'," he said as he chuckled at her response. "I thought you were goin' to wake up for a little bit and actually enjoy the ride a little. After all, I figure I'm your first," he told her as he laughed.

Still seeing no response from her, the sheriff continued to abusively rape the young woman until he finally ejaculated into her. Breathing heavily, he let out a loud sigh as he sat back on the cot.

"That was good little darlin', too bad you didn't want to get into it with me. It's been a while for me you know. Not every woman wants a good, strong man like me. They want men like that piece of trash, Wolfe out there! Now you best not be gettin' pregnant from this all. You are the one that came here, and came onto me, remember. Comin' in here dressed sexy and all. And don't bother tellin' Ms. Dixie about this, I can destroy you in this village. You just remember that everyone will know what a whore you are if you open up your mouth about this little roll in the hay!" he told her.

The young woman slowly took her eyes from the window and looked up at the sheriff again standing over her.

"Now you best be gettin' yourself together and get out of here," he told her as he took a step back from her.

The young woman pulled her dress back up to cover her breasts as she quickly stood up. As soon as she stood, she grabbed at her stomach, bent over and vomited onto the floor.

"You're lucky I'm not goin' to make you get down on your hands and knees and clean that filthy vile puke up!" he told her in disgust. "I'll make that waste of a man come in here later instead and do it. It'll help him pay for his keep. That kind of work is all he's good for anyway, cleaning up other people's slop!"

Standing back upright, the woman grabbed what was left of her torn bloomers from the floor and pushed past the man as she headed for the door.

Josiah looked up when he heard the door to the back room open. As the young woman exited the room, she was shoved hard from behind by the sheriff. Stumbling across the floor after the shove, the young woman fell forwards and into the wooden desk. Seeing that the back of her dress was torn open, and that the young woman had tears streaming down her face, it made Josiah fume inside. The sheriff again walked up behind her and shoved her off of the desk, and this time the young woman stumbled and fell to the floor.

Josiah looked towards the young woman and saw that she had blood smeared on her upper thigh and down to her knees. Pulling the skirt part of her dress up from around her feet, she got up again and moved beyond the sheriff's reach. Once she got far enough away from the man, she desperately ran for the door.

115

"Now you come back anytime sweet thin', you hear," the sheriff called after her chuckling to himself as he watched as the young woman bolted out the door.

"What are you gawkin' at boy?" the sheriff asked as he looked over at Josiah. Josiah just glared back at the man as he watched the sheriff zipping his pants back up, and buckling his belt once more.

"That sweet thin' ain't no a virgin any more, that girl is a woman now," the sheriff stated. "She was as sweet as a plum just ripe for pickin'. She was ripe to, let me tell you," he said as he chuckled to himself. "Did you see that blood runnin'? They don't get no fresher than that! You'd think that she'd be more grateful to me for gettin' her ready for a husband someday," he said as he slapped his leg and laughed at his own nasty joke.

Still rather pleased with himself, and with what he had just done, the sheriff walked back over to his desk and sat down. Glancing over to the corner of his desk, he reached out and pulled over one of the trays of food.

"You know, that Ms. Dixie, that woman knows how to cook. She ain't much to look at, but she makes the best damn meatloaf and tators in town. Too bad you ain't gonna get any of it though," the sheriff said as he laughed. "After that workout I just had with that little wildcat, I need both of these here trays to just build back up my strength," he added while continued to laugh.

"You're a pig!" Josiah yelled at the man.

"Who, me?" the sheriff asked a little surprised as he glanced over at Josiah and chuckled. "Well, let's just look at who is on this side of them bars, and who is on that side of them bars, before we start to doin' any name callin' here boy. Besides, I'm not the one who just butchered my wife and kid, remember?" he added.

Josiah glared at the man. He opened up his mouth to say something, but then changed his mind. Instead, after glaring at the vile man, he turned and went back over to sit back down on his cot.

"Yeah, you better back off boy, or I will come in there and give you a workin' over that you won't soon forget," the sheriff threatened.

The sheriff finished the food on the first tray, and then pulled over the second tray as well.

"I'd let you lick the left-over slop off of the trays, but that would be too good for a pansy dog like you Wolfe," the sheriff added as he snickered to himself.

"I gotta go take a piss, so now don't you go nowhere you hear," he cackled. After taking two steps, he paused and turned back and looked at Josiah. "Oh, but that's right, you can't go anywhere even if you wanted to, you're locked in, and I have the only key," he chuckled as he jiggled the keys hanging from his side before turning and heading for the door. Walking out the side door leading to behind the building, the sheriff glanced around into the darkness, and then urinated against the small tree just outside.

117

Josiah didn't know what to do. There was no way he could escape, and even if he did, where would he go. Deep down in his heart though, he knew that if he stayed behind these bars for very much longer, that the sheriff would see to it that he would never live long enough for a trial.

The sheriff, still zipping his pants, returned after only a few minutes and walked back into the middle of the room where his desk was.

"I left that back door open some, I think that pretty little thin' stunk the place up a bit, don't you?" he said cruelly as he chuckled. Josiah glared at the sheriff with hatred in his eyes. He didn't know how anyone could be so cruel to another human being as he was to that young woman.

The sheriff was a harsh man, he was cruel to everyone, but especially to women, and to anyone of a color different than his, male or female, it didn't matter. He was racist to the point of comparing anyone that wasn't white, and anyone who spoke with an accent, even if they were born in this land, as not human at all, and nothing better than the dirt beneath his feet where he had just relieved himself. And that twisted way of thinking, did nothing for his popularity in town.

After turning up the flame on his wall lamp so he could see better, the sheriff pulled his chair out and sat back down at his desk. Pulling an old newspaper out from a drawer, he leaned back and began to read it.

Josiah was the first to hear what sounded like something scratching at the doorway that the sheriff had left open. The sheriff turned and glanced over at the door, but seeing nothing, went back to reading his newspaper. Then Josiah heard the sound of a deep guttural growl emanating from outside the open doorway.

"Shut up boy!" the sheriff yelled at Josiah. "What do you think you are, a dog or somethin' over there growlin' like that. Do I need to throw you a bone, would that shut you the hell up?" he yelled as he slammed his fist down on his desk and turned and glared at Josiah. "Maybe you need fixin' like they fix them male dogs that go around gettin' all those mongrel half-breed female dogs pregnant. I bet that would fix you, and you won't be feelin' the need to be doin' all this ridiculous growlin' then, huh!" the sheriff told him. "Hell, I'll even do it myself," he said as he pulled a knife from his drawer and stuck the tip of it in the top of his desk.

Surprised, Josiah looked over at the double-edged knife. There was something familiar about it, but he didn't know what.

Seeing Josiah's eyes widen, the sheriff chuckled. He was pleased with himself for getting this kind of reaction from his prisoner.

Out of the darkness, another growl broke through the silence. This one was even louder than the precious one was.

The sheriff slowly turned and looked at Josiah again. "Was that you boy?" he questioned as he stared intently at his prisoner. Josiah only looked back at him wide-eyed, and silently shook his head no. Slowly the sheriff stood up from his chair and looked over towards the door that the young woman had run out of, and was still closed. So, whatever it was, it was at the back door.

"I might step outside for a few minutes," the sheriff nervously told Josiah as he started to nervously walk to the closed door.

Before the sheriff took two steps, there was another scratching sound that came from beyond the open door, and the sound of something sharp striking the cobble stones just outside.

Turning towards the open door, the sheriff anxiously took a step forward and looked in its direction. Looking at the open doorway and then back towards Josiah, the sheriff just didn't know what to make of the situation.

"Who the hell's out there?" he called out into the darkness. His question was only met by silence. He could still hear something rustling around outside the door, but whatever it was, it was just out of his line of sight. "Who the hell is out there!" he again demanded as he put his hand on his baton.

Starting to walk towards the door, he only got two steps past his desk when he saw a large set of glowing amber eyes in the darkness staring in at him. As he stood frozen, he stared back at the eyes and a body began to slowly take form out of the darkness.

"What the hell...," He started to say before a large wolf type creature leapt in through the open door and stood on all fours in front of him snarling with hatred in its eyes.

The sheriff screamed out as the large wolf type creature again leapt forward and was now only inches from his face. The sheriff quickly backed up and bumped into his large wooden desk making a loud noise. Before the sheriff could move, the creature jumped on him and they tumbled to the floor.

The sheriff quickly reached for his gun, but upon drawing it, the animal immediately knocked it from his grip with one swipe of his clawed hand. The gun flew through the air until it hit the wall on the other side of the small office, and then it dropped to the floor with a thud.

The creature stood hovering over the sheriff who was now lying on his back. Bending over, the creature put its muzzle down closer to the sheriff's face and maliciously taunted him. The sheriff could feel the hot breath coming from the creature's nostrils blowing against his skin. As he snarled at the man, the creature's saliva began to trickle down onto the sheriff's face. Fearful and disgusted, the sheriff turned his head off to the side as the spital drooled onto him and ran down his cheek.

As the creature snarled once more at the man, a bright yellow puddle began to form on the floor underneath where the creature was kneeling. Out of fear, the sheriff had begun to lose control of his bladder, and urine vacated his body.

The creature sat back upright and stared at the sheriff as it let out a loud guttural growl. The sheriff's eyes got wide as the creature raised up one of its massive hands, and swung it at him. The large claws cut through the man's chest, leaving large slices in the sheriff's shirt, and the flesh that lay beneath. The cuts were deep, but not deep enough to be life threatening. The creature was only playing with the sheriff now, tormenting him as the sheriff had done to others in the past.

The sheriff cried out as he felt the claws of the animal slicing through his skin. Leaning his head forwards and looking at his chest, he saw his blood begin to pool up and run out of his wounds. The creature then swung at the sheriff again, but this time coming from the opposite side of his body. His claws again ripped through the man's clothing and went deep into the flesh beneath it. The sheriff didn't see that attack coming, and as soon as the claws began to cut through his skin, he cried out in agony.

Bending forward and sticking his muzzle down close to the sheriff's face, the wolf type creature menacingly snarled at the man and spittle once more dripped from his mouth down onto the sheriff's chin. Still lying beneath the creature, tears of sheer terror began to run down the man's face.

Standing back up, the creature now towered above the helpless man. *"Judged Guilty,"* the creature silently growled at him as he kicked at the man before him. The sheriff started to speak but the creature bent over and swung his clawed hand again, this time at his face and as the sheriff turned away, he ripped off one of his ears. Putting his hand up to the side of his face, and feeling nothing where his ear had been, the sheriff rolled onto his side in front of the creature and sobbed like a baby. He no longer was the man that he thought he was, and he was getting what he deserved.

Seeing the keys to the cell dangling from the side of the sheriff's belt, the creature reached down and took them into his hand and threw them towards Josiah's cell. They fell just short of the cell bars, but at this point, Josiah wasn't going to try to reach for them. He had no idea what this creature was, or where it had come from. He was in his own state of shock and disbelief.

The creature's attention was drawn back to the sheriff as he saw the man grab for his baton lying next to him on the floor. As soon as the man had it lifted up, the creature lunged downward and bit into the man's arm, crushing it within his powerful jaw. Quickly jerking his head off to the side, the creature easily ripped the man's lower arm off from the elbow down. The sheriff cried out in horror as he saw his arm being torn away and only leaving a shredded stub behind.

"You will never touch our brother ever again," the creature growled loudly at the sheriff in a low, rumbling inner voice. It was a voice that was being mentally projected at the man, and one that the sheriff heard loud and clear, even though it was being said without true sound behind it.

The creature's muzzle was now only inches from the man's face, and he could feel its hot breath breathing down upon him. The sheriff's eyes widened from the intense fear coursing through his heart, and this time he defecated in his pants as he realized that he was done for, and that what he was seeing before him was the eyes of death. In one final quick swipe of the creatures massive clawed hand, the sheriff's head ripped away from his body and went rolling across the worn wooden floor.

After the sheriff's head came to rest several feet away from his body, the creature stood up and pointed his penal sheath downward and urinated on the decapitated body of the sheriff. He was marking his territory to prove that he was the stronger, and more dominant of the foes.

At the sight of the sheriff's head being ripped from his body, and the smell of the fresh urine, Josiah turned and threw up onto the cell floor. The creature, hearing Josiah retching, straightened up and approached the cell bars and peered in at him. He stared at him and sniffed the air that stood between them. Josiah quickly stepped back from the bars and looked up at the creature as it reached out and wrapped its clawed fingers around the bars. The creature was massive and stood at least a whole two feet taller than Josiah's own six-foot frame. Shocked by being so close to it, Josiah didn't know what to say or do.

"Innocent brother," he said mentally to Josiah in a rough, broken speech. *"Innocent,"* the creature said as he released the cell bars and took a step back away from Josiah. The two then stared deeply into each other's eyes. There was a faint sign of familiarity to both man and wolf, as if somehow, in some way, they were connected. Slowly the creature started to back away further from Josiah's cell. Breaking eye contact, the creature turned and started to head towards the back door.

"Wait!" Josiah called out to it. The creature paused and turned back towards Josiah, but before he could say anything else, it turned and ran out the open back door on all fours. As Josiah watched the creature disappearing into the darkness, deep down, and without question, he now knew what and who had likely killed his family, and now he wanted to know why.

Josiah looked over at the sheriff's headless body, he hated to admit it even to himself, but he was glad that the man was dead. He was glad that the sheriff had suffered so much while the creature tortured him as well. If nothing else, it was some payback for what he did to the young woman earlier, and for what he had done to him and others as well.

Turning his head to the right, he then looked at where the keys were now laying on the floor before him. He had to get out of there, and to do that, he had to get the keys. Getting down on his knees, he reached through the bars with his good arm, but the keys were just out of his reach. Looking around his cell for something to use to pull them to him, he realized that there was nothing there that could be of any use. He then looked at the sheriff's dismembered arm that the creature had ripped off. It was lying close by, and possibly could be close enough for him to try to get a hold of. He had to try.

Pausing for a moment, Josiah stared down at the lifeless arm lying on the floor and resting in a pool of blood. Once more, Josiah turned his eyes away and retched. Taking a deep breath and getting his composure back, he knew that using the dismember arm was his only way of getting out of there. He had no other choice, and he knew it.

Josiah slowly reached his hand out targeting for the arm. Gagging, he grabbed the sheriff's arm by the bloodied stump and began to pull it nearer to him. Diverting his eyes from it, he put his other hand over his mouth as he tried not to vomit. The bloodied arm was slippery as he tried to get to get a grip on it. He had to readjust his grip on the bloodied stump twice before he was finally being able to bring it up to the bars of his cell.

Pausing for a moment to take a deep breath, Josiah looked down at bloodied arm in his hand. Taking the time to try to get a better grip on the sheriff's dismembered arm, Josiah aimed the arm out the bars and pointed it towards where the keys lay.

Stretching his own arm out through the bars, he tried to position the limp above where the keys were lying. Lowering the arm down until the lifeless hand now lay on top of the keys, he slowly began to drag them to him. The keys started to move underneath the weight of the sheriff's hand, but then Josiah's hand slipped on the bloodied stump, and he lost his grip on the arm. Grimacing, he picking the arm up again and reached it back out, once again placing it over top of the keys. This time as he dragged the keys towards him, Josiah managed to get the keys to within his reach. Breathing deeply, he collapsed onto the cell floor, exhausted.

Getting back up onto his knees, and now holding the keys to his cell in his hand, Josiah again gagged. Using his good arm, he then threw the sheriffs severed arm away from him. Looking down at his wet, sticky hand, Josiah walked over and wiped the sheriff's blood that was on it onto the thin, worn mice infested mattress that lay on the rickety cot. Then he wiped the blood off of the keys on it as well.

With shaking hands, Josiah fumbled with the keys until he found the correct one that with a loud click, unlocked his cell door. As soon as he had heard the click, he took a deep breath and began to push his cell door open. It creaked loudly with age as he began to open it.

Pushing harder on the heavy metal door to his cell, he opened it all the way. He silently stood and stared at the sheriff's mangled body as he relived in his head what had just happened, and how easily the creature had been able to kill the large man. Still not knowing where the creature had come from, or if it would be back, Josiah quickly glanced over at the still open side door. Staring out into the darkness, he didn't see any movement at all, and began to feel more at ease knowing that the creature wasn't still outside waiting on him to escape.

As Josiah stood at the open cell door in silence, the sound of voices drawing nearer broke his concentration, and interrupted his thoughts. The voices were quickly coming closer and getting louder. Panicking, Josiah began to look around him. Looking over at the door where the creature had run off through, he knew that was his only way out.

Looking one last time at the sheriff, and then up to the knife still stuck down into the desk, Josiah ran over and grabbed the knife. With the knife now safely in hand, Josiah darted out the back and into the night. Behind him he could hear a man yelling for someone to get the doctor. No doctor could help the sheriff now though, nor could anyone help Josiah. He knew he would be blamed for the sheriff's death, as well as the death of his family. He knew it wouldn't be long before

127

they realized he was gone and began to search for him. He didn't have much time to get away, but he had to get as far away as he could. He only had one stop to make first before putting as much distance between him and the men that would be searching for him as possible.

Chapter Four

A loud noise from outside of the cave awoke Josiah from his restless slumber. As he awoke, he could see that a storm had moved in, and the lightning was brightening up the sky. Though it was raining, Josiah didn't care, not as long as he was dry inside of his den. As the thunderstorm continued to rumble heavily over the village for hours, rain also unceasingly fell from the darkened clouds and watered the earth below.

Josiah sat lazily on the dirt floor of his den and watched an ant as it ran as swiftly as its little legs could carry it from one area to another in search of scraps. Quickly getting bored with the ant, Josiah leaned down to it, and with one quick snort, sent the ant tumbling away from him and back into the shadows where it had originally come from.

Stiffness began to settle into Josiah's muscles and bones from dampness from outside. Slowly getting up, he stretched out his aching body. It felt good to him to have a full stomach again, it was a feeling that he hadn't been accustomed to as of late. The venison that he had ate the night before had strengthened him, it not only fed his body, but it fed his confidence as well.

Walking over to the mouth of the cave, Josiah looked out into the night. There was no reason good enough to go out into a stormy night such as this, and after watching the lightning flash a few more times, he went back into the depths of the cave and sat down. It was at times like this that he found himself feeling lonely. He missed the companionship of having another to talk to the most. It was a solitary life that he now led, but it was the way it had to be, he was not given a choice.

Josiah decided that being there was nothing that he could do about the weather, and there was no reason to go out, that he would lay back down and try to get some more sleep. Sleep was not kind to Josiah most times, when sleep would come to him, it would almost always be an unrestful sleep, full of foul dreams and nightmares. He rarely remembered any of his dreams after he awoke; he mostly would only awaken afterward to a sense of loneliness, and a feeling of deep emptiness from inside of him. After stretching out his muscles one last time, Josiah leaned back and shut his eyes. Now with his stomach still full of venison, and the new feeling of satisfaction that it had provided him, he comfortably, slowly drifted off into a deep sleep.

In his dreams this night, as with most nights, Josiah again dreamt about when he was still a man, freshly escaped from the jail cell that he was unjustly imprisoned in, and running away out into the night. He knew that he had to get back to the field, and to the house before they came looking for him. He knew that the house, his house, was the first place that they would look for him. He had to be quick though, he had to get in, get his rifle and shells, and then get back out swiftly. He knew that he had to attempt to put as much distance between him and the posse as possible. He knew that once they found his jail cell empty, that they would blame him for the sheriff's death, and with the village's southern justice, this time he would be immediately hung, guilty or not.

As Josiah hurried away from the village under the cover of darkness, he could still hear the men in the jail house calling for the dogs to be brought in. When he heard one of the men say that they had a murderer on the run, that confirmed it, he was now not only a man on the run, but a man marked for death.

Making his way along the darkened wood line, Josiah tried to put some initial distance between him and the posse of men that would be after him. When he got to the wide-open field that stood between his land and the town, he paused to look at the field before him. He knew that he would have to run for it, because crossing the open field was the quickest way to get to his house. The only problem was, the moon was almost full and not leaving much darkness to use for cover. Turning around, Josiah looked back for any signs of a search party gathering, and seeing none as of yet, he took his chances and dashed through the open field, aiming for the farmhouse at the other side.

When he reached the house, Josiah ran around the back of the building and entered in through the exterior ground level

131

door that led into the root cellar. This room was not only built for the storage of their food, but it served as a storm shelter to protect him and his family from the ravages of the twisters that would occasionally sweep through the land. By using that entrance, Josiah would be able to climb back up the ladder on the other side of the room, and into the first-floor pantry through a hidden hatch in the floorboards. For him, he knew it was a way into the house where he would be less likely to be seen. The two front doors would be too obvious if anyone were watching for him, as well as where the posse would head first to find him.

Once inside the house, breathing heavily, Josiah tossed away the sling he had been wearing and headed for the upstairs bedroom that he had once shared with his wife. That is where he had kept his gun and the ammo that he would need to take with him.

As Josiah began to pass by the door to his oldest daughter's room, he paused and choked up. Knowing that he didn't have time for grieving, he forced his emotions deep down within him. Taking a deep breath, Josiah continued down the hallway before running up the stairs to the master bed room. Reaching for the door latch, Josiah was again overcome with grief, and a tear escaped his right eye and ran down his face. In his mind he was remembering the sight of his wife laying on the kitchen floor ripped to shreds, and his unborn son gone, torn from his mother's womb.

Shaking his head to clear his thoughts, Josiah reached down and pushed on the metal door latch. The steel latch creaked, and the hinges whined from age as Josiah went into the room. Without taking the time to look around, he headed straight for the closet and pulled out his Winchester lever action rifle and tossed it onto the bed. He then turned back to the closet and reached up onto the top shelf to feel for the box of shells that went with it.

The house was completely dark but for the few wisps of the moons glow that would come in the window from time to time. Feeling for where he thought the shells should be, his fingers finally found them. Taking the box into his hand, he took them down from the shelf.

Josiah paused to listen for any noises coming from outside, any sign that the posse was on its way, satisfied that it was still safe, he set the box of shells on the bed next to the gun. Turning back to the closet, he reached in and grabbed his coat from one of the hangers and put it on. He then loaded his gun and shoved the remaining shells into his jacket pocket. Just before he went out the door to leave, he stopped. Looking over at the nightstand by the bed, he saw the picture of his family that was in an old wooden frame. He walked over to it and picked it up. He looked down at the picture in the moonlight, and realized that was now all he had left of his family. He felt that he had to take it with him. He put it into the pocket of his jacket along with his shells, and headed for the door.

Josiah hurried out of the room and headed back down the stairs. At the bottom of the stairs, and to the left was Ava's room. He knew he didn't have time, but he felt that had to go into his youngest daughter's room. The door was already partially open, so he just pushed it in with his foot. The moon

133

light illuminated the room just enough so that he could see. He looked at the bed in which she had lain, and the small teddy bear that she had always slept with. Reaching down, he picked up the teddy bear and held it tightly. Bringing it up to his face, he smelled it to see if he could still smell his daughter's scent. As he did, a wave of emotion came crashing down on him, and tears freely ran from his eyes.

Hearing the dogs in the distance brough Josiah out of his sorrow and he knew that he had to get out of there quickly. Shoving the teddy bear in his other pocket, he quickly headed for the hatch that led to the root cellar. Once in the root cellar, he paused to peek outside before he opened up the outside door to exit. Seeing no one within sight, he hurried up the stairs and darted outside. His only hope for escape was to head for the hills where he would be harder to track. He could hear the dogs and their handlers as they entered the field and headed in his direction. He knew he had to now move, and move fast.

"They will stop at the house first," he mumbled out loud to himself as he gazed out over the field. That will give him time to make his way up and into the forest before they press on further to follow him. Once he reached the tree line, he looked back once more at what was once his home, and what had now become nothing more than an empty shell full of bad memories of what had just happened there to his family. He had no reason to ever go back there now. He had no family there, all he had left was his youngest daughter, Ava. He was sure that the great beast that he saw slaughter the sheriff less than two hours before, was the same creature that had killed his livestock and murdered his wife and daughter. And he was sure that the same creature very well could still have his youngest daughter, Ava, with him.

As he heard the dogs and their handlers arrive at the house, he saw lantern lights begin to shin through the darkened windows. He knew at that point that they wouldn't be far behind him. He had to move, and get as far up the mountain as possible before they discover what direction he was taking.

Josiah stirred and moaned restlessly in his sleep. As he slept, his legs began to involuntary move as if he were hurriedly running away from something chasing him. Now panting heavily, he began to sharply turn his head back and forth as he looked around behind him. His dreams were always very vivid and seemed so real to his unconscious mind. Though he never remembered them, his body always did.

Awakening with a sudden jolt, Josiah quickly jerked his body upright into the sitting position. Wildly looking all around the darkened interior of his den, he felt like it was as if he had suddenly woken up in a strange place, and not his cave. The suddenness of it left him frightened and out of breath.

While trying to control his nerves, Josiah yet again looked around at his surroundings inside the cave. After not seeing anything that could have led to his uneasy feelings, he began to calm down, and his breathing slowed to where he could begin to relax again.

Glancing outside, Josiah saw that it was still dark outside, and the moon continued to be unwavering in its refusal to fully show itself through the darkened storm clouds that still lingered above the land. He could still hear the occasional rumble of thunder and the unceasing rain as it continued to steadily drop to the earth as the storm rallied on.

Sleep, a real restful sleep, still remained just out of reach for Josiah. He never remembered what he dreamt about on the nights such as this, but he wished that he could. With nothing else to do, Josiah decided to just go and lie down at the mouth of his cave so that he could watch the rain and the storm as it continued to roll through. With the storm continuing on outside his cave, Josiah had no cares, no worries, and was just content to remain where he was and rest.

The rain continued to drench the earth for one more day and night. When it finally did stop, the sun rose high up in the sky, the clouds changed to a puffy white and everything smelled fresh and new again.

Josiah was getting anxious to get out of his den. Though it offered him protection from both the weather and from outsiders, it also at times felt like a prison cell, and it left him feeling as if he were a caged animal just waiting to escape.

Looking out at the new day, Josiah could see and hear the various song birds as they were fluttering back and forth above the field looking for bugs to catch and eat. He even saw a rabbit as it gently leapt across the field, and a skunk that was over by the wood line hurriedly digging up grubs.

"Tonight, I will go out and hunt. I will go out and see what game I can find in the woods on the other side of the hill

again. Game seems to be plentiful there," he said to himself as he turned and sat down. Leaning his back up against the rocky edge of the opening, Josiah shut his eyes and took a deep breath of the fresh air. As he did so, he let out a deep sigh.

The rays of the sun penetrated his exposed fur, warming his body and taking the dampness from his bones. For once instead of the sun's bright rays giving him a feeling of uneasiness, it was now giving him a feeling of contentment and pleasure.

Josiah continued to sit at the entrance of his cave until late afternoon, when the sun's rays shifted and moved on to another area. Getting up, he stretched his weary muscles, and the joints of his legs cracked and popped as he extended them to their full length.

Getting back down on all fours, Josiah walked back into the depths of his cave. Reaching out into the darkness, he drew out a weathered cloth bag. It was an old feed bag with a tie on it that someone had left behind high up the mountain long time ago. He took the bag back to the mouth of the cave and began to dig out its contents one by one. There was an old blanket, far too small now for his large body, but he kept it anyway. It was the only thing in the bag itself when he found it. Next, he drew out an old photograph. It was a photo of his family, an old black and white one that had now been yellowed by age. He looked at it closely and ran his finger over his wife's face. It seemed like a lifetime ago since he had seen any of them. Not a day went by that he didn't think of them though, and wonder where his youngest daughter, Ava,

137

was. *"She was three when she was taken,"* he thought to himself, *"she should be..."*, and then his thoughts went silent. He was having a hard time remembering how many years had passed by him since the day that his family was tore apart. He thought harder about it, but he still couldn't count the days, weeks or years that had gone by.

Touching his youngest daughters face in the photograph, Josiah shed a single tear. *"I will find you little one, someday I will find you,"* he promised her. *"And when I do find you, I will give this back to you,"* he whispered to himself as he dug out the small teddy bear that he still had with him. It too had begun to show the wear of time, and it was a little dirtier then when he first took it, but that little bear and the photograph of his family, they were his most prized possessions.

The photograph of his family and the teddy bear were the only true memories he had left of what once was for him, and the only thing that he could consciously remember about the past life he once led. Other than knowing he had a family and that he missed them, everything else about the life he led before was a blur. Consciously, he remembered very little of his previous life. His only true memories from back then were locked away in his subconscious, and in his dreams. If it weren't for the picture and the teddy bear that he carried with him as a constant reminder, he would have had no way of knowing if what little he did remember, were true memories or not.

After shoving everything back into the bag, Josiah returned the bag back into the shadows where it would be safe.

Evening would be moving in soon, and the sun's rays were quickly beginning to once more descending below the tree tops. It was his time now, the hour of the predators.

Walking back to the mouth of his den and into the fresh air, he put his nose to the wind. Everything still smelled clean and new. Old scents had been washed away, and the world was ready for new ones to take their place. He could smell the rabbit that he had seen earlier in the day, and he could even smell the field mice and the moles that ran across the thick growth of wheat, timothy and sage grass in the field directly in front of him.

Josiah scanned the field once more before he came out of his den and into the open. After stretching his limbs, he then turned and headed up the slight incline to the backside of where his den was. Looking once more back towards the field, he turned and moved off into the forest beyond. He was heading for the hunting ground he had last used, and where he had been so successful at finding that lone doe. He never did make it back to finish off her carcass though, but he was sure that nothing went to waste on it. There were many smaller animals in the woods that he wasn't even aware of, and he knew for sure that they would have taken care of all that remained of what was left hidden beneath the hollow log. Nothing ever goes to waste when there are hungry animals just waiting for a free meal.

It didn't take Josiah long for him to get to the other side of the hill where his hunting grounds now were. Because of his physical make-up he found out early on after he had changed, that navigating through dense brush and fallen trees, weren't even a problem for him anymore. This ability has also worked in his favor at other times, it helped to ensure that when needed, he could disappear into his surroundings swiftly and easily, especially when he needed to avoid the prying eyes of the two-legers.

Upon reaching the other side of the hill, Josiah took the time to sit with his back against an old oak tree and relax. He just wanted to take a few moments to sit and observe what was before him, and to see if there was anything of interest moving in the woods before he began his hunt. Though now hungry, he still wasn't in a hurry to make his next kill; he was just happy to be able to be in the woods again.

It wasn't long though before he heard a rustling noise coming from just on the other side of a small clump of trees to his left. He sat motionless and listened. He heard some more rustling of the leaves, and then it suddenly stopped. He could no longer hear whatever it was. He couldn't smell anything either, the breeze was not working in his favor in the least. He decided that either the animal had changed the direction that it was taking, or that it might have frozen due to some other danger it sensed lurking close by. Either way, it didn't look good for him.

Staying silent, Josiah continued to wait to see if what had been there, would decide to still chance coming out into the open. Though not scenting this one, he could still smell several different distinctive scents in the area, so he knew that there was no shortage of prey animals around, and if this one didn't work out to his favor, then there would certainly be another.

After a few more minutes, the animal again made a rustling noise, and he now knew that it had returned to where he had first heard it. Getting to his feet, Josiah readied himself for the impending hunt. The animal before him nervously stepped out into a break in the trees. The deer was acting uneasy and anxious as it slowly came fully into his sight. Nervously, the deer kept glancing back over its shoulder and into the darkened woods behind it. It knew that something was stalking it.

Josiah looked past his intended prey, and into the woods behind it where it had been staring, but he saw no signs of anything hiding in the darkness. Putting his nose to the breeze didn't help either, for once more, it was traveling in the wrong direction for him to try to pick up the scent of whatever it was that was making the deer so anxious. Continuing to watch the deer as it made its way out of the trees, Josiah silently held his position.

Getting impatient and deciding not to wait any longer, Josiah leaped from his hiding spot and grabbed the large buck around the neck with one arm. He then grabbed it around the head to control its antlers with the other arm. Frightened, the deer kicked up with its front feet and tried to throw Josiah off of it, but he was far too strong for it, and continued to hold on securely. As the deer continued to try to fight off its attacker, it began to thrash its head back and forth as it snorted loudly.

Josiah was using up energy that he didn't need to waste, so with one swift twist of the deer's head, he snapped the spinal cord in its neck and then allowed it to crumble to the ground.

141

The deer made one last defiant kick of its legs as it laid on its side, and then it was done. It was a swift kill, and the deer did not suffer long this time. It was able to die with dignity, swift and true.

After quickly glancing around at his surroundings, Josiah reached down and picked the deer up by its hind legs. Holding the legs tightly in one hand, he dragged it back up towards the wood line and out of the semi-open area. Just as he approached the darker shadows of the tree canopy though, he caught sight of movement, and a set of pale-yellow eyes.

Josiah gave a loud gutter growl as he scowled at the faceless creature of the night. The other animal didn't move. Staying hidden in the darkness, it stared intently at Josiah as it answered his growl, with a growl of his own.

"Be gone with you! Leave this place and go back to where you have come from," Josiah mentally ordered loudly. The animal didn't move off, but instead it chose to hold its ground. Dropping the hind legs of the deer that he was dragging, Josiah stood ready to defend himself, and his prey from the unwanted intruder.

The piercing yellow eyes began to move sideways, and to circle around Josiah in the darkness. The animal's footsteps could barely be heard as it moved around and in between the trees of the forest.

"What is your business here?" Josiah gruffly mentally spoke as he kept a wary eye on the moving animal. As it moved, it

gradually made its way out of the protection of the shadows, and into the clear area where Josiah could get his first glimpse at what, and who he was up against.

A full-grown six foot long, 200-pound grey wolf was what was now circling Josiah, and it was preparing to fight for the carcass that now lay at the creature's feet. It was the deer that it had been tracking first, and the wolf was what the deer had been so nervously glancing back at in the shadows. The large grey wolf now began to snarl threateningly at Josiah, as it snapped its large teeth.

"You dare to threaten me dog," Josiah growled back at it menacingly. The threat had no effect, and the wolf continued to circle him. Josiah kept pace with the wolf as he rotated his body to keep up with its movements. *"You, lone wolf, where is your pack? Why did they leave you to fend for yourself?"* he growled as he egged it on. *"You are no match for me and you know it!"* he snarled aggressively at it.

The wolf, with its head laid low, continued to circle around Josiah, moving closer and decreasing the distance between them with each pass it made.

"You stand no chance wolf, and you know it," he mentally told it. *"You would do best to back off and leave,"* he added.
At one point the wolf got close enough to reach out and grab the deer carcass by the neck, and in one quick motion, it began to pull the carcass away from Josiah. Seeing what the wolf was doing, Josiah reached down and grabbed the deer's hind legs, jerking them back towards him, and ripping the deer from the wolf's mouth.

143

"You won't get my food that easily dog," he told it. Josiah now got down on all fours, and readying himself to do battle against the large grey wolf. The wolf lunged at Josiah, and when it did that, Josiah took one of his large hands and swung it at the wolf. The wolf was able to turn and duck just in time to avoid the impact as Josiah's hand swished through the air above it.

Again, the large wolf bared its teeth and lunged at Josiah, and as it did, Josiah also took aim and swung at it as well. This time his aim was more accurate, and he made contact with the large wolf. The impact of the blow knocked the large wolf off its feet, and sent it crashing to the ground a few feet away.

Infuriated, the wolf got back up onto its feet snarling its distaste for what had just happened. Bending its legs to gain momentum, the wolf quickly rushed at Josiah. With great speed, it jumped onto Josiah's chest, and knocked him off balance. Losing his footing from the force at which he had just been hit with, Josiah fell backwards and together they both tumbled to the ground.

With the large wolf still on top of him, Josiah grabbed the wolf by the scruff of the neck and held it fast as it snapped and tried to lung at his face. Saliva sprayed from the angry wolfs mouth and dripped onto Josiah's fur. Turning over onto his side to gain an advantage, Josiah was able to forcefully toss the wolf off to the side of him towards the trees beyond. When the wolf came back down to the earth, it did not land on its feet, but instead came down onto its side, impacting the ground with a thud.

Quickly getting himself back up onto his feet, Josiah rapidly prepared himself for another attack. He saw the large wolf attempting to stand back up while shake its head back and forth. He knew that it had been left dazed from the hard impact that it had with the ground. On its second attempt, the grey wolf was able to get to its feet, stumbling at first, and as it rose, it turned and once more snarled at Josiah.

Now steady on its feet again, the wolf charged at Josiah once more. He quickly stepped aside this time, and when the large wolf passed by, Josiah turned and leapt onto its back. Grabbing it from behind, he straddled its back and forced it to the ground. The wolf tried to shake him off, but it couldn't dislodge the larger beast.

"I don't want to hurt you dog," he told it as it continued to struggle against him. Having Josiah on its back though, only infuriate the wolf even more. *"Calm down!"* Josiah yelled at it. But all he was answered with was more snarling and aggression.

"Don't make me do it dog, because I will take your life!" Josiah said to it as he tried again to calm the wolf down. Seeing that the wolf was not going to give up its fight, Josiah knew what he was going to have to do. He did not like to kill just to kill, but this wolf was giving him no option.

Pausing for a moment as he looked down at large grey wolf below him. He admired both the beauty and the tenacity of the beast that he had just fought. *"It didn't have to be this way,"* he thought to himself. *"Last chance to give up and go,"* he told it, almost as if pleading with it to give up the fight and

145

to move on under its own power. When the grey wolf didn't concede, and it continued to fight against him, it left him no choice. With his hands already around the wolf's neck, he extended the fingers of one of his hands and in one quick draw of his claws, he ripped the wolf's throat out.

The wolf let out a loud whine as it felt the creature's sharp claws dig deeply into its flesh, and then there was nothing, all went silent as the wolf's lifeless form now lay limp on the ground. Still straddling the dead body of the wolf, Josiah looked up towards the star lit sky and howled into the night. It was a howl of mournful despair, he felt bad about doing what he had just done, but again, the large wolf had given him no choice, the wolf would not relent, nor would it walk away. It sealed its own fate by doing what it did, and in the end, it cost it it's life.

All the creatures of the night went silent upon hearing the mournful howl. The echo of the howl carried far on the breeze, and it put all the other nocturnal animals at alert. It told them all that there was an apex predator now in their midst, and they needed to be wary of what might come.

Looking down at the lifeless body of the wolf before him, Josiah felt remorseful for what he had to do. It was a senseless death, a death that didn't have to happen like it did. The wolf could have hunted elsewhere that night and left him be with his prey, but it pushed him too far. The deer was his, it didn't belong to the wolf. They could have even shared it, and the wolf could have had its fill after he was done with what he wanted. But now it was too late for sharing, now he was all that remained after the battle was done.

Josiah bend down and took the hind legs of the deer back into his hands, and pulled it off into the depths of the darkened woods. He didn't feel he would have to hide his prey's remains this time, he would just eat what he wanted and leave the rest to the other animals in the forest to consume. He was also sure that if a two-leger would happen to find it, they would just assume that the wolf itself was the one that made the kill before falling victim to another of its own kind. And as he thought further, if the couple that were in the field that night said anything about something hiding in the shadows, he knew that this wolf would now also take the blame for that.

Reaching out with one of his hands, Josiah carefully took hold of the thick skin of the deer, and then by using one of his claws, he carefully cut a slit across the back haunches of the animal. Working quickly, he skinned the backside of the deer, and then continued to skin it up the back to just below the rib cage. After skinning out the area he was most interested in consuming at the moment, he again used one of his claws to cut the connective tissue and then remove the muscular upper portion of the hind leg.

Sitting back on his haunches, he used both hands as he ate. Blood dripped from between his fingers as he took large bites of the tasty meal that the deer had provided to him. After he devoured both hind quarters of the deer, he moved his attentions up to the spinal area of the animal. Carefully, and again using one of his claws, he cut through the hide of the deer to expose the loin area of the back. After pulling the hide free from the back, he gently ran one of his claws along the spine, and then again above the rib cage to cut through

147

the silver skin coating to expose the tender loin area of the back.

After running one of his claws deeper down along the spine and curling it up underneath the meat, the best and the most tenderest part of the deer fell off into his hands. This was the part of the deer that was treasured the most, and with that, the best part of the large buck now lay within his hands. He drooled in the anticipation of the flavor that awaited, and the feeling of the tender sweet meat in his mouth, for him, it was the part that he usually enjoyed the most. But tonight though, his heart just wasn't in it. He was still thinking about the wolf, and how he had chosen to die instead of backing off. After he finished with the first loin, Josiah then went back for the second one. After both of the loin strips were consumed, he then moved to the meaty area of the upper front legs.

Josiah used to hunt often like this when he lived up in the mountains. At one time the prey was plentiful up there, and there was no worry of going hungry. That was before the two-legers had expanded into his territory though, and forced him out. They gave him no choice but to leave, and after that, his life had only gotten worse as time went on.

Humans are like that, they always destroyed what lay before them, and they always take more from the land than what they are due. When the two-legers moved into his mountainous home, he had no choice but to move on, and by moving on, he not only ended up moving away from what he had been unconsciously searching for, but he was also being forced downward, and that made him move closer to the

148

two-legers in the village, and the humans that he despised the most.

Josiah had lived in the mountains for years after he escaped from the jail cell and his certain death at the hands of the posse. Up in the mountains, he hunted for the creature that had killed his family, and took his youngest daughter from her bed. But as time went on, the land was not kind to him, and his thoughts had begun to become clouded and the memories of his earlier life had begun to become distant. Slowly, and without realizing it, Josiah had begun to change, and become one of the creatures that he himself had been hunting.

The change came up on Josiah very slowly. It started when he began to have problems remembering various things from his past, his own childhood and his parents, then it went to intense body aches that made his joints feel as though they were twisting out of their sockets. As time went on, he began to have difficulty with walking, and hunting had become almost impossible for him. He found that even surviving in the wild as he was now, had become a struggle between life and possible death.

Then one day Josiah began to become very ill, and a great fever began to rage through his body. He had delusions and nightmares about creatures that couldn't possibly exist. He didn't understand any of what he was seeing or how he was feeling. His mind was playing tricks on him all the time, and when he would look down at himself during what he thought were one of his few lucid moments, and look particularly at his hands, they didn't appear to be his hands at all. Nothing seemed real to him. Josiah felt as though he was losing his mind, and deep down in his heart, he was sure that he was going to die alone on that mountain side.

Josiah was in and out of consciousness for a week at a time. He would become aware of his surroundings for only a short time before he would recede back into a world of nightmarish, unbelievable creatures. He thought that there was someone, or something that was there taking care of him, but he didn't know if they were real, or just another part of his continuous nightmare. His thoughts were scrambled, and he was having a hard time telling what was real, and what wasn't. Josiah spent most of his time delusional, and living in his own nightmare of a world.

Eventually his fever did break, and the strength in his muscles had returned back to him. Whoever it was that had been taking care of him the whole time that he was ill; they were now no longer anywhere to be found. There were no signs to even let Josiah know who they had been, or where they had come from. He did know though that whoever it was, that they had kept a fire burning to keep him warm throughout the whole duration of his illness, and that it hadn't been that long ago that they had left, because there were still smoldering ashes remaining in the firepit, and they were still throw off heat. Not only that, but there were also two freshly killed rabbits left for him laying at the mouth of the cave.

Immediately Josiah noticed the change from within himself. He looked at his hands first, and couldn't believe what he was seeing. *"This must be some kind of a dream, am I still dreaming?"* he asked himself as he held one of his hands out and made a fist. He watched his hand, and watched how the clawed fingers curled and uncurled again. Flipping his hand over, he looked at the back of it. It was covered with short black hair of some kind. Looking up from his hands to his arms, he saw that they were muscular and covered with denser black hair than what his hands were. He then looked down to his feet; they too were covered with dark coarse hair, and were shaped differently than before. His feet now looked elongated, much larger than they had been before. They too, like his fingers, had long claw like nails that extended from the front of his feet where his toe nails used to be. *"This can't be,"* he nervously told himself over and over.

Putting his hands up to his face, Josiah let out a small gasp when he felt a long protruding type structure in place of where his mouth and nose had once been. Looking downward with his eyes, he now saw that he had a long black muzzle in place of his nose and mouth. His body began to tremble from the shock of what he was seeing before him. He didn't know what to think, and couldn't comprehend what had mysteriously happened to him.

Looking down over the knoll just outside of his cave, Josiah stared at the fresh water of the creek below. Leaving the safety of his cave, Josiah hurriedly half walked and half ran to the creek below. Kneeling down next to the water, Josiah apprehensively he leaned over the water's edge and looked at himself in the clear refection.

Josiah jerked backward and came to rest on his buttocks as he cried out at what he had saw staring back at him in the

151

water. His heart began race, and he started to hyperventilate from the shock. He turned and looked frantically around him in a failed attempt to see if the person who had helped him earlier was still nearby and could tell him what was happening to him, but there was no one there. With his heart still racing, he didn't know where to turn or what to do. After gaining control of his breathing, he again got to his feet and slowly approached the water's edge. Looking into the crystal-clear water, his eyes only confirmed what he had previously saw in his reflection, and that he was no longer a man, not a real man, but some kind of great beast instead.

With confirmation of what he had now become, it was then that he reluctantly had to accept that the image that he now saw staring back at him, was indeed a true reflection of himself as he now appeared. He was no longer a man, at least no longer the man that he used to be, but instead, he was now an animal, a large wolf type beast, the same wolf type beast that he saw in the sheriff's office that one night long ago.

Josiah wanted to kill himself, but he couldn't do it. If he would do that, then there would be no one to continue his search for his daughter, and to rescue her from the beast that kidnapped her. He was now afraid that even if he could locate her, that there was no way that she would recognize him, and he feared that she would run from him in terror. How would he be able to explain to her about his appearance, and explain to her about her mother and siblings, when he couldn't even explain it all to himself. Still though, the one thought that remained strong within his mind, and the pact that he made with himself, on the lost life of his wife, daughter, and unborn child, that one day he would find the creature that killed his family, and took his little girl. And then he would make it pay for what it did to his family, with the price being its own life.

From that point on, Josiah had to adapt to his new body, and the new appetite that came along with it. Because he no longer had a need for them, he left his Winchester and most of his belongings behind in the small cave when he left. He only kept the worn blanket that he had used, the cloth sack that he had found, and the memories that it held within. Overtime, he would still occasionally take out the photo of his family, and the small bear that belonged to his youngest daughter. He needed those items to help remind him of who he was, and what he had lost years earlier. And most importantly, he needed them to help him remember what he still had to do, and that was, to find his daughter.

As time went on, it didn't take Josiah long to learn how to use his new abilities to hunt, and capture game. Though he would still eat fruit from time to time, he really only craved raw meat. He had become more animal like in both appearance, and instinct. Unlike before when he was still a man, he could travel swifter and further than ever before without tiring. Over time he adapted to his new abilities well, and he learned to become one with them. His attitude had also changed along with his appearance. He was no longer the mild mannered, quiet man that he had been before, but now, he was stronger and wiser, forceful and cunning. He was, and had become, half wolf, half man...he had become, a Dogman.

B.J. MOORE

In the shadows,
Dark and dim,
An old owl calls,
With tales of him.

Warnings are shared,
Of a wolf in wait,
Run away, run away,
Before it's too late.

The claws of a Dogman,
Are razor sharp,
Don't make him mad,
Or he'll rip you apart.

Not all are bad,
But how do you tell,
For once you see them,
You are under their spell.

BJ Moore

Chapter Five

Josiah glanced over at the body of the grey wolf as it laid on its side next to a small stump. Looking down, he shook his head, he felt that the wolf didn't need to die like it did, not at all. Looking away, he slowly went back to eating the front quarters of his kill, though he ate it, he didn't take much pleasure in it because of the end results of what happened afterward. After Josiah finished his meal, he left the remains for the other creatures of the night. They would all feed well tonight, not only on the remains of the deer, but on that of the wolf as well.

Josiah got to his feet and started his long walk back to his cave. He was in no hurry this night; daylight was still hours away. His stomach was full, and as he walked, he enjoyed the feeling of being free, free of human contact, and free to walk in peace. In the woods, there were no restrictions, he could go where he wanted, and go without fear of being seen.

As he approached his den, Josiah's ears perked up and he quickly froze in place. Silently, and without making a sound, he slid over the small embankment and hid in the shadows behind the trees. Rotating his ears back and forth, he listened closer to pinpoint the area from where the voices had emanated from. After a few moments of silence, he began to realize that what he had picked up on was some of the two-legers from the village, and not anyone close to him or nearby in the field below.

It was late and the tavern in the village was just closing for the night. There were half a dozen drunken men stumbling off in different directions, laughing and joking with each other as they went. *"It would be so easy to take one or two of them just for spite"*, he though, but he knew better and fought off the temptation.

Thought it would be very easy for him to seek revenge and kill the two-legers that he hated, taking a human would do nothing but bring him more problems than it would be worth. He knew how the two-legers could be. His torment, and the cruelty inflicted upon him from the sheriff of the village, was just one of the few memories that he still retained, and that one alone would probably be burned into his soul forever.

When the creature from all those years ago attacked and killed the sheriff, the town's people automatically assumed that it had been Josiah that was responsible for the man's murder. From what he had overheard the two-legers saying, they even blamed him for sadistically rip off the sheriff's head, and arm from his body as if he had the strength to do that in human form. He knew that being the Sheriff's arm was found in his cell, it didn't help matters any. But it wouldn't matter to them anyway even if they knew the truth, and that it was only there because he had to use it to get the keys so that he could get out of the cell.

They, the sheriff and his men, had also unjustly accused him of butchering his family, and of somehow disposing of his youngest daughter's body somewhere on the property before the sheriff and his deputies got to his house. When he was fleeing for his life, one night he snuck back in close enough to hear what some of the posse was saying about him around their fire. Without them knew the facts about what had happened, they had all already unjustly declared him guilty of everything.

The two-legers searched for him with their dogs for weeks, but Josiah had managed to move high up into the mountains where even the dogs were not comfortable going. They could feel that the mountain was different, and they could sense the dangers that were hidden there. Josiah could feel it himself as well. At a certain point, the dogs just refused to go any further. Assuming that Josiah was now beyond their reach, and without the aid of the dogs, the posse gave up on their search for him, turned around and headed back to the village.

It wasn't until much later, when the logging companies moved in that the two-legers had a reason to venture higher up into the mountains again. Big saws cut the virgin timber down and horses were used to haul it back down off the mountain. The loggers set up camp sites up on the side of the mountain, and they hunted for game to feed the men. They used big guns, not the common Winchesters 1886 that most homesteaders still used, but a new gun out, called a Marlin

1895. These men also shot for fun, more so than for food. They killed just to kill, and left much of it to rot where it lay. Eventually, there was no more large game left to roam that side of the hillside. They had wiped out several entire herds of the white tail, and mule deer both. The mountain not only became barren of trees, but it was barren of food. All because of the outright arrogance of the loggers, Josiah then had no choice but to leave, and then once again, lacked a place to call his own.

More often than not, Josiah's memories were blurred now, with many of what he had held dear, now totally gone. Only bits and pieces of memories would still come to mind at times, but nothing consistent or complete. It was like miscellaneous puzzle pieces, with no definitive puzzle to put together for the larger picture.

Sometimes when it was quiet, he would wonder about his life, wonder how and why he got to be what he is now, and more so, where his humanity left off, and the creature had begun. His identity was so intermixed now, that there was no distinction between man and beast. For Josiah, the only thing that remained as proof of his old life, was the picture of him and his family together, and his daughter's teddy bear.

Standing in front of his den, Josiah relished at having a full belly again. He had gorged himself on venison until he could eat no more. Looking up at the moon, he paused to wonder if the deer had moved back up the mountain yet. *"The two-legers that had cut down all the trees had left awhile back, two winters ago, or was it three,"* he wondered. He wasn't really sure. *"It might be time to go back, time to leave and head home to the mountains. This land holds nothing for me now, the memories of it are gone. What once was mine, the two-legers now claim, and as far as I am concerned, who needs it,"* he mournfully lamented.

While contemplating the thought of leaving and heading north, Josiah stood and watched as the last of the two-legers went out of sight. Turning around and looking at the opening of his den, he then glanced once more at the full moon above, and sighed. His heart was no longer here, he was realizing it more and more as time went by. He was now not only thinking about it, but he was longing to head north, back to his mountain home where he could again be free.

Walking over to the face of his cave, Josiah bent down and went inside. He had thought about leaving this valley before, many times actually, but something from deep within him always held him here. Now even the reason behind that eluded him, he no longer could remember it, and that bothered him. *"Why can't I remember why I am still here!"* he asked himself in frustration. He blamed the valley itself for his lack of memories, and the stress he was feeling from being here.

Off in the distance the mournful howling of a wolf caught Josiah's attention. The eerie sound that it made carried far across the land. *"That must be the mate to the big one,"* he told himself as he walked over to the opening of his den and looked out. Again, he heard the howl, and this time it sounded even more mournful than before, and after a third final lowly howl, it trailed off to silence. At that, Josiah bowed his head in respect for a formattable foe.

159

No longer hearing the howling any more, Josiah lifted his head, turned and went back inside of his den. He went over to the side of the stone wall and sat down. *"I think I will leave tomorrow. My time here is now done,"* he told himself in contemplation. *"I will sleep now to save on energy, and then tomorrow night at dusk, I will begin my journey back up the mountain, and to the land that I had once called home. I will go back up and also search for what I have lost. I will search for my Ava."*

With that, Josiah leaned back and stretched out on the cool floor of the cave and shut his eyes. Though sleep was rarely peaceful for him, this night with his stomach full, he quickly fell into a deep restful sleep. He needed his rest, for the next evening he had a long journey ahead of him, a journey that would take him past where he had previously lived, to new points, and higher peaks on the mountain than he had ever thought about going before. He would have a lot of ground to cover, and many days of travel ahead of him, but to put as much space between him and the two-leggers as possible, it would be worth it.

Later in the day, with the sun still shining brightly in the sky, Josiah was awoken by the sound of two-legers out in the field again. He could smell their presence even from within his cave. He knew that they were nearby, and far too near for comfort.

"It is good that I am leaving tonight," he told himself. *"Two-legers are getting too close,"* he thought, *"and their females, they are becoming too tempting,"* he said as he sniffed the air.

It was then that Josiah realized that one of the two-legers was a woman. This one was different than the last though, this one smelled younger, purer. Her scent was very enticing to him, even more so than the other woman had been. Getting up on all fours, Josiah put his nose into the slight breeze that was entering his cave. Flaring his nostrils, he breathed the alluring scent of the young woman deep down into his lungs.

"Mmmm," he said as he closed his eyes and lightly groaned. He could feel a tingling in his groin, and he knew what was going to happen next. Unable to control it, the pressure began to build, and he began to grow firm again. The aching and the deep-seated burning sensations in his groin began to get stronger and more uncomfortable for him.

Taking two steps towards the entrance to his cave, he could feel a light whimper starting to emerge from within him, and he did his best to silence it.

"No!" he silently screamed at himself to calm himself down and to regain control. *"No! Ignore the female!"* he told himself as he forced himself to go no further.

With his groin area now aching, he reached down and cupped his firm sacks in his large hand. *"Calm yourself,"* he told himself as he took a deep breath in, in an effort to regain his composure. After taking his testicles into his hand and holding them tightly, he gained no relief, if anything, it only again made the sensation he was experiencing worse. The intense feeling, and his need to take care of that feeling overcame him, and he moved his hand up to his penile

161

sheath. He was already almost fully erect at this point, and as he pushed the penile sheath the rest of the way down the shaft, he gave his penis a strong jerk that caused it to enlarge to its full size. *"Get it over with fool!"* he told himself as he now jerked his penis until the hot fluid rose up and shot from his loins. *"There, it is done,"* he told himself gruffly as he took in a deep breath and then exhaled. *"Yes, it is good I leave, and the sooner the better,"* he disgruntledly told himself as he quickly turned. Disgusted with himself, and walked back into the depths of his cave once more.

The next night as the darkness fell across the land, Josiah gathered up his meager belongings, and left his den for what he felt would certainly be the last time. Turning back, he paused and looked at the entryway. It felt as though he was leaving an old friend, one that's path he would never cross again. His den was like close friend that offered him both safety, and shelter from the elements. A friend that kept him hidden, and out of the sight of prying eyes. He would miss his den, but it was time to part ways. *"Good bye old friend,"* he thought to himself as he took two steps backwards, then turned, and walked away.

Heading for high up in the mountains would take him two weeks or possibly more of constant traveling depending on how quickly he walked. He could make it much quicker if he really wanted to, but he decided he would play it by ear. All he knew, was that he planned on going even higher than he ever had before. He was in no hurry, and he also knew that after he left the valley there would be little chance of human interaction, no one to push him, and for that he was glad of. Josiah knew he was heading for rough terrain, terrain that he knew nothing about. He had no idea what to expect when he got there, he just knew that he needed to go.

When Josiah left the valley behind him, he was not heading in any certain direction. As he walked, he felt glad to be leaving his burdens behind him, and was enjoying the new found freedom he felt as he increased the distance between him and the two-legers. Not having any firm destination in mind, Josiah believed that when he got to where he was heading, that he would just somehow know, and it was then that he would be where he was destined to be all this time.

Josiah had traveled three full nights on his journey up the mountain side. Resting by day, and traveling by night, he had covered many miles of terrain, and left many miles of wilderness behind him. It wasn't hard traveling, he took his time and enjoyed being one with nature. Now that the sun's rays were beginning to peek out brightly over the horizon yet again, he would have to find somewhere to hold up for the day, and then it would be the time for him to rest once more.

With the last of the night sky giving way, Josiah come upon a creek bed and he knelt to drink of its cool, fresh water. Leaning down close to the water, he saw his reflection looking back at him. He paused for a moment and looked at himself. *"How long has it been since I've become what I am now?"* he wondered to himself. Josiah over the years had lost all concept of time, time no longer meant anything to him. Looking away from his reflection, he put his muzzle down and lapped up the cool water. It tasted good to him, sweet and untarnished by man. It had been quite a while since the two-legers were on this land.

163

Just beyond the creek, Josiah spotted a tall rock ledge with what looked like darkened gaps in the face of it below. Getting back up to his hind legs, Josiah walked towards the ledge to get a closer look at the openings. Stopping just 15 feet shy of reaching one of the cavities, he paused. Putting his nose to the breeze again, Josiah began to sniff the air around him. He was picking up on a scent, a scent that he hadn't smelled for years, but yet a scent that he would never forget. He had dealt with this animal many times before when he lived on the mountain side, and every one of them was as ill-tempered as the next.

As he stood before the rock ledge watching for the animal that he had smelled, he heard rustling coming from within the opening. It was obvious, that what lie within the darkness, had also picked up on the stranger's scent as well. He heard more rustling and could tell that the animal was coming closer to the mouth of the cave. Josiah watched as a pair of yellow eyes began to appear and silently stare out at him with suspicion.

Josiah could hear a low rumbling growl beginning to be emitted from the animal that was hidden and watching him from just inside of the darkened entrance. Instinctively he began to growl back at whatever lay inside. Dropping his pack from his shoulder, Josiah got down on all fours and stared back at the animal as it hid in the darkness before him.

As Josiah stared at where the animal was, a large mountain lion slowly took a step out of the darkness and stared intently at him with its large golden eyes. Unfamiliar with what it was seeing, the large cat was sizing up this new intruder.

Josiah was much larger, and stronger than the big cat was, and the mountain lion instinctively knew that it was definitely at a disadvantage. It didn't stop the large cat though; it was not allowing itself to be intimidated. As the mountain lion slowly emerged the rest of the way out of the darkness of its den, it began to snarl and aggressively circle Josiah. Though Josiah was familiar with the large felines, this cat had no idea what, or who Josiah was.

"I do not want to hurt you cat," Josiah mentally told it. But the big cat didn't understand, it couldn't comprehend what Josiah was trying to say to it. It heard the words that Josiah was telling it, but it didn't understand the language. Again, the big cat snarled at Josiah. Raising up its front right leg, the large cat swatted at the air that stood between the two of them. Far from connecting, the mountain lion appeared to be testing the parameters of its opponent, trying to see what the larger animal's reaction would be.

Keeping his eyes on the snarling cat before him, Josiah followed its every move as it continued to aggressively circle around him. Then when the cat took another swipe at him and almost made contact, Josiah was infuriated. Bending his front legs and crouching to the level equal to that of the cat, he extended his neck, laid back his ears and let forth with a loud, guttural growl that echoed off the trees, and the rock walls around them. As Josiah growled, the sound waves from the growl were so intense that it hit the cat with such force that it pushed its ears and fur backward as if a strong headwind was blowing forcefully directly into its face. Taken aback, the large cat looked confused and silently stared at the great beast before it.

Alarmed by what it had just experienced, the cat took a step back from Josiah and intensely stared at the massive creature that stood before it. It had never seen a creature such as Josiah before. Even with the creature down on all fours, it still towering dangerously over the cat.

The large cat snarled as it took another step backwards and then a step off to the side, all the while, not taking his eyes off Josiah. Looking up at Josiah, the large cat took in the full magnitude of the creature that stood before it. Reconsidering the large disadvantage that it was now realizing; the mountain lion decided that it was no longer sure if this was a fight that he really wanted to pursue. Beginning to back off even further, the cat lowered its head and lightly hissed when it saw Josiah clench one of his fists, and turn his body to follow its direction.

Josiah took a step towards the large cat, forcing it to rapidly take another step backward in retreat. Still keeping its eyes on Josiah, the large cat turned its body sideways as a gesture of submission, then slowly proceeded to move back away from him a little more with every step.
Josiah watched as the large cat slowly began to walk away from him and head towards the safety of the trees beyond. After reaching the edge of the forest, the large cat stopped and took one last long stare at Josiah. It glared at the larger animal, but didn't make a sound. When satisfied that Josiah wasn't interested in pursuing it, the large cat walked off and disappeared into the woods.

The mountain lion had chosen its battle wisely this day, if it had stayed and chose to fight for its den, it most assuredly would have not had only lost the battle, but it also would have lost its life as well. For the cat, it was better to live to fight another day, then to waste its life on something as insignificant as this.

Josiah rose back up onto his hind legs and watched as the cat slowly disappeared into the trees. Reaching down to pick up his sack, Josiah again turned and approached the entrance to what was the mountain lion's den. Getting back down on all fours, Josiah crawled in through the crevasse like opening in the rock.

The inside of the den was larger than it had appeared from the outside. Sniffing the air within, Josiah was repulsed by the strong odor of the cat that was ingrained within its stone walls. Looking around the interior of the cave, Josiah walked over to where he could tell that the large cat had been bedded down and resting. Leaning forwards with his hips, he proceeded to urinate on the spot. He was getting rid of some of the odor left from the cat, as well as now marking the territory of this cave as his own.

Josiah felt good, he felt strong, and he felt alive. More alive than he had in a long time. Being away from the valley was having a good effect on him. He wasn't constantly looking over his shoulder, nor second guessing himself every time he had a close call with a two-leger. Nor was he always having to be careful to ward off discovery at all cost.

Going to the back of the cave, Josiah laid down his pack and sat next to it. His life had begun to feel stagnant in the valley below. His movements had become very restricted, and he felt too closed in there to be comfortable. Up here in the mountains though, he not only felt free, he was free.

Josiah decided to lie down for a while and rest. He knew that the big cat would not return tonight, nor would anything else dare to bother him either. The first leg of his journey had been a tiring one. He had walked all night and covered many miles, and now he needed to rest. He needed to rebuild his strength so he could continue on his way when the darkness would once again fall the very next evening. The night time was good to him. It gave him safety and comfort; the darkness of the night was his only true friend.

Josiah woke just as the evening hours were at hand, and darkness was replacing the light of the day. He had just slept better than he had in years. He did not dream, no nightmares playing themselves out in his head, just sweet, restful sleep. His rest had fulfilled him and renewed his body, and his mind. He stood up on all fours and stretched his limbs. His muscles rippled beneath the layer of the thick dark fur that covered his body. He was strong now, no longer a weak two-leger as he had been in his previous life, but strong and demanding his rightful place at the top of the food chain. As the mountain lion learned, he was a dangerous predator not to be messed with, he was, Josiah Wolfe.

As he came back out of the cave and into the darkness, Josiah paused to sniff the air. There were no other creatures close by that he could pick up on. Everything was peaceful for him now, no sounds of any two-legers, or the smell of their foul smoke. All he heard now was the occasional owl calling, and the crickets that were now chirping their songs. As he stared out into the darkness, he watched the lightning bugs as they were lighting up the night in unison, and he could hear the water as it rippled against the rocks as it made its own journey down the hillside. *"If only the water knew what awaited it down below in the valley…"* he thought to himself as he continued to listen. He always found the untainted night time sounds of nature soothing, and now they truly comforted his soul.

Josiah had awoken thirsty, so he decided to head back over to the small creek to get himself a drink of the cool mountain spring water. Getting down on all fours, Josiah leaned down to lap at the water. After getting his fill of the fresh spring water, he filled his hands with it and splashed it upward onto his face. It felt refreshing against his toughened, weathered skin. Taking another scoop, he repeated the process, and then shook off the excess water before turning and looking up towards the top of the mountain.

The top of the mountain still seemed so far away to him. It will still be quite the trek to get there, but he would not be dissuaded into ending his journey early. As he continued to stare upward, he watched as the clouds moved across the sky, and engulf the mountains snow-covered peaks high above. Everything that high up just seemed so familiar to him, it was as if he had seen it all before. But he had never been this far up on the mountain side before, not even when the two-legers had pushed him out from where he had lived below.

Closing his eyes, Josiah imagined that he could hear the mountain itself calling out to him. Its words were getting plainer the higher up he climbed. It beckoned him to come to it, and now it was also calling out to him by name.

"I am coming, I hear you, and I am coming," he loudly called back to the cloud covered peaks above.

Grabbing his sack, Josiah turned and headed back out into the moon-lit wilderness. Taking long strides, and feeling driven, he was able to cover more territory than usual with each step. He needed no map; instinct seemed to lead his way. Every so often as he limbed upward, he would stop and smell the air. With his senses peaked, he was more aware of all his surroundings than ever before. He now sensed everything, both the seen and the unseen. For him, it was like an awakening.

He had plans to hunt again this night before the light of the new day would rise, but before doing so, he still wanted to cover many more miles. His intentions were to wait and then christen in the new days rising while feasting on his latest kill.

He had traveled upward for hours before he caught the scent of something that interested him. It was the scent of fresh blood. Somewhere close he could tell that there was a fresh kill made by another. The sweet aroma of blood filled his nostrils and tantalized his taste buds. Getting closer he could tell that the kill was done by another large predator, but not one like the cat that he had just dealt with the night before, but one that was much larger and more dangerous.

Sticking his nose to the air, he could tell what direction that the fresh meat was in. He was hungry and was not beyond

170

scavenging for a meal, and it wouldn't be the first time he had stolen a kill from another either. He knew that even with a large black bear, that he could easily take a kill from it. But he also knew that this was no black bear that he was smelling, that it was a large grizzly bear that he would be facing instead.

Josiah was sure that the bear would challenge the taking of its kill, but he knew that with his size and strength, that this bear would pose only a minor threat to him. He had dealt with bears this size before when he lived on the mountain side. Though the large bears are dangerous, he was even more so deadly.

As Josiah found where the fresh kill was taken, the grizzly bear saw him as well and rose up onto its hind legs. This bear didn't back down from Josiah as he thought it would, but instead it stood its ground. Josiah saw that it had killed a large mule deer buck, a good size meal, and more than he was sure it would eat. Josiah had no intentions of taking the entire deer for himself, he only wanted a portion of it, but he wasn't so sure that the large grizzly was willing to share.

The big male grizzly bear snarled at Josiah as he began to come closer to it and its kill. Snarling even louder, the bear warned Josiah to come no closer, and that it fully planned on keeping this kill for itself, and that it had every intention of aggressively defending it against him.

As Josiah slowly took another step forward towards the carcass, the grizzly bear got down on all fours and moved over in front of its kill.

"I only want to share your meal, I do not intend on taking it all," he told the big bear mentally, but it was apparent that it did not understand what he was trying to say to it. Kicking up dirt with its large feet, the big grizzly did a mock charged at Josiah, and after stopping short, it swatted at him with its claws. Josiah quickly got down on all fours and into a defensive position while snarling back.

The bear swung at Josiah again, and as it did so, Josiah swung back, narrowly missing the bears face. His swinging back at it surprised the large bear, and it took a step back. Josiah then jumped threateningly at the large bear, and growled menacingly at it. The bear snarled and snapped its jaws at Josiah before standing upright on its hind legs, and roaring angerly at Josiah.

Josiah too stood up onto his hind legs while leaning forwards with his arms curled up and positioned for a fight. Showing his power, Josiah slowly and with authority approached the mule deer that the bear had killed. The grizzly bear angerly shook its head and snap its teeth at Josiah as he approached. Keeping an eye on the bear, Josiah reached out with one of his large hands and took hold of the hind leg that was laying on the side of the deer that was facing upward. Then as he stepped on the body with his heavy foot to hold it down, he jerked the leg upwards and ripped the leg off from the carcass. Laying the leg off to one side, he glanced up at the grizzly. The large bear roared in anger as he watched Josiah stealing a portion of his kill. Ignoring the bear now, Josiah turned the dead deer over and removed the other back leg from its body. Again, glancing up at the bear, Josiah brought the leg up to his muzzle and sniffed its freshness.

The large bear glared at Josiah and snarled loudly at him. It didn't like losing any part of its hard-earned meal, especially to a creature such as this, a mysterious interloper that chose to wander into its territory. The grizzly bear, though standing the same height as that of the dogman, remained cautious because had never seen a creature such as he before in the forest. That was the only thing that kept the large grizzly bear from further attacking and the confrontation coming to body-to-body combat.

As Josiah once more stood upright with both legs of the deer in his grasp, he stepped back from the rest of the carcass to give the grizzly bear room to retake its prey. As Josiah took another step away, the bear dropped back down onto all fours and slowing made its way back to its kill as he knew it would.

Feeling confident with himself, Josiah turned his back to the bear and started to walk away from it. After only taking two steps, he instinctively knew something was wrong. He knew that he had let his guard down to soon. As Josiah turned back around to look at where the bear had been, he caught movement out of the corner of his eye as he saw that the bear was now charging directly at him.

Instinctively, Josiah swung one of the large deer legs that he still had in his hand at the bear, but it had no effect. The large bear hit Josiah full force and knocked him backward and off of his feet. The impact had knocked the air from his lungs as he landed on the ground with a thud. Josiah now found himself laying on top of the damp leaves of the forested floor, panting as he tried to recover.

After a few seconds, the large bear got up onto its hind feet again and began to ready itself for another attack. But this time Josiah lunged first, in one swift motion he had rolled off to the side and got up onto all fours and charged back at the large grizzly bear. Knocking the large grizzly bear off of its feet. The strength of the hit forced the bear backward on the wet leaf litter. Trying to recoup, it quickly fought to regain its footing.

Josiah stood in front of the bear and growled menacingly at it. He and the large grizzly bear were both worthy adversaries, and almost of equal strength. The large bear had definitely gained the dogman's respect.

Getting back up onto its feet, the bear stomped one of its huge front paws down onto the earth below it as it threateningly glared at Josiah. This time it did not charge at him though, it only stood its ground and continued to snarl at the dogman with hatred in its eyes.

Josiah began to back away from the bear and went to where his scavenged meat still lay on the ground. Not willing to take his eye off of his adversary this time, he did not fully turn around while he reached down and picked up the two dismembered deer legs. He refused to turn his back on the bear again until he had put some distance between him and the angry grizzly bear.

He knew that he could have killed the large bear if he wanted to, but killing it would serve no purpose. He would never kill another without good reason, and he definitely would not kill just for the sake of killing, it was not his way, that was the way of the two-legers, and he refused to stoop to their level.

After traveling a few more miles over the rough upward terrain, Josiah found a place that suited him well that he could sit and rest. He still had not eaten his dinner yet, and after putting many miles between him and the large grizzly bear, he decided that it was now a good time for him to feast.

This meal alone would not be enough to satisfy him though, but it would be a start. If he found no other prey animals this night to finish filling his stomach, at least he would have this to hold him over. Lifting the fresh venison up to his muzzle, he took a long, deep whiff of the sweet meat. The aroma alone made him drool. Taking his first bite, he savored the flavor as he moved the fresh meat back and forth over his taste buds. He always enjoyed fresh meat and it was what he as a predator was meant to have to satisfy his hunger. That was not how it had always been for him though, in the past when times were tough for him, he had been forced to eat the rotten maggot infested meat left-over from another to survive. Now, never would he have to stoop to such a degrading level as that again.

Rolling the fresh meat around in his mouth just made his salivary glands water even more so. Not wanting to waste a drop, Josiah licked at the blood that had coagulated on the stub where it had ripped free as well. What he had now was not as much as he had become accustomed too, but it also was not his kill that he ate. For him to take more than he did, it would have been unfair to his worthy adversary. Instead, he was fair-minded with the large grizzly, and only took an

175

amount that was equal to what he thought the large bear would probably not be eating itself.

Getting back up to his feet, Josiah continued to walk up the mountain side. He felt good. The further he went, the better he felt. It was like the fresh air had rejuvenating properties to it, and every time he took a deep breath, it was healing both his body, his mind, and his spirit, from the inside out.

With every step that Josiah now took, he knew it was one more step closer to where he needed to be. He could still feel the pull that the mountain had on him. He still didn't understand it, but he felt as if maybe he wasn't supposed to. As he climbed further upward, he began to notice a difference in the air temperature. It was getting cooler. As the cooler air made its way through his thick fur, it felt comfortable and invigorating to him, it felt good and it was as if it was the temperature, he was meant to live in.

Day break would be coming soon, but Josiah didn't care. He decided that he was going to continue on and try to cover more territory before he had to stop. He knew that underneath the sheltering canopy of new growth trees, the sun wouldn't be as bright as it was in the field where he had been living below.

As the hours passed, he found that he was correct, and that the sun's rays did not penetrate well through the thick leaf covered tree tops. Only every now and then, would small wisps of the sun's rays make it all the way through to the ground below, but that made no difference to him. He knew that with the shade of the trees, and the coolness of the air, that he would have no problem traveling comfortably now. In the back of his mind, he was hoping that more of the ground that he would be traveling in would be like this. He was truly enjoying himself now. On occasion he was even seeing some of the other forest creatures, the smaller inhabitants of the woodland, that he rarely seen in the darkness of the night.

Josiah could feel the forest creature's eyes watching him from where they hid. They were all paying close attention to his every step, and every sound he created. Hidden by their own disguises, they sat quietly in the brush as he passed them by. Only on a few occasions did he smell the fear growing within them, but today they need not fear him, he did not intend on wasting his time to hunt them.

Night time had again fallen over the forest, and after walking the previous night and all of the next day, Josiah was physically exhausted, and now had no choice but to rest. He had been walking for a long time, longer than he had ever walked before, and he was tired, very tired. His gait had begun to slow, and the area that his steps covered had been getting shorter and shorter with each step. Extreme fatigue was evidentially beginning to set in for him, and he knew it.

Josiah had walked for so long, not because he was in a hurry to get up the mountain, but because he couldn't remember the last time that he had been able to walk in the daylight. The forest looked totally different in the day time than it did at night. In the light of day, it looked alive. Colors that were normally dim for him, were now bright and vibrant. He saw animals and birds that he had not seen before, or maybe just didn't notice before because they were animals of the

177

daylight, and not of the night. He found them all very intriguing, and curious in a way. Walking in the daylight had opened up what was now a whole new world for him, and he enjoyed it.

Surveying the area around him, Josiah looked for a sheltered area in which to rest. Dark clouds were quickly moving into the sky above him, and he could tell that rain was on its way. He did not like to travel in the rain, he never did. Not seeing anywhere to keep himself dry, he had no choice but to continue to walk. As the ground began to become rocky and larger boulders were now in sight, he saw that as a good sign that a possible shelter may now not be very far.

Josiah continued to walk for another half a mile before he came upon a cliff side that held a partially hidden opening much like the one that he had taken up residence in down in the valley, only with this one appearing to be much larger.

Josiah surveyed the outside of the opening carefully before slowly making his approach. Sticking his nose towards the opening, he tried to see if he could pick up the scent of anything else that may be already living in it. Not smelling any recent scents, he then paused to see if he could hear anything moving about. Hearing nothing, he carefully approached the opening of the cave.

As Josiah reached the opening, a movement off to the side caught his attention. The movement was upwind from him so he stuck his nose to the breeze again to see what it was. It was a deer that had caught his attention, and it was moving in his direction.

Taking the pack from his shoulder, he set it down on the ground at the mouth of the cave. Quietly backing away from where he stood, Josiah got down on all fours. He watched the deer as it mingled amongst the trees, stopping off and on to nibble on a new seedling here and there as it walked. It was obvious that it was still totally unaware to his presence.

Staying downwind from where the animal was as to not give his own scent away to it, Josiah cautiously began to approach the deer.

Carefully Josiah continued to noiselessly creep through the trees, while using the groups of larger trees for cover. He was going to try to come in from behind the deer, and he didn't want it to see him approaching until it was too late. Josiah's stomach chose that moment to grumble from the hunger that it was feeling, and he quickly put his hand over it in an effort to silence it.

The deer heard the noise, and stopped. Raising its head, it looked up in Josiah's direction. Seeing the deer look up, he froze and knew that he didn't dare even to move a muscle. The deer, using its front hoof, stomped the ground once and snorted, and then it did it again as it looked out into the shadows. After staring into the darkness for several minutes and not seeing anything moving, the deer slowly lowered its head, and went back to feeding.

Josiah was angry with himself for almost letting his hunger give his position away like that, and nearly taking away any advantage that he currently had over the deer. Carefully moving a little faster this time to make up for the extra distance that the deer had created between it and him, Josiah silently proceeded bit by little bit.

Sensing again that there was something amiss, the deer once more looked up from where it had been feeding and stomped its feet. Twitched its tail back and forth, the deer looked towards where Josiah was now hiding behind a large group of trees. It seemed like it could sense that something was hiding there in the shadows, but because of him being downwind from it, the deer wasn't able to pick up on his scent.

Pawing at the ground with its front hoof, the deer again began to stomp its front feet at Josiah as it continued to snort. As the deer stood erect and held its head high, it continued to stomp its feet as if it were trying to appear larger than it really was. Taking a step closer to where Josiah was hiding, it again stomped its front feet out of frustration.

Knowing that he would soon be discovered if he stayed where he was, Josiah decided to take his chances and go for the deer. Coming out of hiding, Josiah charged on all fours at the deer. He moved faster than any normal creature in the woods could. The deer saw Josiah coming at it, and it quickly turned away from him and began to bolt through the trees.

Josiah quickly weaved around various trees as he pursued the deer. Though the deer was running for its life, he knew that the deer's speed was no match for that of a wolf. Josiah quickly caught up to the deer, and jumped upon its back. After digging his claws deep into the deer's sides, he opened his mouth wide and sank his fangs into the flesh of its neck. The deer tried to fight back, but the extra weight upon its back was too great for it. No longer able to run, and exhausted from the chase, the deer bleated its final cry, and quickly dropped to the ground.

After the deer so suddenly stopped and dropped to the ground, the impact threw Josiah off balance and sent him and the deer tumbling down the declining grade of the hillside. After the deer was able to stop its downward tumbling, it quickly was able to catch its footing again, and as it did so, Josiah lost his grip on it, and he continued to roll down the slope.

After regaining its footing, the badly wounded deer, fueled only by adrenaline, took off running again. With the surge of adrenaline coursing through its body, and its heart still strongly pounding, the deer's blood now began to pour out from its wounds, leaving a heavy blood trail behind.

Josiah had no sooner stopped his downward decline, before he had regained his own footing, and was back to chasing down the deer again. As the deer weakened from blood loss, Josiah quickly caught back up to it and immediately launched himself back up onto the deer. With one quick bite at the base of the neckline, Josiah severed one of the vertebrae in the deer's neck, and it went down. When the deer went down this time, it was done.

Still on all fours and full of adrenaline himself, Josiah quickly looked around with wild eyes and growled as he protected his kill from unseen forces around him. Though there was nothing there to challenge him, his reaction was purely instinctual. His animal instincts were growing stronger by the day now, and he could feel them rising up inside of him. It was as if he was losing more of what had originally made him, him. He now had very little left in him of the man that he had used to be, and it was being replaced with more of the beast that he had now become.

With the adrenaline still coursing through his body from the hunt, Josiah looked up towards the moon resting high up in the sky and let out with a long, loud ominous howl. It was a release of penned up tension, and a warning howl to all that was within earshot, that Josiah Wolfe was here, and he wasn't going anywhere.

Reaching down with one of his hands, Josiah ripped through the hide of the deer with one rake of his razor like claws. Still feeling anxious, Josiah didn't take the time that he usually would with his kills, instead he ripped the hide from the deer in one pull and began to grab at the meat that lay underneath. Wrapping his fingers around the muscle tissue on the hind leg, Josiah pulled at it and ripped it off the bone in one piece. Still lightly growling and nervously glancing out into the darkness, Josiah brought the venison to his mouth and ate. As he chewed, he continued to anxiously look off to the sides of him every few bites to scan the trees for any intruders.

When he was finished eating, Josiah stood up on his hind legs and stretched. Now that he had consumed almost all of the large doe that lay at his feet, he had satisfied his hunger. With his stomach again full, his nervousness, and his tiredness both began to ease up as well. Josiah looked down at what was left of the venison, and not wanting to waste any of the meat, he reached down and ripped off the last remaining hind leg of the deer before standing back upright once more.

After climbing back up the small incline, Josiah looked back to where he had originally been when he saw the deer, he also now could see where he had left his sack, and where the entrance to where his temporary den for the night now was. Taking his time, Josiah slowly finished climbing back up the small incline with the hind leg of the deer in hand. As he got closer to where he had left his worn sack, he looked up and saw that a large raccoon was clawing at it, and chewing at the drawstrings that kept it closed.

Josiah, now enraged, growled angerly at the raccoon as he quickly approached it. Startled, the animal turned and looked up at the great beast. Seeing the larger animal quickly approaching it, the raccoon spun around and hissed as it menacingly growled back at him. The raccoon, showing no fear, foolishly stood its ground against the great beast.

"Go!" Josiah mentally bellowed at the creature. Ignoring him, the raccoon continued to growl at him as it turned its attention back to what it was doing, and went back to digging at his sack. Josiah growled again snapped his teeth together at the raccoon in an effort to scare it away, but his efforts didn't work. The raccoon would not be intimidated by the larger predator.

"You do not know how to pick your battles little one," Josiah said as he menacingly snarled at the raccoon. Just as Josiah finished speaking, the raccoon managed to dig out the small teddy bear that had belonged to his small daughter.

"No!" Josiah yelled as he dropped the meat he was carrying and charged at the raccoon. The raccoon looked up just as Josiah reached it. He grabbed it by the neck and took the bear from its grasp. *"I told you no!"* he yelled into its face while baring his teeth. Terrified, the raccoon began to twist its body back and forth as it tried to escape the larger creature's grasp.

Snarling at the animal and snapping his jaws just inches from the raccoon's face, the animal's eyes grew wide. Josiah glared at the smaller creature within his grasp. Instinct told him to snap its scrawny neck, but instead he turned and forcefully hurled it back towards the forest edge. When the raccoon landed on the ground, it hit hard against the base of one of the trees. From the force that Josiah had used to throw the smaller animal, when it hit, the bones in its body gave way and shattered. Lifeless, the dead raccoon fell over onto the damp ground at the base of the tree.

Looking down at the teddy bear that Josiah now held within in his large hand, he felt a twinge of pain in his heart. Josiah slowly bent down and carefully placed it back into his sack where it had come from. He would have to be more careful the next time that he laid his sack down. *"I can't lose all I have left of my family, all I have left of Ava,"* he thought to himself as he now hugged the sack close to his chest. Then as he looked around at his surroundings again, he said to himself in a whisper, *"must never leave Ava alone again..."*

Josiah held his sack in one hand, and then picked up the left-over venison in the other before stepping closer to the opening of the cave. Instead of stopping again to check it out for inhabitants, he just walked right in. It was empty inside. It looked like nothing had actually lived there for a long time, and any scents that were there at one time, were now old and stale.

Carefully laying his pack off to the side, Josiah sat down next to it. Looking down at his left-over meat that he still had in his hand, he huffed as he tossed it a few feet away from himself to save for later. He was tired now, very tired. Opening up his mouth, he let out a loud yawn. Now that his belly was full again, he needed to rest. He had traveled many miles since he last slept, and his mind was becoming fuzzy from exhaustion, and irritation from the racoon still ate at him.
Curling up on the floor of the cave, Josiah laid his head down onto his sack and closed his eyes. As he dozed off, the last thing that went through his thoughts was, *"Ava…..I will find you."*

Chapter Six

Josiah began to slowly awake from his restful slumber. Stretching his arms and legs out to alleviate some of the stiffness that he felt, a wave of contentment rushed over him. He felt good, the higher up the mountain side he went, the better he was feeling both mentally and physically.

Slowly getting up from where he was lying, Josiah walked towards the mouth of the cave to look out into the night. He had slept peacefully through the last rising of the sun, as well as through most of the night time hour in which he usually would have been found traveling higher up the mountain. He had risen during the fullness of the moon, but instead of moving on, he sat on the ground in front of the cave contently watching the night sky, and listening to the animals around him. He just had no desire to leave. He had no one pushing him this time, no two-legers were after him, and he felt content right where he was. Strangely, Josiah also had no desire to hunt again either, his stomach was still processing the kill from the previous night, and because of that, he felt no desire to replenish what had already passed through.

Looking out at the forest floor, he could tell that it had rained the day before, he could smell the dampness of the leaves, and the freshness of the air even before he reached the outside of his den. The forest smelled alive and renewed again, and that alone helped to increase the feeling of contentment within him.

Josiah turned his head and looked over to where the dead coon was still laying at the base of the tree. Nothing had even attempted to scavenge the deceased animal during the previous day, nor during the darkness of the night that followed.

"You should have minded you own business coon," he told the dead raccoon. *"You stuck your nose where it didn't belong. I gave you a chance to turn tail and run, but you didn't, and it cost you heavily,"* he huffed at it.

Looking up into the sky, Josiah again took in a deep breath and smelled the freshness of the air around him. He relishing in the coolness of it on his face and body. Yawning and stretching once more, he turned around and went back into the cave.

Remembering that he had brought the left-over hind leg from the deer that he had killed earlier with him, Josiah glanced over to where he had tossed it. Walking over, he sat down on the cool soil next to it and picked it up in his right hand. Raising it up to his muzzle, he lazily began to eat it. He didn't eat as feverishly as he did when he had first killed it, but instead he now took smaller bites and took his time with it. The meat was good, just not nearly as fresh as it had been,

188

and it had dried out where it had been exposed to the air. He wasn't really hungry, but he just ate to eat. Not completely finishing the leg, Josiah again laid what was left of the meat off to the side. He decided that he would take it with him when he did leave the next night coming, it would again give him a nice snack as well as an energy boost for when he traveled.

Looking out towards the crevasse from where he sat, he could see out the mouth of his cave. He could see that the sun was now getting brighter the higher up in the sky that it climbed. Because of the altitude of where he was, it was now going to be far too bright for him to travel by day. With more rocky outcrops and fewer trees around him, he would no longer have any protection from the direct rays of the sun. Although he enjoyed his walk in the daylight, the suns bright rays that shown down on the earth now bothered his eyes far too much. Because of that, he decided that he would have go back to traveling the way he had done for many years. For a creature of the night, it was the way it was meant to be.

After watching the dawning of the new day, he stretched his muscles, leaned back and rested his body on his elbows. The sounds of songbirds caught Josiah's attention and he looked over again at the mouth of the cave. He could see the rays of the sun dancing around in the tree tops, and making a light show on the bare ground below. He missed spending time out in the light of day, but things were different for him now, a lot different.

Leaning to the side, Josiah reached out for the sack and pulled it over towards him. He opened up the top and took out the small bear that had belonged to his daughter. Carefully holding it in his hand, he gently outlined its shape with his fingers. Bringing it up to his muzzle, he sniffed the bear. He could no longer smell the scent of his daughter on its fabric; all he could smell on the teddy bear now was the scent of the raccoon, and it made his lips curl in disgust.

Josiah put the bear close to his chest and rolled over onto his side. He needed to feel closer to his daughter, she was the only connection he had left from the past, that connection helped him to cling onto what humanity that he had left in him. As he laid there holding the small bear in his massive arm, a single tear ran down his weathered cheek onto the ground.

How he missed his family. His wife was gone, brutalized and her life viciously stolen away, and his other daughter, Anna, killed and left lying in her own bed. There was nothing he could do for either one of them. But Ava, Ava was still out there. He could feel it in his heart. Her heart beat with the same blood as his, and he could feel it pulsating strongly, calling out to him. And that feeling was getting stronger the further he went up the mountainside.

"I'm coming Ava, I am coming for you..." he told her as he laid with the bear clutched close to his heart. He took a deep breath and very lightly, mournfully howled. As he laid there, another singular tear escaped his eye just before he fell asleep.

When the sun began to recede down out of the sky, Josiah reached for his sack and put the small bear back into it. He securely closed it and put it over his shoulder. Reaching over to his other side, he picked up what little was left of the hind leg from the deer before walking over to the opening of the cave. Pausing at the mouth of the cave he looked out into the twilight. Putting his muzzle into the breeze, Josiah sniffed the night air. It still smelled fresh and clean, nothing like the air did in the valley below. Things were much cleaner here, and nothing was tainted by man.

Glancing off to the side, Josiah noticed that the coon was now gone. Sniffing the air in that direction for clues, he knew it had been a coyote that took the coon for its own. *"At least it was of use to something,"* Josiah thought as he walked the rest of the way out of the cave and into the night.

Josiah turned and walked around the corner of the boulders to where there was a narrow game trail leading up through the side of the rocky ledge. Looking upwards at the incline, he took a deep breath, and once more began his climb up the mountain side.

At this altitude, the ground had become rockier and the earth was now more uneven beneath his feet. Stones were shifting precariously under his weight with every step he took, but he didn't allow it to slow him down, he pressed on and continued to climb. When he got to the top of the embankment that he had been climbing, the terrain leveled out and formed a medium sized plateau. Walking out through a small grove of trees and onto the plateau, he saw that there was a thick carpet of native grasses covering the ground around his feet. He also noticed that the only trees that were there, were in thick clumps along the edge of the plateau in various places, and none in the clearing itself. That left him a wide span of little to no cover for protection. He was uncomfortable here; he didn't like traveling where there was no cover. No trees meant nowhere to hide from prying eyes, and nowhere to run if he needed to. But then he realized that there were no humans this high up, no two-legers anywhere close by to put him in jeopardy. He was now safe from their judgements, and their vindictiveness for acts that they accused him of, heinous acts that he didn't do. Taking a deep breath, Josiah now calmed himself and continued on.

Josiah slowly walked out further into the small field and then suddenly stopped. He thought he had heard a noise. Putting his nose to the wind, he inhaled deeply, but he didn't smell anything. He then realized that what he had heard, had come from behind him, and downwind from where he now stood. Slowly he turned and looked back into the darkness from where he had just come. He didn't see anything, but he knew that there was something there. He moved his ears forward to try to figure out which area of the darkness that the sound had come, but nothing was giving him any clues. All he could hear with his sensitive ears was silence.

He was beginning to realize that there were more animals higher up on the mountain side than he had though. He believed that most of the game animals on the mountainside had been driven downward towards the valley when the loggers had moved in, but he was now finding that he was mistaken. Many of the animals were instead pushed upward, along with the other predators that followed them. He now wished he had read the signs better himself, and if he had, he would have gone upward himself too. Under the pressure of the two-legers though, he felt he had no choice but to go down.

The number of predators that he was finding here on the mountain were much higher than what he found in the valley. In the valley there were no mountain lions, and only the occasion wolf that came around. Over the last week that he had been making his climb, he noted that he was also seeing more signs of predators than he had earlier on too.

Mountain lions seemed to flourish here, he observed many tracks along the way, along with several piles of their scat left behind. It wasn't much wonder that it was a mountain lion that was the first animal to giving him issues on his trek. There was just far too many of them living here in his opinion.

Breaking his train of thought, Josiah heard what sounded like the snap of a twig from the thin wood line that he just came out of. Turning around to look out into the darkness, he still saw nothing.

"Come out and face me!" he loudly called out into the night. As expected though, the only reply he received was silence.

Now he was starting to think that he was hearing things, or that if there were something there, that it was not foolish enough to try to approach him. Josiah took a few steps backward as he continued to stare into the darkness where the moons rays didn't quite shine. Then out of the blackness, he heard the noise again. He heard the sound of small stones shifting and rolling down the incline to his right, and then the sound of dry grass being walked through to his left. Looking one way and then the other, he now knew that there were in fact two animals hidden in the shadows, and not just one. And that both of them, were now stalking him.

"Come out and face me!" Josiah mentally called out again, following with a loud menacing guttural growl. This time his growl was met by a growl that was from of another. The first growl emanated from one side of him, and then a growl from the other direction broke out into the night as well.

Two large wolves stepped out of the shadows, and made their presence known. Both wolves lowered their heads, and laid back their ears as they approached Josiah from opposite directions. Josiah knew what they had come for. They could smell the meat that remained on the deer leg that he still carried with him. They had probably picked up on its scent miles before, and just trailed him until they could get him in an open area.

"You do not want to take me on wolves," he told them as they began to flank him from both sides. Seeing this, Josiah stepped backward to reposition himself so he could see both of the wolves at the same time. Both wolves menacingly growled in unison as they saw him moved out from between them. Their yellow eyes pierced the darkness as they continued to stare at him. All that Josiah could do was to stare back at them as well as he waited for one of them to make the first move.

"Come on you cowards, what are you waiting for?" Josiah sneered as he taunted them. Both wolves bared their teeth and snarled back in response.

Josiah slowly lowered his sack to the ground, and then tossed the left-over deer leg a few feet away from it as he prepared himself to take on the two new challengers.

After getting down on all fours, Josiah still towered threateningly over both of the wolves. They looked like small dogs in comparison to his hulking stature.

Sticking his muzzle out, Josiah gave a loud roar type growl towards the wolves. Refusing to turn and run, the wolves displayed no fear of him and stood their ground. As the wolves began to draw nearer to him once more, Josiah snarled and snapped his teeth at them aggressively.

The wolves again began to try to flank Josiah. In response, he once more began to back up to keep them both within his sight, but this time they were too quick for him. Coming in for the attack, both wolves ran at Josiah and jumped at him in unison. Josiah turned and grabbed one of the wolves in his mighty hands and forcefully flung it several feet away from him. The wolf landed with a loud thud against a rock. As it hit, he heard it loudly cry out in pain. Just as he let go of the first wolf, the second wolf sunk its teeth deep into the flesh of Josiah's shoulder. This infuriated him and he roared out loudly in anger. Reaching back, he dug his claws deep into the animal's neck and back, dragging it upward over his head, he forcefully catapulted it to the ground before him.

The wolf, though injured, got to its feet and once more jumped at Josiah, and as it did, Josiah swung at it and caught the animal across the side of its face with his massive clawed hand. The large wolf cried out as Josiah's claws ripped into the wolf's flesh and tore its ear and surrounding skin away from its skull. Now partially blinded by the slashing and in pain from its wounds, the wolf got up and made one last lunge for Josiah. This time as the wolf charged at him, Josiah reached out with one clawed hand and caught the wolf by the throat. Slowly drawing the struggling wolf up closer to his face, Josiah glared at it eye to eye, muzzle to muzzle. As Josiah continued to hold the wolf firmly within his hand, and without warning, he suddenly thrusted his free hand into the chest of the male wolf. With no resistance, his claws easily ripped through the wolf's chest wall, and in one fluent motion, he tore out the animals still beating heart from within.

Josiah threw the dead animal off to the side and turned to look at the other. The female wolf was laying on the ground in agony from her badly hurt leg as she watched her mate being killed.

"You want food, here is your food," he said to her angerly as he threw the bloody heart of her dead mate at her. The heart of the dead male came to rest next to her, and in fear, she painfully tried to push herself backwards to move away from it.

Looking at his bloodied hands, Josiah raised his head up towards the sky and let out an icy, haunting howl. The howl echoed off the side of the mountain before expanding out into the night. Hearing the howl, the female wolf slightly bowed her head to Josiah as she showed submission. She had learned who the alpha was in this situation, too late to save her mate, but maybe not too late for her.

"You will not die tonight, but do not cross paths with me again," he told her harshly as he walked towards her and towered over her injured body. The female wolf refused to meet Josiah's stare, instead she continued to look submissively to the ground.

Turning his back to the female wolf, Josiah walked over to where the lifeless male wolf lay and paused over it. He did not enjoy killing it. Not killing it like this. *"You wolf did not know who you were up against,"* he said quietly. *"But you died in battle, and with honor,"* he finished.

Josiah turned from the dead wolf and walked over to pick his sack back up. As he stood back upright with his sack in hand, he heard a young wolf pup whine just inside the shadows. The female wolf tried to move to where her pup was, but her injured leg would barely hold her weight, and when she tried to get up, she immediately collapsed back down onto the ground.

Josiah scanned the shadows for the pup, and then caught sight of its movement. The young pup whined again for its mother, and she tried to get back up once more. This time she was able to get to her feet and take a small step forward. Her injuries were very painful for her, but she did now manage to put a little weight on her injured leg, and as she did, she started to limp over towards her young pup.

A single young pup peered out of the shadows towards his mother. It was leery of leaving the cover that it was hidden in, but it desperately wanted to be by its mother's side and as she got closer, it walked out into view. Josiah saw the female

197

wolf try to tuck the pup in behind her to protect it from him. When he looked down at her pup, the female threateningly growled at him. He now understood why the pair had wanted his left-over meat. Looking down at the ground below him, Josiah bend over once more and this time picking up the hind leg into his large hand. He looked back towards the female wolf and her pup, he then tossed what was left of the hind leg over to them.

"You hunt when you can, but take this now and feed your young," he mentally told her in a slightly softer voice than he had used before towards her. The wolf stared at Josiah uneasily. She didn't trust him, but now that she was badly injured, she knew she was in no condition to decline what he now offered. Not taking her eyes off Josiah, the female reached out for the deer leg and slowly took it into her mouth. Still keeping a close eye on Josiah, the female wolf carried the hind leg with her as she limped off into the darkness with her pup. She was badly bruised, but she would heal. The main thing was, was that she was alive. The cuts would scar, her leg would heal, and she would forever remember the half wolf, half man that gave those injuries to her for the rest of her life.

After watching the female wolf and her pup heading for the shadows, Josiah turned and looked back towards the other side of the field. It was there that he would look to see if he could find shelter, something that would shield him from the brightness of the coming day. Looking up into sky, he could see that the dawn was already beginning to peek over the horizon, and he knew that his time was now limited before the full days light hit once more. Josiah glanced up at the moon lit sky once more before turning and beginning to walk towards to the tree line at the other side of the plateau.

As the minutes passed, the sun was starting to peek through the trees that were on the edge of the plateau. Pausing, Josiah lifted his hand up to shield his eyes from the light and glanced back across the width of the plateau to where the female wolf had been. As he expected, she was no longer in sight. She and her pup were back into the safety of the trees where they belonged. Turning his attention to where the male wolf still lay partially hidden by the tall field grass, Josiah felt bad that the fight for leftover food had come to costing the life of a majestic animal such as this. He was not without mercy though, or kindness, but the male wolf had been the aggressor in the attack, not him. It had left Josiah no choice but to defend himself. The wolf had died with dignity though, and for Josiah, or really any predator, that is all that mattered in the end.

After reaching the woods at the far end of the field, Josiah momentarily paused and looked into the darkness of the trees before him. They seemed to welcome him. He could feel the cooler air as it circled around his feet, inviting him into the shadows of the trees. The trees were thicker here, and they shielded the sun's rays more so than they did on the other side.

Josiah looked around at his new surroundings as he entered the tree line. There didn't appear to be anything in the area where he would be able to settle in to get some rest for the day. There were no outcroppings, only trees for as far as his eyes could see. Seeing nothing that stood out to be of any use to him, Josiah decided to continue walking and see if he could find something further along the way. What he was looking for didn't have to be anything big, he only needed something that was large enough to accommodate an animal of his body size, and not much else.

The ground beneath his feet had begun to get rocky again, with large boulders and other rock type formations scattered amongst the trees that surrounded him. This part of the mountain side began to look more promising to him. As Josiah continued to climb higher up the mountainside, he finally caught sight of something that might be of interest to him in the distance.

He could see what appeared to be a small opening between two of the massive boulders in front of him. As he drew nearer to it, he walked over to inspect it. There was an opening that went back between the two large boulders, and it appeared to lead back into a cave type formation beyond.

Sniffing the air from where he stood, he was pleased to find that there didn't appear to be a scent of anything in the area that may have already been residing in the cave. After dealing with the mountain lion earlier in his journey, he was in no mood to have a confrontation with another one of the big cats over a den.

With the sun rising higher up in the sky, Josiah walked closer to the opening between the two larger rocks. After pausing momentarily for one more sniff, he then entered through the opening. He hadn't gone far into the opening, before he had to get down on all fours to maneuver himself around in it.

The side walls tapered inward at the top and it was becoming a tight fit for him, but with some effort he was able to work his way through the narrow sections, and into an area where he found a much larger room. Once inside the more spacious cave area, he was well pleased with his surroundings. It was large enough for him to rest comfortably, but also somewhere that was warm and dry as well.

Josiah removed the sack from his shoulder and leaned it up against the side of the cave before sitting down. He was exhausted from all the walking that he had done over the course of the last several days, and he was tired from the battle that he had just had with the two wolves on the plateau. Though neither wolf had been able to seriously injure him, he still had to expend unnecessarily energy acting in his own defense.

Josiah laid down on the cold rock floor of the cave and immediately drifted off to sleep. He was exhausted. He would sleep all day and well into the next night before he would wake again. With no light shining into the depths of the cave where he rested to let him know what time of day it was, he had easily lost track of time and over slept far longer than he had planned.

When Josiah awoke from his deep sleep, he stretched and looked around. Cocking his head to the side, he struggled to focus his eyes in the darkness. To see in the dark, even a creature of the night still needed a certain amount of light to bounce off of the rods in its eyes to see, and within the confines of the stone walls that now were surrounding him, there was no light present to even be seen.

Once he regained his bearings, Josiah grabbed his sack from where he had left it and headed for the mouth of the cave. Twisting and turning to work his way back out, he finally exited the cave and entered out into the night. Tossing the pack over his shoulder, Josiah tilted his head back and looked up into the sky. The stars glowed brightly against the dark sky above him, and by looking at the position of the moon above, he knew that he had slept far too long.

Looking out into the woods that lay ahead of him, Josiah paused and put his nose to the air. To him, it smelled earthy, with a slight hint of mustiness to it. He didn't detect the scent of any prey animals or other predators that were in the area though. Satisfied that nothing lay ahead, he headed out. His stomach, now almost emptied from his last meal, grumbled loudly. He knew that he would have to hunt again this night. He was holding out hope that he would be able to come across something large such as another mule deer that would fill his stomach as he continued to travel, but considering the late hour of the night, he had also resigned himself to taking something smaller such as a rabbit or a woodchuck if necessary.

Josiah could hear scurrying coming from all around him within the leaves that lay on the floor of the canopy. He paid no heed to them though; he had no interest in rodents. At one time early on in his new life, that is all he was able to catch for food, but as time went on, and he got more cunning and skilled in his hunting, he moved his way up the food chain. Over time, he had progressed his way up to the much larger game animals. At that point, he was then able to take down a fully grown deer as easily as if he was swatting a fly.

When he was forced to leave his mountain home by the two-legers years before, he was also forced to again consume the smaller animals that he despised eating. At that time, larger animals in the valley had become harder to find, and those that were there, they were always greedily taken by the two-legers, leaving him no chance for them himself. But now, no longer being in the valley, he did not have to worry about the presence of the two-legers ruining his life, and determining what he could and could not eat. Leaving the land of the two-legers was an easy decision for him, and one he would never regret. He knew that because of his new-found growing desire to mate, that he could no longer live amongst the two-legers and their women. It was time to leave for his own safety as well as theirs.

Leaving the valley and returning back to his mountainous home meant that he could feel safe once more. Safe from the two-legers, and safe from their desire to kill what they do not understand. He also returned back to his life in the mountains to find his daughter, she was his only connection left to what he once was. He knew that somewhere on this mountain is where she had to be. He could feel her presence getting stronger and stronger the higher up the mountain that he climbed. In his heart, he knew that she was alive, and that no matter what, he had to keep looking for her.

Josiah continued to walk until it was almost day break again. He had not found any prey along the way like he had thought he would, and his stomach was now totally empty. More important than food though, was that it was time for Josiah to find shelter for the day. Looking at the rocky embankment in front of him, he scanned the side of the cliff. He saw what he thought might be a cave, and started to walk towards it. What had looked like an opening though, was just a dark shadow cast on it by the light of the moon. He continued to look further down the cliff, but nothing was making itself evident to him.

Discouraged by the lack of a den where he thought that there was one, Josiah walked over to a downed tree and sat down upon it. His stomach rumbled noisily as it showed its disapproval of not being satisfied with food. It had gotten use to the new time of plenty that he had been living in. As he sat on the fallen tree lamenting, he heard a rustling in the leaves off to the side of where he was. As he silently sat on the log, he watched as two does naively wandered through the trees in front of him, oblivious to his presence. One doe was much larger, and probably the mother to the other.

Quietly Josiah slipped the sack off of his shoulder and left it lay on the log next to him. As he slowly slid off the log and onto the ground, he silently crouched down onto all fours. One of the deer stopped and twitched its ears as it glanced around into the darkness that surrounded it. It hadn't heard him, but it was like the doe could sense that something about its surroundings was off.

Seeing both of the does now stick their noses up into the air and sniff in his direction, Josiah froze in place and did not move. After a few moments, he realized that neither deer could pick up on his scent. He knew that he could reach them quickly and easily if he were just a little bit closer, but he also knew he couldn't begin to approach them while they were looking directly in his direction. He needed them to look away in any direction other than towards him. That would give him sufficient time to chance getting into a better position, and then he could go in for the kill.

Surveying the distance between the deer and himself, Josiah wondered how many foot-falls it would take for him to reach them. He figured that with where they were located now, he could do it easily within only four or five hits of the ground. That is all it would take for him to be on them and making his kill. He could easily leap 10 feet or more at a time when he was on all fours. But again, as long as they were looking in his direction, any movement he made would alert them to his presence, and they would run before he would even get one step in.

For a long while, Josiah continued to crouch down on the earth and silently watch the deer. Finally, when the deer turned their attention away from him, and continued walking through the trees, Josiah took his cue and went after them. Neither of the deer hear him coming until he was upon them. Everything had happened in the matter of seconds, and the deer had no time to react to their attacker.

Leaping upon the back of the larger of the two does, the deer let out with a loud bleat as she crumbled to the ground and onto her side from the pressure of his massive weight. Startled, the younger deer turned and kicked its feet at Josiah in defense of the larger doe. After unsuccessfully trying to fight off the large predator and get him away from her mother, the smaller deer gave up, turned, and ran deeper into the woods. Josiah, unphased by the smaller does attack, stayed where he was on top of the larger does back and watched as the smaller deer continued to run until it disappeared into the darkness.

The larger doe, still struggling beneath the creature's massive weight, bleated and kicked its feet into the air. Taking one of his clawed hands, Josiah pulled up the head of the doe towards him. He could see the intense fear that she felt as they looked into each other's eyes, and without breaking the stare, he reached down with his other hand and cut through the does juggler vein. Now silenced, Josiah respectfully laid the does head gently onto the ground and stood up. This deer had just died for him to live, he was not so much of an animal yet, not to realize that this animal had just given up its life for him.

As Josiah stood next to his kill, he began to feel uneasy for some reason. It was a feeling that he wasn't accustomed too, nor did he understand it. Josiah carefully looked around the area and into the shadows that the trees were creating. He didn't see anything within the area for him to fear. There was nothing in the woods that he was afraid of anymore. The only thing that he feared now, was man.

Reaching down, Josiah grabbed the deer by the back legs and pulled it back to where he had earlier sat down upon the log. Still, he felt uneasy. He dropped the deer's hind legs and scanned the area once more, smelling for a scent, and listening to the wind. Nothing came to him to explain the nervousness that he was feeling from deep withinside of him. Looking down towards the deer, he reached down and grabbed one of the back legs. He held the body down with his foot and twisted the leg until he heard a loud snap signifying that the leg bone had just separated from the hip joint. With that, the meat then easily lifted free from the body.

Josiah didn't like this new feeling that he was experiencing. Feeling fear and anxiety were foreign feelings to him now, at least it was since he had left the valley for the mountain. It was just an odd feeling that he had been experiencing from deep down within the pit of his stomach since he got to this upper elevation of the mountain. The uneasiness at times and the nervousness of the unknown were now weighing heavily on him. He felt like his every move was being watched, like he was being stalked for some reason, but he didn't know why.

Still feeling uneasy, Josiah silently sat down on the log and continued to scan the darkness before him. He had never felt this way before. Never had he felt the presence of something equal to, or greater than himself in the forest, something that he felt leery of, something that might threaten his very own existence.

Not taking his eyes from the woods before him, Josiah took the leg he had just removed, and quickly pulled the skin away from the meat. Bringing the leg up to his muzzle, he paused before taking a large bite of the venison. He ate in silence as he constantly scanned the woods and wondered what was hiding out there and watching him from the darkness. This would be an uncomfortable night for him, and an even more uncomfortable day ahead. He continued to eat his kill until he had almost all of the venison consumed. With the newfound uneasiness that was now growing from within him, he knew that he needed to be cautious and ready for what trials he felt sure still lay ahead.

Josiah got up and with his foot, moved what was left of the carcass out of his way. As he once more scanned the darkness for anything out of the ordinary, he still didn't see anything that stood out as a threat. Feeling more secure that there was nothing there, he slowly felt his uneasiness begin to dissipate. Though he still felt apprehensive, he had begun to feel slightly more assured that there was nothing hiding in the shadows.

The sun would soon be rising high in the sky once more, and he still needed to find somewhere that he could rest. Reaching down, he picked his sack back up from the log, and began to venture further up the wooded hillside. Josiah kept his eyes open for any signs of shelter, but he also was keeping them open for whatever, or whoever may possibly be following him.

Just as the sun was climbing skyward, Josiah saw something that looked promising to him. He had spotted what looked to be a small cave, and headed in its direction. The entrance was small, but just as long as there was enough room for him to lay down inside and get out of the direct sun, that is all he needed. It wasn't that he couldn't be out in the sunlight, he enjoyed the heat it provided against his skin, but he just found it visually uncomfortable for him to be out in it. The sun didn't use to bother him as much as it does now. His eyes had just become so accustomed to the darkness, that the bright sun now made them uncomfortable, stinging and watering.

Josiah set the sack down just inside of the small entrance, and then he climbed in himself. The inside wasn't as larger as he had hoped it would be, but he was able to turn himself around in it enough so that he could lay down. After getting comfortable, he extended his front legs outward and proceeded to lay his head down upon his hands. He wanted to be able to keep an eye on the area beyond the mouth of the cave. Though he could no longer feel the mysterious entities presence around him any longer, he still wanted to keep a watchful eye out just in case. That way if there was something or someone that was still following him, he would be able to see it first, before it had a chance to possibly make any aggressive moves towards him.

Though the remaining uneasiness from the anxiety that he was feeling earlier made Josiah want to fight sleep and vigilantly keep watch for anything that may still be out there, the content feeling provided by his full stomach, and the exhaustion that he felt from the journey he was on, sleep won out and eventually overtook him.

He needed to rest, but his slumber this day was anything but restful. Shortly after falling asleep, Josiah began to dream. It was one of the few bad dreams that he had had since his journey north had begun. He dreamt that he was out in the woods walking and he could hear something following him, but every time he turned to look, there was nothing there. He could feel a hot breeze blowing on his upper spine as if something was breathing down heavily upon the back of his neck. But again, when he would turn around, there would be nothing there. He could hear strange noises in the woods around him, and strange birds were flying above him. He walked and walked, but the further he walked, the less ground he seemed to be covering. Then he started to notice the same patterns on the trees, and the same rocks on the ground. He then realized that he had been walking in circles.

Along with strange noises, he began to hear twigs breaking in the woods from all around him now. Turning wildly, he looked all around the area in which he now stood. Again, he didn't see anything, he knew there was something there, and more than one of whatever it was, but he just couldn't see anything.

"What do you want?" he called out loudly into the darkness. He was only met with silence. Squinting, he tried to look closer into the darkness that surrounded him, but again there was nothing to see. Frustration and fear began to creep into the pit of his stomach. He didn't have a good feeling about who, or what it was that was now surrounding him.

Josiah got on all fours and began to run in a different direction than he had been walking. He ran quickly, dodging around trees and rocks, but then he began to again recognize the same patterns on the trees even though he had taken a different path. He began to realize that he couldn't get away from whatever it was that was taunting him. He felt like someone was playing a cruel joke on him, and it was making him very angry.

"Where are you?" he bellowed out into the darkness. *"What do you want from me?"* he asked. Again, the only response was silence. Out of frustration, Josiah put his hands up to his head and screamed as loud as he could into the night, and then that scream turned into a blood curling howl. Exhausted, Josiah sat down, put his hands up to his face and was silent.

That is when he began to hear the faint sound of a crackling fire coming from behind him. He turned and looked off in the direction of where the noise was coming from. That is when he saw a large golden glow peeking through the trees. Mesmerized by the flames, Josiah walked towards where the fire was burning. As he got closer, he realized that there was a small field there that he hadn't notice before. Josiah paused and gazed at the flames as they illuminated the immediate area around it.

As he watched the flames dance before him, he became aware that he was no longer alone. He saw others appearing from what seemed like out of nowhere. Others like him. Half wolf, half man. They were all slowly walking in from the wood line towards where he now stood. They didn't even look at him as they approached, they just seemed to ignored his presence.

"This must be who has been following me in the woods. It has to be," he thought to himself. Josiah watched the others as they walked up to the fire and stretched their hands out to it. They didn't stand in front of the fire warming themselves for very long though, before they turned to face Josiah. He was too busy watching the two creatures like himself that were next to the fire, to see the other two that had approached him from the rear. As Josiah watched and was mesmerized by the two creatures standing by the fire, he felt the two others grab him by the arms from either side. He struggled against them, but they both had strength equivalent to that of which he possessed himself, if not stronger. With barely any effort on their part, they had quickly immobilized him and were able to hold him firmly in place.

The two dogmen that had grabbed Josiah by the arms then roughly forced him to walk forwards and up to face the group that had congregated in front of the large fire. The others all stared at him intensely, but none uttered a sound towards him.

"Who are you? What do you want with me?" Josiah loudly mentally demanded as he struggled against the secure grasp that they had on him. Looking from one face to the next, he demanded again, *"What do you want!"* The only response he got from them was their constant silent menacing glare.

One of the dogmen that stood in front of Josiah looked at one of the others standing next to him. Slowly leaning over to him, he silently mumbled something into the others large pointed ear. That dogman then turned and disappeared to the backside side of the fire. When he returned back into view, he had with him a small framed young woman. She was blond with long tangled, dirty looking hair. She was very small and petite in stature and dressed in a simple, dirty, cream-colored dress. Looking downward, he took note that she was also barefoot. There was no shape to the dress, nor any form to it. It just hung from her shoulders straight down with its only purpose being to cover her body. It wasn't thick enough to even provide any warmth against the cooler mountain air. By all appearances, he knew that the young woman definitely wasn't one of them. Looking at her, Josiah wondered where she had come from, and why she was there.

The two dogmen that were holding Josiah's arms began to drag him forward to force him to walk closer to where the young woman now stood. When he saw her from up close, and without the blinding fire behind her affecting with his vision, he began to realize that she was not a young woman after all, but a young girl, barely of teenage years yet. Fearful, the young girl wouldn't look up at Josiah, instead she kept her eyes facing down at the ground. Even if she had been looking up at him, he couldn't have clearly seen her face, for her long scraggly blond hair hung down over it, concealing her face from view. Josiah wanted to reach out to the young girl, but the two dogmen continued to hold tightly onto his arms, and wouldn't allow it.

"Are you alright?" he mentally asked her. He felt sympathy for the young girl. Without looking up at him, the girl slowly shook her head yes, but did not utter a spoken word.

"What are you doing here?" he asked her as he once again tried to get her to talk to him. This time though, she didn't respond at all to his question.

"What are you doing with her, why is she here?" he mentally yelled angerly at the others standing in front of him. One of the dogmen looked over at him and grinned before speaking.

"You do not recognize her, do you?" the dogman asked as he sneered at Josiah.

Josiah looked at the girl again, but he still didn't recognize who she was. If he could see her face, maybe, but probably not, why would he recognize her, she was a stranger to him.

"She was taken by our brother years ago from her home. She has lived here amongst us, serving us, and doing our bidding

213

ever since. She is our pet, serving us is how she earns her keep." The dogman said as he glanced back down at the young girl and then back to Josiah before continuing. *"Now, do you still do not recognize her?"* the dogman asked as he continued to glare menacingly at Josiah.

Josiah looked at the young girl and shook his head from side to side to signify that he still didn't recognize her.

"I can't even see her face. I don't know why you think I should recognize her anyway, how am I to know who she is?" he gruffly told him as he tried to pull his arms away from his captures.

The leader of the dogmen reached over and roughly placed his hand under the young girl's chin. Jerking her face sharply upward into the glowing light of the fire, her hair parted some and the illuminated light from the fire lit up her pale face and made her blue eyes shine brightly. When Josiah saw her eyes, the bright blue eyes that held seeds from his past, he realized that they were the eyes that he now only now saw in his dreams, they were eyes that he could never forget.

Josiah's mouth opened, but he was without words. He was shocked to be looking at what was the spitting image of his wife when they had first met in the village. She too had looked younger than her age back then. The high cheekbone structure, the sky-blue eyes and full lips were all features that his wife had held. This girl looked just like his wife would have when she was of this age. Reality then began to set in with Josiah, and he began to realize who this young girl really was to him, and what relationship she held to him.

"Ava?" he mentally called out to her as he cocked his head and looked closely at her. *"Ava, is that you?"* he asked her once more. The girl only looked back blankly at him and stared. She didn't recognize her own father, any more than he had recognized her. Time had erased most of her memories, and Josiah definitely no longer looked like he had appeared to her the last time she saw him. He was no longer the man that was her father, but instead he had changed into the creature that he now had become.

"Ava honey, it's me, it's your Papa," he told her. He tried to reach out to her, but the other two dogmen continued to hold firmly onto his arms.

"What have you done to her?" Josiah demanded of the other dogmen.

"We have done nothing to her that what we have not done to many others like her since the beginning of time. She has been with us so long that she has forgotten where she had come from, and anything about her life before she was taken. All she knows is her life here with us now, and that she is, and always will be, one of us," he told him.

"No! She is my daughter; she is not one of you!" Josiah mentally yelled at him. The dogman that seemed to be the leader of the pack looked down at the young girl, and then with his hand, signaled one of the others to come over and take Ava away. Taking the young girl roughly by the arm, she immediately and submissively bowed her head as to dare not make eye contact with her captures, and then without struggle, she willingly allowed herself to be led away.

As the young girl turned to leave though, her foot caught something on the ground and she stumbled forwards. As she stumbled, a strong breeze caught her dress and blew it snugly up against the front of her body. Josiah's eyes widened as he saw that his daughter now had a large rounded abdomen that had been hidden by her loosely fitted dress.

"What have you done to her! What have you done to my daughter!" Josiah demanded angerly.

"We have done nothing to her. She is only with child. She will bear a pup child for us soon. That is what females of any race are for. When they hit first blood, they are ripe, and it is time for us to breed. She will breed many times and bear us many pups before she is no longer of any use to us."

"No! She is only a child herself you bastards! You raped my little girl! You can't do this to her, I won't let you hurt her anymore!" he screamed menacingly at him.

"She has known no other life. She is ours to do with as we desire," he told him. *"She is fertile and as I said, will bare many pups for us now. We, our race, will continue to live on through her and the others we have here with us."*

Josiah stomped his feet in frustration and growled loudly. *"Ava!"*, he shouted after her. *"Ava!"*

"She will not respond to you. She doesn't even know her given name any longer. When she first came here, she used to cry out for her daddy, but you never came. You never came to find your little girl, you never even looked for her. We told her

216

that you didn't care about her then, and that you don't care about her now, and that she never meant anything to you as well! And now, she doesn't even remember you. All she knows is life here with us, our ways, and what is expected of her. She is ours now, and will be until the day she dies," he told him.

"I tried to look for her! I didn't know where she was. I knew that the beast had taken her with him after killing her mother, sister and baby brother, but I didn't know where he took her! I tried to look; I really did!" he yelled back at the larger dogman.

"She is lost to you now. She doesn't know you, and she doesn't want you. We only brought you here so you can see that she is no longer yours and to make you give up on her. She hates you and blames you for her being here with us. Now you go! You leave this mountain, and do not come back! Do not look for her again, and do not fight to get her back. If you do, we will kill you, and her both. She is ours now!" he bellowed at Josiah.

Those words now echoed over and over again in Josiah's ears, *"Do not look for her again, and do not fight to get her back. If you do, we will kill you, and her both. She is ours now!"*

"No! No, give her back!" Josiah yelled out loudly in his sleep as he jumped up, and hit the back of his head on the ceiling of the small cave. Turning his head wildly back and forth he looked around the cave as he quickly took a defensive stance on all fours. Growling intensely into the darkness, he was prepared to fend off whatever or whoever it was that was out there.

217

Josiah, realizing that he must have been having a horrible nightmare, tried to calm himself down. He could still feel his heart racing from within his chest, and it was pounding so hard that it felt as though it was going to burst out of his rib cage.

Laying still, he began to take in deep breaths in an effort to try and calm his nerves. He had never woken up from a dream like that before, not this frightened or this angry.

Slowly climbing out of his cave into the dimming light, Josiah dragged the sack with him. He sat down upon the ground and opened up the bag and took out the small teddy bear from within. Looking down at the small bear, he brought it forward and held it up against his still pounding chest. Closing his eyes and taking more deep breaths, Josiah finally began to calm down. His heart rate began to slow, and his breathing once more began to return to a normal rate as well.

Taking the bear from his chest, he looked at it. *"Do not look for her again, and do not fight to get her back. If you do, we will kill you, and her both. She is ours now!"* he repeated to himself as he stared at the bear. He didn't remember the dream itself, but he remembered the feelings he had felt during it, and after when he woke up. But there were no other details. The only thing that stood out above it all, was the sentence that still echoed in his mind, *"Do not look for her again, and do not fight to get her back...."*

"Why can I remember that, but not the rest of the dream? Why would my dreams be trying to tell me not to look for my daughter?" he pondered to himself.

Josiah pulled the small stuffed bear back up to his chest again and held it firmly against him as he stared out into the forest in front of him.

"I will look for her, and I will find her!" he yelled out into the shadows. *"She is my daughter, and like it or not, I will find her! Whoever you are out there, hear me, I will find her!"*

Josiah bend over and put the small bear back into the sack. He wasn't going to let anything, or anyone keep him from finding his daughter. He knew she was out there somewhere, and if someone was going to this extent to try to keep him away from her, he knew that he must be getting closer.

The evening was quickly approaching, so Josiah decided to head out early. As he continued to climb upward, he once more had the feeling that he was being watched. He didn't care any longer though. He wasn't going to allow anyone, or anything to keep him from his little girl. His every thought now was of her, and finding her. *"How long has it been?"* he wondered to himself as he pressed on. He had no idea how long he had been living this new life, he had no idea about any of it, he no longer had any concept of time. His days, weeks and years all ran together now with no distinction between them. He wasn't even sure of how old his daughter was now, but he did know that he would recognize her when he seen her. He had no doubt about that. He just hoped that she was okay, and that she would want to see him as much as he wanted to see her.

Pressing on, Josiah started to recognize some of the rock formations though he knew that he had never been this high up on the mountain before. But yet he had a sense of familiarity about the place. *"I must have been here before, I had to of been this way at some time for me to remember this place,"* he thought to himself as he continued to look around at his surroundings. Taking this familiarity as a sign, he now knew that he must be going in the right direction, and that feeling alone made him press on harder.

Looking at the rock face that stood before him, he envisioned it covered with snow and heavy ice. Even now he could see the ice crystals on the loose rocks shimmering in the light of the full moon. He knew that up this high on the mountain top, that it had to get very cold in the winter time, both very cold and very windy. *"If she is up here, how could she have survived the winters, she must have been so very cold,"* he sadly thought to himself.

Shaking the thought out of his head, Josiah once more looked up at the sheer face of the cliff before him. Not liking what he was seeing and judging it too difficult to climb, he looked over to the left and saw that the rock face was not nearly as steep as it was over on the side where he was at. After walking over to the far side, Josiah took hold of the ledge and began to climb. He scaled the rock face easier than he had even imagined he could, and he amazingly did it with little effort at all. It was like he had already done this many times before, and his body retained the memory of it, even if his mind didn't. He didn't understand it. As he climbed, he realized that his muscles had become stronger during this journey, and that he had become more confident in himself and his abilities as well. All this combined gave him the motivation and the determination to reach the top.

As he climbed up the steep cliffside, he began to allow his mind wander. Josiah had begun to think more about his daughter and his desire to find her than paying attention to his ascent up the cliffside. Slipping on some loose rocks, Josiah began to tumble downwards. Extending his arms out, he tried to try grab onto anything that he could to keep himself from falling further. Failing to do so, Josiah continued to tumble downward until he finally came to rest on the jagged edge of a small ledge. Josiah moaned as he laid motionless on the rocks edge as he tried to catch his breath. Every muscle in his back and neck screamed out in agony at him for being so stupid. Knowing that he was not badly injured, did not stop him from being very upset at himself for being so careless.

"Idiot!" he yelled at himself as he clenched his fists. *"You are so close, so, so close to finding Ava. You cannot be so stupid!"* he said as he severely admonished himself. He could not believe that he had let his guard down like he had.

After laying on the platform with very little room to move for a few more minutes, Josiah regained control of his breathing and sat up. Shaking his head to clear the fog that he had experienced after hitting his head on a large rock during his rapid descent down the mountain side, he was now ready to continue on his upward climb back up the mountain.

Taking his time and testing his footing, Josiah once more began to climb up the face of the cliff. Small pebbles began to give way and fall with every hand and foothold he took. After slowly and carefully progressing upward, Josiah caught sight of the top of the ridge above him.

After climbing to the top of the roughly 450-foot-high sheer stone cliff, he looked down over the edge and viewed what he had left below. The fully grown trees at the base of the cliff looked so tiny from this high up, that to him they looked as if they could be nothing more than small saplings.

Lifting his gaze from what he had left below, Josiah looked out across the large plateau that lay before him. Through the trees, he saw that there was a small grass covered field that lay on the other side. Though it was much like the other plateaus that he had come across, this one seemed different. As he scanned the plateau further, he could also see that there was a thick grove of trees surrounding it on all of the interior edges like a secured fortress of timber. Slowly walking into the wooded area before him, he could tell that it felt different there.

The field looked vaguely familiar, but like with the rock formations, he just couldn't place it. He didn't remember ever being in this place before, but something definitely seemed familiar about it. *"Maybe I've been elsewhere, and there had been a place that looked close to this,"* he told himself. But yet it still bothered him, he wondered what it was that he wasn't understanding about this place, and why couldn't he remember its significance when it was so clear to him, that he had been there before.

As Josiah continued to look at his new surroundings, that same strong uncomfortable feeling of being watched began to come over him again. Looking back from where he had just come, and then around at the edges of the tree line, he still saw nothing that could be making him feel that way.

Everything about this place felt different though, but he had no idea why.

Looking upward beyond the plateau where he now stood, and with the aid of the moon light above, Josiah could see that the mountain still continued upward beyond his line of sight. He saw that more peaks and plateaus rose upward even higher to new heights until they eventually poked through the clouds and extended further yet. He knew that he had to be well over 6,000 feet in the air, higher than most other living creatures have ever dared to go. He could tell that the air was thinner here too, but it didn't seem to bother his breathing. There was just so much to take in from where he now stood. But even with everything before him, despite its beauty and its majesty, that nagging uncomfortable feeling of being watched was still there.

B.J. MOORE

Chapter Seven

Josiah slowly walked out into the field and looked around at the vastness of the plateau. It was much larger than he had originally thought, but other than its size, nothing looked different than any of the other plateaus that he had seen earlier in his trip. Yet, though he knew that he had never been this high up on the mountain before, there was still this intense sense of familiarity that it held for him that he couldn't shake.

Looking up into the sky, Josiah gazed at the full moon that was shining brightly above him. As he looked up at the moon, the uncomfortable feeling that he had begun to feel earlier, had now suddenly increased in intensity. He felt as though he had eyes boring into him, like something was now watching him with great interest and he began to feel very uncomfortable.

Turning around and cautiously looking out into the darkness, Josiah looked for any sign of eye shine. He knew that something was there, but he just couldn't see it. Without hearing any sounds from movement, or even catching a glimpse of the eye shine that whatever or whoever it was would crate, he had no way of pin pointing where whatever it was that was hiding from him within the darkened tree line was.

"I know you are out there," he forcefully called out to the unseen stalker. *"I know you have been following me for a while. Why don't you come out to where I can see you?"* he mentally called out into the darkness of the shadows. *"Where are you, what are you afraid of,"* he asked from where he stood.

"Who are you that comes before us?" came a voice out of the darkness from somewhere behind him.

Not expecting to hear an answer, Josiah was startled and jerked around quickly to face the direction that the voice had come from. He recognized the voice, *"...but from where?"* he asked himself.

Staring out into the darkness, Josiah looked deeply into the shadows, but he still couldn't see any movement or eyeshine from whoever it was hiding there.

"Where are you?" Josiah mentally asked as he continued to stare out into the shadows.

"We are here. Now you answer us, who are you?" the voice asked.

"Who is 'We'?" Josiah demanded.

"We are the one, and the only. We haunt the hills and put fear into the hearts of man," the voice told him. *"We have been waiting for the one that remains. Now I ask you, who are you?"*

"You aren't answering my questions, and stop talking in circles! Who are you? And why won't you show yourself to me?" Josiah demanded.

"We are like you, we are one," was all he said.

Josiah turned and looked in every direction, but still didn't see any movement.

"Show yourselves! Show yourselves now!" Josiah demanded in anger. He could hear the rustling of leaves from within the tree line, and he turned to look in the direction that the sound had come from. It was then that he saw a shadowy figure standing alone in the darkness.

"Who are you?" Josiah mentally asked. The figure stood still, not moving, and still not answering. Josiah was now getting very frustrated with the figure that stood silently in front of him.

"Why won't you talk to me?" Josiah gruffly asked the mysterious figure. In frustration, he took his clawed hand and ran it over top of his head and let out a low angry growl at the figure.

"If you are not going to talk to me, I am leaving!" Josiah called out in frustration. *"I am not going to stand here and talk to*

someone, who will not talk back to me," he told him harshly as he turned his back to the mysterious figure and began to walk away.

"Wait!" came a voice out of the darkness. Josiah stopped, breathed deeply and huffed loudly as he turned back around and looked angrily at the shadowy figure. *"You cannot leave,"* the voice added.

"Why can't I?" Josiah demanded with irritation still showing in his voice.

"Because you cannot. We had to be sure of why you were here. We had to feel what you were feeling inside, we had to see what you see for us to be sure that you were the one. And we now know that you are. We have been waiting for you to come to us for many years, and you are finally here where you belong. You are part of us, as much as we are a part of you. That is why you could feel us with you."

"I don't understand what you are talking about, what do you meant when you say that I am a part of you?" Josiah asked the mysterious figure. It was then that the figure that was standing in the shadows began to walk towards Josiah. When he stepped out into the moonlight, Josiah couldn't believe what he was seeing.

"You are like me?" Josiah said in astonishment.

"Yes, I am like you, and you are like us," the figure told him as he held his arms and hands slightly outward from the side of his body.

"What do you mean by us?" Josiah asked as he looked behind the mysterious figure and then off to the sides of him.

"I mean us," the dogman said as he raised his arms up higher and held them off to the side of him, and with that, others like him began to slowly emerge from the shadows. Josiah stood still and watched them one by one as they all walked towards him from out of the shadows. In amazement, he counted ten dogmen now standing before him.

"Why have you been following me, I felt you, and where did you all come from?" Josiah asked the dogman that now stood in front of him.

"We all come from the same place as you," was the answer that he was given.

"You are doing nothing but talking in circles, and I don't like it!" he told him as he raised his voice. *"Just give me a straight answer!"* he now loudly demanded.

"We all come from the same place. You were born to a human mother, just like the rest of us here were. You grew up in family other than the one you were born into, did you not?" the dogman asked.

Josiah tilted his head and just looked at the other dogman, uncertain as to what to think about what he just said.

"How did you know that? Who told you that about me?" he asked uneasily. Josiah still didn't know what was going on, and the unknowing is what unnerved him. It made him feel

229

uncomfortable for them to already know so much about him, when he knew absolutely nothing about them. Looking from one dogman to the other, he looked for any kind of a reaction at all from them, but they all stayed stoic and were silent but for the one who spoke to him.

"This is how it was for all of us."

"I'm not understanding you. Stop talking in riddles and just tell me what is going on!" he growled at the dogman that stood before him.

"We are all part of the same pack. We all have different adoptive names, but we still all carry the same bloodline. We all also have the same birth-rite, the same family sir name," he told him.

"You need to start at the beginning. I have no idea what you are talking about. You need to explain it all to me, and I want to hear it now!" Josiah told him while trying to quell his frustration and anger.

"First, your name. Tell us your name. And did you keep your adopted name, or change it back to your rightful name when you became a man?" he asked.

"My name," Josiah quietly began, and then paused. It had been so long since he had said his own name out loud, so long in fact that it now seemed almost foreign to him. He no longer was that man any longer, he had left that man behind many years ago. Looking at the other dogman in the eyes, he told them, *"My name is Josiah."*

"Josiah Wolfe? Am I that correct in that?" the other dogman asked.

"Yes, yes, it is, but how did you know that?" Josiah responded questioningly.

"What was your adopted name?" he asked already knowing the answer.

"Cullen, why?" Josiah asked. *"And how did you know I changed my last name?"*

"I know a lot of things, past and present. As I said, we are one," he replied. *"What made you decide to drop your adoptive last name, and go by the name of Wolfe? That part I do not know."*

"Wolfe was my given middle name. I came to those who adopted me with no name as a baby, and they were the ones to name me. I asked them at one time why I had such an unusual middle name, and they told me that in their hearts, they felt like that was my true name. So, when I became an adult, I dropped the Cullen and went by Wolfe with their blessings."

"Your parents had good insight for humans, an unconscious knowledge of what they could have never known otherwise," he told him.

"So, who are you?" Josiah asked him back.

"I am Daniel. Daniel Wolfe."

"Wait, I don't understand, are you saying that your last name is also Wolfe?" Josiah said as he stared at the man. *"Are we related by blood?"* he asked.

"Yes, we are. Here on this mountain top, we are all brothers by blood."

"How can we all be related? I want, no, I need to know everything. Tell me all of what you know of this," he demanded of Daniel.

"Come brother. Let us go over to the pit, we can sit and talk there," he told him.

In the darkness, Josiah hadn't noticed the large earthen circle that laid in the middle of the field. It was barren of any grass, or any greenery at all, and within it, there was a large pile of ash that lay in the middle. One of the other dogmen took a piece of flint, and lit a small fire in the center of the ashes and fed it more wood from a small stack nearby. They then all went and sat upon rocks that were placed in a rectangle in front of the fire. As they sat, the dogmen all faced each other. Josiah looked at the two empty seats left on the end of one row. He looked up at Daniel, but before he could ask, Daniel began to speak.

"Now I will tell you the story of how we came to be," Daniel said as he looked directly at Josiah. Josiah, still trying to take it all in, only nodded his head at him in reply.

"It is important that you listen closely to what I am about to tell you. This is our past; it is our history. It was long ago when

232

our race began. Some people out of fear referred to us as monsters; creatures of the night would be more accurate though. Some humans even gave us the name of Werewolf, and here in this land, our southern brothers are often referred to as the Rougarou, and in other areas they use other names, but some call us what we go by here, and what we refer to ourselves as, Dogmen.

We all were once normal men like you were at one time. We were good men, some of us had good jobs in the towns where we lived, and some of us farmed the land. We lived what were normal lives for humans. But that was before the change. Here in our society, you will notice that there are no females, that is because this is a male dominant gene that we carry within our bloodline. Females in our bloodline that carry it are not healthy, and most perish young.

We, as in the Wolfe clan, came to be from the blood of a woman, a female two-leger, and a rogue wolf from many, many years ago. More years ago, than any of us, our fathers, or their fathers before them, have been around. We came into existence from the tainted blood of a child that never should have been born, a child that was born from an unholy union between a human female and a male wolf type creature.

The lone wolf had a sickness that boiled from within its blood. I'm sure you have felt the same cravings boiling from within your own blood by now. That sickness is within all of us, and not something that we can control. That is one reason why we live here. It is an intense burning fire that is hard to put out. This wolf was one of the first of its kind that could either travel on all fours, or walk upright like a man. No one knows

233

where it had originally come from, or where it had traveled through on its journey. But that wolf, he was our great, great, great grandfather.

Our pack is still young in comparison to others, and has been around for hundreds of years, or possibly for even more, but we are only ones left. The two-legers have written stories about us. They say that by day we are two-legers like them, but at night, by the light of the full moon, that we change into wolves. What they do not realize though, is that this is the way that we are. Their fables and stories are nothing but that, only stories that they like to pass around and tell to all that will listen," Daniel told him.

"What happened to the original wolf, the one that we all came from? What happened to him, and how did we come to be?" Josiah asked.

"Our original ancestor had attacked a young woman. He had attacked her and almost killed her, and the two-legers would not allow that to rest. The act that was portrayed by that lone wolf went further than the two-legers knew about though. It was more than just a mauling. The young woman out of fear had kept some of the details of what had happened to her during the attack to herself. Our ancestor had not only attacked the young woman, but he defiled her as well. He viciously raped the young woman before mauling her, and leaving her in the woods for dead.

It was said that some children from her village were playing in the woods when they found her barely hanging onto life. Some of the children then ran back to the village to get her help, while others stayed. Then after some of the men from the village came to her aid, they found her to be gravely injured and unconscious. They returned with the young woman back to the village. She had managed to survive the attack put forth by the lone wolf, but the attack left her badly scared, both physically and mentally, and she was never be the same afterward.

After a few months, the rogue wolf was found and killed. The hunters had never seen an animal such as he before. The towns men brought his body back to the village and displayed it before they publicly decapitated it, and burned his remains. The village deemed him a Demon Wolf. He was only one of the wolf type creatures that spawned the creation of the fables of the werewolf though, and many of the other stories known by the two-legers today. If only they knew the true story that lies behind it though...." he said before he let his voice trail off.

Josiah sat in wide-eyed amazement at what he was hearing. As Daniel continued on, he was having a hard time believing that what he was being told was true, and that it had really happened. It all just didn't seem real.

"Things had settled in the village after the death of the strange wolf, but when the young woman started to show to be with child though, and being unwed, the villagers openly mocked her for her pregnancy. They were cruel to her, kicked dirt at her and called her ugly names. The other woman demanded to know what man from the village that she was cavorting with, and if it were one of their own husbands who had impregnated her.

She tried to tell the people of the village that she had been with no man, and that it was not any man in the village that had impregnated her. But after their continuous abuse and belittling, she relented and admitted to them that it was the wolf type creature that had attacked her. She told them that it had raped her, and that it was the one who was responsible for her being with child.

The villagers were all horrified. They then turned their backs on her and shunned her for being in league with the Devil himself. After that day, they exiled her from the village and forced her into the wilds to fend for herself. As they chased her away, her own parents, ordering her never to return again."

"What happened to her then, where did she go?" Josiah asked.

"People from another town had found her wandering alone in the woods. She was barely lucid at that point after being alone in the wilds for months. When they could not console her or alleviate her unwarranted fears of them, they had no choice but to send her an institution for the mentally disturbed.

From the time that she got to the institution, all they could get out of her was her name and where she had once lived, so they sent word to her family there. Her family sent a message back to them denying that she was their daughter. After months had passed, they still denied her, and would not claim a daughter that they felt had done such vile things as to cavort with a Demon Wolf.

At the institution, she had begun to grow larger and her delivery time was nearing. After being prejudiced by what they had been told about her from the village that she had come from, they too felt that her condition, both mental and physical, were direct results of her own perversion. They were now fearful of her, and believed her to be a witch, and that the wolf type creature that bred with her, had been her familiar. She then only remained there because of the innocent baby she carried in her womb.

This woman, our great, great, great grandmother, later gave birth to a son in the institution, and the child was sent out for an elderly farmer named Jacob Wolfe and his wife to raise as their own. His wife was barren due to an accident, so when the child was offered, they gladly took him in. They did well with him, taught him a trade and raised him up as their own child. He was never told that this couple were not his real parents, and this is where our pack name came from.

When the child grew to be an adult, he took himself a wife, and through her, they had six sons. As he aged though, he began to change. As he saw what was becoming of himself, he went up into the mountains on a hunting trip, and he never returned. He was assumed to have been killed by wild animals, or more specifically, a large wolf. They found large wolf prints all around the area of his campsite. But it wasn't a wolf that had killed him. He had transformed, and became like us. He was the first. Story has it," Daniel continued on, *"that a few months after his disappearance, his wife was struck ill, and she later died. With no family to take the children in, their six young sons were separated and farmed out to six different families across the land to be raised as* laborers to help to earn their keep. All the younger sons had then taken on the sir names of their adoptive families but for the eldest, who kept the name Wolfe, none of the brothers were ever reunited, or had any contact with each other again.

As each son grew to adult hood, they too took wives and had sons and daughters of their own. And by doing that, the gene and the legacy of the one lone wolf, continued to be passed on down the line to all the male offspring born. The female offspring of our pack were never were affected as we were, but they were affected in other ways. You see, as I said, we are all brothers here. We all have the same blood coursing in our veins from the original ancestor. We are one."

"How many are there of us now?" Josiah asked.

"We are all that is left on this side of the bloodline, the direct descendants of the one brother with the sir name of Wolfe, and we are now slowly dying out. When a male child is to be borne by one of us in our old life as a man, we can sense it, we can feel it from deep within ourselves. Our ancestors chose as a group to end the Wolfe bloodline and to not allow a child borne like us, or if it is, to put it down as soon as possible afterwards."

"You are murdering innocent children though!" Josiah yelled at him as he stood up. "What if there is a male child born that doesn't have this curse, can you tell the difference, or do you just go ahead and kill it anyway?"

"I will further explain, but for now, please sit, there is more to hear," Daniel told him calmly as he motioned with his hand towards the stone seat. Josiah was upset, but the calmness that Daniel retained in both voice and action, began to bring him back to a calmer state as well. Josiah looked down at Daniel for a few seconds more before taking a deep breath, and then sitting back down on the rock.

"How do you know if they are all affected? How can you tell?" Josiah calmy asked Daniel.

"We can tell. We can always tell. Within our direct bloodline, we can feel it. There is no question, and we have never been wrong. There has not been a male child borne to our blood line in the last two hundred years that we haven't known about. You are now the last of this bloodline, and now you have come here to be with us. You were the last of the Wolfe's to be born. I have a question for you, you did not know your mother at all, nor did you even know your father, am I correct?"

"You already know I was adopted, and no, I never knew my father, nor my mother," Josiah said impatiently. *"My mother was said to of died when I was born, and I could never find out who my father was, no one would say, but what does that have to do with any of this?"* Josiah asked.

"Because sometimes the mothers do not survive when they give birth to one of us. Depending on the circumstances behind how we come about, whether the pregnancy happened through marriage to one of us in human form, or by an assault by one of us that have already changed, that is what makes the difference. Your mother was attacked by one of our kind after he had changed. She was viciously attacked,

239

and left impregnated from that attack. Just like our ancestorial maternal line, your mother too went mad from her experience, and because of it, she took her own life. After your mother gave birth to you and your brother, she killed herself that same night. She never even had a chance to see either one of you before she hung herself in her room."

"What? Wait, are you saying that one of you...that someone here, raped my mother, and that I have a brother out there somewhere?" Josiah stammered.

"Yes, on both accounts. Though he still loved her, your mother's husband left her after he realized that she had been impregnated by the attacker, and he knew that the babies she carried weren't his. He knew that you were the product of the rape, and he didn't want either one of you as a constant reminder of it. After your mother's death, he had nothing left in the town where they had lived but for bad memories, so he gave you both up for adoption and then left town without looking back. He just wanted to get as far away from you and your brother, and the all the bad memories as he could."

"Who here is my father, which one of you raped my mother!" Josiah questioned as he looked around at all who sat nearby.

"He is no longer with us. After such an act, he was no longer trustworthy and had to be dealt with harshly."

"Is he dead? Tell me that he is dead!" Josiah angerly asked as his eyes seethed with hatred.

"Yes, he is no longer here with us," was Daniels only response.

Satisfied with the answer he was given, Josiah calmed down and looked at the ground as he shook his head.

"I thought you killed all the male children when they were born? Why didn't you kill us then?" Josiah asked as he looked back up at Daniel again.

"We try to, but we couldn't get to you and your brother. There was no way we could get into the hospital without being seen to take care of the task, so we had to wait. As time went by though, the two of you were separated by the hospital staff and then sent away to different families to be raised. At that point we lost our opportunity to act. We instead then chose to followed you and monitor your progression and movements. We knew where you both were at all times as you grew; we always knew."

"What about my brother? Where is he now? Is he here in this place as well?" Josiah asked.

"Yes, he is here with us. He came here to be with us many years ago. He changed long before you did, and it was hard on him. He was barely an adult when he began to change. He never had a chance to have a wife, nor did he know what it was like to have a woman. All that and more played a factor in his actions of the past, and how he is now."

"Are one of you my brother then?" Josiah asked calmly as he glanced back and forth between the dogmen.

"He is here, but he isn't sitting here with us right now," Daniel told him as he glanced at one of the unoccupied seats.

241

"Normally he would have been seated here with the rest of us, but I wanted to talk to you about him first," Daniel told Josiah.

Josiah had so many questions he needed to ask, things he needed to know, but he didn't know where to begin.

"The dogman that you saw in the two-legers jail that night so long ago, that was your brother. He went there to set you free. As you know, that night didn't go so well though, and a two-leger was killed. He still struggles with the balance between the human side, and the animal side of his existence. He is unpredictable because of how he changed, and more so, when he changed. His human body was raging with hormones at the time, and even then, his human family found him uncontrollable as well. Not much has changed for him unfortunately, even after he transformed, it is still hard to keep him under control at times. His human hormones never had a chance to settled down, and because of it, it has affected his mental stability. We have to keep an eye on him at all times. He can be unstable and dangerous at times to both himself and others. We thought for a while that he was doing better, he seemed mentally stronger, but we were wrong. He isn't the first dogman to have a problem adjusting to their new life, and what they have now become."

Josiah only nodded his head.

"Like I said though, we here are the last of our direct bloodline, which includes you. But the bloodline from the other five brothers that were borne still do exist, we tried to find the ones we could from those bloodlines too, but there

are male children that were missed such as yourself, ones that we could not get to, and ones that we just could not find. We couldn't feel them like we could feel our own. They are foreign to us.

We tried our best to keep track of the other bloodlines, but those lines have broken off and scattered far and wide, and many of those dogmen have gone rogue as well. Once rogue, there is no way to follow them, so we don't even know where those ones all are. The other lines stretch far across this land and dispersed throughout the whole northern hemisphere. They also are not only in this land, but they have migrated to other countries as well. Some traveled to other countries while still in human form, and not knowing what was yet to come for them in their future. Being that we cannot travel to other countries ourselves, obviously we have no idea of the extent of the spread that our kind has there. We have only heard rumors that it is extensive."

Josiah didn't know what to say, and only sat staring at Daniel in silence.

"The ones that went rogue here in the North American territory; we hear of them occasionally coming into contact with two-legers. Most of them try to stay hidden and out of sight, but others don't. For some reason those ones unfortunately seem to need and crave that connection to what they once were. They sometimes allow themselves to be seen by the humans, to just try to make some kind of a connection with their past, or they go mad like your brother has, and terrorize the two-legers. Some have even attacked the two-legers, and the humans are never to be seen again.

243

Usually, wild animals are blamed for the attacks, but we know, we know deep down inside what, and who, was at fault.

We have gotten word that there has been speculation by the two-legers about some of the sightings that the they have had of werewolf type creatures, and of the many mysterious disappearances of humans as well. The humans that go out into the wilds either for hunting or for the tending their cattle and never return spur most of these stories. The rogue dogmen do us no favors, they make us all out to be blood thirsty animals, and as you know, that is not true."

"For so long, I thought that I was the only one. Originally, I thought that the dogman who killed the sheriff was just something that I imagined because of my head injury. Then I realized though that it must have been real, because it killed my wife and other children, and after that, it took my youngest daughter from her bed. I had so many thoughts going through my head at that point, I just wasn't sure of anything. It all is still a blur for me. I had no idea that there were more dogmen other than just myself, and the one I saw at the jail until now? How many more are out there? And what about the ones in other countries?" Josiah asked inquisitively.

"There are thousands of dogmen across this land, and many more that live in other countries as I said. We are the last of our direct blood line though, the last of the line borne from the one older brother named Wolfe. The others are off-shoots borne from the other five brothers. They are the ones that either could not, or did not hear their own calling like the one

that you heard that brought you here to us. They may also lack the knowledge that was handed down through our lineage. The old ones here, including your father, have all passed long ago, but they have left the Wolfe heritage with us, and as new arrivals came over the years, we shared that legacy with them. That is why I am telling you this all now. You are the last of our line.

Long ago, we were told by the old ones that there are other packs of dogmen like us all over the world that are not even of the same bloodline as us, and that those bloodlines could be older than ours is. They are packs that were created much as we were, but from a different rogue lone wolf. Unlike us though, these packs are said to have females of their breed, but we have no way of knowing for sure. We only know what we were told by others. We also have heard from others that some of the rogue packs here have also managed to somehow produce females that transition, and through mating with those females, dogman pups have been born, but again, we don't know for sure because we do not have contact with the other packs in this country.

Our pack though, the Wolfe's, we made a promise over a century ago to our forefather's that we would allow our bloodline to die off and not permit it to be carried on. Our forefathers knew long ago that our line, like all the other lines, are lines that never should have occurred, and never would have occurred in nature if it weren't for the lone wolf all those years ago. If it hadn't somehow been created and then went rogue and mated with our maternal ancestor, then none of this would have happened, and none of us would have ever been born."

Josiah sat on the rock and stared at Daniel as he took everything in that he was telling him.

"Tell me, does the memory of your past life still fade in and out from time to time, and do you still feel drawn to it?" Daniel asked Josiah.

"I have a hard time remembering what is real and what isn't as far as my past goes," Josiah admitted.

"That is normal. We all have felt like that after we changed over. Some of us can still remember who we were, and we remember most of our lives that we had before. Some of us have problems remembering like you, once you get here though, for most it all begins to come back again. I think it is being here with us, and being as one pack that brings that about. But a few sometimes do not remember their past lives at all. Many of the rogue ones are like that, they do not remember anything before they became dogmen. They are now only animals with no humanity left in them, and if pushed, they are dangerous to the point of being murderous. We have seen it happen. Unlike us, they are the ones to be feared by the two-legers. They have taken women into the forests with them, they rape them and keep them as slaves, and they are even forced to bear their offspring. Those ones are now multiplying quickly. The young know nothing of their history, all they know is how to be dogmen. Where game is now dwindling, they are beginning to encroach on the two-legers farms on a regular basis, and they are taking their livestock. They are playing a dangerous game with the two-legers. A game that if they are found out and seen, will eventually cause them to be hunted down and killed."

"I never had any idea about any of this. I had no idea," Josiah said in astonishment. *"If you remember your past life. Who were you then, and what did you do in that life?"*

"I used to be a doctor when I was still in human form. I attended a prestigious medical school and graduated top of my class with high honors. A well to do family had adopted me after I was born and gave me a good life, and in return, I made them proud. After having my own practice for several years, that is when I began to slowly change. I was not married at that time, but I was seeing a young woman named Grace, who was also of privilege.

One night when we were out taking an evening stroll, a large lone grey wolf jumped out in front of us and readied itself to attack. Grace screamed and ran, while I stayed and stood my ground. Just as the wolf began to approach for the attack, something else stepped out of the shadows, something large and unlike anything else I had ever saw before. As the wolf leapt at me, in one quick movement, it knocked it out of the air, and when it hit the ground, the wolf was dead. It was that fast. That mysterious creature was the original leader for our pack that came to the mountain top. He was our grandfather. From that moment on, I knew who I was, and what I was to become. I went back to town that night and packed up all my belongings. I told my parents and my girlfriend I had a sudden trip out of town I had to make. When I left, I never went back. They found some of my belongings torn to shreds just outside of town lying next to the dead wolf. The rest of my belongings, medical books and basic equipment I thought that I may need, I brought here with me. I had a long journey to get here, by far longer than you.

247

I did stay close for a short time after I left, but not for long. I just had to make sure that no one would come looking for me. In a newspaper that I found one day that had blown into the woods, I saw where the authorities assumed that the dead wolf that was found, was just one wolf of many in a local pack. They theorized that the rest of the pack had most likely killed me and dragged me off, and that is why they found no body. After that, like you I traveled here, our grandfather showed me the way. Here is where I changed, and now, where I live."

Josiah nodded at Daniel. *"Now I understand why you seem to be so different; you just have a presence about you. Though I have not heard the others speak, you are well-spoken, and more educated it seems. What about my brother though?"* he asked.

"Your brother, like I said, is one that has a problem with distinguishing between who he was, and who he is now. He remains volatile at best. He is getting to where he can no longer be trusted. We try to keep him here on the mountain top with us now at all times, but every so often he will still wander off without us knowing."

"He's the one that attacked my wife and unborn son, and killed my little girl, right?" Josiah asked with anger building in his voice.

"Yes, he was. We knew that your wife was to give birth to a male child. We thought that your brother would be a suitable choice to follow through with the task that had been bestowed upon him. He had been doing so much better at

248

that time. But he slipped out one day without us knowing, and he left far earlier than we had planned. And because of that, he acting before the child was born. He was told that when he did go, that he was to stay hidden and out of sight of all two-legers, and to just wait until after the male child was born, and then when he was able to safely get in to your house undetected, he was to take him from you, and bring him here to live with us. Instead of killing him like is usually done, we were going to raise him until you came yourself. But he didn't do that, he didn't follow the instructions he was given and he went rogue.

When he got to where you lived with your family in the valley, he could smell the pheromones that your pregnant wife was emitting and it was too much for him. We didn't take the huge shedding of pheromones into consideration when he was sent to retrieve the baby. We thought that he would be okay, and he knew that you were his twin brother, that you were direct family to him. We hoped that the relationship that you shared would make a difference, but the pheromones that your wife was emitting as she neared delivery time, they had a stronger effect on him than we had anticipated, and because of that, he lost control."

"Why did you send him when you knew he had problems to begin with!" Josiah demanded to know.

"As I said, we thought that he was strong enough to handle it. He knew what had to be done, and we thought that he could be trusted. He isn't like you though. He had changed earlier then you, his memory of being human has totally faded for him. After he killed your family, he rapidly declined even

249

further and into a much worse mentally deficient state. He is now more animal, than anything."

"Still, why did you send him? You had to of seen some kind of signs that he wasn't well! He killed my family because he is the one you sent!" Josiah told him almost shouting.

"We just didn't know that he was digressing so quickly. He had appeared to be handling his condition better, and accepting how things were going to be for him now before he left, but it was apparent when he returned back to us, that it had only been a temporary state of lucidness that he was in. In reality, it turned out to only be the calm before the storm.

What happened to him mentally between the time that he left here, and when he returned back to us, we don't know. Over the several weeks that he had been gone, he apparently regressed so badly that when he got close to your woman, he couldn't handle the scent of her, and he had to have her for himself. I know that you must have had felt the struggle within yourself by now as well. Imagine that temptation, and that struggle when you no longer were in your right mind. That is the state that your brother was in."

"Yes, I have been there. I was tempted, I was very tempted, but I didn't do anything about it, I fought the urge! I didn't go after the human woman when I easily could have. If I can control myself, then why couldn't he?" Josiah asked as he raised his voice in frustration.

"Like I said, he wasn't in his right frame of mind, and he was not mentally, or morally as strong as you. After the death of

your wife, he thought he saw the boy moving within his dead mother's womb, so he cut it out to deliver it. But he was inexperienced, and the child was born dead."

"Well, what about my little girl, why did he have to kill my daughter!"

"She had witnessed him raping your wife, and cutting the male child from her womb. When he realized what she had seen, he knew that we couldn't take the chance on anyone knowing about our existence. She had seen far too much. She could have told. He didn't want to do it. But he had no choice, one way or another, he had to silence her."

"And my son's body, what did he do with my son's body?" Josiah asked.

"He didn't know what to do with your dead son's body, so he brought his remains here. Your son was already dead when he removed him from your wife's body, he didn't suffer. We then cremated your son and spread his ashes here amongst us," Daniel told him. *"This way he could always be here, and when you got here, you could be together again as well.*

"Well, what about Ava? What about my youngest, he took her? I know that she is still alive, I can feel her inside of me. I also know she is here. Finding her is all that has kept me going."

"Yes, we have her here with us, and she is safe. Don't worry, she has been well taken care of."

Josiah jumped to his feet and towered over Daniel as he stared down at him.

"Where is she? Where is my daughter!" he demanded.

"She is here with us; you will see her soon."

"Where can I find her, I want to see her now!" Josiah demanded loudly as he started to quickly glance around into the darkness.

"You just have to wait. Do not look for her right now. Do not fight us on this, she is not here at this moment, but you will see her when the time is right," Daniel told him.

"Do not look for her again, and do not fight to get her back. If you do, we will kill you, and her both. She is ours now!" Josiah repeated back from the newly triggered memory in his mind. As he took a step closer to Daniel, he again spoke, *"Has that been you in my head all this time? I have been hearing that phrase over and over again. Why don't you want me to look for her? She is my daughter, not yours!"* he screamed.

Two of the other dogmen stood up and quickly began to approach Josiah as he now menacingly towered over Daniel. Daniel looked over at the others and raised his hand to signal for them to stop.

"No, that was not me in your head, but it was your brother. He didn't want you to find her. He felt your presence as you began to get closer, and he wanted to keep your daughter as his own. We didn't know about the messages that he was

sending you telepathically, he was trying to shield them from us, at least until we were able to break through his thoughts with those of our own. We found out that he was doing his best to dissuade you from coming after your daughter, to make you turn around and leave, but I am glad that he failed to do so.

I was the one that you heard earlier than that though. The calling for you to climb higher and higher. The one drawing you closer to us all," he added. "You will see your daughter soon though. Just do not look for her right now, if you do, you will not see her because like I said, she isn't here with us at this moment. All will happen in due time; you have to be patient and wait. She has to be prepared for your arrival. You do not look the same as you did when she saw you last. You are totally different. And she will no longer look the same to you as well. She is no longer that little girl that you remember her as, she has grown over time and is approaching womanhood. We can sense that about her, and considering the urges that we get when around women that are shedding blood, it is no longer good for her to be here. She has to go back to where she came from."

"I want to see her, I don't want to wait, I want to see her now!" Josiah demanded.

"No. I already asked you not to fight us on this, and I've told you why. After what happened with your brother, we have to be sure that we can trust you enough with the safe return of your daughter back to the valley where the two-legers live. We don't want anything to happen to her, she is family to us, more so than you realize," he told him.

253

Josiah silently stared at Daniel for a long moment before setting back down on the rock and lowering his eyes towards the ground.

"Why didn't he just kill her like he had killed the rest of my family?" he asked after a long moment of silence between the two of them. *"He murdered all of them, why not Ava too. What was the difference between them?"*

"Because this one is special, and even he could sense it. She has pure blood. Your other daughter had tainted blood, much like the daughters who were born to all of us that had them. She never would have lived to see her next birthday. Though she was not like us in a sense, and she would not have change like us, she still had enough of your blood in her veins, that her body was constantly fighting against itself. She would have suffered greatly in the end. The two-legers, when they discovered the mutation years ago, they called it a type of childhood cancer, but that isn't what it is, it is beyond their realm of understanding. The reason why they have no cure for it, is that there is no cure. Your brother didn't want to take your daughter's life, but she had seen him, and with being able to smell the bad blood coursing from within her veins, he knew he had to do it. In the end, it was kinder to put her out of her misery before she began to fall ill. Your daughter's symptoms would have started within a few short months, and she would have suffered great pain before she ultimately succumbed to it. Now though, she no longer had to suffer through that. Her sickness and her pain had been removed."

"But you said before it was only the male children that would be killed, you didn't say anything about the female children. I

254

thought they would be okay, you said that the gene was in the male bloodline!"

"Yes, I did. But with the female offspring, they all eventually succumb to an early death. I know I mentioned this, but I didn't continue on to explain it. Yes, there was no need to hasten it with her, but as I said, she saw too much. Usually, we just allow the female offspring to live out their naturally shortened lifespan, and then pass over," Daniel told him.

Josiah just stared at Daniel. He didn't know what to think. There was just too much information being told to him, for him to try to comprehend all at once.

"But your Ava, she was different, like I said, she has pure blood. What your Ava is, is a rarity. She is something that we have never seen before. Though she is your daughter, she has an immunity to your tainted blood coursing through her veins. Your daughter, she is the first to survive out of any of the female children born from our loins. That is why she is here with us. But she is aging now, and she is maturing. She now needs more than we can give her, and soon it will not be safe for her to be here any longer. Once she becomes a young woman, her scent will change, and it will be too strong for any of us here to bear. The scent of first blood is stronger than any. I'm afraid that not one of us would be able to resist her."

Josiah's eyes got wider at the thought of what could happen to his daughter if she were to stay here on the mountain top. Josiah could only stare intently at Daniel; he didn't know what to say. With so much backstory being revealed to him about what had happened to his family, Josiah felt as though

255

he was being overwhelmed. Putting his hands up to his face, he took a deep breath to clear his mind.

"Your daughter needs to return. She needs to return to where the two-legers to live. She needs to adjust back into the world of the humans, and forget about us here. We don't know what will happen when she does go back, or what life holds for her as she gets older. But she can't stay here. She is the only female child to survive the affliction, and we just have no others to compare her situation with. But she needs and deserves to have a normal life, to be able to marry and have children of her own someday. The legacy of our descendants will now continue in a different direction. With the purity of her blood, it is hoped that she may pass on what immunity she has to what we all suffer from to her own children and grandchildren. We will never know though; we most likely will not live long enough to see it come to fruition ourselves. Our blood line as we know it now will end when we pass, it will finally be done."

"But I want to spend some time with her. I am her father, I want and need to get to know my daughter again, and she needs to get to know me as well. Surely you won't deny me..., deny us that time together," he told him.

"I know how you feel, and you will have a chance to spend some time with her before she goes, but it can't be for very long. She has to be returned back to where you lived with your family, and it has to be soon because we can sense that every day that she remains here with us, it is one day closer to when she will experience her first blood. We were all hoping that you would come to the mountain long before this so you

256

could see her and spend more time getting to know her. I have been calling to you for the last few years, but you apparently either couldn't hear me, or you weren't ready to heed the calling."

"Who is to take her back?" Josiah asked.

"It can be you if you wish. We just needed to know that we could trust you, and now I think that we do. I am concerned that once you see her though, that you may not want to let her go back to the life she must lead. You must fully understand that she cannot stay here much longer, nor can she stay with you either. As I said, she is going to be becoming a young woman soon, and it will be too dangerous for her to be here. We cannot protect her, not from ourselves, and not from you. One of us will go with you when you do leave to return her to make sure that you can truly let her go."

Josiah nodded his head. He understood what Daniel was telling him. When Ava becomes a young woman, and goes into estrous and begins to bleed, it will drive them all wild. The wild animal instincts in all of them would take over, and they wouldn't be able to control themselves. Josiah knew far too well what that all-consuming animalistic drive is like, and what control it can have over them. He though back to both of the human women in the field that were within his reach. It was so hard not to go after them both, but even harder not to go for the one that was experiencing first blood herself. He could not imagine how hard it would be for all of them here to be isolated on a mountain top with a young girl of first blood. He understood the importance of why his daughter had to go back, and he would see to it that it happened.

"I will take her back, but I'd like to take her back by myself. I want us to spend what time we have left together alone. I want to get to know my daughter again with no distractions from another. I really want to see her now. Where is she?" he asked.

"She is not ready to see you yet," Daniel told him.

"Why not? I want to see my daughter, and I want to see her now!" he forcefully told Daniel as he stood to tower over him again.

"Your brother Kendal is with her. He has raised her, and has been responsible for her since he brought her here all those years ago. He, for the most part, with our input, has brought her up as his own. Right now, he is telling her about you being here. She has to be able to understand that you are her father, and not him. When she understands that, then you can see her."

"My brother's name is Kendal?"

"Yes, that was his given name by the family that raised him. He grew up differently than you had though. He grew up in a loveless home. His adoptive parents were abusive to him, and beat him often without reason since he was small. He was kept from school, and forced to do the work of two men in the coal mines when he was but just a boy. They refused to even allow him to sleep in the warm house with their family. They made him sleep in the barn with the cattle. They treated him more like an animal than a child. He was their slave. We feel that with that kind of an upbringing, it is why he is the way he

is now. He had run away as a young boy, barely a teen, but five years later when he had returned, he returned as an angry wild animal.

When he began to turn, the first thing he did was kill the family that raised him. He ripped their bodies to shreds out of anger, and left their bodies strewn through their house. He showed them no mercy. When their bodies were found, the doors were still open to the house, and the killing was blamed on a pack of wolves that had moved into the area. They had no reason to think otherwise either. Kendal was out of control at that time. That is when he headed for the mountains, and found us here. We tried to be his family, but at times he made that very tough for us. He was always so angry. After what had happened to your family, we have never allowed Kendal to leave the mountain top again. He has tried, he has walked off, but we always found him quickly and brought him back. He must never be allowed to leave the security of this plateau again.

When you had your dream and your other experiences, that was when Kendal had got into your mind. When he was sending you those messages, that is when had found him standing at the edge of the cliff. He was just standing there staring off into the land below. He was mentally projecting himself to you, and fully entering into your mind. None of us have been able to do that before. We didn't know that it was even possible, but he did it," Daniel told him.

"I kept sensing that someone was there, it felt like someone was watching me, but I couldn't see, nor smell anyone there. The further I came, I would sometimes here a rustling of

leaves, but there was never anything there to be seen as well," Josiah told him.

"That was all Kendal's doing. He made you sense all those things, and hear the leaves rustling and other things as well. It was him all the time. As soon as we picked up on what he was doing, we broke the connection. After you take your daughter back to the two-legers where she belongs, she will be too far away for him to communicate with her any longer. At that point, he will have no influence over her any more. She will be able to make a life of her own, making her own decisions, all while living with the two-legers as she should have been to begin with."

"How did he treat my daughter? Was she happy here?" Josiah asked.

"He treated her very well actually, well beyond belief. For Kendal, having her with him here was a blessing. She always appeared to have a calming effect on him. She was never afraid of him either. Not even once. She saw past his wild dogman exterior, and into the soul of the man that he once was. She could see the hurt child that he had once been, and she comforted him. She could touch that inner child and draw it out of him. He loved her as if she were his own, and she in turn, returned that love back to him ten-fold. Your daughter is a very special girl in more ways than one."

"Right from when she was born, I always felt that she was special. I loved both of my daughters equally, but even I could sense that there was something different with Ava. Even as a toddler she was carefree. She wasn't afraid of anyone or

anything. She would walk right up to a wild animal and show no fear," Josiah told him.

Daniel nodded to Josiah.

"She has special qualities that were born into her, and as she grows older, I hope that she understands the importance of who and what she really is," Daniel told him.

Up on the mountain,
Where the land meets sky,
A secret is well hidden,
One they cannot deny.

There the dogmen wait,
For the last one to arrive,
Once thought to be dead,
But still very much alive.

A brutal fight occurs,
As brother's hatred swarm,
A secret is revealed,
And a child's heart is torn.

The wisdom of a child,
So young and so sweet,
Now sent home to strangers,
With secrets to never repeat.

No time for goodbyes,
Only the howl of gloom,
When the child looks back,
Solitary darkness looms.

BJ Moore

Chapter Eight

As Daniel and Josiah continued to talk, they began to hear the rustling of grass, and the crunching of dry leaves underneath heavy foot falls.

"That must be Kendal now. You must wait here, don't follow me," Daniel sternly warned Josiah.

Josiah stood upright and closely observed Kendal as he stood in the shadows at the other side of the clearing. Silhouetted by the moonlight, Josiah could see the size and the strength that his brother possessed. Though it was hard for him to remain where he was, he abided by what Daniel had just asked of him to do.

Daniel walked over to where Kendal stood, and they began to talk. Josiah tried to listen closely to them with his mind, but it proved challenging for him, for Daniel had closed his mind to him. As he continued to watch the two other dogmen talk, Josiah noted how Kendal was looking back over his shoulder at times. Josiah looked in that direction as well thinking he would be able to see his daughter, but he saw nothing. Again, he turned and looked towards the other two and once more tried to see if he could hear what they were saying, but it was futile.

Josiah could see that his brother kept shaking his head as if he was saying "no" to Daniel, and it looked as though tempers were beginning to flair and that an argument was about to happen between the two. Seeing this, Josiah took a step forward towards where the two dogmen were standing. When the two dogmen that were seated closest to him saw him begin to move forward, they quickly stood up and swiftly moved to position themselves in front of him, blocking his path.

"You have to stay here and let Daniel take care of this himself. He is capable of handling Kendal, he has done it before," one of the other dogmen said to him as he blocked his way. This was the first time that any of the other dogmen besides Daniel had spoken since he arrived.

Listening to what the dogman had said, Josiah realized that he would not be allowed to go any further. Still wanting to see what was going on though, Josiah took a step off to the side so that he could look around the two dogmen that were now blocking his way. As he did this though, he heard a low growl coming from the other dogman that had stayed quiet. Looking at the second dogman in the eyes, he saw that they were serious about him going no further.

"Don't worry, I'm not going over there," he told them out of frustration as he turned and went back to his rock. *"I only*

wanted to watch what was going on with Daniel and my brother," he huffed as he sat. Following suit, the other dogmen also returned to their seats, and sat back down as well.

After what seemed like hours to Josiah, Daniel finally turned and headed back towards the fire where the rest of the group were waiting.

"Kendal says that your daughter is confused about everything he has told her, but that she is ready to meet you. He was reluctant to bring her out to the clearing with you already here, but I reminded him of the reasons why he has to allow her go back to her own kind, and reiterated that she cannot safely stay here. Like it or not, he does understand. He went to get her, and will be bringing her back here to meet you soon," Daniel told Josiah.

"I'm not even sure what to say to her when I do see her. The last time I saw her, she was only three years old, and I was still a man, unlike now," he said as he looked down at his open hands. *"Does she know about her mother and sister?"* Josiah added.

"She does know that her mother is gone, just like she thought that you were gone as well. She was too young to remember anything about when she came here and why, other than that she came here with Kendal. When she comes out to meet you, you will know what to say at that point, and when the time comes, you can tell her what you feel she needs to know of her past," Daniel told him. *"But for now, just give her time to take it all in, and don't rush it. She will need time to mentally*

265

understand what is transpiring now, just like you had to do since you first got here."

After half an hour passed, a figure of a young girl in a flowing light blue dress came walking out of the shadows. Josiah at first had a déjà vu moment, and his heart began to beat wildly. Looking over at Daniel, he saw that Daniel had been looking over at him as well to see how he would react.

"Calm yourself, and breathe deeply my brother," Daniel told him.

Taking a deep breath, Josiah tried to calm himself down as Daniel had suggested. He had to remind himself that none of what was coming back to him from his dream was real, and that it was only what Kendal had been putting into his head. Looking back towards his daughter, Josiah began to realize that in his dream, Kendal's version of Ava had appeared much different than she looked to him now, and with that, it was easier for him to only concentrate on the here and now.

As the young girl progressed further out of the shadows, the moon illuminated the fringes of her dress, and made her appear to glow like an angel. At that point though, another figure stepped out from behind her that towered over her. Josiah glared at the larger figure, knowing that it was his brother.

Together the two of them walked towards where the group sat. As they approached, the young girl momentarily paused and looked over her shoulder at her companion behind her. He looked down at her, and silently placed one of his large hands on her shoulder. Together they continued to slowly approached the area where the others waited.

As they got closer, Josiah stood up and faced them, quickly followed by Daniel doing the same.

"Stay here, let them approach us," Daniel told him as he put his own hand on Josiah's shoulder.

Josiah stood still as he watched the young girl and her escort walk towards the group. When they reached the outskirts of the range of the bright light that the fire had created, the girl and her companion stopped. Using the back of his hand, Kendal nudged the young girl forward one more step so that she now stood before them on her own. Raising her eyes up, she looked at Daniel, and then over to Josiah.

"Stay here and let me go to them. Ava is unsure about all that is going on," Daniel told Josiah as he left his side and walked towards Kendal and Ava. When he got to them, he was the first to break the silence.

"Ava, come forward," he told the girl. Ava nervously looked up at Kendal, but cautiously did as she was told. Kendal began to follow her, but Daniel put his hand up and motioned for him to go no further.

"Let her come alone. Your job with her is now finished. You raised her, you loved her, and now it is time for her father to be reunited with his daughter again," he told him. Kendal looked up and glared at Josiah before reluctantly relenting to Daniel's wishes and staying where he stood.

The young girl slowly walked up to Daniel and stopped in front of him. When she looked up at him, she had the look of fear in her bright blue eyes. Turning her head, she looked back towards Kendal, and then nervously down towards the ground. Anxiously biting her lower lip, she began to fidget with her hands as she held them clasped in front of her.

"Ava, look up at your father," Daniel gently instructed her. Ava only glanced in Josiah's direction, and then back at the ground again.

"Ava, look up at your father," Daniel repeated.

Doing as she was told, Ava slowly raised up her head and looked back at Kendal.

"No child, look up at your real father," he gently told her in a softer voice.

This time when Ava looked up, she looked over to Josiah. Slowly as she looked up to his face, she finally made eye contact with her father. He felt very nervous about how she was reacting, and her reluctance to even look at him. As often as he thought about it, he could never truly imagine what this moment was going to be like for him, the moment when he would finally see her again.

"Ava, it's me, I'm your father," he mentally told her. *"Do you remember me?"* he asked her.

Ava quickly looked away from him in apprehension and quickly shook her head from side to side to indicate that she did not. The young girl began to quiver and bite her lower lip again in apprehension.

"Ava, I can understand you not remembering me, you were only three years old when you were taken from me. Do you remember living in a big house with your mother, and your older sister?" Josiah asked.

Ava paused this time before she answered in a very quiet whisp of a voice. *"Momma?"* she mentally said.

"Yes, your mother and your older sister, we all lived together in a big white house that was surrounded by fields," he told her.

Cocking her head slightly to the left, she quickly looked up into Josiah's eyes, and then swiftly looked away again. Cautiously she slowly raised her eyes again and stared directly into her father's eyes. Her sky-blue eyes shimmered in the darkness as the light from the fiery flames sparkled in them.

"Father?" she mentally asked.

"Yes, yes Ava, I am your father!" he cried out to her as he went towards her to give her a hug. The sudden movement startled her, and she quickly backed away from him in fear. Seeing her reluctance, Josiah stopped and put his eyes down to the ground.

"I'm sorry, I didn't mean to scare you," he told her in a softened tone. *"I should not have approached you so quickly*

like that," he added as he looked back up towards his daughter.

"Where is my Momma and my sister?" she quietly asked. *"I don't remember you, and I can barely remember them. You do not look like my father would; you are only a stranger to me. I know that I had a family a long time ago, but now Kendal and his brothers are my family. They are all I need,"* she told him.

Josiah looked over at Daniel and raised his eyebrows. Daniel looked directly at Josiah, and lightly shook his head no. He knew what Josiah was thinking about, and told him telepathically not to tell her mother and sister. Not to share with her what Kendal had done to her family, it was not the right time.

"Your mother and your sister, they aren't with us any longer. They both died in an accident a long time ago. The night you disappeared, is the night that they left us," he told her. Josiah looked over at his brother Kendal and glared. Kendal bowed his head, and looked down in shame.

"But you lived, didn't you? You didn't die, weren't you in the same accident as they were?" she asked in rapid succession. *"Why didn't you come for me sooner if you wanted me? Kendal told me that my family didn't want me, and that is why I was here. If you wanted me, why didn't you come to find me then, why did you wait until now to find me?"* she asked him as tears began to softly run from her eyes. "What did I do, why didn't you want me?" Ava cried out as she wiped the tears from her eyes with the back of her hands.

"I wasn't home when the accident happened, I was in the fields bringing in the crops before a big storm hit. When I came back in, your mother and your sister were both dead, and you were missing. I had no idea where you were, or how to even find you. I looked for you, I did. I looked for you for years, but not knowing what direction you were taken, I just had no idea where to even look next for you," he explained.

"If you did look for me and couldn't find me then, then how did you find me now?" she demanded as she grew in confidence.

"I finally got close enough that I could feel your presence. I could feel your closeness inside of me, like a missing part of my heart wanting to make me, make us, complete again. Something inside of me began to draw me to you. I don't know what it was, but I knew I had to follow it, I had to follow the calling, and when I did, it brought me here to where you have been," he told her. *"If I had felt it sooner, I would have done everything I could have to get here for you, but Daniel said I just wasn't ready."*

Ava took a step closer, and now stood in front of her father and stared up at him. She stared deeply into his eyes; it was as if she were trying to see through his exterior dogman persona, and into his soul. After staring into her father's eyes for a few seconds, Ava looked down and took a step backward.

"I have something in my bag for you Ava," Josiah said as he turned his head around to look for his sack. Seeing it lying next to the rock he was sitting on, he walked over and picked

it up. As he walked back over to his daughter, he untied the top and opened up the bag. Placing his hand inside of the sack, he took hold of one of the items that it contained, and brought it up out for his daughter to see. What he had withdrawn was the small brown teddy bear that he had carried with him for years, and held it out to her with one of his large hands. Turning the face of the bear towards his daughter, he motioned for her to take it.

"Here, take this," he told her as he held it in front of her to see. *"Do you remember this? I saved it for you and kept it with me for all these years so that when I saw you again, I could give it back to you."* he told her.

Ava looked at the small teddy bear that her father held out to her. Slowly she reached out and touched the bear. She ran her fingers over its face, and then down one of its arms.

"Take it, it belongs to you," he told her.

Ava wrapped her fingers around the bear and took it from her father's hand. She held it in front of her and studied every crease and every fold in the fabric. She touched both of the eyes of the bear with her fingers, and then touched the nose. Then slowly turning it over in her hands, she looked at the back of the bear. Looking at the back of the bear closely, she cocked her head again and paid even closer attention to it as she ran her fingers over some off-colored stitching that held it together.

"Do you remember it, Ava?" Josiah asked his daughter with hope in his voice as he saw how closely she was looking at it.

272

"I remember," she told him. *"I think it was my favorite toy when I was little. I remember that I accidentally put a small tear in the back of it, and Momma sewed up the hole for me to make him all better. The tear was here,"* she said as she pointed to the hand stitching on the back of the bear.

"You slept with that little bear every night. You took it everywhere with you, the two of you were inseparable," he told her.

Without taking her eyes off the small bear, Ava nodded to her father.

"I remember," she quietly told him.

"Your Momma and I used to tuck both of you girls into bed at night. You always wanted the lamp left on; do you remember that?" He asked.

Again, Ava nodded to her father.

"I wanted the lamp left on to keep the monsters out of my room," she told him as she tilted her head again. In her mind, she was reliving the memory from long ago when she was but a toddler. *"But what I had considered monsters back when I was little, I came to soon realize weren't to be feared, and then my monsters turned out to be all of you instead. And you are not monsters at all,"* she said as she looked up from her bear.

"You never said you dreamt about us child," Daniel told her as he stepped closer to her.

"It was so long ago, and it just came back to me," she told him as she looked up into is eyes.

Daniel and Josiah silently looked over at each other as they both began to realize that Ava was even more special than either of them had realized. In her dreams Ava apparently knew about the dogmen from the time she was born. The blood that ran through her veins had revealed all, but she was just too young to understand the importance of what it was showing her.

As Ava continued to look at the small bear that she held in her hands, she looked up at her father standing in front of her, and tears began to slowly run down her face. *"You are my father,"* she quietly cried as she looked up at him.

Josiah knelt down on one knee and opened up his arms and extended them to his daughter. Hesitating at first, Ava then ran into her father's waiting arms. Josiah began to weep as he finally got to hold his daughter in his arms again for the first time since she was little.

"Daybreak will be here soon," Daniel announced to them all around them. *"We should go and get back to our caves now. We live over on the cliff side of the embankment. It is hard to see for anyone who doesn't know that they are there,"* he told Josiah as he looked down to him.

Josiah nodded his head to Daniel.

The others, who had been quietly observing the interaction between father and daughter, got up and began to slowly walk back towards the shadows that engulfed the cliffs. After they disappeared into the darkness, all that remained were Daniel, Kendal, Josiah and Ava.

"Kendal, Ava and her father will stay with me now until they are ready to leave when the next moon rises. Your brother needs to spend some time alone with his daughter, and you can say goodbye tomorrow evening before they go," Daniel told him.

"No, I will not leave her!" Kendal hostilely responded. *"She is my blood, and I raised her! She is mine!"* he snarled aggressively at Daniel as he took a defensive posture.

"You will not fight me on this Kendal! You will do as I say," Daniel told him forcefully as he raised his voice, but again Kendal resisted and snarled at them.

"No!" he said as he took a threatening step towards where Josiah and Ava stood. Josiah quickly reached down to his daughter and picked her up into his arms. Now with her secured in his grasp, he quickly turned and moved her protectively behind him. Ava now positioned behind her father, leaned over and peered out from around him to look at Kendal.

"Ava, stay behind me and do not come out. It isn't safe," he told her as he used one of his hands to nudge her back out of sight, while keeping his eyes and full attention on Kendal.

"Kendal, do not do this!" Daniel sharply ordered him while baring his own teeth and snarling.

275

B.J. MOORE

Ignoring Daniel, Kendal menacingly took another step towards Josiah. Josiah then took a protective defiant step towards Kendal as well.

"Daniel, you need to get her out of here, take Ava away to safety," Josiah quickly told him as he kept his eyes on Kendal.

Knowing that Kendal was now beyond the scope of his control, Daniel quickly moved in behind Josiah, and in one swift move he scooped Ava up into his own grasp and quickly lifted her up into his arms. Without even skipping a step, Daniel quickly carried Ava to another part of the field that was only a short distance away, but yet far enough to provide a safe retreat if necessary.

The other dogmen that had left heard the loud confrontation beginning between Kendal and Josiah, and stopped where they were and turned back to see what was happening. Seeing a fight brewing between the two brothers, they quickly began to run forward towards Kendal to stop him, but Daniel motioned for them to stay put. This battle was between the two of them, and Kendal had to learn that Ava was no longer his. If Josiah proved not to be able to stand up to his brother, then they would step in and take control of the situation, and of Kendal himself.

"She belongs to me brother!" Kendal aggressively growled at Josiah as he leaned in closer towards him.

"No Kendal, she is my daughter, not yours! You have no right to her. You stole her from me after you murdered my wife and children. And you stole her mother, sister and baby brother

276

from us both!" he growled back. *"We may share the same blood, but you cannot have my daughter!"* he told him.

Daniel held Ava close to him as they both watched and listened to what was transpiring between the two brothers. Ava looked up at Daniel with shock on her face. He knew that she had heard what her father had just said about what Kendal had done to her family.

"You weren't to know about this child, you weren't supposed to know, not yet and not in this way. I wanted to protect you from ever knowing what really happened," he told her as he gently held her head against his chest. Daniel could feel Ava starting to softly cry in his arms.

Kendal was the first to get aggressive and make a hostile move as he took a swipe at Josiah with one of his large clawed hands, but Josiah being quicker than his brother, moved out of the way just before he could connect with his blow.

"Don't do this brother, I'm begging of you. It doesn't have to be this way. Even though you took so much from me that day, I still do not want to hurt you, you don't know what you are doing right now," Josiah told him.

"You don't tell me what to do! No one tells me what to do any longer," Kendal roared as he leaped at his brother. The two dogmen aggressively pushed each other back and forth, kicking up dirt with their feet as they struggled with each other in the darkness. The blood curdling snarls and the snapping of teeth echoed in the air around them, causing Ava

to shudder at the sound and bury herself in deeper into Daniel's chest.

As they fought, Kendal saw an opening and temporarily seized that moment to take the advantage. He grabbed a hold of Josiah, and forcefully shoved him off to the side of him where the rocks were placed in the circle. As Josiah stumbled backwards, he lost his footing and fell over the rock that he had been sitting upon earlier, and tumbled to the ground behind it.

With Josiah now on the ground, Kendal quickly turned and began to run towards where Daniel and Ava stood. Seeing this, Josiah quickly got to his feet and ran after his brother. Running as fast as he could, he caught up to him and leapt onto Kendal's back. He grabbed at his brother's shoulders and dug his mighty claws deep into his flesh. First blood had now been drawn, and the real battle would ensue.

Kendal cried out in pain as he reached behind him and grabbed at his brother while he still clung to his back. Reaching for whatever he could get within his grasp, he was finally able to grab hold of one of Josiah's forearms. As he took Josiah's arm in both of his hands, he heaved him up over his shoulder and flung him forcefully down onto the ground before him.

As Josiah hit the ground, Kendal leapt down at him again. Josiah saw him coming and swiftly rolled off to the left side to get out of Kendal's way. After quickly getting back up onto his feet, Josiah turned to once more faced his brother. Snarling at him, Josiah clenched his teeth.

Now on all fours, Kendal laid his ears back and snarled at his brother. He now had a different look to him, and his eyes showed every bit of animalistic fury that there was within him. Josiah now fully understood what Daniel meant when he told him about Kendal being more animalistic than human. The wild look that Kendal had in his eyes at this moment, the hatred he was putting forth, just proved to him how truly unpredictable that Kendal really was.

Josiah stood and stared at his brother. He didn't want to fight him, but Kendal was giving him no choice. As Kendal leaped at his brother again, Josiah also dove forward. They impacted against each other with a loud deadened thud. The echo of the collision carried through the air and was heard over and over again as it dissipated in the wind.

Snarling and scratching at each other, the two dogmen fought furiously. With Josiah gaining the advantage this time, he bit down hard into the flesh of Kendal's upper arm, and as he did so, his teeth sank down into the bone itself. Hearing the bone crack under the strength of his jaws, Josiah quickly let go of his brother and backed off.

Kendal howled out in pain as blood began to run from his wound. Glaring at his brother with hatred in his eyes, Kendal once more turned and prepared for another attack. Bleeding heavily from his injuries, Kendal continued to want to fight on. With his arm now rendered useless and hanging limply at his side, Kendal used his other arm to yet again take a swing at Josiah, but he missed. Though Kendal was the larger of the two brothers, there was no way he could now effectively fight against Josiah, who had proved to be a worthy adversary.

"I don't want to do this Kendal! I don't want to hurt you!" Josiah told his brother. But again, like a rabid animal, Kendal charged at his brother. Josiah quickly moved out of the way and pushed Kendal into the rocks that he himself had just previously fallen over.

Kendal cried out in frustration and pain as the already damaged arm slammed into the corner of one of the rocks. Getting to his feet, Kendal again charged at Josiah, and again Josiah dodged him and moved out of his way. With his own ineffectiveness now being shown, it only served to add to Kendal's extreme animalistic rage.

"Kendal No!" Ava screamed at him from where she now stood in front of Daniel. She had used her real voice for the first time since her father had arrived. Daniel reached out and put one of his hands on her shoulder offering her his support and backup.

Kendal stopped and slowly turned his head to look at the girl. His hardened face and blazing eyes immediately began to soften when he saw her.

"Kendal, my dear Kendal," she said softly to him. *"You must stop. If I mean anything to you at all, you must stop fighting with him now!"* she mentally told him. *"He is my father. I love you dearly, but he is my real father. I don't want you to hurt him, and I don't want you to be hurt either,"* she told him calmly.

"He is taking you away from me," he told her as he looked over at Josiah and growled.

"He is my father, Kendal. You raised me, you took care of me and protected me for most of my life, but now it is time to let me go. You told me yourself this evening that it was time, and that I had to go back to the village where I had come from before you brought me here. You cannot keep me here any longer. I have to return to my own kind, to people who look like me," she told him in a soothing voice as she and Daniel began to walk closer to him. Daniel allowed her to walk in front of him, to let her be the center of Kendal's focus, but yet staying only a few steps behind her, and still within reach if necessary.

Kendal stood up and cautiously slowly backed away from Josiah. While still keeping a close eye on his adversary, Kendal walked over to where Ava and Daniel now stood. Now feeling safe enough to take his eyes away from Josiah, he lovingly looked down at the girl.

"I do not want to lose you little one," he told her. *"I am afraid that you will forget me."*

"I will always love you, and I will never forget you. If you love me like you say you do, then you must let me go," she told him as she looked up at him.

Kendal slowly reached out with his good hand, and she carefully placed her hand into his. They looked deeply into each other's eyes, and as he stared into the bluest depths of her being, it was as if her heart beat was now that of his own, and her breaths, were also part of his. He felt as if they were once again as one. Still looking deeply into her eyes, Kendal then saw himself in their reflection. Lowering his head, he nodded. Ava was showing Kendal in her own way, that he will always be a part her, and that she will always be a part of him as well.

"You are hurt, and you need to heal now. You must go and rest your arm," she told Kendal as she looked up at his still bleeding upper arm.

Daniel now took a step forward and protectively came to stand beside Ava. Looking up at Kendal, he then spoke.

"You must go now. Go back to the shelter with the others and rest. Your arm is broken, and it will need time to heal. I will make sure that you will see her again before she goes," he told him with a tone of authority in his voice. Kendal shook his head in agreement. Lowering his eyes in submission, he turned to leave. Before he did though, he looked over at Josiah and paused for a moment.

"I am sorry brother for what I have done," he said to him before he turned back and continued to walk to where the others still waited. He only took a few steps before he heard Josiah speaking back to him.

"I am sorry as well Kendal," Josiah called after him. Kendal stopped and started to turn and look back towards Josiah. As he took a step towards his brother, he suddenly stopped and looked over to where Daniel and Ava still stood watching him.

"Kendal, you go must now," Daniel told him. *"You must go back to your cave and stay there until you are called for. You do not have a choice in this matter."*

Looking back at the others who still stood watch, Daniel motioned for them to come and escort Kendal away. After looking back at Daniel, and showing little resistance to the order that was made, Kendal turned his back on the three of them and walked off into the darkness, while flanked on either side by two of the other dogmen.

"Josiah, you and Ava will come to my den for the night. You will be safer there with me in case Kendal decides not to obey again. We have our own laws and rules here, but he never ceases to put them to the test. He is unpredictable at best as you can see, so as I said, you both will be safer there with me than you would be by yourselves. Ava was able to stop him this time, but I don't know if she could do it again if he once more lost control," Daniel told him as he motioned with his hand for them to follow him. Josiah reached down and grabbed his sack up off the ground and carried it with him as he and Ava followed Daniel as he headed to the edge of the woods.

As they entered the tree line, Josiah looked up and saw where there was a series of caves that were strewn throughout the cliffside. They were barely visible to the naked eye, and were so well hidden by the trees that had grown from the crevasses around them, that he now understood when Daniel said that even by the light of day, that they would remain quite well hidden from the prying eyes of others. For the dogmen, it was a perfect place for them to live in seclusion.

"Come, this one is mine," Daniel said as they got closer to where they were going. Daniel led Josiah and Ava up a small

283

path until they came to the highest entryway in the network of caves. Daniel paused at the entrance, and motioned for Josiah and Ava to go in first. As they entered, Daniel turned and scanned the path below them for any signs of movement before following the other two in.

"You can sit anywhere you would like," Daniel told them as he entered the cave. Ava knew the cave quite well, but Josiah curiously looked over the interior. Navigating by the bright light of the moon, Daniel went to the far corner and picked up a blanket. He handed it over to Ava, who then spread it out on the floor before she sat down upon it. After reaching over and picking the stuffed bear back up from where she had temporarily set it while laying out the blanket, Ava began to look at it and run her fingers over every seam and to inspect every inch of it.

"Where did you get your blankets, and the clothes that you needed for Ava?" Josiah asked Daniel after seeing the various items he had for her there.

"We would make trips down the mountain as we needed things for her. We would take blankets from the two-legers as well as clothing that they had left hanging out overnight. We would gather what we could, and then return back here with it. The last trip down we made was two years ago. We always got clothing of differing warmth's, and in larger sizes than she wore when we went so that it would allow for her to grow into them."

"Surely you had more than just blankets for her to keep her warm in the winter," Josiah commented.

"Yes, we also had skins from deer that we fed upon. I tanned them made her a warm coat and warmer blankets to use, she used them for extra warmth during the coldest months. They are in Kendal's cave though and not here," he told him.

Josiah nodded.

"The rest of her things are in Kendal's cave as well, and we will get them for you later. The hides have to stay here though. She cannot have them with her when she goes back, it would cause far too many questions," Daniel told him as he slightly paused.

"At sundown, we will pack her a bag and you and she can head out. It will be just the two of you as you requested. I know now that we can trust you to do what you need to do. We will make sure that Kendal remains here with us after you leave. If he tries to follow, we will be forced to take action against him. I don't wish it to come to that, but we will do what we must to ensure everyone's safety."

Josiah looked up at Daniel and nodded. He understood what Daniel had meant. If Kendal tried to follow them, or to interfere in any way with them leaving, he would be harshly with dealt with by the others, and maybe even lose his life in the process. Josiah hoped that it didn't come to that though. Even though Kendal had killed his family, he loved his daughter and raised her as his own. He protected her and nurtured her for years on this mountain top. Ava loved Kendal as much as he loved her, and Josiah did not wish her hurt by what may happen to Kendal if he tried anything. She has already lost so much in her life as it was, he didn't want

285

her to lose more. Josiah also knew that Kendal was not right mentally, and that is what had caused him to do what he did. He couldn't hold his brother's mental condition against him, not now knowing what had most likely caused it.

Daniel watched Josiah carefully. He knew what was going on in his mind.

"Yes, what you are thinking is correct. Kendal is progressing more towards the animal side of his existence than the human side, much like the others have that have gone rogue. If it comes to that, we cannot allow it, and he will have to be dealt with. We don't want it to come to that, but we cannot permit him to leave this plateau in the mental state that he is in now. We must keep him here at all cost, and if he ever were to escape, it would be necessary for everyone's safety, dogmen and human alike, that he be put down."

Josiah shook his head in understanding. Daniel was right, if Kendal were ever leave, he was too much of a danger to others, that was already proven.

"I didn't realize that Ava still knew how to use her voice to communicate. How long has she been able to do that? I just assumed that being raised by nonverbal creatures such as ourselves, that the use of her vocal cords would have not been necessary," Josiah quietly said to Daniel while Ava was distracted by her stuffed bear.

"Ava has always known how to talk by using her voice. When she first got here, she had a limited vocabulary because of her age. I saw to it that she retained her ability to verbally

286

communicate, and gave her probably more than what is now considered a basic education so that when the day did come that she had to go back, she would be ready."

Josiah nodded to Daniel as he looked lovingly over at his daughter.

"Ava," Daniel began.

The young girl looked up at him.

"You do realize that you can never speak of us when you return to your kind. The two-legers like yourself must never know about us, or that we ever existed. If they did, they would do everything in their power to destroy us. Humans have a tendency to destroy anything and everything that they do not understand. And the fact that we are so vastly different than they are, they would never stop hunting us down until we were all no more."

Ava shook her head yes. Through Daniels influence and teaching, the girl was wise beyond her years. Her vocabulary was better than many humans of her age, and she fully understood the importance of the situation they were now in because of her, and the importance of her vow of silence.

For only the second time since her father had arrived, Ava chose to speak out loud. "Yes, I understand. I could never tell anyone about you, you are my family. I know that to do so would mean the death of all of you here, and others elsewhere, and I can't do that to you. I love you all too much," she told him. And then looking over at her father, "I did hear you asking Daniel about my ability to talk, it is your blood in me that gave me the ability to hear thoughts and communicate through thoughts, but it was also Momma's blood that gave me the ability to retain the human side of what I truly am. Daniel has taught me well during my time here, and through him I lack nothing. When I return, I will be fine, I know everything I need to know and more," she told him assuring.

Josiah moved over closer to his daughter, and carefully put his arm around her to give her a reassuring hug.

"Ava, now that you are leaving us, I think it is important for you to continue to use your voice instead of your mind to communicate. You need to become accustomed to it, you need to fit in with the other two-legers in the valley below," Daniel told her.

Ava nodded to Daniel and said, "I will do that."

Josiah turned his head, and when he did, he caught a reflective glint of something metal off to the side of where Daniel now sat. Looking at it curiously, he cocked his head off to the side. Daniel looked over to where Josiah was looking and then reached over and held the item up in front of him.

"How did you get that? Where? Wait...I thought I had lost that knife a long time ago," Josiah stated with confusion in his voice.

"You didn't lose the dagger; I took it back from you. It is a ceremonial dagger that had been handed down through the

generations of our pack. It has been here on this mountain top for over one hundred years. It was created by one of the first dogmen of our bloodline. When I saw that you had it, I had to bring it back to where it belonged before it was lost to us again."

"How did you get it? I know I had it with me when I fled into the mountain's all those years ago. After I had went through the change, that is when I noticed it missing, I thought that I had somehow managed to lose it."

"Do you remember much from when you changed? Do you remember that there was someone there that was taking care of you?"

"Yes, I do but I have no idea who it was. I was so in and out of it, I don't remember much other than that," Josiah said.

"That was me. I was the one there with you for weeks to make sure your change was successful. You were having problems, and you were very ill and almost died. I hunted for you and made sure that you were well fed and kept warm. Without me, you would have died during the change."

"Is the change that hard for everyone else as it was for me?"

"No. For some it can be easy, but I could sense that you were very ill, so I came to you. It was then that I found the ceremonial dagger. It was something that Kendal had taken with him when he headed for the valley. We didn't know that he had taken it until after he had gone. It is what was used to take the life of your oldest daughter."

289

"If you were there when I changed, why didn't you bring me here at that point?" Josiah asked him.

"Because you were not ready. You had to deal with your change, and come to terms with what had happened to your family, and we couldn't do that for you. It wasn't until after you dealt with what had happened to you, that you could then hear the calling to come here."

"I have noticed that my memories are slowing returning from my past as I spend more time here with you, just like you said they may. I remember that after Kendal killed the sheriff, that the knife was there at the jail. It had been stuck down into the top of a wooden desk. When I escaped, I grabbed the knife. I don't know why, but something inside of me just told me to grab it, so I did."

"I am glad that you did. It is now in its rightful place again, here with us," Daniel told him. *"More of your past memories may return to you when you come back here to live permanently. It has that effect on some, but like I also said, not on all unfortunately though. The fact that you are already beginning to remember is a good sign though."*

Josiah nodded to him.

"Now, both of you need to get some rest. It is best if you leave here shortly after dusk to make your way back down the cliff side. It is treacherous for one, but you will be climbing down for two. I will pack some food for Ava to eat while you both sleep. She does not eat what we eat, we never allowed her to consume raw meat like we do. We did our best with her, to

rear her up and provide her with what she needed emotionally, physical and mentally," Daniel told Josiah.

Josiah nodded to Daniel. *"Thank you for what you have done. I can see that you took good care of her,"* he told him. Josiah was grateful for what Daniel had done for his daughter, and the influence that he had over her rearing in the time that she had been there with them.

"We are all family; we knew that the girl that Kendal had returned with was also family, but after knowing the situation with you and what you were then facing, that there was no way that we could safely return her. We all had a part in Ava's raising. Rest assured, it wasn't only Kendal who took care of her, we all monitored everything dealing with Ava from the start," Daniel told him. *"Now go ahead and get settled in, you both will need your rest so you can get an early start. You have a long trip ahead of you."*

Daniel went over to where the small pile of blankets was laying and brought over another one for them to use. He then handed it over to Josiah. Looking to his daughter, Josiah motioned for Ava to follow him over to a darker area of the cave that was further away from the entrance. Ava followed her father and then laid upon the blanket that he had spread out.

"Where are you going to lay?" Ava asked her father.

"I don't need the blanket, it is for you to use," he told his daughter after she laid down. Josiah then took the other blanket and placed it over top of her to keep her warm.

291

After Josiah laid down on the floor next to his daughter, they both quickly fell asleep. Josiah didn't have any bad dreams that night, and for the first time in years, he slept totally unencumbered with his soul truly at rest.

As Ava laid next to her father, he felt her small body shiver from the cold. Instinctively, he rolled over and put his arm up over her small frame to help share his body heat. Upon seeing this, Daniel got up and retrieved another blanket from the shadows in the cave. Taking it over to the sleeping duo, he carefully unfolded it and gently cover them both up with it.

Chapter Nine

Josiah awoke to find that his daughter was already up and dressed. Daniel had fixed her a breakfast of fruit and a variety of cooked edible plant roots that he foraged for earlier. Daniel had also had her dressed in more appropriate traveling clothes for her long trip down the mountain. Two years prior to her leaving, their scouts had secured a pair of long pants, and a heavier shirt that would keep her warm. Though still a little baggy on her, both items would serve her well. This particular outfit was obtained in preparation for the time that they all knew was soon to come. The time when Ava would have to go home.

"Ah, I see you are awake now my brother, did you sleep well?" Daniel asked Josiah when he noticed him beginning to sit up.

"Yes, I did. Is evening now approaching?" he asked.

"Not yet, but the hour is drawing near. I went to Kendal's earlier and retrieved the two dresses that Ava's had from when she was little. It was all she came with. On the way back

here though, she decided that she wanted you to have them to remember her by. I will keep them here for you until you return back to us. Kendal still is not happy about her leaving with you, but I do not think he will cause any further problems with the two of you when you go. You proved yourself last night to him, you were a worthy opponent. Even though the fight between you was halted by your daughter, you have gained his respect. If he does try anything when you get ready to leave, we will deal with it then. I allowed him to say goodbye to the girl while I was there, I felt that he at least deserved that right," he told him. *"He will not be present though when you leave, he was told to now stay in his cave until you were gone."*

"Good. I didn't want to hurt him yesterday, but he left me no choice," Josiah said as he nodded to him. *"And I want to thank you for everything, and for keeping the dresses here for me."*

"I know you didn't want to hurt him. Because of the animosity he holds though, I thought it best that the two of you did not have any further interaction until you return from taking your daughter home. We will deal with any problems or issues that remain between the two of you at that point," Daniel told him.

Josiah nodded in agreement.

"When do we leave?" Josiah asked Daniel.

"You may depart for the valley again as soon as we finish getting everything ready. Dusk will be upon us shortly, and

then when it is dark, you can leave at any time. Like I said, I already have a pack readied for Ava. I put two blankets in there for her. She gets cold up here on the mountain this time of the year, and she needs the extra warmth that they will provide her. She also has more than enough food to get her down off the mountain contained in her sack as well. You will have to hunt for yourself though, I'm sure you will have no issue with that," Daniel told him.

"Thank you. We will be fine. Thank you for taking care of my little girl, protecting her and watching over her for all these years. She is one special little girl; I just didn't realize how special until now."

"I think that what she told us earlier about her dreams she had as an infant of monsters, of monsters that later eventually became us here, proves that she is more special than any of us have actually realized. It also explains why she wasn't afraid of Kendal when she first saw him, nor of us when she first came into contact with us. It was because she already knew about us and had already lost her fear of us by that point. It was almost like a premonition of sorts, just explained out to her so that a small child like her could understand it," Daniel stated.

Josiah nodded and turned and looked for his pack. Upon seeing it laying behind him where he had been sleeping, he got up to his feet and went to retrieve it. Bringing it back over, he sat down on the floor of the cave and opened the bag up and took something out.

"Ava, come here," he said as he called out to his daughter.

The girl did as she was told and happily came over and sat down next to her father. He slowly handed her the time worn photograph of her family that he had been keeping for her to see.

"This is your Momma and your sister, and that there, that is you," he told her as he pointed to the infant in the picture.

As Ava lightly touched the faces on the worn photograph with her index finger, a tear began to run down her cheek.

"I think that remember all of you now," she told him. "I now remember how you looked before I left and was brought here. I remember how you would come in from the fields, and we would all eat our dinner at the table. I remember laughing at the faces that you..." she began until she momentarily paused in mid-sentence to looked up at her father. "The funny faces that you would make at us, and how you would tickle us as we played," she finished.

"I want you to have this picture now. I don't want you to ever forget us again. I will keep you all alive in here now," he said as he pointed to his head with one of his fingers, *"and in here,"* he told her as he then laid his hand over his heart.

Ava smiled at her father and then rose to take the photo over to Daniel so he could see it too. He looked at the photo and then over at Josiah, before then turning his attention back to Ava again.

"Very nice, you were but a young pup then," he told her. *"I do see the resemblance between you and your mother. Your*

mother was a fine-looking woman, and you will be as well when you are grown."

Ava smiled at Daniel and then looked over towards her father and smiled at him again as well as he came to stand beside them.

After Daniel handed the photo back down to Ava, she carefully put it away in her own bag. Standing next to Daniel and her father, she noticed how dwarfed by the two of them that she actually was. Standing next to two eight-foot plus dogmen made her almost four-and-a-half-foot frame look much tinier, and her petite appearance made her age look much younger than she really was.

"How old are you now?" Josiah asked his daughter. *"You had just turned three when you were taken from me all those years ago, and for me, the years have all run together after that day."*

Ava looked up at Daniel and shrugged. She had no idea herself how long she had been there.

"I believe that she has been here with us for nine winters now. It is hard for us to keep track of time. As with you, our time runs together because there is no need to keep track of it. We only estimate time when we need to."

"So, my little girl is 12 years old now, going on 13," Josiah said as he smiled at his daughter, and she smiled back. *"Your birthday was in March…. March 19th, I believe,"* he told her. *"I guess you need to know that for when you go back."*

297

"You must get yourself ready to go now little one, it is time. Darkness has settled over the mountain top now, and it is time for the two of you to get ready travel," Daniel told them as he picked up Ava's bag and headed for the opening of the cave.

Stepping outside into the cool night air, Ava shivered despite her warmer clothing that she now wore. Some areas higher up in the peaks of the mountain had already begun to see snow, and the rest, including the one that they were on now, were not far behind. The clouds that had covered the peaks that Josiah had saw earlier, were now blackened and carrying the threat of bad weather. He knew that winter would soon be settling in, and by the signs he was seeing, it would come early this year, and when it did come, the snow and ice would again take over the earth.

Josiah looked over at Daniel with concern. He too looked up at the dark clouds and sighed.

"I think the storm will hold off long enough for you two to make some good progress downward, but you will need to be swift," Daniel told him.

Josiah nodded to Daniel and looked back down at his daughter.

"Come, you must leave now before Kendal comes out of his cave. I still do not fully trust him not to try something. Darkness will only be with you for so long, and you need to cover much ground before daylight breaks again," he told them.

"I feel as if a whole new life is beginning here for me," Josiah said as he looked at Daniel.

"That is because it will be a new life. You will have no fear here, no one hunting you any longer, and you will be free," Daniel told him. *"And this new beginning also holds true for Ava as well. She is going to be beginning a whole new life of her own, and that new beginning will be with humans like herself."*

Josiah nodded his head to his new friend before putting his hand on Ava's back and pulling her closer to him.

"You will travel faster if you are on all fours as you already know. Ava has ridden before, and knows how to hold on well. The travel will be more dangerous for both of you now with her being with you, but I know that you will protect her. I know you well enough now to know that you would give up your life for your daughter," Daniel said as he looked at Josiah.

"Yes, I would. My daughter will be safe, I can guarantee that. I will travel as you suggested to make better time. When I have returned her back to the two-legers, and when I know that she will be safe, then I will return here. I do not belong down in the valley any longer, not now with what and who I am. Our kind will never be accepted by the two-legers. We are far too different than they are."

Ava turned and looked up at Daniel with tears in her eyes. She was going to miss her mountain family, she would miss all of them, but she was going to miss Kendal and Daniel the most. They were the only family she had known for so many years, and it was hard giving them up.

"Good bye little one," Daniel told her with love in his eyes. Letting go of her father's hand, Ava turned back to Daniel and gave him a big hug. He gently put one hand on her back, and the other on her head and stroked her long blond hair. He was going to miss her as well.

"Have a good life little one. We will all miss you, and we will never forget you. You are one of us and you always will be," Daniel told her. *"Now go and be with your father. You have a long trip ahead of you."*

Ava nodded to Daniel and then as she wiped away the tears from her eyes, she again joined her father.

"When you return brother, we will welcome you back here to live and be one with us. Even Kendal will come around in time. The others have come out to say good bye to you and Ava," Daniel said as he motioned to the mouths of the other caves along the pathway that they took to get to where they were. In front of all the occupied caves, a single dogman stood. *"I will walk with you to the edge of the plateau to see you off,"* Daniel told them as they began their decent down the edge of the cliff.

As the three of them walked past the others on their way back down the path, the other dogmen all nodded their heads, put their clenched fist over their hearts, and said, *"Safe travels brother and little sister, safe travels be with you."*

Josiah looked at them each individually and bowed his head to show them respect, while Ava slightly raised her hand and waved to them as more tears flowed from her eyes. She was really going to miss her mountain family, as they will miss her.

Memories of Ava's old family, her human family, were still just vague glimpses of what at one time her life was like. She didn't want her new memories of her mountain family to get lost like these ones did. She was hoping that someday she would begin to remember more of her human family, but for now she would take what memories she still had and cherish them forever.

When the three of them reached the grassy area in the center of the plateau, Josiah turned and looked at Daniel. He extended his hand out to him in gratitude and they shook.

"Thank you for looking after my little girl while she was here. With how I am now, and what I went through to get to where I am today, I don't think that I would have been much of a father to her even if she had been with me. To watch me go through the change, I think that would have been very frightening for her, especially after what you told me I went through," he said to Daniel as he glanced down at his daughter.

"Yes, even though Kendal didn't follow direction and went only by his animal instincts, him bringing the girl here was ultimately what needed to be done. Leaving her there while you were being charged with murder, who knows where she would have ended up. At least here she had freedom, and she

301

had family. He did what needed to be done, just like you taking her back now, it is what needs to be done for her own good."

Josiah nodded to Daniel in agreement.

"Good luck to you," Daniel told him. *"And you little sister, you remember to keep our secret. We will miss you here, but hold you here and here,"* he said as he motioned to his head, and then to his heart before kneeling down to give the girl a hug.

"Are you ready Ava?" Josiah asked as he looked down at his daughter. She nodded to her father and then watched as he got down on all fours in preparation of her mounting his back.

After taking the strings from her sack and securing them around her waist, Ava carefully climbed up onto her father's back. Josiah looked down at his own bag. There was no real need for him to take it with him now. What were the most important items to him that were in there, were now in the possession of his daughter anyway. In Ava's bag, Daniel had packed two warm blankets, along with some food, but it now also contained her small teddy bear as well as the picture of her family that Josiah had given her. It was that picture, and the small teddy bear that had meant more to Josiah than anything else, and now it means just as much to his daughter.

Daniel, reading Josiah's thoughts nodded to him. He would take the bag back with him and store it until he returned.

Ava looked up and smiled at Daniel one last time before reaching down and burying her hands deep into the fur on her father's back. After she knew they were tight, she gave them one final tug.

"I am ready father," she told him.

"Good bye my family, swift and safe travels," Daniel told them as they started walking off across the open grass. Daniel remained vigilant where he stood to keep a watchful eye out for Kendal in the event that he would decide to come out to watch the two of them leave the mountain top. He did not totally trust that Kendal would allow them to leave without making a scene.

Pausing at the edge of the field where it met the wood line, Josiah turned and looked back towards Daniel, and the place that he was now going to call home for the rest of his life. With the exception of Kendal, the other dogmen now were all standing with Daniel watching them as they departed. Then, as if in unison, the group all began to howl. Their voices carried and echoed in the air around them. Tipping his own head up, Josiah answered them back with a long-drawn-out howl of his own.

When silence again took over the mountain top, Josiah turned back and looked out into the darkness before him. Taking one step after the other, they entered into the shadows of the trees and disappeared into the blackness of the night.

They had traveled a good distance before Josiah decided to stop and rest. After he found a good spot for them, Ave climbed down off of her father's back and sat down on a rock.

303

"There is fresh water there if you would like to go and get a drink," he told her. He had stopped near a small creek that he was familiar with, and had visited himself on his way up the mountain.

Ava got up to her feet and they walked a short way over to it. Lowering down onto her knees, Ava dipped her hands down into the cold spring water and brought it up to her lips. After she was satisfied, she stood back up. Josiah waited until his daughter was done drinking before he bent down and began to lap up the water to quench his own thirst.

"Are you hungry?" Josiah asked his daughter as they walked away from the creek side. Ava looked at her father and shook her head no. The little girl was being very quiet. She hadn't said a word since they had left the plateau of the dogmen many hours before.

"Are you okay? "I You are being very quiet," Josiah gently asked.

"Yes, I'm fine. I am just nervous about going back to a place and to people that I don't know. Maybe they won't want me there," she told her father in a quiet voice.

"Well, I know that they will want you. You will have a home there, and you will be with your own kind. You will have other children your own age to play with too. This is what I want for you. A normal life. This is also what Daniel and the others want for you as well."

Ava silently nodded to her father.

"When you get there, make sure to tell them who you are. Tell them that your name is Ava Wolfe. Tell them that your father was innocent of what happened that day so long ago, and that it was someone that you had never seen before in town who murdered your mother, and sister Anna. Can you do that for me? I don't want you to go through life with people thinking and talking behind your back that your father had killed your mother and sister. Tell them that this man had kidnapped you, and that when he died, you were finally able to escape and came home. Don't tell them from where you came from, just tell them you walked until you found your way back."

"I will. I will tell them you weren't at fault for anything that happened to Momma and Anna," she told him.

"Thank you," Josiah told her as he carefully gave her a hug.

As Josiah hugged his daughter, he heard the rustling of leaves. Ava nervously looked at her father and moved closer to him.

"It's okay, look," he told her as he pointed in the direction of the noise. Just then they saw a rabbit come out of the nearby brush pile and begin to hop down to the creek.

Josiah looked down at his daughter and she nodded her head to him. She knew what he wanted to do, and she wanted to let him know it was alright if he needed to hunt. She had seen the others do it many times in the past, it didn't frighten her. She knew that he needed to hunt to eat, it is how they survived.

Josiah hugged his daughter again before getting up and disappeared into the shadows. Not long after her father left, Ava heard the rabbit squeal, and her father quickly returned with his prey in hand.

Josiah sat down and looked over at Ava before he turned his back to his daughter. Though he was sure that she had seen the other dogmen eat their meals, how couldn't she not have, but she hadn't seen him eat like this, and at that moment, he felt almost ashamed of what he had become. Sensing her father's discomfort, Ava got up and moved to his side.

"It is alright," she told him as she stroked the hair on his back. "Go ahead and eat, you need your strength. I will go over to the big tree and wait for you to finish," she told him. Still uncomfortable, Josiah glanced up at her and nodded. Then he turned to finish his meal.

Daybreak would soon be rising over the horizon, so he knew that they needed to begin to look for shelter. Remembering where the cave was that he had used before, he took his daughter by the hand and headed for it.

Pausing at the entrance of the cave, Josiah bent down and carefully sniffed the air to see if there was any sign of anything that may have moved in. It was still empty, so Josiah motioned for his daughter to go in first and then he followed right behind her.

"I can't believe how much you have grown since I saw you last. You are turning into a young lady right before my eyes,"

he told her as he watched her spread out one of the blankets on the cave floor. *"You were so tiny when Kendal took you from me,"* he then added.

"He did take good care of me; I want you to know that. He played with me and taught me the way of the woods, and a long with Daniel's help, he taught me how to hear and speak with my mind. Daniel then also taught me how to talk with my voice. Each of the dogmen took a part in my learning, some told me of the outside world below, things that they had learned while on their trips down to get me clothing. They wanted to make sure I would be ready for the day when I would have to return."

"I'm glad that they took good care of you while you were gone from me. I wish I could spend more time with you now though, I feel that I have missed so much of your life," he told her. *"After all this time I've lost with you, now that I have found you again, I am once more forced to give you up. It isn't fair."*

"I know, I would like to be able to spend more time with you as well. Just know that I was happy there. Daniel made sure that I had what I needed. I had a life different than any other young girl ever could have imagined, but it was a good life, and one that I would not want to trade for any other. Yes, I would have rather have spent it with you, but being I could not, I spent it with those that were as close to family as I could get."

Josiah nodded to his daughter. He understood what she was saying to him.

After spreading out one of her blankets, Ava laid her bag down on top of it to use as a pillow, and then laid down herself on the hard surface of the cave floor. Reaching down, Josiah picked up the other blanket that she had with her, and used it to cover his daughter's sleeping body to help keep her warm.

Josiah sat and lovingly watched his little girl as she drifted deeper off into sleep. He loved her deeply and wanted to keep her with him, but he understood why she had to go back to the two-legers. She needed to have a chance at a normal life, a normal life amongst other humans like herself. As time went by, he was surprised to find that his hatred towards the two-legers was starting to dissipate the more that they talked of her going back. He realized that his hatred wasn't aimed at all the two-legers in the village, and that not all two-legers were bad. It was only the ones that had unjustly accusing him of murder, the ones that insistently hunted him down like an animal when they had no proof that he had done anything, those are the two-legers that he still felt hated and distaste for.

Josiah knew that his young daughter was getting close to coming of age, so he had to hand her over to the two-legers whether he wanted to or not. He hoped that a good family would step up and take her in. He knew it would be far too dangerous for her to be around the other dogmen like him. They all knew it, he knew it. He had felt the urges within himself, not towards her, but towards the two-leger women in the field, and it was an urge that even he found hard to resist. Only after Ava return to her own kind would she truly be safe from them.

Josiah looked out towards the entrance of the cave and saw that the daylight was getting brighter. He needed to get some rest as well in order to prepare for the next nights long travel that they had ahead of them. Although he wanted to spend as much time with Ava as he could, he knew that time was of the essence, and he needed to get her home. He was traveling much faster now than he had on his way up the mountain, and though he spent roughly two weeks' time on his trek upward, he was hoping that he would be able to make it back to the valley below by the sixth or the seventh days dawn.

Looking back to his daughter, he could feel the love growing up in his heart for her. *"You need to be amongst the other two-legers just like yourself. You deserve the normal life that you can have there. I just hope you never forget me,"* he thought to himself as he watched his daughter sleeping comfortably.

Moving to be closer to his daughter, Josiah laid down next to her and closed his eyes. Sleep came easier now for him. No more nightmares came to haunt him and nothing more was there to disrupt his sleep. He was finally free of the horrible memories that had haunted him for years. He felt as though his soul had now been freed and made whole again.

Josiah awoke from his slumber just as darkness was beginning to take over for the light. Ava was already up and gotten herself something to eat for her breakfast. She still had an apple in her hand that had been packed into her sack, and had some venison that Daniel had dried into jerky over the fire for her as well.

Josiah sat up and watched his daughter as she sat by the entrance to the cave eating her meal. Slowly eating each bite, she seemed lost in thought as she stared out into the shadows beyond.

"Are you okay?" Josiah asked his daughter. *"I know that I keep asking you that, but I am worried about you,"* he told her.

Ava turned around and looked at her father.

"Yes, I'm fine. I think I'm just a little homesick is all. I already miss my pack. They are my family, the only family I've had for most of my life," she told him.

"I know, but your home is with the other two-legers now. You must forget the pack and accept that you cannot be with them any longer. You need to get on with living with your own kind."

"I know I have to go and live there with them now, but I will still never forget the pack. They will always be a part of who I am inside," she said as she ate the last bite of food in front of her.

"That is because they truly are a part of you. Because of the bloodline that Daniel told me about, they are all your family in a way. They also reared you as one of their own. Kendal is your uncle. He is my brother by birth. A piece of them will always be with you, like a piece of me will always be with you as well. They will never forget you either," he told her. Ava smiled lovingly at her father.

"Did you get enough to eat?" he asked her.

"Yes, I had enough. I still have plenty left over for the rest of the trip too."

"Are you ready to leave now?" he questioned as he looked around the cave to make sure that everything was packed back into her bag. "Do you need to....., do you have to...?" he stammered from not knowing how to properly ask her.

"No, I don't," Ava chuckled. "I have already done that," she chuckled at her father. "And yes, I am. I am ready to travel," she answered.

Josiah walked to the front of the cave where Ava was. Standing at the opening, they watched as the sun began to set and drop down beyond the tree tops. Josiah pointed towards the stream to see if she needed a drink before they left. Ava nodded her head yes and they both walked towards the crystal-clear water.

When they got down to the creek, Ava bent down and dipped her hands into the cold water and then drank. After she drank a few more mouthfuls, she splashed some onto her face and droplets of water fell from her chin making her giggle. Josiah watched his daughter with great interest. She seemed very mature in a lot of what she did, and he knew that was only from the way she was reared. But when she giggled like she just did, he could see the true child that was still inside of her.

As Josiah bent down and lapped up some of the cold flowing water himself, his stomach gurgled and churned. He knew he

311

would have to eat again before the nights end. Ava looked at her father as she heard his stomach growl.

"If you need to hunt before we leave it is okay, there is time," she told him.

"No, I am fine. I will watch on our way, and if I see game, then I will hunt," he told her.

Ava nodded back to her father.

"Are you ready to travel now," he asked his daughter. Again, Ava nodded and Josiah turned his back to her before get back down on all fours so that his daughter could once again climb back up and onto his back.

Ava once more dug her fingers deep into the hair on her father's back. Feeling that she was secure, Josiah began to trot down through the darkness and deeper into the forest. The only light to brighten their path now, was that of the full moon above their heads.

They had covered a large distance of territory before Josiah decided to stop to let his daughter rest. Ava was getting tired and Josiah could feel her grip beginning to loosening on his back.

"Are you okay up there, do you need to rest?" he asked her.

"Yes, I just need a short break to rest my arms and stretch my legs," she told him. "I have never ridden for this long before," she added.

312

Josiah slowed his pace and then stopped near some rocks. Ava got down from her father's back and stretched. She was getting physically exhausted and he knew it.

"Rest for a bit. Regain your strength," he told her as he sat off to the side and motioned for her to do the same. Ave leaned back against a fallen tree and closed her eyes. The trip was harder on her than she wanted to admit to him, but Josiah could still see it.

They had rested for only a few moments before Ava told her father that she was ready to continue on.

"Are you sure, we can rest longer if you need to?" he asked.

Ava nodded to her father and got up onto her feet. Josiah again got down onto all fours and positioned himself for her to mount. He could feel that her grip still wasn't as tight as it had been before. Knowing this, Josiah decided that he would travel much slower this time so that Ava didn't have to try to hang on so tightly.

Shortly before dawn, Josiah stopped so his daughter could rest again. There wasn't much darkness left in the sky, and he still needed to hunt. The lack of food in his system was making him weak. The rabbit that he caught was nothing more than just a morsel of food to him, and it gave him little to no nourishment. First, he would look for shelter though. He needed to find a secure place for Ava to safely rest for the day. He didn't realize how hard the trip was going to be on her when they left. Though she didn't complain about how tired she was, he could still tell. *"This is why the two-legers don't ascend this high up the mountain, it is too rough and too hard of a climb,"* he thought to himself.

Looking around into the darkness surrounding them, Josiah didn't see any prey animals within sight, or within hearing distance either.

"Leave me here and you go and hunt. I will be alright staying here alone, really, I will be," she told him after seeing him looking around.

"No, I won't leave you here alone. It is too dangerous. You will stay with me and I can still hunt while we look for shelter," he told her.

Ava, too tired to argue with him, nodded to her father in agreement.

With Ava again on his back, Josiah slowed his pace even more than he had before and just walked silently amongst the trees. While keeping a keen eye out for both food and shelter, he continued to press on. He had to find shelter for both of them, more so than food. Above all, his daughter had to be kept safe. If he had to, he could go without food for one more day.

"Look! I think there is a small cave over there," Ava said excitedly as she pointed to a small rock formation partially hidden within the trees.

Josiah looked at where his daughter was pointing and sure enough, there was a small cave hidden in the shadows.

Turning towards the cave, Josiah headed over to where it was to get a closer look and to see how large of a structure it truly was. When he got closer to the mouth of the cave, Ava got down from her father's back, and Josiah went over for a closer look by himself. Sticking his nose to the air, he sniffed to see if he could tell if there were any signs of any other animal living there. Smelling nothing, he stuck his head into the opening and looked inside.

Just as Josiah stuck his head in and looked into the cave, he began to hear a rattling noise. He instantly froze and did not move. He listened closely to see from which direction the rattling had come from. The rattling was coming from beside him, just under the barberry bush at the mouth of the cave.

"Ava, stay back!" he yelled to his daughter. She had already heard the rattling as well, and she silently stood frozen in place. Josiah cautiously looked down and saw where the snake was coiled. Slowly he turned and began to back up little bit by little bit. The snake, picking up on the motion though and raised itself up to strike. Josiah quickly backed up and as he did so, the snake opened up its mouth and launched itself into the air as it struck out at Josiah. Josiah quickly moved off to one side when he saw it coming, causing the snake to miss its target.

The large rattlesnake swished its tail back and forth as it again prepared to relaunch itself at Josiah. This time Josiah was ready for it though, and as it struck out, he swung his large hand around and grabbed the snake behind its head in midair. The snake wiggled and tried to free itself, but Josiah held on tightly.

315

Josiah snarled at the snake in his hand as it did its best to still try and strike out at him. It couldn't get to his large hand though, because of where Josiah had managed to grab it at.

Glaring down at the snake still struggling within his hand, Josiah took his other hand and firmly wrapped his fingers around the snake's body just below where his upper hand was positioned, and then in one swift motion, he yanked his hand downward and ripped the snakes head from its body.

The snake, as if not knowing that its head was no longer connected to its body, continued to squirm and writhe about within his hand. The bodiless snakes head hissed and continued to try to strike out as well until it fell from the top of his hand to the ground. He stared at the still moving head of the snake for a moment longer before picking up a stick and using it to lob it off to the side away from the caves opening, and away from his daughter as well. The snake itself as prey wasn't much, but now he at least had some food to hold him over.

Josiah held onto the dead snake's body as he again poked his head into the cave. He still didn't smell the odor of any other animal that may be living there, but if there was one rattlsnake there, there could be others. Looking off to the left he saw a rock and he picked it up. Josiah tossed the rock inside of the cave and bounced it off the walls. Not a sound was emitted other than the echoing of the impact that the rock itself had made. If there had been any other rattlesnakes present in the cave, the disturbance created by the rock being thrown in would have caused them to announce themselves with a wave of rattles.

"Ava, come now, I think it is safe to go in," he told her.

Ava came to her father and waited as he entered the cave first. Looking the interior over better, he then motioned it was okay for her to follow.

"This will definitely do for the day. You did very well," he told his daughter.

Ava smiled and nodded at her father. As she began to lay out the blankets, Josiah went back to the cave entrance and began to eat the snake. The rattlesnake had been nearly nine feet long, so it made a decent meal to get him through the day. He rarely ate snake, it wasn't something that he enjoyed, but it was still meat all the same. And right now, he needed the energy that it would provide him until he could hunt again.

Ava had the blankets laid out and was sitting on them eating some more of her dried meat when Josiah came walking back in from eating his meal. She offered him some of what she had, but he shook his head and declined her offer.

"Are you about ready to bed down now," Josiah asked his daughter. Ava nodded to her father as she finished eating her last piece of meat that she had in her hand before putting the rest away for later.

"She doesn't eat much," he thought to himself. *"No wonder she is so skinny. She needs more than dried meat and fruit to be healthy and to grow. She will get that and more in the village, it will be good for her to be there,"* he thought to

317

himself. He was in a way still trying to convince himself that letting his daughter go was the best thing for all, but especially for her. He had just found her though, and he knew that his time with her was now growing shorter by the day. He was not looking forward to the last goodbye that they would share before she was gone.

Josiah looked out towards the cave entrance and saw that the morning was quickly approaching. He looked down at Ava, who was now laying on her spread out blanket. She was a beautiful child. She looked so much like her mother. Unlike her mother though, her skin was pale from the lack of exposure to enough sun light. She lived in the darkness, and playing in the shadows of the night. Night time was all that she knew ever since she went to live on the mountain top.

"Good night father," Ava tiredly told him as she yawned and closed her eyes. With as exhausted as she was, it wasn't long before the young girl drifted off to sleep.

Josiah walked back over to the entrance of the cave and looked out. He watched the sun as it rose up high into the sky. He began to again think about how pale his daughter's skin was, and again he began to realize how backwards her life really was. She should be out playing in the sunshine, not just settling down for sleep as she was now. She needs the sunlight to help her to be healthy, and to grow stronger. The realization of all this was now settling any questions that Josiah had about taking her back, and it also solved Josiah's inner turmoil about having to say goodbye to her. *"She has to go back,"* he said to himself. *"She has to live in the daylight like she was always meant to."*

Hearing her father's thoughts, Ava softly mumbled something in reply as she rolled over onto her side and fell into a deep restful sleep. As she slept, Josiah noticed how she tightly clutched her teddy bear to her chest that he had carried with him for all those years. He realized that the bear had now become a safety net for her, and he was sure that it, in addition to the photo that he gave her, would be one of her largest reminders of him in the days to come.

After watching his daughter for a few more moments as she slept peacefully from the entrance of the cave, Josiah stood up and went back over to where she lay and sat down next to her. As he sat in contemplation, he continued to stare out into the daylight for a long while. Now with having some food in his stomach, sleep began to creep into his body and his eyes began to become heavy. Laying down next to his daughter, he then also easily then drifted off to sleep.

Past histories are told,
As old hurts are unfolded.
The truths are age-old,
About those departed.

Brother against Brother
A great battle is fought.
Monster against Monster,
Or so she thought.

As a little girl cries,
Tears run from her eyes.
Her family was gone,
With only silent goodbyes.

But the healing can begin,
For not only one, but two.
Though lives had been stolen,
Others now, can continue.

BJ Moore

Chapter Ten

Josiah awoke early and went to just the inside of the mouth of the cave to sit and watch the sun as it slowly began to receded down from the sky. As he stared out at the sun slowly fading before him, he mulled over all the events of the past few days in his head. Though he was aching inside over knowing that he must soon leave his daughter with the two-legers, he was also beginning to better understand how Kendal himself felt when he showed up to reclaim her from him. The hurt that he felt was the same hurt that he himself was now feeling knowing that his own time with Ava was soon going to be coming to an end.

While looking out through the trees, Josiah thought that he caught movement. His first assumption was that it may be a prey animal, and that he would finally get an opportunity to hunt. It wasn't until the sun had fallen below the horizon that whatever it was that was hidden in the darkness to move again. A flash of tawny brown dashed from behind a large tree and disappeared behind a big rock. Seeing the all too familiar color flashing before him, Josiah instinctively now knew what was outside of his den, and unfortunately it was not prey.

Getting up from where he was seated, Josiah moved to just outside of the mouth of the cave and stood. Cocking his head to the side, he put his nose to the wind. As the slight breeze swirled around where he stood, a scent was beginning to register with him. Inhaling deeper, he recognized the scent easily because it was one that he knew well. And it was a scent of an animal that he really did not want to deal with right now.

Josiah continued to watch the shadows as he waited for more movement. Again, he put his nose to the wind and the scent seemed even stronger now than it had been. He knew that the animal was coming in closer to where he and his daughter were, and he didn't like it. A deep-seated animosity began to build up within him, he knew that the situation was now getting serious.

A low snarling growl came out of the darkness and Josiah answered it with a growl of his own. Getting down on all fours, he laid back his ears and prepared to fight in defense of his daughter who was still asleep in the cave.

The tawny colored animal was a mountain lion, and he was far too close for Josiah's comfort. He knew how dangerous this large cat could be to his daughter. He had dealt with these tawny cats before on his way up to the top of the mountain, and though he knew he could easily handle it on his own, he had his daughter with him now, and that changed everything for him.

Watching the cat closely, Josiah saw that the animal was discretely working its way to the left of where the cave was positioned. Not wanting to lose sight of it, Josiah continued to watch it intently so that he could see what direction that the animal was heading next. He hoped that it would keep going and would move off in a different direction other than theirs, but it didn't. The large cat showed that it had no intentions of leaving, and slunk back behind a fallen tree.

Josiah stood back up onto his hind legs and looked around to see if he could catch sight of the big cat again. He couldn't hear anything, nor could he see anything. He couldn't smell that cat either. The path in which the air was moving had shifted to a different direction, and now left him clueless as to where the large cat had positioned itself.

Ava awoke and began to stir inside the cave. Looking up and seeing that her father wasn't in the cave with her, she called out to him.

"Papa?" she called to him loudly. Josiah heard her, but didn't respond to her call, he was still watching intently for where the large cat had gone.

This was the first time that Ava had actually addressed her father as Papa like she had when she was little, but Josiah was so preoccupied with protecting his daughter, that he didn't react to it.

"Papa?" she called out again with fear rising in her voice. This time Josiah backed up a little closer to the mouth of the cave and spoke back to her.

"I am still here with you Ava. You stay in the cave and get yourself ready for travel as quickly as you can," he instructed her.

"What's wrong? What's going on?" she asked in a nervous quiet whisper when she heard the distress in her father's voice.

"Just get yourself ready to leave as quickly as you can, okay. Go and pack up all of your stuff, and let me take care of this," he told her.

Hearing the worry in her father's voice, she hurriedly did as she was told. Ava quickly got up and began to fold her blankets. She could feel the anxiety building up within her father and knew that something was very wrong outside of the cave. After the blankets were folded, she then put them on the ground next to her bag. Reaching into her bag, she drew out the small cloth sack that held some of the food that she had brought with her. Taking out some of what was left of her dried meat, she sat down upon the folded blankets and began to quickly eat.

As she hurriedly ate, Ava anxiously stared at the mouth of the cave and watched as her father stood guard. She could hear him emitting a low growl off and on out into the darkness, and she could see the hackles in the middle of his back raise into a piloerection as the hair stood stiff.

As he waited, Josiah continued to scan the trees looking for the big cat. He didn't see any more movement, but he could sense it was still there. He surmised that this is exactly what the large cat had in mind when it found a place to hold up and stay hidden from sight. He was hoping that it had left the area, but he knew better than that, these large cats cannot be trusted. He didn't want to bring Ava out into the open if the large cat was still nearby, but he felt as though he was being given no choice in the matter.

Momentarily turning, Josiah glanced back into the cave and saw that Ava was putting the blankets back into her bag.

"We will need to be quick. Are you ready?" he asked as he turned away from her to again stand guard over her.

"Yes Papa," she nervously replied.

"Okay, come over here close by me and stand behind me for a moment," he told her.

Picking up her bag and securing it to her waist, Ava did as she was told and walked over to her father's side. When she got next to him, she put her hand out onto his back. She could feel his tense muscles nervously rippling beneath his skin. This worried her and made her feel even more anxious to know what was going on outside.

"Papa, what is wrong?" she asked him quietly. "What are you afraid of out there?"

"There is a big cat out there hiding somewhere in the trees. It has been there awhile and has no intention of leaving this area. It is now stocking us," he told his daughter. *"Stalking you,"* he then added.

Ava looked at her father with fear building up from inside her own chest. She knew how dangerous big cats like this were, and to know that one was stalking them and wanting to get at her frightened her.

"Okay, when I lower down, I want you to jump up onto my back as fast as you can and be ready to go as soon as you are on. I need you to hold tightly, as tightly as you can. Hold on like your life depends on it. Can you do that for me?" he asked her.

"Yes, Papa," she told him nervously.

Josiah looked around the area once more. He could still feel the cat's presence, but he couldn't see it and he could no longer hear it or smell it. Slowly, he got down onto all fours and looked back at his daughter.

"Now!" he quietly called out to her. Instantly Ava leaped up onto her father's back and tucked her feet in, in front of his hind legs and grasped onto the fur on his back as tightly as she could.

Instantly Josiah jumped from the mouth of the cave and onto the forest floor beyond, and as soon as his feet hit the ground he began to run. As soon as he left the security of the cave, he instantly could hear the large cat running after him. He knew that with Ava on his back, that it wouldn't be long before the cat would begin to close in on him. There was just no way that he could run as fast as he usual could without taking the chance of Ava losing her grip and falling off, and that put them both at a severe disadvantage.

If his daughter wasn't with him, Josiah never would have run, he would have stood his ground and fought the aggressor. But he knew it wasn't his scent that had attracted the large cat, it was that of his daughters. He didn't care about himself, but he could not live with himself if he allowed something to happen to her.

Ava held on tightly and laid down onto her father back as low as she could. She too now knew that the big cat was in pursuit of them. She could hear the twigs breaking and the leaves crunching beneath its feet as soon as they left the safety of the cave. Fear was beginning to rise up in the young girl as she glanced back and saw the large tawny beast gaining on them. She had seen large cats such as these before when she had been out with Daniel learning about the edible plants in the area, but this cat was much larger than any of those that they had come across. Those cats had also backed down from Daniel's might. Just his size alone had been enough to make the smaller cats shrink back in fear.

Closing her eyes to try to shut out the vision of the large cat from her mind turned out to be a mistake though, she was soon caught off guard as her father swerved to miss some downed limbs that stood in their way, and she almost lost her balance and fell off. As Josiah continued to run, Ava began to lean her body in the direction that her father was leaning as he would dodge and swerve around trees and rocks. That alone helped her hold onto him better, and enabled him to also move more swiftly.

Josiah could sense that the big male cat was getting closer and he knew that he couldn't allow it to jump at him while

Ava was with him, and especially not with her on his back. He would have to stop when he got to where there would be cover, and a safe place for Ava to hide while he dealt with the dangerous cat.

"I am going to have to stop," Josiah called back to his daughter. *"I can't let it attack us from behind,"* he told her. *"I am going to try to find cover, and when I stop, you jump off and run and hide as quickly as you can. I will then face it alone. I am far too large and strong for it to hurt me."*

"Yes, Papa," Ava apprehensively told him as she continued to hold on tightly.

Keeping his eyes open, he watched closely for any available cover. Josiah had to choose his battle site carefully as he continued to course through the trees. Seeing a clearing full of rocky outcrops, he changed direction and headed for the first set of rocks that he saw. He knew that the large rocks would give Ava more cover than anything else available in the area, as well as a tree vacant area that was large enough to do battle in. Heading for the rocks, he dodged around the largest one and momentarily ducked out of the line of sight of the large cat.

"Now!" he shouted to his daughter as she instantly let go and slid to the ground.

"Go!" she told him as soon as her feet touched the earth. As soon as she gained her own footing, the young girl scrambled to the back of the rocks to hide while her father turned and doubled back to face the large cat alone.

As Josiah came out from behind the rocks and stood his ground, the large cat approached him. As the mountain lion slowed down and squinted its eyes to study Josiah carefully, it took note of the missing child that had been with him. Placing one step carefully in front of the other, the cat began to circle Josiah as it cautiously stalked him. As the mountain lion continued to move around him, a low guttural growl began to emanate from within the aggressor.

Josiah watched as the cat's lips curled and expose its large white canine teeth as it began to angerly growl and snarl loudly at him.

Without taking its eyes off of Josiah, the cat began to sniff at the air. It could tell that Ava was still near, it could still smell her scent lingering in the breeze, but it also knew that Josiah now stood between it and where the young girl was hiding.

As the large cat continued to circle around Josiah, it attempted to work its way to the far side near where the rocks met with the tree line. As it started to slowly make its way towards the rock formations where Ava was hidden, Josiah menacingly growled at it. He was not happy with the direction that the cat was now trying to head.

"No!" Josiah shouted as he loudly growled at the cat and quickly moved over to again blocked it from his daughter.

The cat snarled wildly at Josiah's efforts to keep it from going into the rocky outcrop. Taking a step closer to Josiah, the large cat again angerly snarled and sprayed spittle from its mouth. It was growing furious with Josiah, who it now only

329

considered as an annoyance that stood between him and his prey.

"You will not harm her!" Josiah said as he stretched out his muscular neck and roared menacingly at the impudent cat.

Josiah had no sooner finish roaring when the large cat suddenly leapt at him. Raising up one of his massive arms in defense, he swiftly knocked the large cat out of the air and sent it careening through a brushy area and down onto the ground. Through it all, the mountain lion somehow managed to land upon its feet on the leafy ground cover several feet away, digging its toes into the dirt, and leaving deep furrows in the soil from its nails. Furious at what had just happened, the large cat yet again readied itself for battle.

"You are no match for me!" Josiah roared at the cat again.

The large cat ignoring, his warnings, lowered its head to glare at Josiah with hatred. The big cat again began to aggressively circle Josiah much like it had before. The cat reached out a paw and quickly took a swipe at Josiah, but it wasn't close enough for the threatening motion to make any contact with him. The cat knew it wasn't close enough to make contact with the creature before it took the swipe. It was more of a show of intent by the large cat to try to intimidate his opponent, but even that failed to make an impact.

The two adversaries continued to evade each other with eyes locked as they sized each other up. Both challengers took turns at showing their strength, and not letting on about any weaknesses that they may hold. Every once in a while, the cat would pounce in towards Josiah in a mock charge to egg him on, but Josiah firmly held his ground. The large cat was trying to get him to make an unwise move, something that it could take advantage of and use against him, but Josiah had no intent on allowing that to happen, not when his daughter's life was at stake.

The large cat again tried to circle itself towards the rock formation, but Josiah once more turned it back and blocked its way. Out of frustration, the large cat snarled harshly at Josiah. It could tell that the girl was still in there, it could smell her sweet scent, and he was determined to do whatever it took to get in there after her.

All at once, the large cat suddenly stopped its aggressive stalking, and took two steps backward from where it was standing. This unexpected act confused Josiah. Tilting his head, he stared at the animal standing across from him, trying to figure out what its next move was going to be.

"Are you done cat?" Josiah asked as he growled a little less aggressively at the cat. The large cat hissed back at him, but did not rise. *"You need to go!"* Josiah strongly ordered as he raised up his arm and pointed with his fingers.

The large cat slowly got back up to its feet and menacingly stared at Josiah. There was hatred spewing out from its deep amber eyes, and the hatred that it felt was all aimed in Josiah's direction.

"Back off!" Josiah yelled loudly at the large cat as he tried to get it to leave.

Still snarling the large cat took two steps back away from Josiah. Then after snarling one more time, it turned and took a step further as if in retreat. Josiah watched intently as the cat slowly began to walk towards the trees.

Josiah then heard a rustling noise coming from on the other side of the rocks where Ava was hiding. Not knowing if the mountain lion possibly had a mate that had followed them without them knowing about it, Josiah momentarily took his eyes off the large cat and glanced over towards where the noise had come from. Josiah didn't want to look away from the large cat, but he had to make sure that his daughter was still safe.

Taking full advantage of Josiah being distracted, the large cat swiftly turned and silently charged towards the rocks behind him. Leaping past where Josiah stood and up onto the top of one of the large rocks, the cat stopped and turned to snarl defiantly at Josiah just before it leaped back down onto the other side of the outcropping and out of sight.

Josiah, being caught off guard, turned and saw the large cat just as it jumped from the top of the rock down into the area where his daughter was hidden. Panic immediately set into his heart.

"No!" Josiah roared as he leapt up and over the large rock in one swift movement, coming to rest upon both feet on the other side of the rock. Josiah saw the large cat standing before him. He charged forward at the cat in a rage. The cat quickly dodged the larger creature and jumped up onto the top of another boulder off to the side.

"Leave this place or I will kill you!" Josiah menacingly threatened the large cat.

Ignoring Josiah's harsh warnings, the cat turned and jumped onto the top of another boulder further away. Hearing a slight rustle of leaves below, the cat looked down between the gaps. Hidden between two boulders below his feet, the large cat saw the prey that he had been seeking, he found Ava.

Looking up through the crevasse between the two boulders where Ava was hiding, she saw that the mountain lion was now looming over her from above. Fear began to rise up within the young girl's chest.

The large cat jumped down to the ground, and looked intently at what was beyond the crack between the two large boulders. Sticking its paw through the opening as far as it could get it to go, it swatted at Ava with its claws fully extended.

"Papa!" Ava screamed to her father. "Papa! Help me," Ava again screamed as she tried to stay out of the reach of the large cat.

Josiah quickly jumped down onto the ground behind the large cat. Reaching out, he quickly grasped the mountain lion by its hind legs, and forcefully swung the cat's body up into the air before throwing it several feet behind where he stood.

As the mountain lion came down, it hit hard against one of the large boulders. As it hit, it let out a loud yowl before

333

crumbling to the ground. Shaking its head as it recovered from the blow, the cat got to its feet and again faced Josiah.

The large male mountain lion snarled at Josiah as he glared into the larger creature's eyes. Looking deeply into his eyes, the cat saw something it had never saw before in the eyes of any other animal, and it suddenly could understand what Josiah was mentally saying to it.

"Go!" Josiah yelled at the cat with hatred in his voice.

The tawney cat turned its head to the side and shook it aggressively to clear the fog that remained in its head. It had no idea why it could suddenly understand what the larger creature was now saying. Not sure of the situation, the cat took a cautious step backwards away from the mighty creature.

"You go or I will kill you! You cannot have my daughter!" Josiah growled aggressively at the large cat.

The cat looked off to the side where it knew that Ava was still hiding, and then back at Josiah in wonderment. It tilted its head and silently stood as it stared at Josiah in astonishment at the kind of sounds that was now hearing within its head.

Josiah continued to stare menacingly at the large cat. He could tell by the way it looked that at him now, that it was finally hearing his words.

The mountain lion looked from Josiah to the ground at its feet, and then back towards where it had originally leapt over the big rock moments before. Taking a step towards the rock, the cat turned and looked back at Josiah. It now knew that if it pressed further to go after the human child, that it would be killed. He had been told, and now it fully understood the ramifications of the situation that it was in.

The cat knew it was no match for the dogman, and it had no choice but to now back off. This battle was not a wise one to begin with, and the large cat knew it. They were both strong adversaries, but the wolfman type creature had both size and added strength on his side. Josiah was a far stronger adversary than the large cat had counted on.

The large cat kept a close eye on Josiah as it slowly backed away from the fight. After putting a few feet between the dogman and itself, the cat turned and walk over to the large boulder that it had leaped over earlier. Jumping up on top of it, the large cat then leaped back down to the ground on the other side.

Josiah, with his blood still boiling, charged after the cat. The large cat heard him coming and quickly turned and looked back to face Josiah. Seeing him approaching at a rapid pace, the cat turned and dashed into the darkened woods until its footsteps could no longer be heard.

With the large cat now gone, Josiah turned and went back behind the large bolder and towards the rocks where his daughter had been hiding. He went around the back side of the boulder to where she had been, but he didn't see her there any longer. He began to look wildly from one side to the other in search of her.

"Ava!" he called out. *"Ava!"* he called louder.

"Here Papa," she called back to her father. She had gone further down the ledge of the rock formation to hide where the big cat wouldn't see her if it came back. Slowly she carefully climbed back up over the rock shelf and headed for where her father was.

"It is safe now," he told her. *"The big one is gone now. He decided that this was not the battle for him to take on."*

"Good," she told him as she reached out and hugged her father.

"Are you ready to continue on?" he asked.

"Yes," Ava replied as she shook her head.

"Come, lets walk a bit," he told her as he motioned for her to come with him.

This time they would travel at a much slower pace. He knew that the large cat would no longer pursue them, and that Ava was again safe.

Josiah had just expended a large amount of energy being in battle with the large cat over the protection of his daughter, and it was now imperative that he replenished that energy soon. His plan for now though was to find shelter early so that it would allow him time to hunt before daybreak came, and if successful, then to obtain the much-needed nourishment he required.

"We will be to the village of the two-legers in only a few days' time now," he told her as he slowly walked on all fours with his daughter by his side. Ava looked up at her father as she put her hand on his muscular arm and sadly nodded.

Ava knew what her father was thinking, and she too wanted to have more time to spend with him, but she understood why she couldn't. She understood why Daniel said that time was of the essence to her. Daniel had explained to her what happens as a human female matures, and what changes were going to occur within her before her father even got to the mountain top.

"If you want, we can spend one last day together in my old den when we reach the valley. No one will see you there, and you will be safe. I can tell you about your family, or at least what I can remember of them. I know that you were too young when you were taken to remember much about any of us, but I may be able to fill in just a few more of the details for you," he told her.

"Yes, I'd like that," Ava happily told him.

By taking Ava to his den by the village, Josiah knew that he was buying himself one more day with his precious daughter. One more day to be treasured before he knew that he may have to leave her go for good.

The two of them traveled down into an area that was familiar to Josiah. He was now on what had once been his hunting range before he had been pushed further down the hill to the valley below by the two-legers.

337

"Do you want to rest?" Josiah asked his daughter as he glanced back at her. *"There is a spring nearby and you can get a drink if you want."*

Ava nodded her head to her father and he led her to where the spring was. The cool fresh water came up out of the ground in this area, before it then flowed down through the forest in a winding stream. Josiah had no idea where the stream went to, he had never followed it all the way to find out. But he always wondered in his mind how far it ran.

"Here we are," he told his daughter as they began to hear the bubbling sound of water as it spilled out from the ground and formed into a small stream. The water was very appealing, crisp and clear like mountain spring water should be.

"Are you okay?" Josiah asked his daughter as she walked ahead of him. All of her muscles were still aching from the tension that they were under as she had to continuously hold on tightly to keep herself from falling off her father's back when the mountain lion was chasing them.

Ava didn't speak, but instead only nodded to her father as she strolled ahead of him and towards the water.

Ava bent down to the fresh water and stuck her hands into the cold mountain spring. She washed her hands off in the clear water before cupping them together and lifting up the water to her face to drink.

After getting her fill of the cool spring water, Ava pushed her sleeves up and began to lift the water up one handful at a

338

time as she proceeded to wash the rest of her exposed areas. She cleaned the dirt off of her arms and then her face as well as the back of her neck. The cool, crispness of the water felt good to her. There had been a definite temperature change from the mountainous plateau that she had just spent the last nine years of her life at, to here. It was warmer here than she remembered it being when she was little.

Josiah sat and watched his young daughter in amazement. She was so much like her mother. Her mannerisms, her physical appearance and her face, looking at her, was like looking at a younger version of his wife. Since being up on the plateau, a lot of the old memories that he had forgotten of the past, were now quickly coming back to him in flashes. He could now remember the man he used to be before he became what he is now, and he remembered how much he loved his family, his farm and his life. He remembered a lot of the little things too like playing with his children, and helping his wife with her gardens. One by one, the memories were all coming back.

When the young girl finished getting another drink of water, she stood up and looked over at her father. Josiah quietly got up and walked over to her. He looked at her for a moment and felt the loss in his heart of all the time that he has spent away from her. It was a feeling that he would feel deep down in his soul for the rest of his life. Looking away from her, he put his face down into the stream to get a drink from the cool spring himself.

"We are close now, aren't we?" she asked her father as he lapped up more water.

"Yes, we are getting closer now. This is the area that I had once lived in. Over on the horizon just beyond where you can see, is the field where we had lived when you were little. That is the field in which I will leave you in to go and live with the two-legers. We will have two, maybe three more evenings of travel after this, and then when the next day's light begins to wane, you will be home."

"It is not my home, my home will always be up on the mountain with you, Kendal, Daniel, and the others," she told him as she reached up and placed her small hand on the back of his. As she looked up at her father, he saw a single tear rolled down her cheek.

"I will miss you too my daughter, but this is for the best. You have to go back. You no longer belong with us up in the mountains. You belong with your own kind. You need to play in the sunshine, you need to have other children for friends. You need to be with humans like you. Maybe you will even get a new family, someone to love you and that you can love back. Wouldn't you like that?"

"I don't want another family. I have you, and the others. You are all my family, no one else will never replace you," she told him with teary eyes.

"Yes, we are your family, but you need a real family, a family where you can have a mother and a father and siblings that you can be with. We will always be family, but you need a human family too. The two-legers can give you so much more than we ever could. You will see that as you get older. It will become easier for you in time," he told her.

As Josiah took her tiny hand into his, Ava tearfully nodded her head to her father.

"I will try to do as you ask and have another family, but it will be hard," she told her father.

"I know it will be, but do it for us. We all love you Ava, and that is why we are doing this. I would have liked nothing better than to be with you for the rest of our lives, but we can't. It wouldn't be fair to you, nor would it be safe for you. I know that Daniel explained all that to you," he told her.

Ava nodded again to her father as another tear rolled down her face.

"Come on, it is time to go and find shelter before the sun starts to rise. Day break will be coming soon, and I still need to hunt," he told his daughter.

Ava silently nodded as she wiped the tears from her eyes.
Still holding onto her father's hand, the two walked towards the edge of the wood line where a cave was located at that Josiah had previously lived in. It was the perfect place for them to rest.

The stars shined brightly above them, and the position of the entrance to the cave would give them a flawless view of the night sky. It was a clear night with a full moon, and from where they would be standing, they could look out over everything that lay beyond.

"How long did you live here in this place?" Ava quietly asked.

"For a long time, I must have been here for a few years. This is where I lived after the two-legers chased me from the valley below. This is also where I changed," he told her.

Ava only nodded, not wanting to press her father further on a memory that she knew was to be painful. They walked in silence the rest of the way up to where the cave was at.

"Come, this is where I stayed," he told her as he looked into cave to make sure it was safe.

As Josiah entered into the cave, his daughter followed him in. Leading her to an area off to the side of the hollowed-out rock, Josiah motioned for her to sit down.

"You stay here. You will be safe here by yourself. I am going to go and see if there is any game before the sun begins to rise again," he told her. Ava nodded to her father and watched him as he turned to leave.

As Josiah exited the cave, Ava began to unpack her bag and spread out the blankets that she brought with her. When Josiah returned from his successful hunt, his daughter had eaten and was already asleep.

"You sleep. We will talk more when you wake up," he quietly told her when he saw her stir as he entered the cave.

It wasn't long before the exhausted girl fully nodded off once more. Josiah quietly watched his daughter as she slept peacefully under her blankets. He wondered what his other daughter Anna would look like now, but he would never know because Kendal had killed her. A soft grumble was emitted from his chest as he thought about what his brother had done to her. He now knew why he had done it, but it didn't make the loss of his older daughter any easier for him to deal with. He was the one that found his daughter lying dead in her bed, and that was after he had just found her mother butchered in the kitchen. That one horrible day, and the extreme loss that it meant to him, was one memory that is burned into his soul, and one that will haunt him now forever. Even if his daughter Anna was sick, maybe they could have done something to help her. It had been a long time ago that Daniel was a doctor, maybe he was mistaken about there not being a cure, how could he be sure that one hadn't been discovered. Josiah will never know now though because his daughter Anna was now gone, and she had no chance at all for any kind of a normal life.

Josiah got up and walked over to where his daughter was sleeping and sat down on the floor of the cave next to her. As he sat there, he continued to watch her sleep and saw her hugged her small teddy bear even tighter to her chest than before.

"At least you will have a life to live my daughter, you will have the life that your sister never did," he told her in his mind. As he told her that, Ava rolled over towards him and wrapped her arm up over his arm and hugged it.

Ava slept peacefully throughout the next day without even waking up, and into the evening hours as well. When the moon began to rise high up in the sky, she awoke to see her father still sitting next to her.

343

"Did you get enough rest after your big day yesterday?" he asked her as he looked down into her face.

After he spoke to her, it was then that Ava realized that her father was only still next to her because she was still tightly holding onto his large arm. Seeing that, she sheepishly released her grip on him.

Ava yawned and nodded to her father as she sat upright and stretched.

"Is it time to leave already?" she asked her father as she glanced out the entryway into the cave.

"No, we have some time yet. I brought you something to eat last night when I came back from hunting," he told her.

"Here," he said as he handed her a fresh apple from one of the wild trees growing in the next clearing over.

"Thank you," she told him as she smiled and took it from his hand. "Did you eat last night too?" she asked.

"Yes, I ate. I caught a good-sized deer, and that will suffice me for a couple of days," he told her.

"The mountain lion chasing us scared me the other night," she told her father as she took her first bit of the apple.

"Yes, I know it did. But you know that I never would have allowed it to get to you," he told her. *"I would have killed it first before it had the chance to,"* he added.

"I know that. That was a rabbit that almost gave me away in the rocks to begin with. I saw it when it came out and started to dig in the leaves looking for food," she told him. "That is what you and the mountain lion heard before it came over the rocks at me."

"I didn't know what had made the noise, I was worried that maybe there was another large cat, the mate to the large male, that had snuck in from behind, or that you had moved for a better hiding spot. I am only glad that the big cat gave up and left," he told her. *"I didn't want to have to kill it, but I would have if I had to."*

"I'm glad you didn't have to kill it," Ava said as she took another bite of the fresh apple.

After Ava finished her apple, Josiah helped her fold her blankets back up and pack them back into her bag.

As they exited the cave, they both looked out into the night and heard the call of an owl off in the distance. The call of the owl took Josiah back to the night when the two-leger couple was in the field and the female was in heat. It was after they got back to the village, that the owl called out and he howled his mournful howl out into the night. That was not a good night for Josiah, and it just reiterated why his daughter was now going home.

"Another predator hunts this evening," he told his daughter in reference to the old owl. *"Do you want to ride tonight, or do you want to walk?"* he asked as he looked down at his daughter.

345

"If it is okay, I'd like to walk Papa," she replied back as she looked up at him.

Josiah nodded to his daughter. After reaching up and taking her father's hand, they walked through the woods next to each other in silence.

Two more nights of uneventful travel had passed for the two of them. The topography of the terrain had changed drastically and it had gotten less rocky and not as steep as it had previously been. With smoother and easier to travel surfaces now before them, they began to make better time in their decent down the mountain. Josiah took note that the closer they got to their destination, the quieter that his daughter Ava was getting. He was worried about his little girl, and how this was affecting her. It was just before daybreak of their last day of travel that Josiah told Ava that they were getting close to where his old den was.

"We are almost there," he told his daughter. *"Are you okay, you haven't been saying much?"* he asked her.

"I'm okay. I have just been thinking about how things were before up on the mountain, and how they will be now. I am going to miss you all," she told him as a tear slipped out and ran down her cheek.

Josiah put his hand on his daughters back and tried to comfort her the best he could, but that just caused his daughter to begin to cry more. Pulling her to him, he knelt and gave her a hug, which she readily returned with one of her own.

Josiah held his daughter close to him until she stopped crying. After wiping the tears from her eyes, the two of them walked up to the edge of the field and paused as they looked out across it. They could see the early morning lights burning in some of the windows down in the village. Josiah looked down at his daughter's innocent little face as she stared in amazement at the village.

"What is the brightness in the buildings?" she asked without taking her eyes away.

"Those are lanterns. Do you remember how we used to light the house with them when you were little? The lanterns have oil in them and that allows them to burn brightly like those that you can see in the windows," he told her.

"Yes, I remember now. You would light them with a thin piece of wood that you would strike on the stones of the fireplace. They are just like the one that you would light for me to keep my monsters away when I was little," she said as she chuckled and smiled up at her father.

"Yes, just like the lantern that I would light for you," he said back to her chuckling. *"Monsters huh?"* he then added with a smile.

Ava chuckled at her father. The thought of her once thinking of her mountain family, and now her father as monsters in the past, made them both laugh.

"Don't they have flint like our mountain family does to start their fires?" she asked.

347

"Yes, they do, but they don't use them to light the lanterns. The thin wood that they use to light fires are called matches. That is what the thin wood fire starters are called," he told her.

Ava continued to stare at the village as her father spoke.

"Down there, that is where you now belong. That is the life that you need and were meant to live," he told her as they looked towards the village.

Ava removed her eyes from the village and looked up at her father as she apprehensively bit her lower lip.

"You used to do that when you were little too, sucking in and biting your lower lip like that. I think you got that from your mother, she used to do it too," he told her. *"Every time you had to do something that you didn't want to do, you would pout and bite your lower lip like that,"* he told her.

Ava looked up at her father and smiled widely at him. She really did love her father. The love that she felt for him had grown so strong that it was almost as if they had never parted.

"Will I ever see you again?" she asked her father as she held tightly onto his hand.

"I don't know. I will try to come back down from the mountain off and on, but I don't know if we will ever see each other or be able to spend time like this together again. If I can return though, on the inside you will know when I am here. You will

feel me inside of yourself like I was able to feel you inside of me as I climbed up the mountain side to find you. The closer I got, the stronger the feeling was that you were there. And you know my howl, so when you hear me howl again, you will then know it is me for sure, an no other." he told her.

"If you are close enough for me to hear you howl, then you will be close enough for us to talk in our minds then, right?" she asked him.

"Yes, maybe, but Daniel says that for your wellbeing, that we should not meet again," he told her.

Ava looked up at her father sadly and nodded before looking back to the village.

"I don't know anyone there. I'm scared to go," she said nervously.

"You will be fine there. They will take care of you there. I know that you are scared, but you know that you need to be there with your own kind" he told her in a very soft voice.

"Where is your den? You said we could spend a little more time together before I have to go," she asked.

"It is over there just on the inside of the woods. There is a small cave there that has brush and ivy's hanging down over the entrance way."

"Can we go there now?" Ava asked emotionally as another tear began to form.

"Yes, we can go," he told her as he took his daughters hand and led her down the embankment towards where the cave was located.

Once they reached the small cave, Josiah stood in front of it and looked at where the entrance was. Nothing had changed at all since he was there last. Turning he looked to the old downed apple tree as well. For just a moment, he was being torn between returning to the mountain top, or staying here to be close to his daughter. Then he again remembered the two-leger females in heat that had walked by. There was no way he could stay. He had to return, and he had to leave his daughter behind when he did.

Parting the overhanging ivy, Josiah went into the cave first to make sure it was still safe before his daughter entered. As he looked around, a memory of what Daniel had told him about the cave where Kendal had stayed while he was in the valley, and about it being a cave from where he could see everything around him came back to him. This had to be the same exact cave that Kendal had stayed in while he watched his house all those years ago. It was here that he had watched his wife Sara coming and going from the house. He could see everything from here. It was from here that he had prayed on his cattle and his chickens. He just had no idea that he had been here all that time. Then another thought entered his mind. After Kendal had murdered his wife and daughter, could this be where he brought Ava when he took her? Could Kendal have had her here with him while watching everything that happened with him below? Did he watch and listen while he found his wife and daughter dead, while the sheriff and his men rode up and shot him? He must have. He must have had

Ava hidden here when he later came down to the jail and killed the sheriff before setting him free.

Now it was all making sense to Josiah. Kendal was here all that time, and Ava was with him as well. He was also wondering how long he had her here before he headed off up the mountain side. Did he follow Josiah when he left as well, or did they leave and go a different direction? These were all questions that he now wanted answered when he returned up to the mountain top. He didn't know how much Daniel knew about what happened down here, or how much they could get out of Kendal, but he now needed to know for his own piece of mind.

After shaking off all the thoughts that had been pouring through his head, Josiah continued to make sure that nothing was currently in the cave that could pose a threat to his daughter, before calling out to her to let her know that she could now enter.

"Hand me your bag," he told her. *"We will talk for a little bit and then you will need to get some rest. You have had another long night, and we will still have some time to talk more about our family before you have to go,"* he told her.

Doing as her father had instructed, Ava handed her bag to him. Josiah then took a blanket out of her sack and spread it out on the cave floor so his daughter could sit on it.

"You look so much like your mother. Your mother was a lovely woman. Blond hair and blue eyes just like yours," he told her lovingly.

"I can remember her some, but I can't remember a lot about any of you. Tell me about our family. Tell me about you. I want to know as much as you can tell me about all of you," she asked of him.

"It all started when I was adopted as a baby. Did Daniel tell you about any of this?"

"Yes, Daniel wanted me to know about where you had come from, and some other stuff, but he didn't give me a lot of details. I was told about you being raised by others, but I want to hear it from you too, and the stuff that Daniel didn't know about you so I can know myself," she told him.

"Okay. Well, I will just move ahead to when I was a young man. I met your mother when she moved into the area with her family. I lived on a farm that was several miles from here. I had come to the village to buy grain to plant in our fields that summer.

I fell in love with her at first sight, and I think your mother felt the same way. I made a point of coming into the village once a week with hopes of running into your mother again. It was soon after that, that we did see each other again and afterwards I began to court her.

Your grandparents didn't think too much of their daughter being courted by a dirt farmer, but it didn't stop us. We fell in love and then married six months later against their wishes.

After I moved out of the home that I was brought up in, the people who raised me decided to move on themselves. They sold the farm and moved to a town that was in another state where the living wouldn't be so hard on them, and where the weather was not so cold in the winter. It was difficult for all of us before they moved because I was no longer able to be there to help them with the farm as much as they needed me to be. At that point I now had a farm of my own to tend, as well as a new wife to support.

I felt bad because I was all they had. My adoptive parent's natural child had died a few years before they adopted me, so when I left to begin my own family, they had nothing to tie them to the farm any longer. It was a year after they left that I was told that they both had passed on shortly after arriving in the town where they had moved. When they left, I had lost the only family I had known for my whole life. But at the same time though, I also gained another family with all of you.

As I told you, your mother and I had gotten married six months after we started seeing each other. Your grandparents on your mother's side were both older at the time, and it was not long after we married, that they came down with the fever and passed on as well. They called it the scarlet fever back then, and there were a lot of settlers that came down with it, and many died from it. The doctor tried to save your grandparents, but there was nothing that could be done for them. Your mother was an only child and she was very heartbroken when they passed. She got a small inheritance from them, and it was that inheritance that enabled us to build our house on the land that I had secured. So other than myself, you have no living relatives left here. You will unfortunately truly be on your own in the world of the two-legers," he told her.

Ava nodded as she once more bit her lower lip apprehensively.

"We weren't married long before your mother became pregnant with your sister. We had made arrangements with the government to get this piece of property through a land grant," he told her as he motioned towards the entrance of the cave. *"It should still be yours now as the only known survivor. Make sure that you see a lawyer in town to get it transferred over into your name for when you are older. Do not allow anyone to talk you out of it, do not allow anyone else to put their names on it either. This land, this is your heritage, your inheritance from us. This is important, promise me this,"* he asked her in a serious tone.

Ava nodded her head to her father and asked him to tell her more.

"After we married, your mother lived in town for a while and I worked the fields below us during the day, and then worked to get a home built for us at night. Working at night was hard, but I wanted a roof, our own roof, over our heads before your sister came, and that building became our home. Your sister was our first born. She looked a lot like your mother as well, and she was smart just like you are," he told her as a tear ran from his eyes.

Ava too was lightly crying while her father told her of his memories about their family, a family that she barely remembers and will never get the chance to ever see again. All she will have left is what he is telling her about them, and the worn picture of them that he gave her.

354

"I'm sorry Papa, I didn't mean to upset you by asking you to tell me about your past, and our family," Ava told him as she saw the sorrow in his eyes as he spoke.

"It is okay, nothing can bring them back to me now, but I do still have you, and though our time is short, I am treasuring the time that we do have here together," he told her. *"Do you know that your mother and I were expecting another child when she was killed? It was to be a boy,"* he continued. *"Our first son, but he didn't have a chance to be born."*

"Yes, I know about that, Daniel told me about what happened. I know that he didn't tell me everything, but it was what he felt I needed to know. So, you don't need to go on. I know how much it hurts you to think about it," she caringly told him as she reached out and put her hand on his knee.

Josiah looked down and nodded to his daughter as he raised his large hand and put it on the back of her head, and stroked her hair lovingly.

"What happened to the house that you built? I didn't see it when we came in," Ava asked her father as she tried to change the subject.

"After I escaped with the help of Kendal, they tore it down and then burned everything that was left. They even burned the barn down. They destroyed all my hard work, and they destroyed everything that we had built up together. They wanted to make sure I had nowhere to come back to," he told her. *"The two-legers destroyed everything that..."* he told her in sadness before allowing his voice to trail off.

"Papa, you have told me enough. I know that you and Momma loved me, and that you didn't desert me like Kendal had told me that you did. You have told me all I that I need to know. I have the picture you gave me and I will always have it to remind me of all of you," she told him as she laid her other hand on top of her bag.

"I think you should get some rest now. You have to be weary from the long trip we have just made off the mountain top," he told his daughter.

"Not yet, I don't want to go to sleep yet," she responded as she looked up at her father.

"You need your rest though. Later today is going to be exhausting for you," he told her. *"There will be so many questions that people will be asking you, and you will need to be ready, and to be ready, you need to be well rested,"* he told her.

"I know. I'm nervous though. I'm afraid to go to the village."

"You don't need to be afraid. They will accept you."

"I know. I have just never been around other two-legers before though."

"When you go down to the village, it is best if you do not call them two-legers to their faces. That is only a term that we use. They will take offense by it, and they will not understand why you are calling them that when you are just like they are."

Ava nodded to her father and looked down at her own two legs. She hadn't thought of the fact that they were just like she was. She never considered herself a two-leger as well before now.

"It's okay, it will take some time for you to get used to it there, but you will," her father told her.

Ava again nodded and looked up at her father with tears in her eyes. "I'm going to miss you Papa," she said as more tears came from her eyes and ran down her cheeks. "I want to still be able to see you, Daniel will understand, won't he? Please tell him I still need you," she cried.

"I will talk to Daniel about it when I go back, but I can't make you any promises. I will try to explain how you feel to him, that you still want and need to be able to see me. Maybe if he allows it, I can come back a couple times a year just to see you. I will do my best to talk him into allowing me to do that. If he will allow it, like I said, when you hear me howl, I will be here. You will know it is me, you will know it inside," he told her as he pointed to her heart. *"Remember. You are different than anyone else out there,"* he said as he pointed his finger at the village. *"You can feel us, I know you can because of who you are. You are special, unlike any other,"* he told her. *"If I'm able to come down from the mountain top, if you want to see me, I will wait here in this den for you. You can come in the daylight when it is safer for you, and I will be waiting here inside."*

"If Daniel says it is okay, how soon will you come back to see me?" she asked her father.

"Not for a while. You need to get settled in with the two-legers, and it would make it harder for you to do that if I am here. You need to take the time to adjust. You have a lot to learn. Things are different here than they were on the mountain top. Give it some time though, and it will get easier for you there. You will be fine," he told her. *"Then after you have a chance to settle in, and I've had time to convince Daniel that my seeing you is what you do truly need and want so that you can still feel close to me, I will come."*

Ava wrapped her arms around herself and shivered as a cold chill spread throughout her body. Josiah, seeing his daughter beginning to shiver, moved closer to her. Reaching over to her, he wrapped his large arms around her and gave her a gentle hug. Turning into her father's chest, Ava snugged against him and she could feel the warmth of his body entering into her own. Josiah then gently lifted his daughter up and onto his lap. He held onto her and comforted her until her tears had all dried up. Gently cradling her in his arms, and soothed by the sound of his heart beat, it wasn't long until Ava fell into a deep, restful sleep.

When early evening began to settle in, Josiah gently woke his daughter from her rest. Wiping the sleep from her eyes, Ava looked up at her father and realized she was still perched upon his lap.

"It is time," he gently told her as he brushed a whisp of blond hair away from her face.

Ava looked up at her father for a long time with sadness in her eyes. She was studying his eyes, and all of the features of his face; she was trying to cement every aspect of her father into her memory. She didn't want to forget anything about him at all.

"I don't want to forget what you look like, or anything about you ever again," she told him as she saw that he had begun looking at her questioningly.

Josiah took a deep breath and pulled his daughter back into him for a hug. After a few moments he released her from his grip and lifted her from his lap and placed her back onto the floor of the cave.

As Ava watched her father, Josiah picked up her blanket and carefully folded it back up and put it back into her bag for her. He knew that it was going to be the last time that he would be able to do this for her, to help her pack, or do anything else that she needed to do.

Reaching down, he handed his daughters bag up to her and motioned for her to follow him back outside of the cave.

Looking down to the wood line along the edge of the field, Josiah scanned the area for anyone watching, or any dangers that may have been lurking in the tall grass.

"Remember, this is all yours," he told her as he looked down at her. *"When you are old enough, and maybe married, you and your husband can rebuild the house and turn this place into a home you can call your own,"* he added.

Ava met his eyes and nodded with a small smile.

"I would like that," she told him as she looked out over the field.

"Dusk will be coming soon. It is time for you to get ready to go while it is still safe for you to cross the field on your own," he told her.

"You aren't coming? Can't you even just walk with me part way?" she asked him.

"No, I have to stay here. I can't take the chance of being seen by anyone in the village. I will be watching over you though, and nothing will harm you on your way," he told her as he bent down and looked into his daughter's eyes. *"I love you; you know that don't you? Never doubt that love. Never doubt that your mother and your sister loved you as well,"* he said to her. *"And I did notice when you began to call me Papa again like you did when you were little. I didn't say anything at the time because of the mountain lion, but I did notice and it brought me great joy. I have missed you calling me that."*

Ava looked at her father and smiled. Her eyes sparkled in the last glimpses of daylight above them.

"I know Papa. I think I have always known that you loved me. After you came back for me, I realized that the empty part that was in my heart, it was empty because it was waiting for you to come back and fill it again. It was where you had been, but weren't any longer because you were lost to me. Kendal had told me that you were gone and I would never see you again. I always knew that there was something missing though, and when you came back for me, it wasn't missing any longer. You filled all those empty space I had, and now you will always be there now. And I wouldn't want it any other way," she told her father as she put one of her hands up to her heart. "And now I can always feel close to you even if you aren't near. I love you Papa," she told him as she reached out and hugged her father.

"I love you too," he told her. *"I know that I keep reminding you of this, but it is very important that you don't forget it. Remember what Daniel said. Never tell anyone about us, or where you were. No one can know about us; they can't know anything at all. If they do, they will hunt us down like animals and drive us from the mountain. There will be bloodshed on both sides, and we don't want that. We only want to live in peace, and live in a place that we can call our own,"* he told her. *"That is very important,"* he reiterated to her.

"I will remember everything you have said to me, I promise," Ava said as she nodded to her father. "I will tell them nothing of where I had been, and I will make sure that they do know that it wasn't you that killed my family," she repeated back to him so that her father would feel more at ease.

Josiah nodded to his daughter.

"Thank you, my daughter, my little one, my love," he told her softly. *"I know that you will remember, I just needed to make sure for myself. There is so much at stake here that depends on your silence."*

Ava looked at her father and gave him a reassuring smile and nodded her head.

361

Josiah looked out over the field and at the darkness that was quickly falling over the land.

"You have better go now," he told her as he placed his hand on her shoulder.

Ava nodded to her father and looked over at the village. The first glimpses of dusk had already begun to settle in and there were lights being lit in the village now. Ava stared at the lights as they flickered through the trees that stood along the edge of the field. The village now looked intimidating to her, and she was beginning to get nervous.

"Ava," he said to get his daughter to look up at him again. *"When you get to the village, look for the place that they serve food. Look for a woman called Ms. Dixie. Tell her before you tell anyone else who you are, and tell her your story that you are going to tell other people. She will know what to do, and where to take you,"* he told her after remembering how nice the woman was to him and his wife when nobody else in the village was. He unfortunately also remembered the young black girl that worked for her that the sheriff had raped.

Memories, both good and bad were still coming back to him as time went by. With as much as he was now remembering, he was growing even more certain that with Daniel's help, that he would again remember everything from his past.

Looking once more at the village, she then turning back to look at her father for support.

"Ms. Dixie," she said to her father as she nodded to him.

"Yes, Ms. Dixie. She would be much older now than the last time I saw her, but I know that she still lives in the village. Now, her skin isn't the same color as yours is, but don't be afraid. She is still just like you are. Ms. Dixie's skin is brown, and I know that you will like her. She is an angel, and I know that she will help you," he reassured his daughter.

Ava nodded to him and then turned to look out over the field at the village. After taking a few steps forwards, Ava paused and turned back again to take one last look at her father, but when she turned, he was already gone. Looking around into the shadows, she thought that she saw movement just inside the tree line further down from where they just were standing together. Staring at the spot, she still couldn't see anything even with the full moons glow. Closing her eyes, Ava began to scan the wood line in her mind, and when she opened her eyes again, she saw her father stand upright before her.

Josiah was right, she could feel him here just like she could on the mountain top, and she could feel his presence inside of her heart. Though he was now barely more than a black shadow in the trees, she still knew that it was him. She saw him raise his muzzle up to the sky and she heard a howl emerged into the approaching night. Hearing her father howling his goodbyes, Ava lifted her head up towards the sky and howled back. By the time she was done, she looked back to her father, and he was gone.

Turning from the wood line and again facing the village, the young girl began to slowly walk towards the distant lights. She turned and looked one last time to the place where she

363

had last seen her father. And though she couldn't see him anymore, she could still feel him standing there.

Her father in fact was still just inside the tree line, hidden by the darkness, watching over her from the shadows as he had promised her that he would.

When his daughter reached the village and he saw some of the two-legers come out to meet the young girl, he knew she was going to be okay now. Backing up further into the shadows of the trees, Josiah slowly disappeared back into the darkness of the night.

Other books by BJ Moore

Horror Novels:

"The Culebra"   Released in 2020

"The Culebra II"   Released in 2020

Other books released by this author under the pen name BJ LaPier

Educational Coloring Book Series:

"Out of Africa"   Released in 2017

"Out of Africa – Simplified"   Released in 2018

"Out of Africa II"   Released in 2020

"Out of America I"   Released in 2021

Religious Series: Released in 2014

Psalms of Nature Volume One

Psalms of Nature Volume Two

Psalms of Nature Volume Three

Psalms of Nature Volume Four

B.J. MOORE

Made in the USA
Middletown, DE
28 February 2023

25861586R00209